I0535586

CONCEALED

VICTORIA MICHAELS

Crazy-Bee Press LLC

Crazy Bee Press LLC

First Crazy Bee Press LLC edition, December 2013
First Crazy Bee Press LLC trade paperback edition, December 2013

This is a work of fiction. All of the characters, organizations,
publications, and events portrayed in this novel are either products
of the author's imagination or are used fictitiously.

Library of Congress Cataloguing-in-Publication Data

Michaels, Victoria.
    Concealed / Victoria Michaels. — 1st ed.
    ISBN 978-0-9841137-3-6 (Trade Paperback)
    ISBN 978-0-9841137-2-9 (e-book)
    1. Romance—Fiction. 2. Mystery—Fiction. 3. Small Town—Fiction. I. Title.
First Edition: December 2013

10 9 8 7 6 5 4 3 2 1

Book Cover by Barbara Hallworth

Printed in the United States of America

To my beautiful daughter who lets me
borrow her name when I write…

PROLOGUE

THE DARKENED ROAD AHEAD made a wide curve to the left. Where the pavement finally straightened out, the corn had grown tall around Sydney. Gone were the vast mountain landscapes she'd been driving through earlier. In their place were towering stalks that limited her view and made her feel claustrophobic. She already believed her world was crumbling, but now the walls of corn threatened to suffocate her as the air was sucked from her lungs. Disoriented, she turned the wrong way at a 'Y' in the road and found herself heading west.

I'm never going back, she thought to herself as she made a confusing series of turns, trying to gain her bearings.

The intersections flew by, and soon they all looked the same no matter which way she turned. Nervous that she was lost, her breathing picked up. She reached up to brush a stray hair from her face and the rough plastic of her bracelet scratched across her cheek. All of the emotions she had tried so hard to bury with the hours of driving burst from her and she had to pull to the side of the road as her pain overwhelmed her.

"I'm sorry."

The words rushed from her lips like a curse before she had a chance to stop them. No amount of grief would ever make things better. She knew that now. That's why she left. Some things changed a person forever. No worthless mouthful of words was ever going to help. With a quick movement, she wiped the angry tears from her eyes, amazed her body could even produce them after all she had shed in the last twenty-four hours.

Her gaze strayed to the tattered green duffle bag on the floor of the passenger's side. There hadn't been any reason to take more than she could carry, not that she left all that much behind. Being thrown out of the house by your mother and left to fend for yourself tended to make one light on worldly possessions.

Sydney stayed until her weeping subsided, leaving her shaking with grief, but better able to breathe. When she caught a glimpse of her reflection in the mirror, she didn't recognize the woman looking back at her. Gone was the determined eighteen-year-old who, just days ago, celebrated her high school graduation. In her place was a broken, shattered woman, who was fleeing the life she knew in search of something more.

"You can do this. One foot in front of the other, Sydney." The words had become her mantra and had helped her keep it together for the last few hours as she had traveled over endless miles of road. There had to be something out there for her, far beyond this random cornfield in Montana; something that would take away the unfathomable ache in her heart. She'd just have to keep driving until she found it, across the entire country if that's what it took. Even though she was devastated, Sydney had to hang on to that thought, or she would die.

She was finally starting to calm down when something darted out from the cornfield up ahead of her car and startled her. Her heart was immediately thrown into hyperdrive. Nothing could have prepared her for the shocking sight of a bloodstained woman running toward her car.

"Oh, my God."

Sydney threw open the door and gasped in horror. As the woman approached, Sydney could see her long brown hair was matted with blood. She looked exhausted when she lost her footing and stumbled forward. The woman was thin, but managed to loom over Sydney with her height. Her tattered nightgown had red bloodstains splattered across the front of it. The fabric was ripped open in several places where it must have caught on the stalks of corn. The cuts on her face and lips bled openly, making her look like something out of a horror movie. Even her bare feet were covered in blood.

"What happened to you?" Sydney could hear the woman's labored breathing as she stumbled closer. "What's that you're—" She stopped abruptly as the woman thrust a bundle into Sydney's arms then collapsed at her feet. It was impossible to tell which was more horrifying, the sound the woman's head made as it cracked against the asphalt, or the realization that the woman had placed a newborn baby into Sydney's arms.

"Help her," the woman gasped, as she tried to stop coughing. "Don't let him find her."

Frantically, Sydney scanned the area. There was no sign of anyone in pursuit of this woman, but she didn't want to hang around long enough to find out. "I'll call an ambulance." "No!" The woman grabbed her leg. The wet sensation of her bloody hand coming in contact with her ankle made Sydney shudder.

"You need help. We've got to get you to a hospital! There's so much blood. Where are we exactly? I need an address to give 911 if my phone even works out here."

"N-No time. Listen to me." Her voice grew softer and Sydney dropped to her knees, placing the quiet baby girl in the grass beside the road. "Wants to kill her. C-Can't let him have her."

Sydney froze. "The baby? Who wants to kill her?" There was a distant rustle in the corn and Sydney realized that if some man came barreling out of the field, they'd all end up dead. What they needed now was help. Fast. But Sydney needed more information before she could run back to the car for her phone.

"What's your name?"

"M-Marcy."

"I'm S—" Marcy's uncontrollable coughing cut her off. Her color was getting worse by the second and Sydney knew there wouldn't be much time. In the distance, she could now hear a man's voice, angry and cursing, getting louder by the second. Her hands started to tremble as she bunched the woman's nightgown and tried to stop some of the bleeding.

"He's c-coming. Take her. Go!" It came out as a hoarse whisper but the desperation in her tone spiked Sydney's anxiety.

"I'll take her to the police."

At the word 'police' Marcy lunged but her limbs couldn't even lift her weight. The woman's terror was palpable and, on some level, Sydney understood. Everyone had their secrets. Some were darker than others.

She tried to figure out how to talk the woman into letting her call the police, but with the man's voice getting closer, and more blood pooling beneath Marcy, Sydney panicked. There was no telling who was going to come bursting through the corn, but after seeing his handiwork up close, Sydney didn't want to be there when he finally showed up.

"Okay, okay. No police. I get it. Let's get you to my car. I'll drive you wherever you want to go. I'll take you both to your family."

"They're gone. No one…but you…help her."

Overwhelmed, Sydney glanced at the baby in the grass. She couldn't have been more than a few hours old. "I-I can't."

Marcy grabbed her arm, digging icy fingers into her skin. Her voice was surprisingly clear and strong. "Take her, love her, and *protect* her." The man's voice grew louder now, the dry stalks cracking under his rough movements. "Please. Go!" Those were the last words Marcy spoke before she lost consciousness.

Sydney watched as Marcy's chest stopped moving, her ragged breathing turning to silence in a matter of seconds. She was gone, and Sydney was all alone, except for the little girl beside her. Somewhere close, the man responsible for Marcy's horrific injuries could still be heard charging toward them. There were so many things to consider, but no time to think. Any doubts Sydney had evaporated when she

CONCEALED

saw the leaves start shaking on the corn stalks. The angry words he was spewing terrified her. Without looking back, she snatched the baby from the ground and took off toward the car.

Decision made.

Her sudden movements startled the baby and tiny cries echoed in the night. "Shh, sweetie. I didn't mean to scare you." She closed and locked the doors, clutching the wiggling infant to her chest as her heart pounded.

Thankfully, the keys were still in the ignition and the car roared to life on the first try. As her foot hit the gas, a hulking man with blood down the front of his shirt broke through the corn near Marcy's body. He stepped over her and raced toward the car clutching something in his hand. Sydney's survival instinct kicked in. With a rev of the engine, she threw on her bright lights, blinding him long enough for her to speed past. She braved a single glance back in her rearview mirror and half expected to see him chasing after her, but instead, she watched him turn away from her fleeing car, then raise what looked like a bat into the air over Marcy's limp body.

Bile rose in Sydney's throat as the scene behind her disappeared as the car rounded the corner. All she wanted to do was get away from her own sorrow and somehow she ended up thrown into another woman's nightmare and running for her life. Marcy was dead, and Sydney was taking her daughter. Sydney slowed the car and made sure she was going the speed limit. The last thing she wanted was to have to explain the blood on her clothes and the newborn in her arms, neither of which were hers. How had this even happened?

She could feel the hungry baby rooting against her breast and, once again, the hollow ache in her body answered. When the wave of misery passed, terror filled her. What was she doing? This girl had lost her mother. Was this the cosmos' way of fixing things? Replacing all that they had lost? Could two wrongs possibly make a right?

A half hour later, Sydney found herself in the darkened parking lot of a dinky hardware store with a stranger's baby at her breast. She had

11

no idea where she was, where she was going, or what she was going to do. If she were thinking clearly, she would have called 911, explained the whole horrible ordeal, dropped the baby at the nearest hospital, and been on her way.

But she wasn't thinking at all.

So she drove.

CHAPTER 1

"O RDER UP!" PETE MASCA yelled through the large service window of his diner. He watched the leggy blonde waitress approach with a questioning look on her face. "Problem?"

"Are these eggs over easy?" she asked with a smirk, her blue eyes twinkling.

He waved the spatula menacingly through the window. "If he complains, dump them in his lap, Melissa." Pete looked over her shoulder to the grumpy old man in the booth by the door. "Just because I'm from the East Coast, the old bat thinks I don't know how to make a decent steak and eggs. You know how many diners we have back in Jersey?"

"No clue, but we can do an internet search when the crowd thins a little," Melissa said with a laugh as she loaded the steak and eggs in question and three BLT sandwiches onto her tray. Another waitress came to the window grinning as she passed Pete her ticket. "Sydney, quick. Look up how many diners are in Jersey before I serve these eggs to Mr. Franklin. I need to prove Pete can cook."

"His name *is* on the sign." Sydney casually pointed to the menu for Pete's Place on the counter. The diner was actually the biggest restaurant for miles, and before Pete and Cara bought it, the space had been a short-lived barbeque restaurant called Sticky Bones. A fire and an unfortunate case of food poisoning at their first anniversary celebration had them closing up shop well before their second year was underway. Pete and Cara moved to town a few months later and decided to renovate the space. Pete's Place had been open ever since in the heart of Elton, Missouri.

"Besides, Pete," Sydney looked over her shoulder at Mr. Franklin who was holding his glass up to the light, inspecting the clarity of his tap water, "he's here every day, so you must be doing something right." As she swept her long, platinum locks back into a ponytail, Sydney grinned. "I'm with Pete," she told Melissa. "Dump the eggs on him. He stiffed me yesterday because his coffee was too hot. And that's after I saved him a piece of pie."

Melissa went over and quickly distributed the plates to each guest, not lingering to see if Mr. Franklin liked the eggs or not. She turned away to hide her smile. If only he knew how close he'd come to wearing his breakfast.

"Coward," Sydney teased as Melissa scurried back behind the counter.

"Brat."

Pete eyed Melissa through the window. "When do you leave for your trip, Miss World Traveler?"

She reached out and patted his stubbly cheek. "About a week. And you'll miss me when I'm gone."

"I still say backpacking through Europe is a bad idea. What if you fall off a cliff or get kidnapped? Who's gonna know you're missing if no one knows where you're supposed to be? I say keep your money in the bank, buy a book about Europe, and stay home where I can keep an eye on you."

Melissa rolled her eyes. "You sound like my parents."

"I might have called them last night…"

"Pete!"

"I just worry about you going off by yourself, Mel."

"It's an adventure and I've been dreaming about this all my life."Sydney smiled as the two continued bantering back and forth.

"Now, if you go to Italy I have a nephew or two there I want you to meet. Really nice boys. Good lookin', too. They take after their Uncle Pete."

"Maybe she'll come back a married woman," Sydney teased. Pete chuckled while Melissa tossed the rag she was using to wipe off the counter at Sydney's head.

"Bite your tongue."

When Sydney Ross first came to town five months ago, everyone assumed she was a relative of Melissa's because, within minutes of meeting, the two had become inseparable. They acted far more like sisters than strangers. The friendship had bloomed from day one when Pete introduced them. Pete declared them "Two peas in a pod," which was true, and made working together at the diner all the more fun.

It was impossible not to be excited for Melissa as she prepared for this adventure. Her face lit up whenever she talked about the trip. The closer it got, the brighter her smile. But for everyone who cared about her, she was going to be sorely missed. For Sydney, Melissa was the heart of Elton and when she left, it was going to be hard to stay there without her.

While they waited for their customers to finish their food, Melissa and Sydney took care of a little housekeeping, wiping down the long strip of counter seating, refilling the napkins, and the salt and pepper shakers. The chime on the door sounded, making Melissa's head snap up.

"Like clockwork." She giggled, elbowing Sydney in the side when she noticed who walked through the door. "Wanna take bets on where he sits?"

"Stop it," Sydney hissed, trying to make herself look busy. She didn't need to look up to know that the local sheriff, Wade Jenkins, had strolled into the diner. He had a way of filling the place with his presence and she always knew the moment he arrived. Her skin would prickle with awareness when he was close and her pulse would race, like she had a radar for the man.

"Look what the cat dragged in." Mrs. Whittman, one of Sydney's favorite customers, snickered from her perch on the stool at the counter. Sydney watched Agnes not-so-subtly tap the space beside her in invitation as Melissa laid a menu out for him.

The two of them were incorrigible. And two of Sydney's best friends in Elton. For weeks they had been dropping hints about Wade, claiming he had a 'thing' for her, but Sydney didn't see it. He was always polite, kept to himself and didn't talk much to her, or anyone. That didn't stop her friends from playing matchmaker, though. Melissa shared a wink with the gray-haired woman, both openly grinning by the time Wade slipped onto the seat at the counter.

Just as they had predicted.

"What brings you to the diner today, Wade?" Mrs. Whittman mumbled into her mug with a grin, "Like I even need to ask."

Agnes Whittman was a long time staple of Elton and a force to be reckoned with. A widow for the last year, Agnes had remained active in the community even after her husband's passing. Everyone adored her, but knew not to mess with her. Heaven help you if you were to sneak onto her property in the middle of the night. She'd take a shot at you then claim self-defense. Beneath the wrinkles and gruff exterior, she was still young at heart. That's why everyone loved her.

"Hello, Agnes." Wade sat down beside her with a smile then turned his attention to Sydney who always found herself struck mute at the sight of him.If she was looking for a man, Wade Jenkins would definitely be a slice of mouth-watering heaven. At 6'2, he was a head turner for sure. His deep brown hair was a touch on the long side, hanging just over his ears with a sexy curl above his brow. His chiseled jaw and mysterious eyes were enough to make even the strongest woman swoon.

If she was looking for a man, she would have imagined running her fingers through his hair, over the defined muscles in his arms, and kissing his full lips. Beneath the gorgeous exterior there was something dark about him. It seemed like he had his secrets, things he most definitely wanted to keep private. That was something Sydney understood completely.

But because of her own secrets, she wasn't looking for a man.

"Sydney will be right with you, Wade," Melissa said in a voice loud enough to turn every head in the diner. No one saw Sydney pinch her under the counter, but they did take note of how Sydney's cheeks flared red with embarrassment.

"You're dead," Sydney snarled as she turned her back to Wade and grabbed a mug.

"And you're welcome," Melissa sang as she swatted her in the rear with a rag. The yelp Sydney let out caught Wade's attention. He gave a little nod her direction and set his hat on the counter.

The bright green color of his eyes was distracting whenever he would look her way. It took a lot to rattle Sydney, but there was always something about Wade that definitely threw off her equilibrium. He slowly looked her up and down, waiting for her to say something. Her stomach gave a flutter and random words tumbled from her mouth before she could stop them. "H-Hi. Hey. Hello. How are you? Want something? What can I get you to drink today?"

Make an ass of myself? Check.

Out of the corner of her eye, she saw Melissa shaking her head and smiling. She busied herself refilling one of the napkin holders and shamelessly continued to eavesdrop. Sydney would've told her all the embarrassing details later, so Melissa might as well witness her humiliation firsthand. At least that would save Sydney the trouble of having to relive it.

Deep breath. "Sorry, let me try this again. Hi, Wade. How are you today?"

"Sydney," he said in that deep voice of his that made her feel all warm and tingly inside. How could he make a simple hello sound so sexy? "I'm good. Coffee, please." When she slid the mug and the creamer his way, he rewarded her with a warm smile. "Thanks."

"Anytime."

One thing she had learned was Wade Jenkins was a man of few words. Not that she had been watching him. Or pining over him. Or having erotic dreams about him the last few weeks. Definitely not wondering what he looked like naked. Nope. Not Sydney. That would be stupid because she wasn't looking for a man. But she had noticed that when he came in to the diner with other people, he sat back and listened, only contributing to the conversation if asked something directly. It was probably why she always asked him so many questions. It was her feeble attempt to get him to talk a little more.

He was incredibly polite and tolerated her verbal diarrhea, which seemed to strike often in his presence. At twenty-four years old, she should have been over that by now. But not where Wade was concerned. He would politely respond to whatever random thing she prattled on about, but rarely offered information. He was probably an excellent poker player because he gave nothing away with his body language. Sydney had studied him long enough to learn the few predictable habits he had, and the coffee was one of them.

He looked up over the rim of the mug and Sydney realized she was still standing there, ogling and gawking at him. She nervously twirled her pen between her fingers as her mind raced, trying to come up with a plausible explanation for her odd behavior. When her shaking hands sent the pen clattering onto the counter, Sydney wanted to die. Things went from bad to worse the moment she and Wade collided trying to retrieve it. She panicked and her hand landed on top of his with a rough slap, loud enough to startle Agnes.

"Oh, my gosh! I'm so sorry." She tried to cover her embarrassment, but failed miserably. "I don't know what's wrong with me today. That doesn't qualify as assaulting an officer, does it? It was an accident. Did I hurt you? Do I need a lawyer?" Wade didn't say anything, but gave her an odd look. Sydney realized with a mortified start that she was rubbing the back of his hand where she's slapped him. She jerked hers away as if she'd been scalded. He probably thought she was certifiable, and Melissa's snickering wasn't helping.

"Cuff her, Wade." Agnes laughed, thoroughly enjoying their awkward interaction.

"Ooh, I hear she likes that," Melissa teased, adding to the humiliation.

Sydney closed her eyes and prayed Wade hadn't caught either comment, but apparently his hearing was as perfect as the rest of him, and he fought to hide the slightest hint of a smile. He held out the pen. "How about a turkey club?"

Relieved he had a sense of humor and was taking all the rambunctious teasing in stride, Sydney smiled even though her cheeks were bright red. "I think that can be arranged."

She called his sandwich back to Pete and piled another order onto her tray, then hurried off to deliver it to a customer who didn't make her act like a fool. Her reprieve was short-lived when Melissa snuck up behind her and sang softly, "He's watching you."

If Melissa ever gave up waitressing, she could open a dating service. Nothing made her happier than setting people up, even against their will. So far, Sydney had managed to stay out of her crosshairs, but now that she was leaving for her trip, it seemed that Melissa wouldn't be happy until she forced Wade to suffer through an evening out with Sydney. The poor man.

To keep some distance from Officer Sexy, she chatted with a table of ladies from town. They were planning the fall festival, and since she was new to the area, they were sharing all the details with her. Donna Perkins was explaining the dance and bake-off, and how the money raised went to fund the school library when Melissa swooped in.

"Why are you over here? Go flirt with him!" Melissa quickly excused them both and linked their arms together, dragging her back to the counter. Sydney's attempt to give Wade some peace with his coffee was thwarted by the hyper blonde.

"Maybe I don't want to flirt," Sydney snarled through her smile, refusing to give in to her desire to strangle Melissa.

"Liar."

"Let the man enjoy his coffee."

"Let the man look at you, dammit." Melissa wrenched her arm and flung Sydney behind the counter. She hurried up to the window to ask about the turkey club, avoiding Wade for a few seconds longer. Pete slid the order through the window with a grin and, over her shoulder, Sydney could hear Melissa accosting Wade.

"So, do you have plans tonight?"

"No." He took a long sip of his coffee.

"Seeing anyone?"

Sydney almost smacked her in the back of the head with her tray. She showed great restraint, though, but found herself holding her breath, waiting for his answer.

Not that she was interested, but if he said yes, she just might burst into tears.

Without skipping a beat, Wade grinned. "You asking me out, Mel?"

It was such a shame she was standing behind Melissa because at that moment, Sydney would have killed to have seen her friend's face. The unflappable Melissa was actually rendered speechless—a monumental feat, for sure. Agnes snorted, hiding a grin behind her mug, enjoying Melissa's stunned silence as much as Sydney.

Melissa recovered and tried to sputter an explanation. "M-Me? A-Are you s-serious? I-I never, I mean you're cute but…I don't mean like, cute like I want to go out with you, I mean cute like a puppy. No, you're no puppy. Maybe a baby tiger. Or a shark, but they're not really cute. I'm gonna shut up now." Melissa spun around and retreated into the kitchen with Pete.

"Well played, Wade," Agnes said with a laugh, slapping him on the back. "I'm going to go ask the reverend why he talks so damn long during those sermons on Sunday. See if I can't make that vein pop out of the side of his head for a few seconds." She winked at Sydney and excused herself, giving them an audience-free moment.

Sydney offered Wade an appreciative smile. The only thing she though could have derailed Melissa from her line of questioning was and atomic bomb—although apparently a gorgeous sheriff with a sarcastic streak worked too. "You're my hero." She slipped the sandwich across the counter and topped off his coffee. There was one piece of pie left in the case so she quickly grabbed it and placed it beside his lunch.

"Thanks for the pie."

"It's on me. It's the least I can do after assaulting you." She stood there awkwardly when he didn't break their eye contact. Part of her wondered if he had something to say, but then she was startled from her reverie by Pete's booming voice.

"Syd, it's three o'clock. You better hustle over to school or little Faith is going to be ticked at you for picking her up late."

"Oh, my gosh!" Sydney looked down at her watch. She was never late to pick up Faith. Never. She couldn't be. But the distraction of Wade and Melissa made her lose track of time. She had been careless, and that couldn't happen again. She scrambled to get her purse and keys from under the counter then raced out the door. It dawned on her as she tore out of the parking lot that she had walked out on all her customers without a single word.

Including Wade.

Swamped with guilt, Sydney managed to keep it together on the drive to school, but her mind was racing the entire way. How could she have let herself be late? Even five minutes would make a difference. The plan needed to be followed.

Always.

Her fingers tapped out an erratic rhythm on the steering wheel as she tried to stay calm. Years of paranoia never really went away, no matter how comfortable she was in a new location. Something always happened to disrupt her calm. Nine moves in almost six years would do that to a person. Obsessively she scanned the area and noticed an unfamiliar car parked down the street. She tamped down the unwarranted suspicion and tried to get control of her fear.

If only she had been on time!

She leaned across the seat, trying to see around the pickup truck in front of her, but it was impossible. Until she had Faith in the car, Sydney was going to be a ball of nerves. She never liked being apart from her daughter, but now that Faith was in school, Sydney was going to have to learn to deal with that better.

Don't let Faith see you like this, she told herself. When it was her turn to pick up, she took a deep breath and stepped out to take Faith by the hand.

"She had a great day," Miss Westmore said as Faith barreled into Sydney's arms.

"Momma! I made you something today."

"I can't wait to see it." She looked over at her daughter's teacher. "Thanks. Have a nice evening."

Sydney ushered Faith into the car and buckled her seatbelt. The moment she was in the car, the tension and anxiety began to ease. Out of habit, she quickly scanned her surroundings and couldn't help but feel like she was being watched. Her eyes darted to where the car had been parked on the side of the road. She froze when she saw someone standing beside it. Instinctively she reached for Faith, but when she looked back, the figure was gone.

Or it hadn't been there to begin with, she told herself. *Calm down, Syd. You sound like your mother.*

On the drive home, Sydney did her best to reign in her fear. They were fine. They'd always been able to stay longer than this before anything happened. Elton was a blip on the map, if it even was on the map. It was that small. Who would think to look for them there? She made sure everything she did was in cash to keep their trail as invisible as possible.

Sydney glanced at Faith's reflection in the rearview mirror. She was looking out the window, happily singing a song they must have learned at school today. She was happy and healthy. That's all that mattered. There was no way Sydney was going to let anything happen to her.

Ever.

It was a promise she had made, and one she intended to keep.

CHAPTER 2

PETE HAD SOUNDED FRANTIC when he called, asking Sydney to come in for a few hours on her day off. He wouldn't say much, other than something happened and the diner was packed. Luckily, Agnes was willing to give Faith a bath and get her ready for bed, as long as she didn't miss the latest episode of Antiques Roadshow. The woman was a godsend.

As her headlights illuminated the parking lot, Sydney was taken aback by the number of cars that spilled out of the lot and onto the road in front of Pete's Place. Through the windows, she could see bodies milling around or gathered at the tables inside as she drove around back to park. When she got out of the car, she was hit with an icy breeze that sent a shiver down her spine.

Something bad had happened. Sydney could feel it.

Plates were clattering together in the kitchen and the sizzle of the burgers on the grill signaled the rush of hungry customers inside the diner.

"What's going on?" Sydney whispered to Pete's wife, Cara, as she tied an apron around her waist. Cara was piling orders of fries onto her tray as fast as her hands would allow. A group of people were huddled around Johnny Rosley, one of Elton's volunteer firemen and resident idiots, hanging on his every word.

The sadness in the room was palpable. Cara shared the awful news. "They found a woman dead in Greenville. Out past the Richardsons' property."

"Oh, my God."

"The girl was in her early twenties, from what the police can guess. What a shame. Sounds like the poor thing suffered something awful." Cara shook her head. "I hope they catch the bastard."

Across the diner, Johnny's voice continued to boom with more gory details he had overheard on his police scanner.

"It's sick," Cara said under her breath. "A woman's dead and he's acting like it's exciting." There was no missing the dirty look Cara cast Johnny's way as she muscled past the group to serve her table. His voice instantly lowered, but the crowd just moved closer to hear him better.

"I didn't realize we had so many rubberneckers in this town," Melissa said with a huff as she slid two pieces of blackberry pie onto a plate. "They're like old women, the way they gossip. They found the girl around three and by four o'clock every booth in here was full. And they just keep coming."

"Ladies," a deep voice said as someone slid onto the only vacant stool at the counter, "what a sight for sore eyes you both are."

"Laying it on a bit thick today aren't you, Luke?" Melissa said with a laugh.

Luke Carter had grown up in Elton with Melissa and Wade. His dirty blond hair was cropped short at the moment, the bright highlights from a summer spent in the sun gone. Where Wade kept to himself, Luke was outgoing and flirtatious, someone you could easily talk to about any topic. He was a charmer, as Melissa knew all too well. The two of them were hopeless flirts, but after a few attempts at a romance between them, Melissa decided he was more fun to play with than date. They would have made a cute couple, the burly football player tamed by the blonde bombshell, but it wasn't meant to be. Instead, they settled for good friends.

"Just tryin' to raise a few spirits around here," he glanced over his shoulder at the crowd, "because it shakes people up when they realize that bad things can happen in small towns. Even ones as tiny as Greenville. And Elton."

"Johnny seems to be doing fine." The details he was spewing about what was found at the scene was making her skin crawl.

"Well, that's Johnny for you," Luke said with a shrug. "I guess he's always had a fascination with the gruesome. When he was a kid, he used to pull the wings off flies and the legs off spiders just to watch them flop around in his hand."

"That's disgusting," Sydney said as she poured Luke a cup of coffee. "Someone lost their life. He shouldn't be so excited."

"Did you forget he's the county's mortician, too?" Luke asked with a laugh. "Death doesn't bother him like the rest of us. It's what he does."

Overhearing part of their conversation, Pete stuck his head out the window and surveyed the crowd. "Death's good for business."

"That's horribly morbid," Sydney said, shocked, but from the look of it, Pete was right. All around her, people were huddled together talking in hushed voices and when they weren't talking, they were eating. As fast as Pete could cook it, they were shoveling it down.

"Remember a few years back when the Parkers lost all that cattle? The same thing happened. People filled this place, hypothesizing about the cause," Luke offered, trying to distract the girls from the heavy topic.

Pete let out a snort. "As I recall, Johnny insisted it was aliens to anyone who'd listen 'til Agnes came in here and threatened to shoot him for being stupid."

"She did take a shot at him once." Melissa patted Luke's hand, smiling. "Remember in high school when she and her husband had that old mare? One night Johnny thought he'd be funny and scare the poor thing because she made the oddest noise when she was upset. So late at night, he snuck out there howling and growling at it like a coyote. Agnes strolled out in her nightdress, looked Johnny in the eye, and shot the hat off his head. Then she closed the door, turned out the lights, and went back to bed."

"She didn't!" Sydney covered her mouth to hide her laughter.

"Oh, she did," Luke assured her. "The sheriff showed up at her house with Johnny's dad. The sheriff asked her if she fired her gun and she said yes, she shot at a deranged coyote that was squawking around her mare. Mr. Rosley got in her face, yelling that it wasn't an animal, it had been his son. Agnes looked at the sheriff, then Johnny's dad and said, 'Well, he does one hell of a coyote impersonation. Keep him off my property,' and slammed the door in their faces. Her husband, George, never even said a word during the whole altercation."

"To this day," Melissa said, handing Luke a cup of coffee, "if Agnes howls, Johnny hightails it in the opposite direction."

They shared a much needed laugh at Johnny's expense, until Pete motioned toward the door. "Wade looks like hell. Poor guy."

"Wade always looks like hell," Luke mumbled under his breath earning a whack to the head from Melissa. "There he is, moping around for attention."

Sydney looked at Luke, unable to fathom where the sudden animosity came from. A second ago he was laughing and now he was a sourpuss. It was obvious Luke didn't think too highly of Wade, but considering he probably had been dealing with the murder in Greenville all day, a little sympathy was in order.

The diner erupted with questions as soon as people realized the sheriff had walked in. Wade didn't even seem to notice the circus going on around him. Instead, his eyes scanned the room until they locked onto Sydney at the end of the counter. He gave the slightest nod of his head in her direction. There was a deep sadness in his eyes that made her heart ache. Without a word to anyone, he walked through the crowd and slid into a booth in the back corner of the diner.

"I can't even imagine how difficult this has been for him. He's been in Greenville for hours." Melissa shook her head. "You should go talk to him, Sydney."

"Why me?"

"Yeah, why her?" Luke asked with a growl. "The guy's been to Iraq, for God's sake. If he can't handle this, then maybe he isn't the half man everyone seems to think he is." As he walked away he mumbled, "Like I've been saying for years."

"He's such a jerk when Wade's around," Sydney said, incredulous that the same guy who had flirted with them was now storming through the crowd like a missile. "Why the Dr. Jekyll and Mr. Hyde routine?"

Melissa refilled a couple sodas before answering. "The two of them have a history. It goes way back. They've never gotten along well." She shrugged. "You'd have to get the details from one of them."

Sydney could tell Melissa was avoiding the question, but there wasn't time to get into it because they were swarmed with orders. Pete was piling the food on plates as fast as they could take it out. Cara was bussing the tables while Melissa and Sydney frantically delivered items. When there was a lull in the action, Sydney went back behind the counter and her gaze once again drifted over to Wade.

He was deep in thought as the crowd continued to inch closer. They were desperate for information and he was the prize they were after. Once the first question flew, an endless stream of horrible inquiries followed, which were none of their business and completely inappropriate.

"Was she naked?" Johnny's disgusting question had Wade grinding his teeth together. He seemed to be using a considerable amount of self-control to keep from punching someone in the face. Without thinking, Sydney snagged a piece of his favorite pie from the rack and pushed her way through the crowd that had assembled around his table.

"Do you have any manners?" Sydney gave a hard shove through the throng of bodies and found herself stumbling in front of Wade clutching the pie in one hand and a fork in the other. The tired smile he gave when she shooed the gawkers away melted her heart. Before she thought to stop herself, she was sliding onto the bench across the table and pushing the piece of pie toward him.

"Hi."

"Sydney." He plunged the fork into the crust and dug into the slice.

Sydney watched his lips part to welcome the tiny piece of blackberry pie inside. His teeth were gorgeous and white and straight and…she was staring at him again like some sort of lecherous pervert. The man had been working a murder scene all day and she was thinking about curling up in his lap and kissing him. She quickly looked out the window and shook her head.

"What's wrong?" The deep rumble of his voice made her hyper-aware of how close he was. She could feel his leg stretch out under the table and bump against her knee.

"Nothing, I'm just sorry that everyone's forgotten how to behave like human beings." She nervously tugged at her ponytail and twirled it behind her head into a messy bun. She enjoyed the way he watched her so intently. "So, how was your day?" The grunt of laughter he gave in response made her smile. "That good, huh?"

He took another bite of pie, avoiding the topic. "This isn't your night to work."

She hid a smile at his observation. So maybe he had been watching her a little. The thought sent a flutter of excitement through her stomach. She liked the idea of him watching her more than she should have. "Pete needed help when the vultures descended."

Wade shook his head. "Murder turns normal folks into gossipmongers."

"Want to know what the LBI has come up with?"

"LBI? What's that?"

"Lunatic Bureau of Investigation, of course," she said with a grin. There was such sadness behind his eyes she wanted to do what she could to make him smile.

"Let's hear it."

"They said she was a prostitute who was found naked at the edge of town. Old Jim told ten people her body was mutilated with a message scrawled into her skin. He had the whole table believing him, too, until his wife mentioned that was what happened on some police drama he watched last night. Then he shut up pretty quick."

Wade sat back and continued eating his pie, listening. It was strange to be crammed into the tiny booth with him considering the circumstances, but it felt right. All around them people tried to interrupt their conversation, but he ignored them, his full attention focused on Sydney. She found it incredibly sexy.

"Johnny has a theory that it was a mafia hit, revenge for some bad blood back in Jersey. Personally, I think he just said that to piss off Pete because he burned his grilled cheese."

He finished the pie and leaned back, casually draping his arm along the back of the seat. "Any others I should know about?"

Sydney counted off the others on her fingers. "The victim of alien abduction, werewolf attack, and the Sasquatch theories were some of my favorites." She rolled her eyes. "Highly delusional, but entertaining nonetheless."

A group of men barged over to their table and began peppering Wade with more questions. "Was she tied up? Any signs of a struggle? Did you do a rape kit on her?" The improper musing from the crowd continued until Sydney's fist slammed down on the table, rattling the fork on Wade's plate, and stunning the men around them into silence. Wade's head swiveled in her direction but he didn't say a word. There was no need to because, disgust and frustration getting the best of her, Sydney erupted with anger.

"Have you all lost your minds? A woman is dead. Dead. Some psycho robbed her of her life, of a future with those she loved. She has a mother and a father somewhere, a family who is probably devastated, and all you can do is play junior deputy coming up with awful scenarios that might have happened, for your own entertainment. Show a little respect, light a candle, say a prayer or two, and stop all the asinine questions!"

Her temper rarely flared but once it started, it was hard to pull back until it had run its course. There was too much history behind these feelings for her to control it in any rational way.

"Now, for the love of God, let the man eat his pie in peace!"

Silence. The entire diner had gone quiet in the midst of her tirade. The only sound to be heard was the sizzle of the deep fryer working overtime. Melissa gave her a proud fist pump from across the room. Pete pulled Cara under his shoulder and the pair beamed at her like proud parents, but every other eye in the place was incredulous. Luke studied her like she was a stranger. Johnny and his crew were mumbling things under their breath, probably questioning her mental stability, which was understandable. She'd just publicly berated the entire town.

With her shaking hands clasped together under the table, Sydney peeked through her lashes at Wade, the one person whose opinion mattered the most to her at that point. He seemed to be taking it all in stride, as if encountering a rabid woman was a daily occurrence for him. The crowd took her not-so-subtle hint and slowly returned to their tables, giving Wade his space. Unfortunately, that left her to somehow explain what happened. There was no way she could share the origins of that outburst. That would be suicidal, for sure. She closed her eyes for a moment and breathed deeply, knowing her cheeks were flushed.

There still hadn't been a word said between them when she felt the gentle nudge of his knee under the table. At first she jumped, pulling her foot back to give him space, but when his leg brushed against her again, she realized it had been on purpose. Her eyes flew open and found him watching her intently, the green in his eyes looking more cheerful and relaxed.

The tension drained out of her body, replaced suddenly by a rush of desire she hadn't felt since, well…ever. Again, the gentle contact with his leg sent sparks flying between the two of them. In that moment, she realized just how desperately she wanted to kiss Wade Jenkins.

"So, how was your day?" He threw her words back at her with a slow, sexy grin.

"Other than embarrassing myself yet again in front of you, and now the whole town? Perfectly boring."

They maintained eye contact for a few silent moments as the bustle of the diner went on around them. With someone else, it might have been awkward, but with Wade, it was comfortable. And despite everything, she wanted more if it.

"Thanks for the pie," he said, slipping his hat back onto his head, "and the company."

"Anytime," Sydney whispered as he disappeared through the crowd. Once she was alone, Melissa flew to her side. "What was all that about?"

"I have no idea." Sydney grabbed Wade's empty plate and held it with great care. Melissa's lips curled up into a smile.

"You two better get together before I leave or I'm killing you."

"Melissa—"

"You've got it bad for him, don't you?" It was impossible to miss the excitement in her voice. "Are you finally ready to admit you're hot for him?"

"Not to anyone," Sydney said with a wink as she turned away from Melissa, "except maybe myself."

CHAPTER 3

THE DAYS LEADING UP to the festival had been rather depressing in town. It seemed everyone in the county had been questioned about the murdered woman they had found the next town over. She was identified as Samantha Walker, a teacher from Kansas, who was last seen leaving work the day before she was murdered. There was no clear motive and no real evidence to speak of in the case.

Wade had canvassed Elton to see if anyone noticed any strangers passing through town that day or in the days prior. Unfortunately, it appeared there had been nothing unusual in the tri-county area until they found Samantha's body. With few leads, everyone was left wondering what could have happened and, more importantly, was the killer still around? But those questions weren't likely to be answered anytime soon.

By the time the calendar flipped to the first of October, all talk in town shifted to one thing: the upcoming festival. People couldn't wait for the celebration to begin. No one had been sleeping well knowing there could be a murderer nearby.

Everyone was glad for the distraction, including Wade.

The Fall Festival was the biggest event of the year in the tiny town of Elton, Missouri. People came from far and wide to visit. Every fruit or vegetable grown in the tri-county area was proudly displayed over the week, farmers vying for the title of largest pumpkin, apple, zucchini, squash, or gourd in the county. You name it; Elton had a contest or trophy for it.

On the last night of the festival there was a dance, followed by the grand finale, the Pie Auction, where the men from the area would bid on the pies and then, not only win a delicious dessert, but a special something from the woman who had baked it. It was a tradition that dated back a hundred and fifty years or so, to when Elton was first established. Back then, it was the way many farmers would marry off their daughters. Now, it represented an evening of fun and flirting for the single people in Elton before the nights turned cold.

The afternoon of the auction, Wade found himself walking down the main drag of the festival, taking it all in. The street was lined with tasting tents and street carts selling an endless variety of foods. People were shoulder-to-shoulder as they tried to navigate through the crowded road. Kids were running around in the grass, laughing, and people were smiling, visiting with neighbors and enjoying one another's company. Out of the corner of his eye, a flash of blonde hair caught his attention.

"Hi, Wade."

"Melissa," he replied as she fell into step beside him, grinning. In her hand there was a cardboard basket with something on a stick. "Dare I ask?" He warily eyed the stick Melissa waved toward him.

"Fried Twinkie. Want a bite?"

"No."

"Enjoying the fair?" she asked looping her arm around his.

"It's nice to see everyone having fun. How long until you leave for your trip?" Together they weaved through the crowd side by side.

"Less than a week now." Her eyes lit up with excitement at the prospect of her trip to Europe. Ever since they were kids, Melissa had talked about leaving Elton and seeing the world. She had been working since she was fourteen and saved every dime she could to make her dream come true. And now, she was days away from the trip of a lifetime.

"It won't be the same here without you."

"Aww, you gonna miss me, Wade?" She patted his cheek. "Don't worry. I'll be back in six short months."

The bright lights of carnival rides and games lit up the road ahead. Children were everywhere, their parents trying to keep up as they rushed from one ride to the next. Wade caught himself scanning the crowd for Sydney or Faith. Of course, Melissa noticed.

"Looking for anyone in particular?"

"No." Even as he said it, he knew the word rang hollow. For the last twenty minutes, he realized he'd managed to wander around every kid-friendly place at the fair, all in the hopes of seeing Sydney. He really didn't care about the craft center or a lopsided cow made of butter, yet he wandered past every group of children, looking for Faith's tell-tale dark curls.

How pathetic was he?

"You're such a terrible liar," Melissa said with a laugh. "Since you're too macho to ask, I'll help you out, because that's the kinda girl I am. I think you should wander over to the petting zoo area. You might find something nice and soft to cuddle up with over there."

Wade's thoughts immediately went to Sydney, and cuddling wasn't exactly what he had in mind. The images that flashed in his head when he thought of her were far more erotic, not that he'd ever share that with Melissa, or anyone else for that matter. It was hard enough admitting it to himself that the tiny blonde was under his skin. In the months that she'd been in town, she'd captured his attention like no one else had in years.

At first it was her looks that had stopped him in his tracks and her laughter. She was a breath of fresh air and lit up the diner with her smile. The longer Wade was around her, though, the more he saw the other side of Sydney. The side she tried hard to hide from the rest of the world. She was a woman with secrets and a past. There was never a mention of Faith's father, which was odd, but even more telling were the personality quirks that Sydney tried so hard to hide from the people around her. Being overprotective of Faith, constantly looking over her shoulder when she thought no one was watching, the lack of details she offered from her past were all red flags in Wade's mind.

Being in law enforcement, he had become an expert at reading the signs people unknowingly gave off, and from everything he'd observed over the last few months, if he had to hazard a guess, Sydney was exhibiting some of the classic traits of a woman who had suffered some sort of abuse or trauma.

Wade could have done a background check. He'd been tempted to plenty of times but stopped himself. Part of him didn't want to invade her privacy and the other side of him simply enjoyed the distraction she offered.

Melissa cleared her throat, pulling him out of his thoughts. "You might fool other people, Wade Jenkins, but I know you like her. I've been watching you at the diner. Never known you to be such a pie enthusiast until Sydney came to town. You're sweet on her. The sooner you admit it, the sooner I can set you two up on a date. Consider it a farewell gift to me before I leave town."

"I'm perfectly capable of getting my own dates, Mel."

"Really?" she asked as she spun to face him, her chin tipped up defiantly. "I happen to know at least three women who have asked you out and you've turned them all down. Your dating life is dead at the moment."

"So?"

"So?" she sputtered, her hands reaching for his neck like she wanted to wring it. "So why would you pass up perfectly acceptable date invitations, unless you were interested in someone?" She thought about it a second, then paled. "You aren't seeing one of your bimbos from Centerburg right now, are you?"

It was amazing that no matter how discreet he tried to be, still the gossip made its way back to town. Maybe he needed to leave the state the next time he wanted to get laid. Rather than explain himself, Wade shook his head.

"I'm not dating anyone."

The wide smile Melissa gave him in return for that information was blinding. "Excellent. Then you should definitely go to the petting zoo."

"Melissa," he tried to tell her she was wrong, but the words wouldn't come. He tucked his hands into his pockets and shook his head.

"I'm going gray waiting for you to make a move on her."

Wade smiled. "You're so impatient."

"And you're welcome." She popped up on her toes and gave him a kiss on the cheek. "Besides, I'm counting on you to keep an eye on her while I'm gone. Do me a favor. When you see Sydney, tell her to meet me at the dance in an hour so we have time to run home and get her pie before the auction." Wade tried to grab her arm, but Melissa started to slip away. "Don't forget to give her my message, Wade." With a wave of her hand, she disappeared into the crowd but he could hear her exuberant laughter in the distance.

She had a way of getting exactly what she wanted. Wade had to give Melissa that. Before he could stop himself he'd turned around and started heading toward the petting zoo. As a zoo, it was sorely lacking. It was no more than a fenced area where bunnies, goats, and other small animals ran loose for the kids to play with. As he made his way past the last of the carnival rides, he saw the familiar wooden fence and heard the excited squeals of the children as they chased after a lively bunny who was trying to escape. A blur of brown curls darted past the fence in front of him.

"Faith!" Sydney's voice immediately captured his attention, but her daughter was too enamored by a squirming lop-eared bunny to answer. "Honey, be careful. You don't want to hurt him." Sydney cautiously opened the gate to the animal pen, making sure none of the critters escaped, then went inside.

Before he was spotted, Wade took the opportunity to unabashedly admire her body. There was a grace to her movements that was hypnotizing to him. A gentle sway to her hips that Wade couldn't tear his eyes away from no matter how many times he tried. She looked beautiful in her tight fitting jeans and black sweater which accentuated her curves. There was nothing overtly sexy about the outfit but the sleek leather boots she was wearing definitely caught Wade's attention and were sure to star in a fantasy or two in the future. He watched her brow pinch as she debated following after her daughter. When she started nibbling on her lip, all he could think about was kissing her.

Wade forced himself to look away from Sydney and found Faith laughing on the far side of the pen with the other children who had moved on from the bunnies and were now chasing the goats with handfuls of feed, trying to get their attention. Sydney skirted along the edge of the fence as she tried to keep her daughter in view. When one of the goats started eating the food from her hand, Faith's squeals of laughter made her mother smile.

"That can't be sanitary," Sydney mumbled under her breath, so close to Wade that his chuckle of laughter caught her off guard. Sydney spun around, startled to find him along the fence, watching her.

"Hi," he said, offering a smile that only grew as the color crept up her cheeks. Her long hair blew over her shoulder in the breeze as she tried to compose herself. She tucked the stray hairs behind her ear and walked a few steps closer.

"Hi, Wade. Did you come to pet the animals?" As soon as the words left her mouth she shook her head, something she did all the time around him. "Of course you didn't. Why would you? You're not five. Sorry." She paused her rambling and took a deep breath. "How are you?"

"I'm good." He glanced over at Faith who was hugging one of the larger goats around the neck. "She's having fun."

Sydney followed his gaze then wrinkled her nose at her daughter. "Faith, stop that. You're gonna smell like a goat." The little girl waved then skipped over to investigate the squawking coming from the chicken pen. "She really likes animals," Sydney said as if trying to offer some sort of explanation for her daughter's behavior. One of the goats headed in Sydney's directions and she shied away. "Shoo. I don't like you. Go find Faith." The offending animal crept closer, sending Sydney scurrying toward the fence.

"He won't hurt you," Wade said trying to hide a smile, but the way Sydney was eyeing the goat like it was a charging rhino was comical. When a second waddled in her direction, Sydney let out a sound of distress.

"Do they bite?"

"No."

"He looks a little crazed. Do they get rabies?" she asked, her entire body going tense as the half blind animals brushed their mouths against her leg, looking for a snack. Wade was surprised when she grabbed his hand and held on to it for dear life. "I know this sounds incredibly pathetic, but can you get them away from me?"

Never one to deny a beautiful woman any request, he braced one arm on the fence and hopped over, landing at her side. He gave the goats a gentle nudge with his knee and they wandered off in search of food. "I guess Faith is the animal lover in the family?"

When the goats were a safe distance away, Sydney leaned back against the fence beside him, her entire body relaxing. She was so close, their shoulders brushed against one another. Sydney looked up at him from under her dark lashes and burst out laughing. "I'm sorry. I don't know what came over me. You must think I'm more of a raving lunatic than you did before."

Wade laughed, but he wasn't thinking about her being a lunatic at all. His attention was focused on other things like the sparkle in her eyes and bright color in her cheeks. Currently the sexy way she flung her hair over her shoulder had his complete attention. She was irresistible and he wanted her. He had to tuck his hands into his pockets to keep from reaching out and running his thumb across her lower lip.

"Thanks for the rescue, Sheriff." Her hand rested on his arm innocently, however his thoughts were anything but. He wanted to feel her soft curves pressed against him as he pulled her into a scorching kiss. As if she could somehow read his mind she stepped back, putting distance between them. The second her hand left his arm, he missed the contact. "I-I've got to drag Faith out of here and go meet Melissa."

"Wait." Wade reached out and caught her wrist, holding her in place at his side. At that moment she looked more afraid of him than she had been of the goat. He must have voiced the thought out loud because a slow smile spread across her lips.

"I'm not afraid of you."

"Good." He pulled her closer, using his free hand to tuck a stray hair behind her ear. She turned her cheek into his hand ever so gently. Her skin was the softer than anything he'd felt in a long time.

"Are you going to kiss me?" The breathless way the words tumbled from her mouth made his heart pound in his chest. He could tell she was embarrassed by what she said, but since she asked, he figured it'd be rude to not answer.

"I'm thinking about it."

Big brown eyes were looking up at him as she took a step closer. "Me too."

The momentary spell that had been cast between them was broken when Faith ran over with a black bunny in her arms. "Mommy, look! I caught it all by myself." The little girl beamed up at Wade. "Isn't she pretty?"

He smiled down at Faith but glanced back at Sydney when he said, "Absolutely."

"Honey," Sydney said as she crouched down to talk to her daughter, "it's time to go meet Melissa. Can you put her back with the rest of her friends and meet me at the gate?"

"Did you see the goats? They're so friendly!"

When Wade chuckled, Sydney elbowed him. "Yes, I saw them. They seemed to like me, a lot. Now go put her away."

Faith ran back to one of the other kids and handed off the animal. Sydney kept her eyes on her daughter but Wade was fixated on Sydney. He was quickly becoming obsessed. Her lips turned up into a smile as Faith ran around saying good bye to each animal in the pen. Wade couldn't stop thinking about how soft Sydney's lips would be and how responsive she'd be to his touch. He knew she wanted him to kiss her but he'd moved on to wondering how she would feel wrapped around him in a tangle of sheets.

"I'm ready, Mommy." Faith grabbed Sydney's hand and extended her other to Wade. "Will you come with us?"

"I'd love to." Wade took her tiny hand and couldn't help but smile at the surprised look on Sydney's face. He held the gate open and ushered them out of the pen. As Sydney brushed past, he whispered, "I'm still thinking about it."

Sydney shocked him when she leaned closer with a flirty smile and whispered, "Me too."

With Sydney and Wade at her sides, Faith led them down the midway. He thought of all the interesting things he wanted to show them at the festival, but then he remembered the message he was supposed to pass onto Sydney. "Melissa's waiting for you at the dance. Do you know where that is from here?" He gave Sydney an out even though he knew Melissa's plan was for them to be attached at the hip. There was no doubt he wanted to spend time with her, but he needed to know that Sydney was there because she was interested, not because they were thrown together by her friend.

"I think I can find it," she said with a relaxed smile, "but maybe you better show us the way, just to be sure." Gone were her earlier nerves. She seemed more comfortable, and with that, came a sexy confidence that he hadn't seen from her before.

And man, did he like it.

They began the long walk across the festival listening to Faith chatter on about the different things she saw. Wade wasn't oblivious to the way heads were turning as they passed. People had been wondering about his love life, or lack thereof, and now he found himself strolling around the biggest gathering of the year with Sydney. He wasn't sure if he should laugh or run. Fortunately, the beautiful woman walking beside him was more captivating than frightening.

"I hear music, Mommy." Faith stood on her tippy toes to see the large tent in the distance. "Ouch!" With a frown she stuck her foot up in the air at her mother. The little girl's whole body started to topple over but Wade safely scooped her up. While Faith laughed in his arms, Sydney examined her foot and winced.

"That's a big blister you've got there, baby girl." She slipped the shoe off Faith's foot then held out her arms. "I'll carry you the rest of the way."

It took everything in him not to roll his eyes at Sydney. Faith weighed next to nothing and without a second thought he hoisted her onto his shoulders. Her squeal of laugher warmed his heart in places he long thought dead.

"I've got her." He held onto Faith's legs and tried not to wince as she grabbed two fistfuls of his hair to help her balance. "Ready?"

"I'm so big!" Her little feet bounced with each step Wade took, and from the excited shrieks she would let out from time to time, she was enjoying the view. Wade would've carried her up a mountain to keep the radiant smile on Sydney's face. The way she was looking at him made him wonder why he had waited so long to spend time with her. He was enjoying her company, and Faith's, far more than he expected.

"Well, there you are. I was just about to send a search party out for the three of you." Agnes waved them over to a nearby picnic table. The dance floor was set up on a large grassy area behind the supermarket. Wade was always amazed at how many people could be crammed into such a tiny space. With a great flourish, he swung Faith onto the picnic table beside Agnes, taking care to protect her bare foot.

"That was fun!" Faith hugged his leg. "Thanks for the ride, Sheriff Wade."

"Anytime." Wade's hand tenderly brushed over the girl's curls. He wondered if Sydney knew how lucky she was to have this child in her life. What he wouldn't give for someone to unconditionally love him the way Faith loved Sydney.

"You gonna stay and dance, Wade?" Agnes asked with a knowing grin on her face. "Why don't you take Sydney out for a spin on the dance floor?"

As much as Wade had enjoyed himself, he didn't want to push too far, too fast. She was finally more comfortable with him but it didn't take much to make her look like she wanted to cut and run. As a lesson in patience, and to avoid the sinful temptation of her lips, he decided to leave.

"Another time," he said to Sydney, hoping she heard the sincerity in his voice. More than anything, he wanted to get his hands on her, but not with half the town watching. He preferred for it to be much more private. And intense. When he caught Sydney's shy smile, he knew she felt it, too. "You ladies have fun."

Agnes watched him like a hawk, trying to dissect each of his words. He did his best to keep his expression neutral. For now, he was happy to see that Sydney recognized his interest and could feel something starting to happen between them. Let the rest of the town wonder.

"Now, don't go running off like a jackrabbit, Wade. Join us for some music if you don't want to dance."

With mention of a rabbit, Faith's eyes lit up and she launched into the details of her time in the petting area. Agnes' attention was captured by the tiny girl's enthusiasm, so Wade decided to take his leave, but not before catching Sydney's eye.

"Have fun," Wade said.

"Thanks for the rescue earlier."

"Anytime."

The funny thing was, walking away from them was harder than he imagined it would be. He hadn't realized how much he wanted to stay, until he left. He'd gone a few steps when someone grabbed his arm and stopped him in his tracks.

"You know, it's not wise to sneak up on a police officer, Melissa." He tried to be stern, but the peeved look on her face made him grin.

"Where do you think you're going?"

He could tell his exit had derailed some elaborate plan Melissa had concocted, but he wasn't going to make it easy on her. Part of the fun of being friends with Melissa was watching her get herself all riled up.

"I'm going to check out the festival. Want to join me?" He offered his elbow but she just continued to glare at him.

"No. I don't want to join you. Why didn't you ask Sydney to come with you?"

"You two are leaving soon and besides, I left her in Agnes' very capable hands," he said, nodding toward the picnic tables.

Livid, Melissa punched him in the arm. "The only hands she wants to be in are yours, you big idiot."

That comment piqued his attention. Wade highly doubted that Sydney would have voiced her feelings for Wade, or lack thereof, to Melissa knowing how she would react. Her cupid instinct was well known and many in town had succumbed to her exuberant dating advice only to realize that her arrow was a little bent at times and missed its mark more than it hit.

But his curiosity got the better of him. "How do you know? What did she say?"

"Oh my God, what are you, like twelve?" When Wade's only response was to cross his arms over his chest, Melissa's lips turned up into a wicked grin. "Go ahead, play it cool, but I know inside you're dying to know what she might have said, aren't you?"

Wade was, but there was no way in hell he was going to admit it now. In an effort to seem indifferent, he put on his best poker face. "Not really."

"Not even if the things she said were pretty racy?"

That comment made his eyebrows shoot up in surprise. He'd had dozens of erotic fantasies about Sydney but the thought of her having one made him crazy. "Were they? Racy that is?"

"I'm not telling," she laughed, delighted to see him on edge. "But because I'm such a nice person I will make one suggestion."

"What?"

"Go to the auction tonight. There's going to be a little something up for bid you definitely want to get your hands on." As she walked away, she yelled over her shoulder, "Bring your checkbook. I have a feeling you could be in for some competition tonight, Wade."

CHAPTER 4

I T HAD BEEN EXPLAINED to Sydney by half the town that the festival always culminated with the auction. It was considered the event of the week. She thought it was an exaggeration until she started making her ,way toward the hall where the pie auction was being held. The building entrance was surrounded by a thick crowd of people, mostly men, waiting to get inside. A number of them she recognized as regulars from the diner, but there were also plenty of men obviously from out of town who came to Elton just for this event. She held on tight to her pie with one hand and Faith with the other. She didn't want to lose either as she pushed her way toward the door.

There were several categories for the ladies to enter their food into. Many of the local women were serious about their baking from what Sydney gathered from the vigorous conversations in the diner lately. As she walked through the hall taking it all in, she was amazed at the spread before her.

Perfectly baked cakes, brownies, and pies lined the wooden tables in the hall like a showcase of crusted perfection. Jams and jellies and homemade butters glistened on tiny pieces of toast and crackers. Sydney had initially scoffed at the idea of entering the auction when Melissa made the suggestion a week ago, but when she found out that the money would go to the elementary school's library, she couldn't say no. So she spent the last two days creating the perfect blackberry pie.

Sydney began baking her pies on a whim for Pete's shortly after she arrived in Elton. It was an easy way for her to make a little extra money on the side without having to be at the diner additional hours. Having time with Faith was important to her, so this was a great compromise. She could make the pies at home then bring them in to work the following day. Customers loved it when the pie rack was full, slices flying out the door as fast as she could bake them. All the recipes had been her grandmother's, the one piece of her past that she held onto and carried with her all these years. Baking turned into a hobby she loved and one she was able to share with Faith.

"Mommy, you look so pretty!" Faith looked up at her with a glowing smile.

Sydney checked out her reflection in the window. She adjusted the pale blue ribbon that matched the tiny stripes in her sweater. When she and Melissa ran home between the dance and the auction, she spent more time getting ready than she ever wanted to admit. If she bumped into Wade again tonight, she definitely didn't want to smell like a goat.

Inside the hall, her nerves started to get the better of her. The whole town would be at this auction and the last time she saw most of them, she'd been foaming at the mouth like a rabid dog. She smoothed her hands down her hair and tucked the few stray pieces behind her ear, praying that she looked like a stable human being. If she did, they might forget her outrageous display from days earlier at the diner.

"I got the pie!" Faith darted toward her, the large blackberry masterpiece about ready to topple out of her hands.

"Put that on the table here by number sixteen." The dish holding the pie hit the table with a bang, but fortunately, everything remained intact. While Faith toddled around the room checking out the competition, Sydney sliced the second pie into bite sized pieces for people to sample before they placed the bids. When the doors opened in ten minutes, all the interested bidders would arrive and let their taste buds guide them. Melissa said it was a 'blind auction' so the names of the people who baked the pies were kept anonymous so as to not influence the bidding in any way. It all sounded a bit complicated from Melissa's hasty explanation, but the idea of anonymity worked for Sydney. If no one bid on her pie, she'd be the only one to know.

"There you are!" Melissa rushed in looking like the picture of fall with her jeans and cream color cardigan sweater accented by the bright scarf around her neck. She slowly looked Sydney up and down with a smile. "You look super cute! You aren't trying to impress anyone in particular, are you?"

"I do have a knife in my hand." Sydney waved the berry-covered blade toward Melissa's pristine sweater.

"Brat. Come on, you've got to get away from this pie before the guys arrive." She looked at her watch. "It's almost time to start. Let me help you finish." Together they scattered the small plates around the table. Even Sydney had to admit the pie looked damn good arranged in the basket with cute fall decorations around it. Hopefully someone would think it was worth bidding on.

"Perfect," Melissa said as she scooped Faith up on her hip. Sydney followed them toward the door just as a rush of men poured into the hall from the opposite side. "Let's take Faith to sample some applesauce in the apple tent while the auction is going on." Melissa's grip on her arm tightened as she dragged Sydney away from the pie tables.

"Lookie, lookie who just strolled in here looking all sexy in those tight fitting jeans you love so much, Syd."

"Will you please be quiet?" Sydney hissed trying not to laugh. Melissa was outrageous and Sydney loved her all the more for it. She braved a peek over her shoulder and had to admit that Wade did look damn good, but that was nothing new. The man could wear a sack and somehow make it look scrumptious. But the simple jeans and T-shirt he was wearing did send Sydney's heart into overdrive, especially after having spent a little time with him earlier in the day and all the talk about kissing. Her overactive imagination was a very dangerous thing.

"Here for some pie, Wade?" Melissa shouted across the room with a wave.

Wade looked their way and smiled. Whatever else she planned to say was interrupted by the squeaking microphone. Melissa picked up the pace and hustled Sydney and Faith out the door, but not before they heard the opening announcement.

"Welcome, gentlemen, to the Perfect Pairing Pie Auction. It's tasting time! Pick a pie, pick a date," a female voice declared with great enthusiasm as the door shut behind them.

Sydney grabbed the back of Melissa's sweater. "Tell me you didn't do what I think you did."

"I didn't do what you think I did," she deadpanned, hiding behind Faith's brown curls.

"Melissa!" Sydney stomped her foot in frustration. "What did you get me into?"

"I told you it was a blind date pie auction."

"No, no, no, no, no. You said it was a blind auction. As in, they wouldn't know whose pie they were bidding on."

"Yes, that's true. See, I didn't lie. The guys have no idea whose pie they're bidding on!" Melissa put Faith down and ushered her toward the applesauce tent. With a squeal, Faith ran from one display to the next, slurping applesauce off spoons as fast as she could.

Sydney cornered her friend next to a bucket of apples. "Start talking."

"Fine." With an exasperated sigh, Melissa waved her hand through the air. "I might have left out the part where you go on a date with the guy who buys the pie."

"Tell me you're kidding." Sydney didn't go on dates. She kept to herself and took care of Faith. The thought of going on a date with a complete stranger was unnerving.

"I'm serious, but it's all in good fun. It's not like you have to sleep with the guy or anything. For all you know, the winner might be married."

"Wade's in there!"

"Duh," Melissa said with a roll of her eyes. "I'm gonna kill you."

With a wink, Melissa laughed. "Nah, I have a feeling you'll be thanking me by the end of the night. Don't think I missed the big goofy grin on your face when he walked you to the dance this afternoon."

Sydney tuned out Melissa's teasing as her mind raced a mile a minute. She was about to be auctioned off like a head of cattle to a room full of men. A room that Wade was in. Would he bid on her? Would he know her pie? What if he won? Without realizing it, she had made the blackberry pie he ordered every day at the diner. If there was one pie he might recognize by taste, that was it. Her stomach somersaulted, but she wasn't about to let Melissa know she was excited about the prospect. She'd never hear the end of it.

"Faith, don't put the spoon back in the jar if you licked it!" Sydney gave her daughter a stern look. The guilty smirk on Faith's face was almost enough to make her smile—almost. Instead, she glared at Melissa. "Thanking you? What the hell does that mean?"

"It means I'm betting that Wade can identify his favorite pie from all the others in the room. He eats it four times a week at the diner for goodness sake. I'm betting he wins your pie!" When Sydney didn't mirror her excitement, she shook her head.

"There are over twenty pies in there, Mel."

"Trust me. He'll bid on your pie. He'll outbid everyone in town for it."

"Did you tell him which one was mine?"

Melissa laughed. "How could I? I didn't even know your number until I walked into the hall." For the first time Melissa looked nervous. "Are you mad at me?"

"Yes."

"Do you forgive me? And feel no pressure to rush the forgiveness, but I will remind you I'm leaving in a few days."

"If Wade doesn't pick my pie…"

"I'll kill him myself." Melissa placed her hand solemnly over her heart with a grin.

A million thoughts raced through Sydney's head. Strangling Melissa was at the forefront, second only to dying of embarrassment when no one bid on her pie, or Wade walking out with the likes of slutty Pamela Wilson on his arm after winning her pie, or Sydney having to go out on a date with Walter Frist, the man seven months shy of his ninetieth birthday. He probably liked pie.

As a distraction, they busied themselves sampling apples until a shrill squeak of the loudspeaker grabbed everyone's attention. "Good evening! It's time for the Fall Festival Pick a Pie Auction. Will all the ladies who entered please return to the assembly hall for the matchmaking!"

"Come on, Faith. We gotta go get your momma a date!" Melissa yelled, turning every head in the apple tent. Sydney covered her face, not sure how she'd survive the night.

With an excited squeal, Faith licked her fingers clean and clapped her still sticky hands together. "What's a date, Mel? Why does Mommy need one, and can I have one too?"

"A date is when Mommy gets all dressed up and a handsome man comes over to the house to take her out to dinner or someplace nice like that." She bent down and whispered in Faith's ear, "And he might even kiss her when he brings her home!"

"Ewwww," Faith laughed, launching herself into her mother's arms. "Do you really want to go on one of these dates, Mommy, and let some boy kiss you?"

Sydney wanted to strangle Melissa for getting her into this mess to begin with, and now, this conversation with Faith was just the cherry on top. As they walked into the hall she answered as honestly as she could. "I guess it depends on the boy."

Inside the doorway, the trio gaped at the crowd that had assembled. The room was packed with hungry men and the women who had baked pies. Sydney started to panic as Melissa shoved their way into the mob of women.

It didn't take long for her to scan the crowd and find the town's sexy sheriff standing against the back wall. He looked uninterested in the whole event until he caught Sydney's eye. He gave her a nod of acknowledgement and the faintest smile before turning his attention to the woman on stage, addressing the crowd.

"I'd like to thank all the ladies for the delicious pies they took the time to bake. As you can see from the empty sample plates, they were very much enjoyed." A loud round of cheers sounded from the men in the crowd. "And thank you, gentlemen, for opening your wallets for a good cause. Now, let's start the auction!"

Excited cheers filled the hall, but Sydney's palms were sweating as the bidding started with the auctioneer introducing each entry. "Pie number one is a traditional apple pie, made with a recipe that was brought over on the Mayflower." People gasped as if an impressive pedigree would somehow make the apples taste better. Sydney surveyed the women and guessed it was made by the reverend's wife, the proud smirk on her face a dead giveaway. When the reverend's hand shot up first to bid, Sydney's suspicions were confirmed.

"Mayflower my ass," Melissa whispered loud enough for only Sydney to hear.

"Twenty dollars," the auctioneer called and the reverend nodded in agreement, proud as could be. When the auctioneer called for forty dollars and Luke's hand jumped into the air, the reverend made eye contact with his wife and tugged at his clerical collar. He looked quite pained when he accepted the auctioneer's call of sixty dollars.

The men in the room laughed and continued their good-natured ribbing with one another as the bidding went on. The auctioneer loved Luke because he took great pleasure in outbidding the husbands, forcing them to dig deeper into their pockets to win their wives' favor. For the time being, it had Sydney laughing, but as the numbers on the pies crept higher, her hands began to shake. The mere thought of being on the auction block was terrifying.

Where Luke's hand was constantly bobbing up and down to bid, Wade sat back and watched. He hadn't taken his hands out of his pockets, not once tempted to bid, even when the pie that obviously belonged to Pamela Wilson named Silky Strawberry Seduction was on the block. The pink sprinkles and obscene amount of whipped cream on top of the pie made it the least appetizing thing Sydney had ever seen. However, the men in the room felt differently. They flailed about, their hands flying into the air with each call of the auctioneer, bidding each other up to a ridiculous final total of two hundred dollars for her pie. The whole time that was going on, Wade stared at Sydney.

"What a tramp," Melissa whispered, covering Faith's ears. "Did you see Pamela flick open the button on her blouse when the bidding hit a hundred dollars and then again at two hundred?" Melissa rolled her eyes. "So much for keeping it anonymous."

"As soon as I heard the name of the pie and saw the sprinkles, I knew it was hers. So did everyone else in this room. Who else would give their pie such a trashy name?" Sydney whispered as Melissa uncovered Faith's ears.

"When is it your turn, Mommy?" Faith was bouncing with excitement.

"Soon," Sydney said with a nervous laugh. "But we can't tell anyone when it's my pie. It has to be a surprise, remember?" Reflexively her eyes searched out Wade who had moved away from the wall and was slowly inching closer to the front of the room.

Melissa noticed, too, and snickered. "Someone's jockeying for better bidding position." The smug, sing-song tone of her voice made Sydney blush from head to toe.

"Stop it," she said, shooing Melissa away. Her hands went to her burning cheeks. Was he moving closer to bid on her pie or someone else's? Sydney's heart stopped when the auctioneer closed the bidding on number fifteen and introduced the next pie.

"Now up for auction, number sixteen!"

Sydney's heart raced as the panic set in. Wide-eyed, she looked out into the cheering crowd. Wade had moved through the throng of people and was front and center. His hands were out of his pockets and now resting firmly on his hips. From all appearances, there was a distinct possibility he might bid on her pie. The mere thought of it tripled Sydney's pulse rate and made her a little dizzy. Luke was standing behind

Wade, glaring at the back of his head. When the auctioneer asked for an opening bid of twenty dollars, multiple hands flew into the air.

Not one of them was Wade's.

She tried to keep her face calm even though her heart was about to burst from her chest. Hurt, disappointment, and confusion swirled in her mind but she prayed she kept her face stoic through it all. So much for Melissa's brilliant idea. She scanned the crowd to investigate the bidders she recognized. Luke, of course, was one of them. He'd bid on every pie so far. A nice guy, a friend, but if she was being honest, not the man she wanted to go on a date with. That man was stubbornly standing a few feet away with his jaw clenched, watching other men bid on her pie.

Luke was definitely the best of the initial bidders. The other two were Matt Schuller, whose young wife was glaring at him so ferociously, Sydney was certain his hand wasn't going up in the air again and Johnny. There probably wasn't anyone in the entire room more distasteful than him. He was self-centered, abrasive, and obnoxious. If she had to listen to his mortician talk for an evening, Melissa was going to be sorry.

As predicted, Matt's hand remained firmly in his pocket and the others fell by the wayside, but Luke and Johnny continued bidding back and forth. The price of her pie soon reached seventy-five dollars. Luke kept his attention toward the auctioneer the whole time. He was too engrossed in the spectacle of it all to try and match the pie to the woman who had made it. With each dollar that was added, Sydney's hope that Wade would raise his hand faded. Melissa was so annoyed she began to inch her way through the crowd, looking like she might throw his hand into the air herself. Sydney caught Melissa's eye and shook her head.

If Wade wanted her, he was going to have to do it on his own.

The bidding slowed with Luke still in the lead at ninety dollars. Johnny looked back at the table, apparently debating if the blackberry creation was worth a few dollars more. As he opened his mouth to bid, Sydney felt someone watching her. She searched for the only person who made her skin tingle that way. Wade. He looked her in the eye, his hand high above his shoulders. In a deep voice that made her heart squeeze, he called out, "One hundred dollars."

Any thought Johnny had about bidding ended the moment Wade upped the stakes. Where Johnny bowed out quietly, Luke's body language said it all. He was not about to be outbid by Wade. When his hand went back into the air and he called out one hundred and twenty-five dollars, the auctioneer sensed the shift in the bidding. So could everyone else in the room. He quickly asked for one hundred and fifty-dollars, which Wade returned with a subtle nod. He continued looking at Sydney to make it clear he was going to win this auction, and her.

He knows it's my pie. Her heart soared at the thought but she kept her face as calm as she could with Wade's heated stare fixed on her.

"Now this must be a quality pie." The auctioneer laughed as the crowd cheered in return. The excitement in the hall was palpable. "Any other men want to get in on this?" When no one else dared to raise their hand, he focused his attention back on Wade and Luke, determined to find a victor but not before convincing them to part with a bit more of their cash. "Now, let me repeat myself. I have a bid of one hundred and fifty dollars for this delicacy. Can I get one hundred and sixty?"

Melissa was nearly jumping up and down in the audience mouthing, "I told you so!" and pointing at Wade. Faith was perched on a chair watching the two men banter back and forth with the auctioneer.

"Who's gonna win, Mommy?" Faith asked wide eyed as the dollar amounts went higher and higher.

"I don't know. We'll just have to see."

Some of Melissa must have rubbed off on Sydney's daughter because she suddenly whispered, "Who do you want to win, Mommy?"

Sydney felt her cheeks flush with embarrassment as she tickled her ornery daughter. "Don't you worry about that. Now hush and watch the auction."

Luke accepted the next bid, then someone in the crowd shouted, "Come on, Sheriff, raise that hand! You're always at Pete's eating pie." There was excitement in the air now that Wade had entered the bidding.

Luke was furious, but the crowd was thrilled. A few of the older women had followed Wade's attention to Sydney and were nodding their heads approvingly. Through it all, Sydney managed to keep her face neutral and simply looked back at Wade even though the heat of his gaze was so intense she felt like it was melting her bones. There was no doubt he knew the pie was hers and he looked damn determined to win it.

A night alone with Wade Jenkins. The thought sent a delicious shiver down her spine. The chemistry between them was unlike anything she'd ever felt before. Since he admitted he was thinking about kissing her, Sydney's imagination had been running wild.

As if sensing the direction of Sydney's thoughts, Wade winked at her then accepted the next outrageous bid, much to the delight of the auctioneer. Not to be outdone, Luke agreed before the auctioneer finished saying the follow-up price. In the blink of an eye, her pie was up to one hundred and ninety dollars. Feeding off the momentum of the men, the auctioneer rapidly called for two hundred dollars, and you could have heard a pin drop in the hall.

"Whoever she is, she better be worth it," a deep voice shouted from the back of the room. The crowd laughed good-naturedly and even the corner of Wade's mouth turned up into a grin.

"I'm betting she is," Wade said and nodded to the auctioneer.

Sydney could feel Melissa and countless other women staring at her with their mouths hanging open in disbelief. Wade Jenkins always played his cards close to his chest. He rarely shared his feelings and here he was, in front of the entire town, expressing interest in her.

When Luke growled, "Two fifty," Wade finally broke eye contact with Sydney long enough to look at his competitor, the animosity between them clear. "How high are you willing to go, Sheriff?" His nasty taunt reached Sydney's ears. She couldn't tell if he was bidding to win the pie, or simply to beat Wade. Knowing that it was probably the latter left a bitter taste in her mouth.

Wade mumbled something to Luke under his breath, and then turned to the auctioneer. "Three hundred dollars."

A whoop came up from the crowd, as people voiced their excitement. She heard the woman beside her mumble, "That's a new record!" She smiled at Sydney. "You must be quiet the little baker."

It was supposed to be anonymous, but Wade was making it obvious who he was bidding on and Sydney felt exposed to the crowd. In contrast, Luke hadn't once looked her direction, his attention solely on Wade. At a bid of three hundred and fifty dollars, Luke cursed, shook his head in surrender, and stormed to the back of the hall. A cheer went out to celebrate the generous donation from the sheriff.

Wade won her pie. She had a date with Wade Jenkins.

Sydney was in a complete daze as the last few pies were auctioned off without nearly as much fanfare as hers had garnered. It was all so surreal. Melissa was beaming. Faith fed off the excitement in the room and was bouncing up and down at her side. Soon the auction came to an end.

"I'm thrilled to announce that we have set a new fundraising record, nearly doubling the amount we raised last year for the elementary school's library."

A loud thunder of applause rumbled through the room. The principal beamed with appreciation on the stage. Sydney was happy to know it had all been for a good cause and the children in town would benefit from it. She tried to focus on that fact as they called the ladies who had entered the contest to the front of the room for the reveal.

Any questions about whose pie Wade had been bidding on were about to be answered. And who he had a date with.

"Now for the fun part of the evening!" The announcer, who Sydney thought might have had a little too much coffee this afternoon, excitedly launched into introductions. "Pie number one was made by Mrs. Walter, and the winner of that delicious pie and a date with Misty is none other than…Reverend Walter. No surprise there, he's been eating that delicious Mayflower pie for years! Come on up, Reverend, and claim your pie and your date."

Applause rang through the room as the names were read and winners announced. Every pie had been purchased, thank goodness, and names continued to be rattled off. As predicted, husbands were paired with their wives. After some encouragement from the crowd, Pete laid a huge kiss on Cara as he claimed her signature cherry pie.

"It's almost your turn, Momma!" Faith was far more excited than Sydney about the impending announcement. A swarm of butterflies were raging in her stomach, making it difficult to breathe. There was no doubt she and Wade would become the talk of Elton. Even if it was only one date, the gossip mill would be working overtime.

Luke offered her a brief distraction from her panic. "Did you enter, Sydney? I had no idea."

"Funny, neither did I." She shot Melissa a withering look. "Did you have fun bidding on all those pies?"

"Yeah." He rubbed the back of his neck. "You should have told me what number you were and I could have saved you from one of these idiots." He waved his hand at the crowd of men who were left.

"Well, like I said, I had no idea I was being turned into a paid escort for the night. And besides," she peeked toward Wade and noticed him watching her talk to Luke, her heart rate picking up, "I'm pretty sure that's against the rules."

"Momma was number sixteen," Faith whispered with a grin. She was terrible at keeping secrets, unlike her mother. "You almost won her pie."

"Faith," Sydney reprimanded, "you weren't supposed to tell."

"That was you he was bidding on?" Of course Luke would be annoyed that it was Sydney's pie Wade had won, but the venom in his voice was over the top. Melissa didn't hesitate to put him in his place.

"If you would have looked around a little instead of staring holes into the back of Wade's head you might have noticed, Luke," Melissa chastised him. "You really have to let it go. Not everything is a competition."

"Right," he said as he looked at Sydney with a frown then walked away.

"I think he's sad he lost," Faith whispered tugging on her mother's arm. Any further conversation was interrupted by the over-caffeinated announcer gathering everyone's attention.

"Now, for my favorite part of the night. The big winner. The record price for a pie, set a few years back by the mayor's wife has been shattered tonight!" Excited applause came from those still in attendance.

"He's going to have to spend big bucks to reclaim the title for his wife next year. He's such a cheapskate, too, it'll kill him to throw out extra cash," Melissa said with a laugh.

"The highest selling pie, as we all know, was number sixteen. The lovely lady who baked it is none other than one of our newest residents to Elton, Sydney Ross!"

"Hooray, Momma!" Faith jumped up and down with all the exuberance her five-year-old body could manage. "You won!"

"Told you so," Melissa sang with a Cheshire grin on her face as she elbowed Sydney.

With a wave of her hand, the announcer signaled to Sydney. "Could you come up here, dear?" When Sydney was within earshot, she whispered, "Lucky girl."

Sydney prayed she didn't look as terrified as she felt as she stepped on stage. She nervously played with a piece of hair that fell over her shoulder and looked anywhere but directly into the crowd. She could feel him watching her, even now.

"Pie sixteen went to the very generous and high bidding Wade Jenkins! Come on up and claim your pie and your date, Sheriff."

Her eyes immediately locked on his across the room. The applause and wolf whistles faded and all she saw was Wade. Sydney felt like she was going to combust as he pushed off the wall and strode through the crowd with that quiet confidence he had. Everything about the way he moved made her insides melt and her brain short-circuit. She vaguely remembered his massive shoulder brushing against hers as he claimed the pie and then her hand. He led her off to the side where Faith and Melissa joined them, congratulating Wade on his purchase. She dropped his hand like a hot potato when Melissa smirked at their linked fingers.

Sydney pulled out of her fog just in time to hear Faith say to Wade, "You know I helped her make the pie, but I'm not going on the date because I don't want to kiss a boy yet. But Momma's okay with it."

"That's good to know. Thanks, Faith."

"Why is your face all red, Momma?"

Faith's innocent question sent Melissa over the edge into a laughing fit. She scooped the little girl up into her arms and managed to squeak out, "We're just going to go help with the clean-up while you two...chat." As they walked away, behind Wade's back Melissa mouthed, "You owe me" to Sydney.

"So," Sydney said to fill the awkward silence between them, "you liked the pie?"

"I order it every time I'm at Pete's, don't I?"

Her heart soared, and then fell. "Oh, you thought it was Cara's," she mumbled as she looked away.

Wade cupped her chin and turned her face to look at him. "I've been going to Pete's for years. Cara's specialty is cherry, but yours is the blackberry pie." His hand felt warm and strong against her cheek but he held her like she was as delicate as a baby bird. "There's always blackberry when you come to work carrying those white boxes."

Sydney stared at him for the longest time before the corners of her mouth turned up into a little grin. "I guess being a cop makes you pretty observant, huh?"

"I pay attention to things I'm interested in," he said, releasing his hold.

They stood together for a moment, the basket that carried the pie between them acting as a barrier. Thankfully it was there or she might have done something stupid like wrap herself around Wade.

"Give me your phone." When her eyebrows shot up at the command, he sheepishly rephrased his words. "May I please have your phone?"

It was a miracle her fingers still worked, she was trembling so much. She prayed he wouldn't notice as she slipped it into his outstretched hand. He quickly punched in his number and gave it back to her, his hand lingering as his fingertips brushed against the inside of her wrist. "Call me later."

"O-Okay," Sydney stammered as she extended the pie to him. With one hand he grabbed the handle of the basket, while the other brushed against her cheek before it cupped the back of her head and pulled her toward him for a gentle kiss.

The idea of kissing Wade had consumed her every thought since this afternoon, but all her fantasizing didn't come close to doing it justice. Everything stopped in that moment and Sydney knew that she was forever lost where this man was considered.

It was a light feathering of his lips across hers, but it might as well have been full body contact with the way her heart responded. Wade did nothing to hide his desire. It was written plainly on his face. But when he pulled back, he didn't kiss her again. He simply smiled and held her close, promising there was much more to come between them without uttering a single word. Her hands fell against his chest to keep from melting into a puddle at his feet. Everyone in the room could have been staring at them, but Sydney didn't notice. When she looked up into his eyes, there was only Wade. Everything else faded away. And she didn't think that was going to change anytime soon.

CHAPTER 5

Exhaustion was an awful thing which Wade had lived through plenty of times in the past, but this was one of the worst. Not only was his body stretching itself beyond its limits, so was his mind. They had upped their patrols in the area since the woman, Samantha, had been found in Greenville to give the residents of Elton some peace of mind. It had been almost a week and there were still no leads he knew of in the case.

Wade sipped his coffee and forced himself to look out the window into the bright sunlight. If he didn't, he was going to search for her face in the kitchen again.

"You look serious," Melissa said with a nudge to his shoulder before sliding into the seat across from him, refilling his coffee.

"Morning."

They'd been friends forever. No matter how bad things got, Wade could always count on Melissa for a smile and a laugh. She had more spirit than anyone he had ever met, even as a kid. She'd follow Wade and her older brother Matt around everywhere they went. If he and Matt had the hair-brained idea of jumping off a tree branch into the river, she was right behind them. When they stole the tires off Johnny's truck one night, she was the first one caught but she never ratted them out. More than anything, it was her carefree smile and warmth that made her impossible to resist. There was never anything romantic between them—she was too much like a sister to him. When Matt moved away, she would come to Wade with problems or questions, and she helped him more than he could say when he came back from the service. He didn't know where he'd be without the hyper little blonde in his life, and he wouldn't have it any other way.

Her absence over the next few months was going to be difficult, but he was so happy she was following this dream of hers to travel the world. She had set a goal, and now she was making it happen. That's the kind of woman Melissa was. And currently, she looked like she was gearing up for the inquisition.

"So, what's new? You look tired. Been up late dreaming of pie again? Or maybe pretty blondes?"

Wade rubbed his hand against his jaw and smiled. "You're like a dog with a bone, Mel."

"Oh, come on, Wade. This is good for you and for her. She's so sweet. Don't smirk at me, mister. I see the way you look at her and I saw that kiss you laid on her at the auction. So did everyone else in town, in case you were wondering. You might think you're being subtle, but believe me, everyone around here sees it." She gave his hand a gentle squeeze. "She'll be good for you. It's time you start living again, Wade. You've shut yourself off for too long. If anyone can put a smile back on that ugly mug of yours, it's Sydney."

"I would have asked her out on my own, you know."

"Well frankly, I got tired of waiting, Wade Jenkins. I leave in a couple days and there was no way in hell I was gonna wait six months to hear about your first date." She leaned back in her seat, smiling. "Look at it this way: I just gave you two a little shove in the right direction, that's all. You can thank me later." As she scooted out of her seat, Wade caught her wrist.

"Thanks, Mel."

She bent over and kissed his cheek. "Anytime." With a wink she walked away, checking on each of her tables and filling the diner with her infectious laughter.

His thoughts returned to Sydney and the kiss they had shared. He had no idea what made him do it, driven only by the thought that he couldn't not kiss her at that moment. She had looked so sweet and nervous. And sexy. There was something about her he couldn't resist, and he realized he didn't want to anymore. Not after he had a taste of her and what could be.

As luck would have it, just then Sydney's tiny blue car flew into the parking lot, kicking up rocks as she sped around back to park. Fate wasn't going to let this go. And neither was Wade.

The first time Wade saw Sydney Ross was four months ago and it was a sight he'd never forget. She was standing on top of the counter, changing a light bulb in one of the fixtures for Cara. Her laughter and spirit caught his attention immediately, not to mention her killer legs which were on full display that day. He buried his smile behind his mug at the memory. She was beautiful, with the kind of curves a man couldn't help but notice, and hair so blonde it was almost white.

He'd had many fantasies about that hair of hers.

At thirty-four, Wade had been through the relationship wringer and had no interest in doing it again. Even with all her personality, there was something about Sydney, a darkness in her eyes, a mystery that she kept to herself that he had been trying to figure out. Women with secrets were bad news in Wade's book. But Sydney wasn't just any woman; she was the first woman in years to spark his interest and make him even think about what it would be like to have someone in his life.

How stupid was he?

He learned a long time ago, you find out more about a person by watching than talking to them. Staying true to that, he was quite content to watch Sydney every chance he got. Sometimes, he noticed her eyes were full of sadness, but only when she thought no one was looking. She kept it hidden well, probably from years of practice, Wade guessed. When her daughter, Faith, was around, it was the opposite. Her face glowed. She couldn't hide her love for her daughter if she tried. The two of them together were like sunshine, and everyone around was attracted to them.

Especially Wade.

"Sorry I'm late." He heard Sydney's soft voice in the kitchen and Wade forced his eyes to stay trained outside a bit longer. "Faith had a fever when I picked her up from school. I gave her some medicine before I left her with Agnes, but I wanted to see if it went any higher." He heard the kitchen door squeak and his head reflexively turned to watch her make her entrance with two boxes balanced in her arms. As she slipped the golden crusted pies into the rack, Wade knew she had been up late baking.

And she still hadn't called him.

He knew she'd go on the date, since it was part of his bounty for winning the pie and she didn't seem the type to back out of an obligation. But he didn't want her to see him as an obligation; he wanted to be her choice. She had liked it when he kissed her—he'd kissed enough women to know when they were into it, and she was definitely right there with him. But since then, she'd been avoiding him. His damn wounded pride wouldn't let it go. He'd rather not go out with her at all than to have her grudgingly follow through with it because she felt like she had to. The silence was preferred to her pity.

There was no denying the chemistry between them, but she turned skittish whenever she found him looking at her, which was often. Fortunately, Wade was a patient man and he was willing to wait and see what happened between them. He had a feeling when Sydney made up her mind to do something, she did it all the way.

While he finished off his sandwich, he studied Sydney. Her every movement was enticing to him. Somehow the woman managed to make something as simple as slicing pie sexy. He was enjoying the view as she bent over to fill the lower shelf when Melissa appeared at his table with a smirk.

The girl didn't miss a thing.

"Got your eye on anything else? You still look kinda hungry, Wade. Maybe something sweet now that Sydney's here?"

"I'll have some pie." He saw her eyes light up as she scurried back to the counter. She bent her head to Sydney's and whispered in her ear. Sydney's head swung around his direction then quickly turned away, but not before he caught the pink flush of her cheeks. Whatever Melissa had been running her mouth about earned her a playful smack on the shoulder.

From across the diner, Melissa flashed Wade a big thumbs up. "Sydney will be right over with your pie, Wade. I'm going on break." She disappeared into the kitchen just as Sydney made a lunge at her.

He watched Sydney take her time finishing up with the pies before steeling herself and heading his way. She was easy to read, and for some reason he found her vulnerability where he was concerned, cute. There was no point hiding his interest anymore, the auction had taken care of that and the opportunity to watch the sway of her hips as she walked his way was far too tempting.

"Hi, Wade. Melissa, in her own subtle way, hinted you might like a piece of pie." She gently placed a plate on the table with a nervous smile.

"Peach?" he asked as his fork pierced the crust, spearing one of the ripe fruit slices.

Sydney shrugged, but didn't step away. He could tell she was waiting for his reaction to the pie and that brought him more satisfaction than it should have.

"I thought I'd try something new. I also figured you might be sick of blackberry pie, since the auction."

The sweet flavors of peach exploded in his mouth with each bite. The woman had a gift for baking, anyone with taste buds would notice that, but there was something about the idea of eating something she had made herself that Wade found incredibly sexy.

Maybe it was simply because he kept remembering that her lips tasted as sweet as her pies.

"It's delicious."

"Thanks," she said tugging at her ponytail that had fallen over her shoulder trying not to smile at his praise. If only she knew the improper thoughts her fingers put in his head as they glided through her hair.

"You haven't called." It was hard to keep from smiling when her hands went still, her eyes filling with an insecurity that, on her, was charming.

"It's late whenever I think to call you, or I'm in bed. I mean, I-I didn't…" she stammered for a second, like he knew she would when he tossed the questions out to her. He could see her thinking, then with a resigned sigh she blurted out, "The thing is, Wade, I don't know how to ask a man out on a date." He could see how much it cost her to admit it. She was young and lively, but apparently old fashioned on some things.

That made him smile.

He knew she was seconds away from taking off for the kitchen, but he couldn't resist teasing her just a little more to see if he could get that spark of fire to flash in her eyes. "If you'd have called, I'd have done the asking." Right on cue, her arms folded and her temper flared. And all he could think about was kissing her again.

"You've been playing me." Her hip settled against the table right in his line of sight. He took a long, slow appraisal of her curves before meeting her eyes.

"Guilty as charged."

"Then I don't plan on making this easy on you. I may owe you a date but you better show me a good time or I'll tell all your female fans around town that you don't know how to entertain a woman." She leaned forward to take the empty pie plate, but Wade stopped her, catching her hand and holding her close enough to smell the intoxicating floral scent of her perfume.

"I know plenty of ways to entertain a woman, Sydney. Don't you worry about that." Once again electricity sparked around them, the sexual tension palpable. He thought for a second about kissing her again because their first kiss hadn't been enough. He definitely wanted a second taste, but with her impeccable timing, Melissa came screeching out of the kitchen.

"Syd, look!"

Sydney nearly fell into Wade's lap, she was so startled. "What's gotten into you?" she asked her friend as she waved the newspaper in her hand.

"Wade, you've got to see this, too!" She shoved the pie plate toward the window and spread out the local newspaper on the table. The front page story was about the festival and Sydney's record breaking pie. There was a large picture of her and Wade that accompanied the story listing him as the high bidder and her as the baker.

"Holy crap." Her face went white as a sheet as she slid down into the seat across from Wade. With trembling hands she covered her mouth and read the story, her eyes widening as she looked at the picture for the third time. "Faith," she gasped as he finger brushed the corner of the photograph where her daughter's image was captured in perfect clarity.

"Syd, what's wrong?" Melissa asked, looking to Wade for a clue as to what could have upset her so much. All he could do was shrug because he was as confused as Melissa.

"Who did this?" Her voice was barely a whisper as she looked between them.

"One of the local photographers probably."

"I-I didn't sign a release. I wouldn't have." Her head was shaking from side to side, emphasizing each word.

"It was probably on the entry form." Melissa smoothed her hand over Sydney's head. "It's okay, honey. What has you so scared?"

An immediate change came over Sydney at the word scared. Wade watched her put up her internal defenses and collect herself. She quickly wiped her eyes, erasing any evidence of her distress. She straightened her shoulders and stood up, grabbing Wade's plate and the paper in her hand.

"I'm fine. I just wasn't expecting to see Faith and I on the front page. I didn't remember signing the release, that's all."

"O-Okay," Melissa said slowly, trying to follow Sydney's erratic mood swing.

"I have to get to work. I'll call you, Wade," she said dismissively with a forced smile. When she left, Melissa looked like she was going to cry.

"What was that about? I thought she'd be excited."

"I don't know." He had no idea what had provoked that reaction from Sydney, but she was certainly acting like someone in hiding. Since secrets had a way of biting him in the ass, Wade intended to find out exactly what it was that had spooked Sydney.

IN HIS QUEST FOR information, Wade went back to the station for a while and did some research on the sultry Miss Ross. He turned up a few things that left him scratching his head and confirmed his suspicions that she was on the run but he still had no real answers about who or what she was running from. On a whim, he drove to the diner and parked along the street in the deep shadow of a large oak tree and waited.

Pete's was a popular place in town, but it wasn't a late night option. The diner closed at eight and like clockwork, Cara arrived just after seven to help Pete start closing. If it wasn't busy, she'd typically send the staff home and take care of things herself. She and Pete had been doing it that way for years and didn't plan on changing anytime soon.

The light in back of the diner flashed on then headlights came around the side of the building. Sydney was on her way home, so Wade decided to follow her at a distance. Tailing someone in a town as small as Elton was no easy task considering how few residents and cars there were on the road this time of night. Thankfully, the moon was full so for a while he was able to follow without his lights on. It wasn't exactly safe, but he'd been driving these roads all his life.

Wade knew where Sydney lived. The town was too small to keep that kind of secret. But as he followed, he found she wasn't taking a direct route home. At first he thought she might have errands to run from the way she weaved down some smaller streets before circling back. But she just kept going, looping around, and backtracking, as if she was worried about being followed.

"Who are you hiding from, Sydney?" Wade wondered aloud as he pulled off the side of the road, watching her car come in and out of view in the distance. It was too risky to continue following her with the erratic way she was driving, and he didn't want her to sense she was being followed, so he drove straight to her house. He found a concealed place to park his truck on a side street that still faced her house and waited. Ten minutes later, her car rounded the corner and pulled into the driveway.

In the dark, he watched Sydney lock the car and check twice to make sure it was secure. Then she went next door, checking over her shoulder as she made her way across the lawn. She constantly scanned the shrubs and dark spaces between their houses, looking for a sign of anything that might be off. Again, Wade found himself wondering who she was expecting to jump out of those bushes.

At Diablo's deep bark, the curtain tugged to the side in the kitchen and the door slowly opened revealing Agnes Whittman and Faith in the doorway. The gray-haired Agnes was into her seventies and was one of the quirkiest, but most loyal, people in town. If you were lucky enough to call her friend, you were set.

He watched the two women exchange a few words before saying their goodbyes. Sydney held Faith's hand all the way back to their house, still casting an eye over their surroundings with each step. She checked the car doors one more time before they approached the front door. Wade grabbed his binoculars and watched Sydney get out a ring of keys. Once the front door opened, Sydney saluted and waved to Mrs. Whittman who then retired back into her home. It must have been an 'all clear' signal the two women had worked out between them.

There was a methodical way Sydney moved through her home. One he recognized from his military training. She turned on every light in her home one by one, her larger shadow always entering the room first, with Faith trailing behind. Any curtains or blinds that were open, she closed. Once all the lights came on, illuminating the place like a Christmas tree, she slowly turned them off, one by one. Wade had a sick feeling it was her way of checking for any dangers that might have crept in.

But what dangers?

Wade ran his hands through his hair as he watched the house, not sure why he was unable to drive away. He knew he should, but he couldn't make himself leave yet. Faith was up in her room, and Sydney was in the kitchen, near the sink he guessed from the way Sydney's shadow was moving slightly from side to side, probably washing dishes. The list of things Wade didn't know about Sydney was lengthy, but the list of things he wanted to know about her was just as sizable. Not to mention confusing because of the emotions involved. Emotions he had long stifled for the sake of his sanity. But in the dark, he tried to focus only on what he knew.

It was obvious she was afraid; of who or what he didn't know, but most people didn't act that paranoid without good reason. She wasn't crazy. Her fear was genuine. Sydney was expecting something to happen every minute of the day. It explained her odd habit of leaving work in the middle of her shift to pick up Faith when she could have asked Agnes to do it. Add to that the systematic way she moved while driving and entering her home, he could tell she'd been living this way for a while. That routine had been practiced for so many years, it was second nature.

She was over-protective of Faith, and there was probably a very specific reason Sydney had chosen Agnes as Faith's caretaker while she had to work. When George Whittman had been alive, he and Wade had often gone hunting together with a group of men from town. He had enjoyed the older man's company and learned a lot about him, most notably that he and his wife were avid survivalists. They wanted to be prepared for any circumstance that may arise, from aliens, to invasions, to nuclear disasters. His wife was as skilled as he was with firearms and knives, and their house was rumored to have a safe room for their protection. She might be old, but Agnes was quick and agile with self-defense moves that were deadly. All of those things would make Agnes the perfect sitter for Faith in Sydney's mind if she felt they needed protection.

His head was starting to throb when his phone rang. As soon as he heard the voice on the other end, he knew his night was about to go to hell.

"Hello, Wade."

"What do you want?"

"You know the answer to that."

"Don't push me," he ground out between his teeth.

"Then don't make me." He remained silent while her laughter grated on his nerves. "Meet me in ten minutes. See you soon, honey."

Livid, Wade turned on the car, his engine roaring to life as his lights gave away his position. He had his own loose ends that needed to be tied up before he could worry about Sydney's, let alone consider a relationship with her.

Was he really considering that?

As he pulled away, his mind still raced with thoughts of Sydney. Her troubles were something he'd rather focus on than his own. The question still remained: who was she hiding from and why? Witness protection? No. She was too jumpy. A boyfriend? Possibly. He knew it wasn't an ex-husband—she'd never been married, as far as he knew—but it was going to be a bit difficult to corroborate, because he'd found out one very important detail in his search this afternoon.

Sydney and Faith Ross hadn't existed until a year and a half ago.

CHAPTER 6

Tᴴɪꜱ Rᴜʙᴇɴ ɪꜱɴ'ᴛ ɢᴏɪɴɢ to serve itself, Sydney!" Pete hollered from the kitchen as he rang the tiny bell at the window.

"Hold your horses, dear," Cara said with a dismissive wave in his direction. "She's getting ready for her big date with Wade."

"Well I don't particularly care about that, and I'm guessing Carl won't care either. Know what he'll care about? Getting his sandwich before it's cold!"

"This is a bad idea," Sydney said as she swatted Melissa's hands away from her hair and snatched the sandwich instead. With one side of her hair up in a twist and the other still hanging over her shoulder she delivered the food to the hungry customer and his wife.

"Don't know what Wade's gonna think of your new hairdo, Sydney. You might want to fix the other side. You kinda look like you've been brawling," Carl said as he took a big bite.

"Goodness, does this whole town know I have a date tonight?" Sydney threw up her hands in frustration when his head bobbed up and down. She busied herself with a loose thread on her favorite green sweater as she mumbled, "Great."

"My bridge club has been talking about little else since he bought you at the auction," Carl's wife, Anna, said with a wink as she made a puddle of ketchup on the corner of her plate.

"He bought the *pie*, not me." She tried not to think about all of the little white haired ladies in town gossiping about her dating life, or lack thereof.

"I think the pie was a bonus. He's smitten." Anna wiped the edge of her mouth with the napkin. "And I have to say, I agree with Carl. You should do something about your hair before he gets here, dear."

"Thanks," Sydney said sarcastically as she headed back to Cara and Melissa's makeshift beauty salon behind the counter.

"What time is he picking you up?" Cara took her by the shoulders and pushed her back down onto one of the stools.

"In like," she glanced at her watch, "crap, fifteen minutes!"

The diner was busy for a Thursday. A number of people were still lingering from the impromptu going away party Pete had thrown for Melissa. She had refused all offers for a farewell party, so Pete blindsided her by having everyone converge at the diner and give her a big send off. She was supposed to be on her way to St. Louis already. She had an early morning flight but refused to leave town until she helped get Sydney ready for her date with Wade.

"Melissa, will you just go? I don't want you falling asleep at the wheel." Sydney tried to get up, but was held in place by Cara's firm hand on her shoulder.

"Save your breath. I'm not leaving until I see you two walk out that door together. I've waited months for this moment, and I'm not missing it. I'll get there when I get there."

With a rough pull, Cara and Melissa coordinated their movements in an attempt to tame every hair on her head. To distract herself from the pain and the butterflies that were raging in her stomach, she looked around for a distraction.

"Melissa, I think—"

Her friend held tight to her hair and waggled a finger in her face. "No way, scaredy cat. You aren't getting out of this date. Cara said she can handle the diner. Every person in this stinking town was just here to say goodbye to me, even though I distinctly remember telling Pete I didn't want a party." She yelled out the last part loud enough for her voice to carry into the kitchen. "There won't be another customer in this place until breakfast tomorrow. Now you go stare dreamily into Wade's eyes for a few hours, and if you get a little action, well, you can thank me in the morning. Preferably before six a.m. when my flight takes off." Melissa wrinkled her nose. "Is that what you're wearing? You look like a nun."

"Oh, for God's sake."

"See? Nun talk." Melissa walked over and wrenched open the collar of Sydney's blouse, sending the tiny button flying across the counter. "Oh please, he paid three hundred dollars, that's more than a high priced call girl. Give the guy a little look at the goods."

Luke chose that moment to stroll over to the counter, a deep frown on his face. "Nice, Melissa."

"Why am I friends with you again?" Sydney asked rolling her eyes, hoping to lighten the dark mood Luke brought with him. He had said little to her since the auction. Melissa insisted he was pouting, upset over the fact that Wade had gotten the best of him, yet again. Whatever their history, it made Sydney uncomfortable to be in the middle of the latest animosity. She hoped he would have shelved it for the day and just been happy and wished Melissa well before she left for her trip but it didn't look like that was going to happen.

"How have you been, Luke?" Sydney asked trying to make small talk as Melissa tugged the last few hairs into place.

"Fine."

"Good to hear." She tried to meet his eye but he was staring over her shoulder at the kitchen door. "You got any plans this weekend?"

"No."

Irritated with his short answers and bad attitude, Sydney snapped, "You mad about something?"

He finally met her eyes and blinked slowly, not bothering to hide his disapproval. "Would it matter if I was?" Sydney's mouth fell open as he turned on his heel and walked away. Their awkward exchange was missed by her friends, the two of them more engrossed in an unruly section of hair than anything Luke had to say.

Melissa circled around her slowly, resembling a large cat about to pounce on prey. When Sydney turned her head to ask Cara what was going on, Melissa snuck in and pulled the old, green sweater she was wearing off her shoulders revealing the light, gauzy blouse underneath. That and her jeans were much sexier than the homely cardigan she had been rockin' moments earlier.

"Give it back." Sydney lunged for the sweater, but Melissa scooted to the other side of the counter.

"No way," she said as she shoved her arms into the sweater and buttoned it up. "Consider this an intervention. This sweater needs to go. I'll give it a European burial for you."

"If you hate it, why are you wearing it?"

"To annoy you. Is it working?"

"Yes." Sydney bit back a laugh as Melissa tugged her hair into a ponytail and got serious about Sydney's makeup.

"Come on. Let's finish your face before he gets here."

Sydney yanked the bobby pins from one side of her hair, letting it all flow over her shoulder. As she gave her head a shake she said, "I'm done playing beauty salon. I worked all afternoon, so this is me. Wade's going to get me as I am. Take it or leave it."

"I'll take it," a deep voice drawled over her shoulder.

"Wade," Sydney whispered in a rushed exhale as she spun around, sending her hair flying over her shoulder. He was standing so close she could feel the heat radiating off his body. She wished like hell she had that sweater to hide behind. "Hi."

"Ready to go?"

"Get her out of here, Wade. I've got a few lingering customers to serve and she's distracting all the women," Pete said with a huff. "And the men too…"

"Let me grab my purse." Sydney's heart fluttered when she stepped out from behind the counter and Wade extended a hand out to her. His hands were rough but she liked the feel of them and the strength with which he held her.

"You kids have fun," Cara called from the kitchen. "Take good care of her, Wade."

"Don't do anything I wouldn't do," Melissa yelled with an exaggerated wink. Sydney broke away from Wade and ran to Melissa wrapping her arms around her neck and hugging her until she couldn't breathe.

"I'm gonna miss you, Mel."

Melissa wiped her eyes, not wanting it to turn into a waterworks display between them, especially when she spent so much time on Sydney's makeup. "I want a full email or text before my plane leaves, or I'm gonna be really pissed off," she whispered in Sydney's ear. "I'll text you when I get to St. Louis tonight, but hopefully you'll be too distracted by Wade to notice." She waggled her eyebrows at Sydney. "Then I'll be in touch when I can." She pulled back and gave one last teary hug to Sydney before pushing her back into Wade's arms. "If she gets chilly, Wade, just toss one of those big strong arms around her shoulders to warm her up."

"Be safe, Mel." Wade kissed his friend on the cheek, whispering one last message in her ear that had her laughing out loud.

"Take care of yourself. And Sydney." She waved from behind the counter as they headed out the door. "You guys make a really cute couple!"

Outside the sun was setting and the crisp fall breeze sent goosebumps up Sydney's arms, but there was no way she was going to let Wade know she was cold, not after the way Melissa had been carrying on. It was bittersweet that the night she was most excited about since she came to town was the same night her dearest friend was leaving. But the date with Wade was exciting and a great distraction so she didn't spend all night crying and stuffing herself with ice cream. She pushed the sadness out of her mind as best she could and did what Melissa wanted her to do. She enjoyed herself.

"So where are we off to?" Elton was a small town with few date options or hotspots. Part of her was intrigued by what Wade would plan, knowing no matter what he chose, it would reveal something about himself.

As he tugged on the door to his truck and ushered her into the warmed cab he said, "My place."

Sydney's mouth fell open. She wasn't prepared to be alone with Wade. A million thoughts and images filled her head of the two of them at his house, none of which she would ever admit to another living soul.

She thought they might go to Murray's and have a drink, be teased by a few of their mutual friends and that would be the end of it. Maybe a drive down by the lake or a walk down Main Street for some coffee and a donut, but the thought of being so alone with him was completely terrifying, and exciting. By the time they pulled out of the parking lot, she had regained her ability to speak. "So, your place?"

"Yep," he replied with a smirk on his face. "You warm enough?"

"I'm fine, thanks."

The darkness quickly enveloped them, the streetlights giving her little glimpses of his face as he drove until they turned onto one of the more rural roads. The truck was neat and orderly and smelled like soap, the faintest hint of cologne, and Wade. She had the strangest urge to reach out and touch his cheek so she could feel the sexy stubble that shadowed his jaw. To keep from making a fool of herself, she locked her fingers together in her lap instead, and watched him out of the corner of her eye.

Her nerves started getting the better of her in the dark. She had a moment of panic, but then reminded herself Faith was in good hands. Agnes wouldn't let anything happen to her. Knowing her daughter was safe, Sydney allowed herself to relax and enjoy her time with Wade.

She never really thought about where Wade lived, since he always seemed to be working. He slowed down and turned down a hidden gravel drive. They followed it through a dense line of trees for a few yards until, off in the distance, Sydney could see the faint glow of a porch light.

Wade's home was a modest split level with neatly manicured land-scaping, she noticed as he led her up the walkway. There was a rocking chair and a small table on the porch. Sydney smiled, imagining him in the chair with his feet propped up on the rail, taking a nap or reading a book on his day off. What she wouldn't give to be in another chair beside him, having an absolutely normal afternoon, instead of always sleeping with one eye open.

"Come on in." His voice startled her out of her day dream. He held open the screen door and waited. She took a nervous step through the doorway and he followed in behind her. There seemed to be less air in the world when Wade was around and Sydney felt her breathing intensify to make up for the lack of oxygen.

"You have a beautiful home." She couldn't stop herself from wandering around, her curiosity getting the better of her. She was immediately drawn to a series of pictures that hung on the wall, wanting to know more about him. They showed him and his family, in various snapshots of his life. Part of her was jealous that he could so openly put his entire life on display. That was something she would never be able to do, but on some primal level she wanted to know what it would feel like to share that with someone.

Her eyes scanned more photos, finding a small boy who must have been Wade, then more where he had grown up and was more recognizable in his late teens. He'd always been tall, she could see, but the chiseled looks and sex appeal had clearly developed over the years. The photos of him in the military were reverently placed on a small hutch next to an older photograph from around World War II of a young man in uniform.

"That's my grandfather," he murmured proudly very close to her ear making her jump. She was acutely aware of his presence in the diner, but being alone with him, in his house, brought things to a whole new level. There was such an intimacy between them as she looked through the images of his life, learning more about him, Wade so openly sharing information with her. He reached around her and picked up a smaller frame with a picture of a boy holding a baseball bat.

"And that's you?" Sydney asked, trying not to jump when she felt his other hand settle on her hip. She felt like his hand was branding her skin through the material of her jeans.

"We won the championship that year," he said wistfully as he put the picture of himself wearing catcher's gear back on its perch. It was a simple wall of pictures, but to Sydney it was the most precious thing in the world. "It's my mom's favorite picture, and she gets mad if it's not out when she visits." She knew so much more about him after looking at the various snapshots from his life. Part of her wondered what he would do if she had a wall that showed all she had experienced. Would he turn and run? Or better yet, arrest her on the spot?

"Would you like some wine?"

"Yes," she said a little too quickly. "I'm sorry. I'm not very good at this dating thing." She didn't belong here. Wade was a nice guy, honest, respected in the community, and she was nothing but trouble. The things hanging over her head had the power to not only take her down, but everyone around her, and she didn't want that for him.

"You look like you're gonna run for the door."

"Honestly, I'm considering it," she said as she nervously played with her hair. Her eyes met his and she saw he had gone as still as a statue, waiting for an explanation. If she wanted to go, he was going to let her, even if he didn't agree. Knowing he'd do that for her made Sydney crave him all the more, and for one night, just one single night, she wanted to be normal. She wanted to forget her baggage and have fun. More than anything, she wanted that night to be with Wade. "It's a long walk back to the diner. How about that wine?"

"This way." He slipped his hand onto her lower back and led her into what appeared to be a gourmet kitchen. There was a huge cooktop on a large island in the center of the room, and an enormous refrigerator along the wall. The smells coming from the stove made her mouth water. Pots and pans of various sizes hung from the ceiling on a steel rack. Sydney leaned back against the granite countertop and gawked.

"This is the most amazing kitchen I've ever seen." She reverently ran her fingers along the cool granite, tracing every vein of color.

"Thanks. I did most of the work myself when I remodeled after my parents moved to Florida."

There were already two glasses on the counter next to an open bottle of wine. Wade poured a generous amount, the deep, rich color of the red wine swirling into the glasses. He handed Sydney one of them, raising his own and clinking it against hers before taking a drink.

"Is there anything you can't do?" She took a long sip, savoring the woody, plum flavor. Sydney moved around to the stove to peek into one of the pots. Lifting the lid, she saw a delicious red sauce bubbling inside.

"I can't crochet. My hands are like baseball mitts, according to my mother." He waggled his fingers playfully at her. "Or dance, I don't dance." Sydney laughed, remembering back to the night of the festival and what he had said to Agnes when she suggested he dance. It was nice to know he'd been truthful and hadn't made an excuse to escape.

While he drained the pasta, Sydney drank more of her wine, loving the warm feeling that was spreading through her body. It could have been from the drink or Wade, it didn't matter. She felt the tension and worry slowly leaving her body. This time she initiated the contact between them when she reached around him and snagged a piece of spaghetti from the strainer.

"Don't worry, I'm a great dancer." She popped the noodle into her mouth as she leaned back against the counter. "I'll teach you."

"I can't wait," he said with a wolfish smile that made Sydney both excited and nervous.

Working side by side in the kitchen, they put the finishing touches on dinner. It was amazing how comfortable they were together. Sydney set the table while Wade laid out the food. The square shaped table was cozy and intimate, especially when Sydney put the place settings side by side rather than across the table from one another. If she was going to have this date, then for one night, she was going to enjoy herself, and the closer she was to Wade, the better.

When they finally sat down, Wade filled her plate. Each bite was more delicious than the next. Flavors exploded in her mouth, and it was intoxicating knowing that he had gone through so much trouble for her.

"This is amazing, Wade. Thank you."

"I'm glad you came. I know Melissa didn't give you all the details on the auction before you entered and you could have said no." For just a second he lowered his defenses and she could see his vulnerability.

With a sincere smile she said, "I don't think Melissa would have left for Europe until she forced us into this date."

"Forced?" he asked with a smile.

"Coerced is probably a better word." Feeling happier than she had in a long time, she raised her wine glass. "To Melissa and her brilliant ideas." She knew she'd remember this night for the rest of her life and she had Melissa to thank for it.

They spent hours talking and laughing about everything from movies, to music, to the people in town. Their time together flew by. It was great to see him so animated. It was a side of him she hadn't seen before. He shared a lot about his family and she shared pieces of her past, without giving too much away. A part of her wanted to lay it out – the whole ugly truth. There was something about him that made her want to open up and trust him, but she knew it couldn't happen. For a second she allowed herself to think that a relationship with Wade was possible, but then reality rushed back in. They were pathetic fantasies and she knew it, but it felt good to think about frivolous things for a change. All the darkness seemed so far way when she was with Wade.

In the middle of their evening, Sydney's phone beeped. She did her best to ignore it, angry that she hadn't turned it off completely, but if there was a problem with Faith, she wanted to make sure she could be reached at any time. There was no way she could stand to be completely cut off from her daughter. She apologized, but Wade understood her need to stay connected to Faith and didn't seem bothered in the least. When she checked the message, they both were relieved to see it was from Melissa. She sent a picture of the St. Louis Arch, assured them she was fine and sent her love.

"She has always loved an adventure." Wade laughed as he took the last of the dinner dishes and rinsed them in the sink.

"I can imagine running around with you and her brother kept her on her toes and prepared her well for this trip."

"You have no idea."

AFTER DINNER, THEY WENT outside, where Wade led her to a porch swing that was tucked off in the shadows. He lit a few candles on the small table and placed a blanket across her legs as they finished the bottle of wine in the crisp fall air.

"You're so lucky," she murmured turning to snuggle closer to him for warmth. It was impossible to keep from smiling when he slipped his arm around her shoulder and held her tight against his side. Sydney just hoped the darkness would hide her reaction from him a little.

"Why?" he whispered against her temple.

"Because you have all of this." She waved her glass at the house and the property. "You have a town that adores you, a supportive family, you enjoy your job, and we've already established you're good at just about everything." His chest shook with laughter.

"I like this," he said softly looking out into the dark.

"What?" Sydney murmured softly.

"This. Here. With you."

It was as if the world around them had gone silent at his words. After all the months of wanting him, she finally had him all to herself. As Sydney looked up at him, she found herself holding her breath, waiting for what might come next. His eyes were intense and sparkled in the moonlight that played across his face. Eyes that were staring at her lips.

"Wade." She managed to exhale his name before he kissed her, the rich flavor of the wine mixing with his own intoxicating taste. Though his lips moved gently, she could feel the power in his body that he was holding back. This kiss was nothing like the last one. It was so hot Sydney could feel herself burning up under his touch. His hand knotted in her hair, pulling her even closer to deepen the kiss. Sydney felt like the world was spinning and grabbed onto his shirt to ground herself on Earth.

Then, as quickly as it began, it ended. Immediately she felt the loss of their connection. While she tried to regain her composure, Wade stood up and stared off into the dark as if looking for something. His body language had changed from relaxed to edgy in a matter of seconds, and it startled her. Sydney stepped behind him, wrapping the blanket around her arms.

"What's wrong?" She heard the distant rustle of twigs snapping and that tingle of awareness she had went down her spine. Had someone been out there, watching them?

Wade tried to shrug it off, wrapping an arm around her and kissing the top of her head. "Nothing, just a deer. Probably a buck." Another woman might have fallen for his act, but Sydney had been on the run long enough to know when danger was close and she felt it in her gut like Wade did. She scanned the trees, looking for the source of their unease but whoever it was had left.

"Come inside," Wade said as he slipped his hand into hers and led her toward the door.

The danger had passed but Sydney's heart was racing as Wade pinned her against the doorframe with his much larger body. There was something raw and powerful about Wade that Sydney found irresistible, even if it wasn't a good idea. Instead of being cautious, she made the dangerous choice to play with fire. "I *am* a little chilly."

"I think I know a few ways to warm you up," he said in a low, sexy drawl that gave her goosebumps. He ushered her inside, locking the door behind them.

They didn't make it any farther than the entryway before he captured her mouth again. Strong hands settled on her hips then wandered over the curves of her body. In their wake was a burning trail, mapping his progress across her skin. Sydney's arms locked around Wade's neck, pulling them closer together, desperate for more contact. She longed to feel every inch of his rock hard body against hers. She'd dreamt about this countless nights, but the reality blew all those dreams away. There was something erotic about the way his muscles responded to her touch as she, too, explored his body.

Without warning, she felt like the floor had dropped out from under her. Wade scooped her up into his arms as if she weighed less than a feather, and carried her to the couch, never losing contact with her lips. The fire and passion built between them until Sydney was certain they'd both go up in flames. The buttons on her shirt fell open and she couldn't tell if she had done it, or Wade. A flurry of hands and skin found each other, greedy for more. All the months of sexual tension between them came to a head leaving them breathless and desperate for one another. Nothing could have stopped her from sleeping with Wade in that moment, nothing.

"Shit," Wade cursed as his phone started ringing on the table.

"Ignore it," Sydney gasped as his hand found her bare breast.

"Done." With a growl, Wade lowered his head and drew her nipple into his mouth. When his house phone joined and started clamoring, he let out a string of curses. "Don't move." He ran his hand through his hair in frustration, looking at her as she laid spread out on his couch like an offering, panting like she had just run a marathon. There was no controlling his anger when he picked up the phone.

"What?" he barked. Whatever he heard on the other end of the phone made his eyes lock on her like laser beams. Sydney started to panic. "Calm down. She's right here, why?"

What if he found out?

While he turned his back and asked a series of vague, short questions, Sydney frantically searched for her shirt and shoes. She tugged her disheveled hair into a ponytail and was ready to take off if he tried to take her in. He was sexy, mouthwateringly gorgeous and made her hotter than any man ever had in her life, but she wasn't going to jail and she wasn't leaving Faith. She was horrified when she looked down into her hand and saw she had grabbed the paperweight off of the side table. How far was she willing to go to protect her secret? Horrified at her subconscious behavior, she dropped the glass weight to the floor with a thud. Wade gave her a confused look as he set down the phone.

"Sydney." He cautiously approached and settled himself into a crouch at her feet.

He knew. Everything about his body showed he was trying to be calm but she could tell that he was ready to explode with anger.

"You have to come with me."

"No." She was prepared to run when Wade's words changed everything.

"That was Cara."

"Cara?" Confusion was quickly replaced by panic. "Oh my God, is it Faith?" Sydney was on her feet before Wade stopped her and pulled her into his arms.

"Faith is fine, but Cara had quite a scare."

"Is she all right? Pete?" Something awful had happened. She could feel it in her gut. Wade calmly took her hands and Sydney braced herself for the news.

"There's been another murder."

CHAPTER 7

A N HOUR LATER, WADE was still recovering from the sound of
Cara screaming hysterically into the telephone, desperate to
know that Sydney was all right. It took a few minutes for what
she was saying to actually sink in, that a woman was dead behind the
diner. A blonde. And he could only imagine how terrifying it was for
Cara and Pete to see the woman and immediately wonder if it was
Sydney or Melissa. After he calmed Cara down and spoke with Pete,
he'd told Sydney what happened and watched her face go completely
white at the news. She had immediately called Melissa for her own
piece of mind and confirmed again that she was all right and over
a hundred miles away from town in St. Louis. It wasn't until they
pulled into Sydney's driveway that the color started to creep back
into Sydney's face.

Once the shock had passed, Sydney insisted on seeing Faith.
Wade drove her home and led her upstairs where Agnes had already
tucked the little girl into bed. When she saw the five-year-old curled
up, safe and sound, she crawled beside Faith, wrapping her body pro-
tectively around her daughter and let her frightened tears fall. When
she looked over her shoulder at Wade and with weepy eyes asked,

"Will you come back?" he was lost to her. All he wanted to do was pull her and Faith into his arms and calm their fears. Forever.

"As soon as I can," he said as he wiped the small trail of tears from her cheek. "I promise."

Downstairs, Agnes offered to stay with them until Wade got back. She flashed him a Smith and Wesson to prove she had things covered and was able to protect the precious cargo sleeping upstairs. It shouldn't have made him feel better to know there was a seventy-five-year-old woman with a gun protecting Sydney, but it did. Agnes Whittman was a skilled markswoman and knew how to handle a firearm. If anything looked suspicious, she'd take care of it. Of that he was certain.

"Go. They'll be fine," she said ushering him out the door. "On a night like this I plan on shooting first and asking questions later, so make sure you identify yourself when you come back. Understand?"

"I think we've lost enough people. Don't you?" When Agnes simply raised an eyebrow at him he shook his head. "Fine. Do what you need to. Anything seems off, you call me."

"Certainly, Sheriff," she said with a wave of her gun. "Go find the bastard that's doing this."

"I'll find him."

As he pulled into the diner, a sense of dread washed over him. He'd spoken with Sam and was relieved to hear the woman wasn't anyone from town. That made him feel a bit better knowing he wouldn't be seeing a friend's body, but death was never easy to process. No matter how many times you see someone dead, their life taken prematurely, it was a difficult thing to swallow.

The flashing lights from the other police cars were a terrible beacon in the night across the parking lot of Pete's. Wade parked his car and walked to the side of the diner where two of his officers were talking. "Here he is," one said as he approached.

"What happened?" Wade asked, surveying the area around him. The weather had taken a turn, the bitter cold biting against his skin as the wind whipped past. Off to the side, Pete's car was parked diagonally with both doors open.

"It's awful. She's got stab wounds all over her, Wade. It's a nightmare back there," Sam, one of his deputies, said, his voice shaking. There hadn't been a murder in Elton, ever. So this was all new to Sam. Wade felt for him, but there was still work to be done so he pushed on.

"Who found her?"

"Pete and Cara, poor things. They're both in shock. What we know so far is that Melissa had left earlier in the evening for St. Louis so they closed up the diner at the usual time, alone. Pete and Cara went home for a while, but had to come back for something."

"Anything inside that might help us?" Both men refused to meet his eye. They were holding something back and it annoyed the hell out of him. "What aren't you telling me?"

They awkwardly shook their heads. "Nothing, boss. It's just…well, Melissa left a note for Sydney that was kinda personal. She was asking Sydney about her date. With you." When Wade's only response was a cold stare that told them he had no intention of discussing Sydney or his date with them, both of the officers wisely dropped the potential line of inquiry and got back to work.

The deputies quickly gave him a rundown of the scene and who they had called already. Wade wondered if there was a link between this and the girl they found in Greenville.

He'd put it off for as long as possible. Now it was time for him to go to that place inside himself where he could shut off his emotions and objectively investigate the crime scene. He'd done it countless times overseas, but this was the first time he had to do it at home. As he turned to walk behind the diner, Sam grabbed his arm.

"It's bad."

Luckily, Wade was familiar with bad. He'd lived through bad and thought it ended when he came home, but obviously he was mistaken. He knew what Sam meant. He'd barely rounded the corner when he felt like he had been punched in the gut.

The scene turned his stomach. The woman's lifeless body was face down on the asphalt of the back parking lot. She was naked, her arms were splayed out and her legs were bent, making her look like a rag doll that had been dropped onto the floor. Her blonde ponytail fell over her face, hiding it from view. The police photographer was snapping pictures from various angles to document everything he could that might give them a clue as to what happened here. With each flash of the bulb, Wade noticed another detail.

She hadn't been killed here, there wasn't enough blood. The body had been dumped here, her murderer probably far away by now. But was he really? Two murders in a month, a town apart. If there was a pattern or a connection between their deaths, Wade was determined to find it.

Wade cleared his throat. "What've you found?"

"Not a heck of a lot. Melissa was supposed to close, but they let her leave shortly after you and Sydney took off, according to Pete. He and Cara locked up and left here around nine." He handed Wade a clear plastic bag with a scrap of paper. "Melissa left this for Sydney." He recognized Melissa's handwriting from his countless diner tickets.

> *Syd,*
> *Hope you had a hot night with Wade and aren't still mad at me for the auction. He's a great guy and you're a great girl and I just wanted you to see what could be.*
> *Love ya lots!*
> *Melissa*
> *ps: Did you kiss him? I am dying to know and you better text me before they close the door on my plane or I'll kick your butt all the way from Europe. Love you, Syd!*

"Pete and Cara were getting ready for bed when he realized he forgot to take the breakfast sausage out of the freezer, so they headed back to the diner and that's when they found her." Sam shook his head. "I thought Pete was having a heart attack when he called the station. He thought it was Sydney. Cara heard him scream Syd's name and she apparently bolted from the car and took off around back. We found the two of them huddled together against the wall with their phone in hand. I think they were talking to you, Wade?"

Wade nodded his head. "Melissa had called them earlier to let them know she made it to St. Louis so when they came back to the diner, they saw the long blonde hair and thought it was Sydney, but she was still at my place. Sydney called Melissa right away while I kept them talking until I heard the sirens in the background and knew you guys were here with them."

"I take it you asked if Melissa saw anything unusual before she left the diner?" Sam asked, looking up from his notepad.

"She left shortly after we did and saw nothing out of the ordinary. Only three cars in the parking lot when she left, all of which she knew, and each one belonged to someone in the diner. No one lurking in the area, no cars parked on the side of the street. Her car was packed and gassed up for her trip so she left straight from here."

Everything that had been photographed was in plastic bags to protect any trace evidence from contamination. Unfortunately besides the body, there wasn't much that had been dumped with her to give Wade something to go on. A small pile of her clothing was tossed haphazardly beside her body along with a section of rope that appeared to have been tied around her feet. It had come loose and was lying a few inches from her, but other than that, there was nothing.

"Give me a minute." The deputy respectfully retreated around the corner, leaving Wade alone. In the quiet he looked down at her pale, lifeless form, wondering what kind of life this poor woman had been ripped away from and who was looking for her.

"Oh, honey. What happened to you?"

It took a few moments but Wade managed to collect his thoughts and focus. He noted multiple stab wounds on her back that were wet with what little blood she had left in her body. He carefully lifted the hair from her face and he could see a large welt on her forehead surrounded by several scrapes and dried blood. She must have been slammed into something, probably to knock her unconscious, then stabbed repeatedly. The lack of defensive wounds on her hands and arms indicated the attacker took her down quickly. Whoever he was, he had made sure to kill her somewhere else, and left as little evidence as possible.

Using what he had, Wade reconstructed what might have happened, imagining the car pulling in the main entrance to the parking lot. He had probably kept her body in the trunk. Wade looked for any indications on the asphalt like tire tracks that might give them a car model for this bastard, but there was nothing. He'd probably pulled behind the building for cover, popped the truck and tugged her out, tossing the clothing out last. No other buildings backed up to Pete's Place, so the odds of someone seeing anything were slim to none, but they'd look into it, nonetheless. Maybe there was an unusual car driving around that caught someone's eye. He was definitely going to call Melissa again and see if there was anything she could add.

Wade walked around the area, searching for anything they might have missed. He was about to leave when a triangle of white caught his eye, something covered in some kind of liquid that must have oozed from the dumpster. On instinct, he gripped the corner with his fingertips touching as little of the paper as possible. He called for Sam and when he poked his head around the corner Wade asked for an evidence bag. If this was related to the case, he wasn't going to risk damaging the evidence by handling it too much. Of course whatever that foul stain was on the paper might have already destroyed everything. Sam ran over, holding the bag open while Wade gingerly slipped the paper inside.

"I'll go log this in." Sam disappeared, leaving Wade alone again with his thoughts.

It could have been Sydney. The irrational thought jumped into his mind until he couldn't escape it. It could have been a night she and Mel stayed late. They could have been closing up and she could have walked out to this psycho dumping a body behind the diner and then God only knows what would have happened to her. He glanced back and saw the blonde hair and for a split second, it was Sydney lying there on the ground. The anger it stirred in him was illogical, but real.

He had to push the thought from his mind before he hit something. Tonight had been the first time they'd been alone together, so he shouldn't be feeling so strongly about Sydney, but he did. The thought of anything happening to her threatened to send him into a blind rage. It also confused the hell out of him.

"Wade. I think you need to see this." His deputy motioned him over, the evidence envelope still dangling from his fingers. In the distance, Wade could see the county coroner had arrived.

"I'll find the bastard who did this to you." He stifled his rising anger and focused on work. It was the only thing he could do that might make a difference for this woman and her family.

"What?" Wade held out his hand to the deputy.

"Did you look at this at all?"

Frayed nerves and strung out emotions got the better of him and he snapped. "No, I was busy. What's the problem?" Wade snatched it from Sam's hand, careful not to damage the contents but his irritation was obvious in his body language.

"Flip it over."

When Wade did, his rage was replaced by confusion. He held the plastic bag closer to his face to get a better look. A figure was on the paper which now looked to be a photograph. Some of the liquid had oozed off the image and was starting to collect at the bottom of the baggie. With his thumb he wiped a little more off through the plastic. When he did, he nearly dropped the bag.

A face took shape.

Faith's.

Wade stared at it in disbelief until his head began to spin with the possibilities. Was this one of Sydney's picture that had fallen from her purse? Had it been in Melissa's hand before she left? Or maybe it was Cara and Pete's. If not, then he had no idea why there was a picture of her at a murder scene. It was a recent picture of the little girl, her curls neatly combed as she stood in profile.

It wasn't a posed picture like one Wade would imagine Sydney taking on the first day of school. The fact that Faith wasn't looking at the camera and was obviously moving through the picture by the slight blur of her legs told Wade the little girl probably wasn't even aware she was being photographed.

"It looks like she's at school." Sam pointed out the white brick wall and the bicycle rack that was visible in the corner of the frame. Those bricks weren't at all common in Elton except for at the school. He took out his phone and snapped a picture of the image in the bag.

"I'll have to show it to Sydney. It's probably hers or maybe Cara's." The two men stood in silence, until they heard the squeaking noise growing louder. The coroner was rolling his gurney toward the woman's body. Wade glanced back at her one last time and in his head repeated his promise.

I'll find the bastard.

With nothing left for him to do there, Wade rushed past his deputies, barking orders and setting up a time to meet in the morning.

Ideas were spinning through his head as he drove away. Connections were being made in his mind that he wasn't ready to deal with or address. But several things were nagging at him. Two women were dead, both savagely murdered in the last two weeks—one in Elton, and the other just outside the city limits. Was there a connection?

There was also the picture of Faith to consider. Wade learned a long time ago that there was no such thing as a coincidence. He hoped it was Sydney's and that would put everything to rest, but if not, well... he couldn't even go there yet. His head was spinning by the time he noticed he was stopped in front of Sydney's house. And at this moment, right or wrong, he didn't want to think any more about it.

All he wanted to do was get back to Sydney.

CHAPTER 8

THE DAYS FOLLOWING THE second woman's death had been awful for everyone. Sydney was still unable to come in through the back entrance of the diner. She couldn't stomach pulling around back, the thought of seeing where someone had died still too eerie. More than anything she wished Melissa was still in town for her to talk to about all of this.

But she was gone now.

"I'll have a BLT with extra mayo," Johnny said as Sydney's pen scratched across the paper, but she wasn't really listening, her thoughts taking her places in the past she'd just as soon forget.

The anger she felt about the woman's death surprised her. It was bad enough her body had been dumped where she worked, but the discovery of the picture of Faith made Sydney lose all reason. Cold dread had slid down her spine as she had looked at a photograph that she hadn't taken of her daughter. She had managed to calmly tell Wade it wasn't hers, while her deepest fears churned her stomach, nearly making her sick.

They'd been found.

For years Sydney had been running from a shadow. The faceless, nameless, person who would slip into their lives and terrorize her, then vanish. If he even existed. She still had no concrete evidence that it all wasn't a figment of her imagination. But her gut feelings had kept them safe and sound so far, and right now it was screaming one thing:

Run.

For the last few days she had been itching to leave. Ever since she saw that picture, she'd been ready to take her daughter and go. Start over again. But when she hinted it might be time to move on, Faith had burst into tears, saying how much she loved school and begged Sydney to stay. She was looking forward to her birthday party which was less than two weeks away with all her friends from school more than Sydney had realized. They'd picked out the princess plates and the balloons, reminders of the upcoming celebration everywhere in their house. In six short months, Elton had become home to her little girl and the thought of leaving broke her heart.

The crazy thing was, Sydney felt the same way about the town. If only she hadn't let them both get so attached to the town and the people. Melissa had been the biggest reason they stayed in the beginning. It felt good to have a friend, someone to talk to and be normal with. Sydney had never had that in her life before. Her mother had been unstable for as long as she could remember which meant her friends had been few and far between. Who wanted to hang out at their friend's house when her mom might accuse you of trying to steal something every time you left?

And now there was Wade.

"You gonna take my order to Pete or stare out the window all day?" The sharp tone of Johnny's voice startled her back to the here and now.

"Sorry, I'll be right back with your food." She'd become a zombie without Melissa at the diner to keep her spirits up. Sydney missed her terribly and it had only been a few days since she left. Reminders of Melissa were everywhere.

Sydney secretly dreamed of settling in Elton permanently. Faith was in school with friends like other normal kids. That was what she had always wanted for her daughter. Sydney had a good job, with good people around her. She even went on a date and kissed the hottest man in town until she couldn't breathe. She'd also wept in his arms for a woman she didn't even know and he'd held her until she drifted off to sleep. Even in the midst of her unspoken fears, Wade found a way to make her feel safe.

But the two murders had changed everything.

"You okay?" Cara's brow pinched with worry. Sydney realized she had been standing in front of the window holding the order in her hand instead of passing it to Pete. It seemed as if she spent every minute of every day deep in her own thoughts. Planning. Watching. Preparing.

If Sydney had been cautious before, she was on high alert now. Paranoid about every person she encountered and every noise she heard at night. She'd slept very little lately for countless reasons. Thoughts of what she needed to do plagued her when she closed her eyes in the very early hours of the morning, when the rest of the world was fast asleep.

In reality, Sydney knew she couldn't leave. Not yet. There were too many things she needed to do. She had to stay and help out Cara and Pete at the diner until things settled down. Melissa had just left so they were shorthanded at the diner and Pete and Cara were far more disturbed by finding that woman than either one of them let on. Sydney didn't miss the way Cara shivered when she had to take the trash out to the dumpster now. They had been good to Sydney and she insisted on being there for them when they needed her the most.

Then there was Faith she had to protect. The idea that someone could be watching her daughter terrified her. Sydney knew she was smothering Faith with her constant attention and the little girl was starting to rebel. Sydney wanted Faith to live as normal a life as possible but she couldn't comprehend the danger they were in. Sydney needed to remember that.

She also had to find a way to walk away from Wade. That was going to be more difficult than she realized. Her new work schedule had helped. It took Wade a while to figure out when she'd be at the diner and that made it easier on her.

Not seeing him.

As wonderful as their date had been, Sydney knew it couldn't last. It was obvious to her now that she shouldn't have let herself lose control like that with him. It had been selfish. Every time she thought about him, she remembered the feel of his hands on her and the gentle way he held her in his arms. Because of that, she had all these deep feelings for him, ones that were complicated and stupid. Ones that would end in disaster for everyone, including Faith.

Cara knew something was up but she didn't question it when Sydney asked her to switch sections because Wade sat at one of her tables. He knew she was avoiding him, too. He was a cop after all. He knew how to read people and everything about Sydney's body language probably screamed 'stay away' because her emotions were still so raw and frazzled. Like the gentleman he was, Wade kept his distance, which only made Sydney feel worse. She never should have allowed herself that one night of happiness because now every time she looked at him she knew exactly what she was missing from her life.

"Why don't you take a break?" Pete stuck his head out from the kitchen and motioned toward the door. "Get some fresh air, clear your head."

"I'll cover your tables," Hailey offered with a smile. Hailey was the new girl that Pete had hired to take Melissa's place. Not that anyone ever could. Hailey was only nineteen, perky, and not that bright, but she did what Cara asked and she was scared of Pete, so that was good enough for them.

The backdoor of the diner loomed ahead of her through the kitchen. Sydney hadn't been out there since that night. The blood, the violence brought it all back. But it was high time to face a demon—or ten—otherwise she'd never get past it. With a steadying breath she pushed open the metal door and forced her feet to step outside. She imagined there would be markings on the ground, forever indicating the place where someone had died. Angie, her name was Angie and she had been from Greenville. Surprisingly, it looked as if nothing had happened. The area round the dumpster was free of markings except whatever liquid had leaked out of the bottom from all the trash. A few leaves blew across the asphalt in the breeze. But everything looked the same.

How was that possible?

"I'm sorry." Sydney had no idea why she was suddenly swamped with grief as she looked at the barren space behind the diner. It seemed so unfair that there was nothing to mark the passing of this woman's life on this spot. It was almost as if it never happened. But it had. And somewhere, there was someone whose life was changed forever because of it.

A jumble of emotion sent Sydney spiraling deep into the past. When she looked at the ground it wasn't asphalt she saw but gravel on the side of the road. She could hear the brittle cornstalks brushing against one another.

"I don't know if I did the right thing that night," she said to no one in particular, but hoped the words would somehow find their way to heaven. "Maybe I should have fought him." She wrung her hands together and paced across the concrete, but her mind was thousands of miles away. "Every day I wonder if I did the right thing that night. But since then, I know I've done right by you, and your daughter. Our daughter." Sydney turned her face up to the sunshine and felt it's warmth settle deep into her bones, lifting some of the terrible weight from her shoulders.

"Faith had to come first. She always has for me." She wiped the tears from the corner of her eyes. "I'm sorry for everything you went through."

She collected herself and made sure her tears were gone before stepping back inside the diner. Somehow Sydney's mind had needed to purge itself of years of guilt, and seeing where the woman, Angie, had died had given her the connection to death, and whatever came next, to make that happen. With less guilt in her heart, she hurried back to wait on her tables.

"There you are," Hailey said, dropping a mangled piece of pie onto a place. Pete would kill her if he caught her trying to serve that to a customer.

"Why don't you go on break now? Take that piece and go enjoy it. I'll cut a new one and serve it for you." Sydney swiftly cut a perfect triangle of pie and got it onto the plate without smearing blueberries from one edge of the plate to another like Hailey had done. "Which table ordered pie?"

"Wade, of course," she said licking her fingers. "It's all the guy orders."

Sydney closed her eyes wondering if this was the cosmos's way of exacting a little revenge from beyond. "No problem, I'll take care of it." She neatly folded a napkin and slipped a fork onto the plate beside the pie, allowing a few seconds to compose herself. With a smile that felt as forced as it must have looked, she brought over the dessert.

"I hear you ordered blackberry pie."

Don't look at him, don't look at him, she told herself. If she saw any kindness in those green eyes she'd start crying again. She was just about to slide it onto the table when she heard her name.

"I almost forgot," Hailey called from behind the counter, "you got a call when you were out back."

"Who was it?"

Hailey shrugged, shoving a big bite of pie into her mouth, garbling her words. "Some guy. Wanted to know if you were here. I said no. Then he asked if you were with Faith."

The plate holding the pie nearly slipped from her fingers. Wade grabbed it right before the fork went clanging to the floor. "W-What did you tell him?"

"I told him she was in school until three."

"Why would you do that?" Sydney knew she was screaming but she couldn't help it.

Hailey paused. "I thought it was your brother."

"I don't have a brother." The gravity of what happened sank in and Sydney exploded. "Oh, my God." Ripping off her apron, Sydney ran for the door. The bells clanged wildly as she rushed outside. She heard someone shouting her name, but ignored it. Her only thought was getting to Faith.

"Sydney!" Wade's hand slammed down on the door as she tried to free the lock. "Look at me."

Her head was shaking side to side, "I-I can't. I need to see Faith. I have to get to her." She pulled on the door handle but it wouldn't budge with Wade's body leaning on it. Why wouldn't he just go away?

CONCEALED

A firm hand settled on her shoulder. She forced herself to look Wade in the eye and straightened her spine to show him how serious she was. "Get out of my way."

"Fine," he said grabbing the keys from her trembling fingers. "I'll take you to Faith. You can't drive like this, you're too upset." He opened the door and Sydney scrambled across, settling into the passenger's side, too desperate to get to Faith to be mad at him right now. It'd come later, she was sure, but for now all she needed was her daughter.

The car dipped as Wade climbed inside, his long legs crammed under the steering wheel. He moved the seat back and the engine roared to life. Wade pinned Sydney with a hard look. "After this, you and I need to have a long talk. Do you understand?"

She nodded even though she had no intention of telling him anything. Lying was second nature to her and it was the only way to get him to step on the gas. He flew down the road, thankfully rolling through the stop signs. The car had barely slowed in the parking lot when she jumped out and ran toward the school building.

"Thanks," she called over her shoulder, not really caring if he heard or not.

She pushed the buzzer on the intercom repeatedly until someone answered. "Sydney Ross, I need to see my daughter, please." The delay was just enough time for Wade to catch up and follow her inside.

"You need to calm down, Syd. You're going to scare her." Deep down inside she knew she was being completely irrational. The call could have been from Luke, or one of Wade's deputies with more questions. Just because Hailey didn't know who it was didn't mean they wouldn't have offered the information if asked. It didn't mean it was him.

Realizing that Wade was right, Sydney paused and took a deep breath, trying to calm herself down as she stood outside the office. It would do no good to run into Faith's classroom, snatch her from her friends, and toss her in the car so they could run away. It would only upset her more. In plain sight at school was probably the safest place for

Faith right now. She pressed a hand to her stomach then touched Wade's arm as he stood beside her.

"I'm sorry. I know I'm out of control." She adjusted her shirt and ran her fingers through her hair to straighten it right before the principal walked out of the office.

"Miss Ross, is something wrong?"

In a millisecond she managed to wipe the distress from her face and replace it with a sheepish calm. "No. No, sorry. Faith wasn't feeling well this morning and I just wanted to check on her but I don't want her to know I'm here. Would you mind if I peeked in on her through the window?"

The principal seemed to buy her explanation. She led them down the hall to the kindergarten classroom. Inside, Faith sat at a table surrounded by friends making snakes out of paper plates. Watching her tiny tongue stick out of her mouth as her fingers worked the scissors reminded Sydney how precious a gift she had been given and that she needed to protect her. No matter what.

"Thank you so much. I'm sorry to show up out of the blue." The two women walked back toward the office while Wade lingered at the door, watching the children play.

"Um, while I'm here, I wanted to thank you for all you're doing for Faith. This is a wonderful school and she couldn't be happier."

The principal's face broke out in a wide smile. "We're thrilled to have her here. She's such a sweet girl."

Sydney nervously glanced at the security monitors in the office. "And all the teachers and aides know about our arrangement, right?"

"Absolutely," the principal said, laying her hand on Sydney's arm. "Everyone knows that you're the only one who will pick her up from school." She thought for a moment then said, "But don't you want to name one other person who can get her, in case you're sick?"

"No. I'm the only one." Sydney answered way too fast, startling the woman but she didn't care. "Even if I'm sick, I'll crawl from my bed to pick her up and that's the end of it."

CHAPTER 9

MOMMY, CAN I GET this?" It seemed to be the phrase of the day. Faith must have said it a thousand times during their trip asking for everything from a piece of candy to a four foot tall teddy bear.

When Cara came up with the idea of a shopping trip, Sydney could have kissed her. The day long trip wasn't the same without Melissa. Both Sydney and Cara had received a quick call from Melissa as she checked in with them just outside of Paris. Things were wonderful and she was looking forward to the next leg of her trip. She had said it would probably be a few weeks before they heard from her again and to not worry. It had been so wonderful to hear her voice. When Cara suggested the outing, Sydney knew it was the right thing to do.

Cara was more of a surrogate mother for Sydney than a girlfriend, but for today it didn't matter. She was exactly what Sydney and Faith both needed—a little motherly TLC. The most important thing was they were getting out of Elton and leaving all the awful stuff behind them so they could relax.

"No, honey, we don't need a dog toy today. We don't even have a dog. Put it back." Sydney stood her ground, even when Faith put on her best pout.

"Then can we get a dog?" Faith asked excitedly. She used her adorable toothless smile as a weapon when she really wanted something.

"No. Now put that back."

"Are you sure she's only five?" Cara laughed as Faith stomped away, the rubber chicken in her hand dragging along on the ground. "She's adorable. My Jennifer would have screamed her head off if I said no to her when she was that age."

"I think she's over that phase. Now that she's almost six, she's moved on to full-fledged manipulation and her own brand of logic," Sydney said with a grin. "It's kinda scary if you ask me."

"I heard about what she said to Wade at the auction." There was no mistake where this conversation was leading, and Sydney wanted none of it so she tried to change the subject and keep it away from her love life. Or lack thereof.

"That's what I'm talking about. The things that come out of her mouth terrify me." She held up a striped blouse from her bag. "What do you think? Does it make me look fat?"

Cara rolled her eyes. "Nice try. We're talking about Wade, child. Whether you like it or not."

"Not." There was nothing to say on the topic. She was done with Wade, not that anything even got started except an evening of heavy petting and could-have-beens that she would be thinking about for the rest of her life.

Not to be put off, Cara became a walking talking resume of Wade's good attributes. "He's employed. Has been since he came back from the service."

Sydney nodded her head in agreement while inside she had her own internal dialogue going on. *As a sheriff and he'll have me arrested when he finds out about Faith.*

"He treats women well."

Her face flushed at that statement. She knew exactly how Wade treated women and it was spectacular. Unfortunately she didn't deserve any of it. *He'd cringe when he found out the truth.*

"He likes you."

That was the hardest one for Sydney to think about. He was interested, he'd made that perfectly clear the night of their date. *But that's because he doesn't know what a horrible person I am. But I do.*

"Five more minutes, Faith. Then we have to leave." Faith scampered over to admire some toys and it warmed Sydney's heart to see her so happy. Cara was distracted so Sydney hoped the Wade litany would end, but it didn't. It only became more awkward.

"He's very handsome." When Sydney's eyebrows shot up, Cara laughed. "I may be old, but I'm not dead. The guy's gorgeous in that rebel-without-a-cause way. Why, if I were thirty years younger, you'd have some competition."

"Maybe *you* should date him then!"

"Except he wants you." The flush came back full force. "And I know you're attracted to him. Melissa and I talked all about it. I see the way you hide from him or get nervous when you have to talk to him. It's sweet."

"It's embarrassing." Sydney shook her head. "Listen, Wade could do so much better than me."

"I think that's for him to decide."

"I don't even know how to talk to him. I can talk to Luke and any other man in the diner just fine, but with Wade I'm constantly making a fool of myself."

"Luke is a friend, nothing more. Wade gets you excited. You've gotta flirt with him, child. Let him know you're interested. Be playful."

"Even if I wanted to, which I don't," Sydney threw up her hands in frustration, "I don't know how."

Cara patted her on the shoulder. "We've got a long drive home. I'll give you some pointers that worked for me when I was trying to catch Pete."

"Oh, Lord!"

With a wink Cara replied, "Oh, Lord is right!"

They laughed and gathered up their bags. It took Sydney a minute to find Faith, but then the little girl came running right over. Once her hand slipped into Sydney's, she calmed down. Everything was fine. They were safe.

For now.

The day had been exactly what they needed to clear their heads, but now it was time to get back to Elton and so many things Sydney was trying to forget.

"I LOVE MY NEW shoes," Faith sang from the backseat as she had been for the last twenty minutes. Cara had bought her a new doll which was snuggled up beside the little girl; however, the shiny new shoes were definitely her favorite. She couldn't stop talking about them as her feet kicked up and down. "They are so pretty and nice and awesome...I love them."

"I'm glad." The songs had been cracking Cara and Sydney up but Cara still managed to get in her tips and lessons for Sydney about how to flirt. She even suggested that Syd try some of them out the next time she saw Wade at the diner.

It seemed as though Cara had picked up right where Melissa had left off.

The drive was relaxing, a combination of highway and back roads that weren't that heavily traveled so it made for an easy trip. Sydney, as usual, kept herself aware of her surroundings at all times and, after a few miles and a number of turns, she noticed a black car was following behind them; at a distance, but definitely following them. She made a turn in error then looped back around when Cara pointed it out, and the car mirrored her actions.

They were getting closer to Elton so Sydney stepped on the gas, wanting to put more distance between them in the hopes that she might be able to lose them on the next turn. If Cara noticed her increased speed she didn't say anything. She was busy chatting with Faith about the book she bought her at the store.

Ahead, the road veered to the left and then they were going to take a quick right to head straight to Elton. There was a slight dip in the road and Sydney felt like this might be her last chance to get rid of this car so she sped up and whizzed around the curve and took the right hand turn a lot faster than she should have. As soon as she straightened the wheel she glanced in the mirror to see if the black car would follow, but her view was blocked by the flashing lights of a police car that had appeared out of nowhere.

"Shit," Sydney hissed under her breath.

"Mommy, that's a bad word!" Faith gasped, covering her ears. Then the flashing must have caught her attention. "Oh, look at the pretty lights."

Cara mumbled something about being a speed demon, so apparently she had noticed the fast pace Sydney had been keeping for the last few miles. Either way, the black car was the least of her worries. She'd never been pulled over by the police and never had to show her ID.

Time to see if it was worth all that money, Sydney thought as she reached for her purse with a shaking hand. She held her breath and waited for the officer to come to the window. When she heard Cara laugh, her stomach dropped.

Please don't let it be him.

"License and registration, please." Wade's deep voice rumbled through the open window sending Sydney into a tizzy.

"What are the odds?" Cara snickered in the seat beside her.

"Um, sure yeah. Here's my license." She stuck her hand out the window but the card fell from her trembling fingers landing on the ground. "I'll just get the registration." She leaned over toward Cara to yank the papers from the glove compartment.

"Jesus, Wade, do you have to be so intimidating? How about a friendly 'Hello, Sydney?' or maybe a hello to Faith and I before you throw her mother in the slammer?"

"You can't arrest my mommy!" Faith freed herself from her seatbelt and leaned between the front seats, glaring at Wade. "Do you have a search warrant?"

"Faith!" Sydney gasped as she pulled the registration from the compartment, sticking it out the window to Wade. "You apologize to Sheriff Jenkins right now! And put your seatbelt back on before I get another ticket."

"No, he has to tell you about your My Anna rights. If not, he gets in trouble." Her little face lit up in a smug grin.

"Faith, what are you talking about?" Sydney spun around and saw Wade crouched down, looking through the window trying to keep a straight face.

"Mrs. Whittman told me all about the police and how they have to tell people their My Anna rights. Oh, and don't talk to Sheriff Wade. Choose to remain silent! That was the other thing she said." Faith reached around the seat and tried to clamp her tiny hand over Sydney's mouth to prevent her from incriminating herself, apparently.

"This isn't happening," Sydney mumbled as she freed herself and pressed her forehead against the steering wheel. She could hear Cara laughing beside her.

"See, Wade? If you just would have said hello, Miss Faith here wouldn't be all worked up and wondering about her mother's My Anna rights."

"Hello, Sydney, Faith, and Cara. How are you ladies doing today?"

"Much better," Cara grumbled from the passenger's seat. Faith moved and stuck her head out the window to talk to Wade.

"Hi, Sheriff. Please don't arrest my mom."

"Wasn't planning on it, Faith. She was speeding, that's all."

Faith looked him up and down. "So no My Anna rights?"

"Not today." That seemed to satisfy her so she pulled her head back inside and buckled herself back into her seat.

"Give him the stuff, Mom, he's not going to arrest you. We talked about it.""

Thanks, honey." If Sydney could have curled up in a ball and died, she would have. The last thing she wanted to do was talk to Wade, but this made that kinda difficult. "Sorry about that. Here's the registration." This time it didn't flutter to the ground.

With a nod of his head, Wade accepted the paper and headed back to his car. The closer he got to the cruiser, the more Sydney wanted to throw up. For all she knew he was going to run her license and figure out it was a fake and she'd be in jail by dinnertime. Who would take care of Faith? She was lost in thought when Cara pinched her shoulder.

"What are you doing?" Cara said incredulously.

"Ouch! What do you mean?"

"Use what your momma gave you to get out of this ticket!"

"Have you lost your mind?" Sydney hissed, glancing over her shoulder at Faith.

"No. Flirt with the man. Tell him he looks handsome. Offer to make him dinner. Oh, or a pie! He loves your pie! I bet he'd let you go with a warning if you made him another pie."

"I'm not flirting my way out of this."

"What does flirt mean, Mommy?" Faith asked with a tilt of her head.

"It's when girls act silly around a boy," Sydney snapped before Cara could give the child more information than she needed at five years old.

"Does it make your face turn red?"

"Sometimes," Sydney sighed, her nerves frayed as she glanced back in the rearview mirror and saw Wade coming back. His face, as always, was unreadable. With every step he took, her heart pounded faster at the realization this could be the end of everything.

"You know *your* face is red, mom."

"Thanks for the info, Faith." Sydney glared at a now cackling Cara. "You're not helping!"

"I'm sorry, Sydney, but you're flirting needs some work."

"For the last time, I'm not flirting with Wade!"

With impeccable timing, she heard in her ear, "Here's your license back, ma' am."

"Jesus, you need a bell around your neck!" Sydney spun around in her seat, too startled to be embarrassed. Her look dared him to say something but instead he was kind, and all business.

"Everything seems to be in order." He passed the papers to Sydney through the car window and she hoped and prayed he hadn't seen her huge sigh of relief. That relief was short lived however thanks to Faith.

"If mom makes you a pie can you not give her a ticket?"

Wade dipped his head down to Faith's window, ignoring Sydney's sputtering from the front seat. "Did Mrs. Whittman explain to you the repercussions of bribing an officer?"

When Faith's head shook from side to side she asked, "A repercussion? Is that like a drum?" Wade couldn't help but laugh at the innocent question.

"Oh, give me a break. It's not a bribe if a beautiful woman wants to cook for you, Wade. It's called your lucky day," Cara chimed, throwing in her two cents. Sydney swore she could hear Melissa half-way across the planet, laughing at all of it.

"Just give me the ticket, please. Or shoot me. A bullet might be less painful than this," Sydney mumbled through her hands which were covering her face.

Ignoring everyone, Faith kept right on talking. "So Sheriff, do we have a deal?" She thrust her crumb-covered hand out the window, nearly poking Wade in the eye. Someday the child was going to be a lawyer.

"A pie for no ticket?" He winked at Sydney who was now staring at him open mouthed through her window. "I think that can be arranged."

"That has to be illegal," Sydney said, angrily shoving her paperwork back in the glove compartment, "or at the very least coercion."

Wade put his face right up to hers, his massive shoulders easily filling the window. "Relax, I'm just kidding. No pie required. I'm letting you off with a warning. You were going pretty fast back there." Her heart fluttered when he reached in and tucked a stray piece of hair behind her ear.

"T-Thanks."

"Be careful," Wade said as a goodbye with a tip of his hat to both Cara and Faith.

"He's so nice, Mommy!"

"Yeah, Mommy," Cara teased as Sydney started the car and slowly pulled back onto the road. There was no sign of the car that had been the cause of the whole situation to begin with, which was fine by Sydney. She had enough trouble on her own. She didn't need any ghosts from the past chasing her too.

"Sheriff Jenkins is very nice, Faith. If you ever need anything, he'll help you."

They drove in silence for a few minutes while Sydney tried to clear her head. Everything was fine. Wade didn't suspect anything, neither did Cara. Faith was happily kicking her feet and singing in the backseat. Everything was all right.

Except Sydney couldn't shake that feeling of dread that had been lingering for the last few weeks. The picture of Faith, the phone calls, the murders, and the mystery cars, all of that, looming large on Sydney's conscious. She felt the safest she ever had in Elton before all of that had happened. So would it be better to stay there and fight, if that's what it came to, or was it time to run? Even if it broke Faith's heart.

Her serious thoughts were interrupted when Cara erupted in a flurry of words.

"I've been biting my tongue so hard it's starting to bleed, so I'm just gonna say it because it's what Melissa would do. The two of you are making me worry myself gray." She took a deep breath and made sure Faith was occupied before she launched into her lecture. "You care about Wade and don't even try to tell me you don't. It's written all over your face. And that man cares for you, deeply. Even if you aren't in a relationship with him, I've seen the way he looks at you while you've been hiding from him. The way he took care of you after they found the girl at the diner." She shook her head. "He treated you like the most precious thing in the world. A man doesn't do that for someone he doesn't care about."

Tears began to fill Sydney's eyes. Cara was right. Sydney did care about Wade. More than she ever had cared for another man in her life. She could even picture herself sitting on the porch swing with him in the summertime as a hot breeze blew across the yard. And it killed her because she knew she could never have that.

"Cara," she tried to interrupt, but Cara's hand flew up to halt her words.

"Sweets, I know you have a secret and it must be a whopper from how closely you watch Faith." The tears were flowing freely now and Sydney didn't even try to hide them. "But Pete and I love you like you were one of our own. I swear, you deserve to be happy, to have a life, and maybe if you tell me about what it is you're hiding from, maybe I can help you."

The words were on the tip of Sydney's tongue, about to spill out. The whole ugly truth. She was ready to get the crushing weight off her chest and be free of it once and for all. But then she thought about the way Cara might look at her if she knew. The disappointment, the terror, the disgust. When she left Elton, she wanted them to remember her as she was, not like a fleeing criminal. Somehow losing her and Pete, and Elton, would hurt worse than it ever had before. They were different. She was different.

She couldn't lose that.

"Cara, I'm fine. Really. This thing with Wade, I don't know. I think we're too different." When Cara started to protest, it was Sydney's turn to interrupt. "No, you're right. I have secrets. Ones that keep me up at night. And Wade deserves better than that. You all do." She turned onto a familiar road and counted the mailboxes until Cara's house. "If I was a better person, I'd pack up and go."

"Don't say that," Cara pleaded. Sydney had hit a nerve with Cara when she mentioned leaving. "Elton is your home."

Sydney gave her a sad smile. "I know. That's the problem. We love it here. You, Pete, and Melissa, you are our family. But it's selfish for me to stay. It would be better for all of you, and that includes Wade, if we left."

"Just tell me what it is, Sydney. I can help you." But Sydney was already shaking her head before Cara finished.

"No one can help me, Cara." The car came to a stop outside her house. Pete was still at the diner so the house was dark. "Thanks for coming with us. It really helped me clear my head, spending time with you today. You're the closest thing to a mom I've ever had." It was a small detail of her past, but it was all she could give the woman who meant so much to her.

"Nothing you tell me will ever change the way I look at you. You need to know that. If you ever want to share your burden with me, I'm here for you."

"You have no idea what that means to me." Sydney wiped the tears streaking her face and put on a brave smile like the chameleon she was. "Faith, say goodbye to Miss Cara."

"Thanks for the doll. I'll take good care of her."

Cara opened the backdoor of the car to get better access to Faith. She gave the little girl a kiss and welcomed the huge hug Faith wrapped her up in. "You be a good girl for Mommy. I can't wait to see you in those fancy shoes at your birthday party in a few days, sweets. I still can't believe you're going to be six!"

Sydney gave a wave as Cara made her way up the steps to her front door. She was a genuinely good person and she meant every word she said, but it was too dangerous to have her involved with the truth. Her past was a living, breathing entity, set on her destruction. No way she'd let Cara and Pete get caught up in that.

Or Wade.

CHAPTER 10

WADE DRANK THE LAST of the coffee in his mug and slipped a few dollars under the saucer for a tip. He had lingered at the diner as long as he dared. Sydney had been avoiding him since he pulled her over the day before, but if he looked back, the distance started the night of their date. She had definitely put up a wall between them and Wade found himself banging his head against it ever since.

He retreated to his cruiser and parked just around the corner from the diner. To kill time until her shift ended, he ran through the list of things he knew about Sydney in his head, trying to figure out what he was missing. She hadn't existed until eighteen months ago so she was living under an assumed name. He was convinced someone was after them, or at least he knew Sydney believed someone was after them. Her erratic behavior and overprotective nature toward Faith said it all. The obsessive way she left work just to take her home from school and the conversation he overheard between Sydney and the principal all but confirmed it.

He had felt guilty lifting her fingerprints off her driver's license when he pulled her over, but the prints were the best way to get answers. If he came right out and asked her, he knew without a shadow of a doubt Sydney would stay silent and he'd never see her again.

The prints had come back as belonging to a Sydney Jackson who was born outside of Boise, Idaho. It took Wade calling in countless favors, but he finally made progress. Her grandmother's maiden name had been Ross. She hadn't lied about her age. She was twenty-four and had left home right after her high school graduation. The prints were on file for a juvenile arrest for petty theft; charges that were later dropped. As far as family went, her father hadn't been in the picture since she was an infant and her mother wasn't the greatest role model. A religious nut who Children's Services believed suffered from some mental illness. Sydney's life sounded like it was anything but stellar. When she took off late in her senior year she was pregnant, had been shunned by her mother, and was forced to live on her own.

Everything after that was a mystery.

Putting the pieces together wasn't easy, but a rough idea of her life started to form in his head. When she left home, she was pregnant. Odds were, if she was hiding from someone, it was probably Faith's father. Maybe he had been abusive. Just the thought of someone hitting Sydney made Wade livid. The other possibility was Faith's father had wanted custody of her, and maybe Sydney feared he might get it, so she took off running. Or maybe he simply wanted her. Neither scenario sat well with Wade. Either way, it seemed highly likely that another male was after Sydney and he might mean her harm. Jealousy and anger collided inside Wade.

Drama was never his thing, and Miss Sydney Ross was a walking drama department. If he was smart, he'd cut and run. There were plenty of women in the area who'd see to his needs when the occasion arose. He didn't need anything long term or exclusive. It hadn't worked out so well in the past. Why would he think this time would be any different with all the baggage Sydney was carrying?

Unfortunately he still found himself wanting Sydney. Even though it had disaster written all over it, he wanted her in his bed but even more frightening, in his life.

Wade glanced at his watch. It was almost time for Sydney to get off work. He didn't want her to notice him lurking outside the diner, so he found an empty parking lot and waited for her car to pass.

Fear and danger must have shaped her life and hiding was so engrained in who she was that Wade doubted she even realized she did things anymore. Sydney never drove home the same way. There were multiple routes she took and he could find no pattern to how she traveled. When she got out of her car, she was always aware of her surroundings which was why he had to be so careful to not be spotted. Anything out of the ordinary caught her eye.

By the time she drove past, he'd finished his coffee. When he saw her car turn left to take the long way home, he grabbed another cup of coffee from the gas station before making his way to her street. He was about a quarter mile away when his phone rang. The number that flashed brought with it another kind of drama.

"What?" he growled, not in the mood for this conversation.

"Now, Wade," the voice on the other end sneered, "is that any way to talk to your wife?"

He debated throwing the phone out the window. His emotions were already out of control, and she was like gasoline on a fire. Always had been, but he'd been too stupid to see it back then. Wade braced for the explosion. "Ex-wife, Tara. What do you want?"

She tsked him under her breath. "Why are you so crabby? Am I interrupting something?" When Wade didn't answer her voice went up an octave. "Are you with her?"

Her games were getting tiring. "I'm working, Tara." He missed the turn to Sydney's because he was so annoyed. "You have thirty seconds, and then I'm hanging up." He pulled into the nearest driveway and wheeled around to backtrack.

"Who is she? That little waitress who's caught your eye. Did you forget my parents are still in the area and I hear things?" He wanted to ask her if she forgot the part where they got divorced, but he learned a long time ago to not engage her in an argument or that would simply draw things out longer. She kept griping then finally exploded. "Damnit, Wade. Answer me!"

He knew it would piss Tara off, but he didn't care. Sydney's house was up ahead and he was done dealing with her insanity. "Your thirty seconds are up. Bye, Tara." As soon as he hung up, the phone rang again. He let it go to voicemail. Wanting no part of Tara, he tucked his phone into the cup holder and put it on silent. Parking his car in the shadows, Wade watched Sydney and Faith move through their house and begin their nighttime routine.

Once darkness fell, Wade could make out Sydney's silhouette at the kitchen window, washing the dinner dishes. The blinds were closed tight, the house he knew was locked up like a vault, but on occasion she would stop and listen. While her protective mother was watching everything around her, Faith ran around the house, flitting from room to room, without a care in the world. She liked to leave a trail of lights blazing in her path which made her easy to track, the shadows of her dolls' heads bobbing up and down as she played.

Wade stretched his legs out under the dashboard as best he could, trying to get more comfortable, but it was nearly impossible. A man his size should not spend this much time in a car. It was getting to be pathetic and borderline stalker-ish. However Sydney was already edgy and if she knew that he had dug into her past, she'd vanish. The only option he had left was to spend hours in his truck, watching her. Or that's what he told himself to justify his growing obsession. His phone buzzed against his thigh. Tara, again, but this time it was a lengthy text going into great detail about how little she thought of him. He scrolled through to get her latest threat and then, as the ultimate sucker punch, she attached a picture of Max.

He should have deleted it and not even looked, but when he saw the cake covered face, he couldn't help himself. Max had turned three years old yesterday. It didn't take a picture sent in anger to remind him. He couldn't possibly forget the little boy, even if he wanted to. The boy's birthday marked a beginning and an end for him. His thumb swept over the image with longing. Could he have done something differently? Beating himself up wouldn't change the past, he needed to remember that. He tucked the phone away and returned to his vigil. His body froze and went on high alert when he saw a hooded shadow move through Sydney's kitchen.

It wasn't Sydney, it couldn't be. The height was all wrong. He quickly scanned the house, looking for her shadow. Dinner was over so she would be upstairs with Faith. The figure was much taller and definitely bulkier than Sydney. There was also no tell-tale ponytail hanging down her back. The roll of the shoulders, the stance, were all masculine. No way were those movements Sydney's. He'd studied her body enough these last few months to know how the woman moved through a room and that was not it. His heart began to pound with worry. It looked like Sydney's troubles might have finally caught up with her.

"Shit," he growled, leaning forward in his seat to get a better look at the home and confirm his suspicions. The trail of lights Faith had started downstairs was now off, and the only illumination came from the upstairs bathroom where Sydney was probably giving Faith a bath.

There was a second of pause where his jealousy had him wondering if it was possible that this man was an invited guest in her home. A lover. Wade saw red at the mere thought of another man kissing Sydney, or making love to her. His possessive nature and past betrayals clouded his thinking but he forced all of that out of his mind. He had been watching her for over an hour and seen no contact between Sydney and this individual. Whoever it was, Sydney and Faith had no idea he was there. And with two unsolved murders in the area, irrational or not, Wade needed to check it out.

Even if he ended up looking like a fool.

Wanting to be prepared for anything, Wade grabbed his gun and slipped out of his car, taking great care to remain camouflaged. All he needed was a neighbor coming out and drawing attention to his presence for this thing to go south, and quick. He approached the house and immediately found signs that someone had tampered with the security system around back. It wasn't a high tech approach, but it had gotten the job done.

Wade slipped inside, gun in hand. It was a challenge entering a house where there was at least one unknown intruder as well as a woman and a young child. If he wasn't careful, this could end badly, very badly.

Common sense told him to call for backup, but he had rushed out of his car without his phone. In his annoyance with Tara, he'd taken it out of his pocket: a careless mistake he hoped wouldn't be fatal.

The house was meticulously kept with no extraneous things in sight. The furniture was minimal, with very few personal items decorating the space. It made it easier for him to move through the unfamiliar house without knocking things over or missing potential hiding places for the intruder. He could hear the soft sounds of Sydney and Faith's conversation upstairs. Occasionally the gentle splash of water would break the silence as he crept through the house, clearing each room. From the stairwell, he heard a creaking noise and went on high alert.

The kitchen still smelled of the pizza Sydney had baked for dinner. A small plate of uneaten vegetables sat on the otherwise empty counter. Wade slipped past the bar stools and cautiously approached the stairs. When a switchblade struck out at him from the darkened stairwell, he let his instincts take over.

In a flurry of motion, Wade reached into the shadows, making contact with flesh and bone as he grabbed the attacker's wrist and wrenched the person to the floor, landing on top. Once he immobilized their hands over their head so there was no chance of them drawing another weapon, Wade paused, until a knee landed hard on his inner thigh. Years of discipline kept him from budging. He tightened his grip and growled, "Don't move." When he felt the body beneath him shudder, he paused.

There was little muscle on the person pinned beneath his chest. Instead of the hulking form he saw in the window, soft feminine flesh pressed against his straining muscles. Something wasn't right. It didn't even dawn on him that could have been Sydney until he heard her whisper his name.

"Wade?"

"Shh, don't move," he whispered in her ear, now more concerned than ever about the intruder. Faith was unprotected upstairs.

"I swear I would have made you that pie. You didn't need to break in and take it by force." She tried to laugh off his rough handling but he could feel her body trembling beneath him. She was terrified.

He lowered his head until his lips were pressed against her ear. "Someone is in the house."

"Faith," she gasped and with a rush of adrenaline, she gave a shove to try and get him off of her, but her effort was futile. She was pinned there until he wanted her to move. "Let me go." The desperate tone in her voice was like a punch in his gut. When he moved his leg, she scurried to the wall and pressed herself tightly against it.

"Listen," he said, his voice leaving no room for doubt or question of who was in charge. "I want you to get Faith and..." Their conversation was interrupted by a wet little girl in a towel who appeared on the stairs beside them. Wade hid the gun behind his back and tucked it into the waistband of his jeans so Faith didn't see the weapon. Sydney took his hand and he felt her press the cool steel of the blade to him.

"Mommy? Why did you scream?" Water still dripped off her wet curls as Sydney pulled her into her arms.

"That's my fault, honey," Wade said softly hoping if he kept his voice quiet, she would follow suit. "I wanted to surprise your mommy, but I think I scared her instead."

"Oh, okay." She settled into Sydney's arms and put her head on her shoulder.

Wade had to get the two of them someplace safe so he could check the rest of the house. There was a noise upstairs that made them spring into action.

"Let's play a game," Sydney said quickly, picking up Faith and moving away from the stairs. "How about hide and go seek? Faith, let's hide and Wade will come find us." He could see there were tears in her eyes, but she refused to let them fall. She had her daughter to think about. "And we have to be quiet because Wade is very good at this game."

Oblivious to the fact she was soaking wet and in a towel or that their lives were in danger, Faith's head bobbed up and down, then she pointed a finger in his face. "Count to twenty before you come looking," she said in a stern voice as she wiggled out of Sydney's arms, but her mother kept a death grip on her wrist.

Sydney made it look like she was casually hugging Wade but her body was taut with fear. "You cleared the downstairs, right?" Wade gave a curt nod. "We'll be in the bathroom. The door is solid oak with a dead-bolt. The window is glass block so we'll be fine." As Wade turned to leave she grabbed his arm. "Be careful." Again he nodded but she held him in place a second longer. "When things are clear, you need to identify yourself and say 'zyxt' or we're not coming out."

There wasn't time to ask all the questions that came to mind from that exchange, so he simply touched her cheek because he needed to reassure her in some small way, and then he leaned back against the wall and gave the appearance of closing his eyes as he started counting softly. All that mattered was their safety. There was a rustle of noise and then they were gone. He waited until he heard the click of the deadbolt sliding shut before he drew his gun and headed upstairs.

There was a trail of little wet footprints along the stairs and down the hall from the bathroom. There were four doors in all upstairs, lim-iting the options for the intruder. Wade carefully entered the first door, which was Faith's room. The tiny double mattress sat on the floor, the pink bedspread neatly made. The floor was covered with all the dolls he had watched her play with earlier. The only area that a man could conceal himself would be her closet so Wade slowly approached, ready for anything. He opened the door, pointing his gun inside but there was nothing more than clothes and a tiny pile of shoes.

From Faith's room, his next stop was the bathroom, the mirror still fogged over from Faith's bath. With just two doors left, he knew it was only a matter of time before there was a confrontation with the intruder. He tightened his grip on his gun, ready to extinguish the threat.

As he nudged the door to the next room open, he knew it was Sydney's bedroom. He could smell her in the air. It was neat and tidy with little to mark it as hers except for that scent unique to her. He'd know it anywhere, the way his body responded to it. With all the times he had imagined himself in her bedroom, it was never with a gun drawn. That sobered his thoughts and brought him back to the task at hand. He had just cleared her room when he heard footsteps on the stairs followed by a loud crash from downstairs.

Wade took off down the hall, taking the stairs two at a time. Sydney and Faith were still silent which was good because it allowed him to follow the smallest of noises. He slowly crept into the living room and he was immediately hit by a cool breeze. The middle window sash was thrown open wide, the curtains dragged through to the outside where the intruder had made his escape. Wade stepped around the overturned coffee table and looked out the window. There was no sound except for the distant barking of a neighbor's dog.

Out of habit, Wade grabbed a towel from the kitchen and used it to close and lock the window, then he went and quickly searched the house again to make sure the man was gone. Only after he cleared the house was he willing to bring Sydney and Faith out of the bathroom. He went to the door and gave it a sharp tap. There was no reaction from the other side.

"It's Wade, Sydney." Still no sound. "Zyxt." At the mention of their safe-word Faith let out a squeal.

"You found us!" The little girl hurled herself into Wade's arms. "That took you a long time. We were really quiet." Behind her, a visibly shaken Sydney stood up and collapsed against his side. He wrapped his free arm around her shoulders and held her close. He needed the contact more than he wanted to admit.

"Why don't you go get a snack in the kitchen?" He let Faith down and watched her run off, unaware of the danger she had been in. "Zyxt?"

Sydney gave a half-hearted smile. "Agnes' suggestion. It's the last word in the dictionary." A shudder went through her body. "What the hell just happened?" Sydney asked as Wade wrapped both his arms around her, nearly crushing her.

He didn't want to share the whole truth about how and why he was there, so he edited. "I wanted to talk to you, and as I approached the house, I noticed the side door was ajar. I saw a shadow of a hooded man passed in front of the window downstairs while you were upstairs." Her face paled. "I thought maybe you had company until I saw the sensors from the security system tampered with and the side door wedged. I think you know the rest."

"D-Did you see him?" Her voice trembled. "The guy. Did you get a good look at him?"

Wade shook his head. "He went out the window."

"What am I going to do?" she mumbled to herself, but Wade decided to offer a solution.

"How about you tell me what's going on?"

Her brown eyes were full of fear and he could tell she wanted to tell him, but she didn't trust him enough to do it. Instead she shook her head and moved away from him. "I need to go check on Faith."

Wade didn't bother to hide his displeasure. In a rougher voice than he intended he said, "The bastard knocked over the coffee table so I'm going to run out to my car and grab an evidence kit. I'll see if he left any prints on that or your window then I'll be out of your hair."

Sydney reached for him but he moved faster. "Wade, wait."

"Go check on Faith," he said as he walked out the door. The walk back to the car was good because it gave him time to clear his head. He was angry at Sydney, scared for Sydney, and tired of thinking about Sydney, period. But he had a job to do. From the trunk he grabbed his evidence kit. Before he went back to the house, he stuck his head into the front seat to grab his clipboard when he stopped short and a string of vile curses flew from his mouth.

From his evidence kit he grabbed a pair of gloves and a plastic bag. He carefully opened the door and reached to the passenger's seat where he picked up the edge of a piece of paper. Once it was inside the bag and sealed, he stripped the gloves and tossed them onto the ground.

Inside the evidence bag was a picture of Sydney at the diner, her throat with a large red slash across it.

CHAPTER 11

ORNING CAME FAR TOO soon. Or maybe Sydney had been up far too late. Either way, the sun was up with all its blinding brilliance and it meant she had to get out of bed and face the day. And her troubles. The urge to bury her head under the pillow was overwhelming until she remembered she still had a visitor camped out downstairs. In the morning light, her curiosity got the better of her and she crept downstairs.

With one eye open she made her way into the kitchen to put on a pot of coffee. She couldn't believe it was already seven. Last night, when Wade came back to the house and showed her the picture, she had crumbled onto the couch and cried. Amazingly, Wade said nothing, and simply took charge as he always did. He scooped Faith up in his arms and somehow managed to get her to sleep, which was impressive. She had countless excuses to stay up if something was going on she was interested in. Sheriff Jenkins in the house was big time excitement, by Ross standards. She shouldn't have been able to sleep for weeks, but Wade had her dreaming peacefully in record time.

Overachiever.

The temptation to see him called to her as the coffee pot began to brew. Knowing he was only a few feet away was killing her. Sydney tried to fight the urge, but the gentle snores she heard coming from the living room were too much to resist. Before she could stop herself, she was standing in the doorway. From there, she could take her time and observe him.

There were no words to explain how uncomfortable the poor man looked, sprawled across her couch in the early morning light. His arms dangled off the cushions as his subconscious searched for more room. His massive body easily swallowed up the length of the secondhand couch. Maybe it was the lack of sleep, maybe it was her overactive libido. Either way, she found it incredibly sexy to see him like that.

Most men would have run for their lives with the hysterics last night promised. Others would have stormed off the second she wouldn't tell them anything more than, "it's a long story." But Wade had patiently waited until the tears had passed. After Faith was asleep, he called one of his deputies over to take the evidence in and start the paperwork on the break in. The one thing he didn't do the entire night was leave her side.

Sydney's last memory before she fell asleep was sitting on the couch and mumbling that she didn't want any of this to hurt Faith. That she had to protect her. From there, he must have carried her upstairs, her exhaustion so deep that she didn't even wake up during the move. It was a kindness she didn't deserve from him after all the half-truths she had told him. She felt guilty about it, but she also felt herself falling more for him, which was dangerous for both of them.

"You need a new couch, Sydney." Wade opened one eye and winced as he sat up.

Sweet Jesus, he's shirtless, she gasped in her head as she clutched the door jamb for support. The light dusting of hair trailing down his chest had her mouthwatering. Especially where it dipped beneath the waist-band of his well-worn jeans. The man looked like sex and sin in the morning. Sydney clenched her jaw to keep it from gaping open as she continued to ogle him as he stood.

Oblivious to her dirty-minded thoughts, he arched his back and stretched his sore muscles. "Where'd you get this thing, a toy store?"

She had been able to form words seconds earlier, but now, with a gorgeous, shirtless man in front of her, she was reduced to a ball of Jell-O.

"You okay?" he asked, taking a step in her direction. Sydney's hand flew out to stop him from coming any closer. If he did, she couldn't be held accountable for her actions.

"I need a shirt. I mean coffee. I need coffee, *you* need a shirt. Don't get me wrong you look fine without it, but..." His lack of a reaction made her temper flare. "Oh, just put on a shirt."

"Who has to put a shirt on?" Faith peeked around from behind Sydney scaring her half to death.

"Sheriff Jenkins, honey." Sydney picked her daughter up and carried her toward the kitchen to give Wade some privacy, which of course he didn't take. He grabbed his shirt off the back of the couch and followed them. Half naked.

"What's he doing here?" The little girl craned her neck toward the living room. "Is that my old blanket?"

Sydney looked to Wade for some help but he just busied himself slipping the tight fitting T-shirt back over his head. The sight of his muscles flexing completely distracted her and made her bump into a kitchen chair.

"Mommy?"

"Crap. Sorry, yes, it's yours. Sheriff Jenkins borrowed it. He slept here last night."

Her brow furrowed. "He slept in your bed with you? Isn't that how babies are made? Am I gonna be a big sister?"

"Faith Ross!" Sydney felt her face heat up and flush with color. If it was possible to die from embarrassment, Sydney was going to find out. "No, no, and no! Where on earth did you hear that?" Sydney asked as she pulled a box of cereal out of the pantry.

"Anna Jacobs. She told me all about making babies."

"I-I don't even know what to say." She looked to Wade for help, but he was doing his best not to laugh. "I swear I'm going to home school her."

"I get to do school at home today? Cool."

"No, you need to eat breakfast and then get dressed for school."

None of this awkward conversation seemed to faze Wade or Faith. The two of them moved around the kitchen like they were talking about the weather while Sydney felt like she was on the verge of a panic attack. Faith couldn't reach a bowl, so Wade picked her up and stood her on the counter. Once she had the biggest mixing bowl she could find in her hand, she tapped him on the head and he returned her to the floor.

Sydney busied herself by grabbing the eggs, cheese and some ham from the refrigerator to make omelets. She knew what Wade liked for breakfast and figured after he spent the whole night crammed on her couch to watch over her and Faith, the least she could do was give him a decent breakfast.

As she moved around the kitchen, she could feel Wade's eyes on her. Any time she snuck a peek his direction, he was giving her a long, lingering look that made her skin feel hot. There was something so sensual about the way he looked at her that she could almost feel his hands on her. She stuck her head into the refrigerator to cool off when Faith called her.

"Can you get us the milk?"

"Sure, I—" Sydney stopped short. On the table between Wade and Sydney was a large mixing bowl that Faith had filled, pieces of cereal spilling over onto the table. Faith held her hands out and wiggled her fingers toward the gallon of milk in Sydney's hand.

"Gimme the milk."

"What in the world is that?" Sydney motioned to the enormous mountain of bran flakes.

Faith waved a finger between herself and Wade. "We're gonna share. He's big, so I made a big bowl of cereal."

"You know I'm making eggs, too. Right?"

"I like eggs," Wade said with a wolfish smile.

"Me too," chimed his newest admirer. There was something adorable about the way Faith had taken to him overnight. She climbed into Wade's lap and made herself at home. Not once did he protest or seem uncomfortable. "Want to share some of Mommy's eggs?"

"Sure, princess. I'd like that."

The two of them dug into their trough of cereal, Wade doing his part to eat as much as possible so Faith wouldn't get in trouble, if Sydney had to wager a guess. Faith chattered on and on about school and what she liked to do. When Sydney slid the eggs in front of them, Faith was busy trying to convince Wade to come in as her special guest next time she had show and tell.

"Thank you." The deep rumble of his voice washed over her. It was so strange having a man share the table with them, but with Wade it was much more comfortable than she would have expected. He dug into the eggs, still hungry even after all the cereal he had stuffed himself with.

Sydney shrugged. "They're not as good as Pete's, but they'll do."

She leaned back against the counter and took a breath. Having a man spend the night was a completely foreign thing to her, but Sydney had to admit, his presence allowed her to close her eyes and get some rest. Watching the interaction between him and Faith had distracted her for a while, but the events of last night were a clear warning, Sydney could feel it in her gut. Nothing that happened to her over the last few years was an innocent coincidence. Each marked when it was time for her to pick up Faith and move on to the next city and now, things were escalating way too fast. He'd *never* gotten this close before. They had stayed too long.

This time it was going to be harder to leave. Elton *felt* different and so did Sydney for the few short months she and Faith had spent there. It was going to hurt to leave, and the man sitting at her kitchen table was a big reason why.

Over the next ten minutes, Faith filled in Wade about her upcoming birthday party and ran around the house showing him everything from the decorations to a picture of the cake Sydney was going to make. She even badgered him until he agreed to come. Wade was attentive to the little girl, but it was hard not to be when she was climbing all over him. Sydney had never seen her be so animated with a man, and Wade had this tender smile when he spoke to Faith that further melted Sydney's heart. If he just would have been put off by the shared cereal, or the climbing, or her daughter's incessant talking it would have been easy to ignore her feelings for him, but now, with him genuinely appearing to enjoy breakfast with a rambunctious five-year-old, she knew she was a goner.

"You better go get changed," Sydney said as she collected the plates from the table. "Your clothes are on your dresser."

"Okay." Faith spun around and placed a big kiss on Wade's cheek, startling him. "Will you come visit us again? I want to play more hide and go seek. You didn't get a chance to hide yet."

Wade glanced at Sydney, so she kept her expression neutral. "You bet, princess. You and your mommy still owe me some pie, as I recall."

"Oh, that's right! Mom, we need to make Wade his pie."

"Wade?" Sydney asked, her eyebrows shooting up in surprise. She was shocked to see Wade's cheeks turn red.

Ever the drama queen, Faith rolled her eyes. "Yeah, Mom. That's his name!" The laughing little girl ran as fast as her feet would take her out of the kitchen and up to her room.

Sydney busied herself at the sink. "I'm sorry. She's not usually so lively in the morning. I think she was just excited to have company this early in the day."

"She's fantastic." Sydney nearly jumped out of her skin when she felt his hand settle on her hip. He was so close his chest brushed against her back as he reached around her and placed two forks into the sink. She was hyper aware of his presence, and that was dangerous. Slowly she turned to face him, her eyes locking on his lips.

"Thanks. She's a lot of fun."

They stood there awkwardly until Wade mumbled a curse then dipped his head and captured her lips with his. Sydney clutched the countertop behind her to keep from wrapping herself around him and never letting go. The kiss was quick, and gentle, and exactly what Sydney had been thinking about doing since she saw him on the couch. It was as if he read her mind.

"Thanks for breakfast," he said, stepping back to give them both some breathing room. He picked up the coffee pot and refilled his cup. "You know we need to talk about what happened."

It was the conversation she had been equal parts dreading and avoiding. She hated lying to him after all he had done for her. It just didn't sit right with her anymore. So instead she decided to avoid every question with the hope he'd get annoyed and leave. Annoyed, she could deal with, but an interrogation would be more than she could handle. Unfortunately he was like a dog with a bone and wouldn't let it go.

"Now that you've slept on it, is there anything else you can tell me that might help me figure out who was here last night?" There was no beating around the bush with him, no games. Wade was as direct as they came. If he had a question, he'd ask. And now that they were both caffeinated, it was game on.

The cat and the mouse.

"I'm not sure."

Wade dug his heels in. "That's not what you said last night. You said it was a long story."

"I was upset." She turned her back to him and started loading their dishes into the sink. If things weren't so dire, she'd think it was funny how their roles had reversed, with Wade talking all the time and her being the one with the short answers.

"Sydney," he turned her, and tipped her chin up so he could look her in the eye, "let me help you."

Something about his eyes made her want to spill her guts, but she bit her lip and refused to cave. "I don't need any help."

"Really?" He caged her against the counter with his massive arms, holding her in place to hear him out. "A strange man was in your house last night. You're running around here with a knife. Someone left a picture of you with your throat slit in my car, and the person who killed a woman and dumped her body behind the diner may have been carrying a picture of Faith. I think you need a lot of help, but you have to talk to me."

She was in a world of trouble, there was no denying it. If he was to blame for all of this, it might be too late. He'd been in her home, he'd followed her daughter. Maybe it was time to lay all her cards of the table.

"Mommy, I can't find my other sparkly shoe!"

"Coming," Sydney called, ducking under Wade's arm and running from the kitchen.

She knew it was the coward's way out and he'd still be standing there waiting for an explanation, but for now, she hustled upstairs and busied herself with getting Faith ready for school. She had to get to Pete's, and didn't want to be late or Hailey might try and make coffee again, something that could end in a catastrophic coffeemaker explosion if they weren't careful.

Fifteen minutes later when she returned to the kitchen, Wade was gone. On the table was a note that said *I'll be by the diner for lunch. We'll talk then.* Sydney crumpled the paper and buried it deep in the trashcan as if somehow that would make it go away.

Avoiding Wade was going to be harder than she thought.

THE EARLY BIRDS WERE already at the diner when Sydney pulled in just after eight. Mrs. Whittman's car, as well as Luke's, were both in the parking lot beside Reverend Jacob's ugly, white, conversion van. Sydney hurried in before Pete noticed she was late.

"Well, look what the cat dragged in," Pete's voice boomed from behind the grill. The acrid smell of charred something filled the air.

"Did you let Cara cook again?" Sydney teased as she hung her jacket on the hook.

With a growl, Pete waved the spatula at her. "Hailey almost burned down the place. She's grounded from the toaster now, too."

"That's gotta be a record." Sydney laughed as she tied her apron around her waist and grabbed a pad of order tickets and a pen and headed into the dining room. The minute she hit the counter, every head in the place turned to stare at her.

"Morning, Sydney," Hailey said in a singsong voice as she put a plate on her tray.

"Hi," she said cautiously, feeling like she had somehow stepped into an alternate reality with half the restaurant still staring at her.

"You're in late," Cara said, barely containing her laughter.

"I'm sorry. Faith couldn't find her shoes and we woke up later than usual. Spent the whole morning playing catch up."

"Mhmmm," Cara smirked, not making eye contact.

"What's going on?" The way people were looking at her, watching her every move kicked her paranoia into high gear.

Had Wade told them what happened? Did one of his deputies spill the details about the man in her house? What else did they know?

God bless Agnes Whittman, but she didn't beat around the bush. When she cleared her throat at the counter, Sydney knew she'd finally get some answers.

"They're all snickering because of your *houseguest* last night." She motioned to her mug.

Cara brought over some fresh creamer and hissed, "Spoilsport."

None of it made sense. How had Agnes found out about the man? Who told her? What did they think about it? Her face turned red and her palms started sweating. "W-What are you talking about?" She scanned the diner and saw Luke sitting at a booth nearby, but he refused to make eye contact. Instead he fixated on his omelet like it was the most interesting thing in the world.

"Oh, come on!" Cara's hands flew up in the air. "We all know!"

"Know *what*, exactly?" she asked, genuinely confused. They were all too giddy to be talking about the intruder.

Agnes smiled like the cat that swallowed the canary and Sydney's pulse raced. "That Wade's cruiser was parked in front of your house all night. Doesn't take a genius to figure it out."

Oh, hell.

"Figure *what* out?" Her only defense was to keep throwing questions back at them. It was like she was talking to Wade all over again as she dodged their assumptions.

"You and Wade," the gray-haired Agnes said as she speared a potato chunk with her fork and popped it into her mouth, "and your illicit all-night rendezvous."

"My illicit what?" Her voice rose to near hysteric pitch. Everything suddenly made sense, the looks, the stares, the glares and the giant smirk on Cara's face. They thought she and Wade had slept together, and they wanted details.

This was bad.

"His car was there when I walked Diablo at midnight, and it was still there when we went for our walk at dawn." Cara stood off to the side, wide eyed, nearly holding her breath in anticipation. "Cara thinks you were up all night talking." Agnes actually made air quotes on the last word, which made it that much worse. "Hailey thinks you screwed like bunnies." She hitched a thumb over her shoulder. "The reverend's wife over there is praying for your soul, and Luke is busy pouting."

"Shut up, Agnes." Luke barely glanced her way as he said it.

"Personally, I'm betting you made Faith a big sister, but only time will tell." She eyeballed Sydney's waistline for good measure and nodded.

"You have all lost your minds," Sydney muttered from behind her hands. She had covered her burning cheeks and closed her eyes, hoping it was all a bad dream.

"Did you kiss him?"

"How does he look naked?"

"Did he let you hold his gun?" At Agnes Whittman's question everyone burst out laughing, except Sydney who did her best to remain straight faced.

"Agnes," Cara gasped between laughing fits, "you're a hoot!"

"What are you all laughing at? I'm serious. He had a really nice piece."

At that comment, even Sydney couldn't hold back her laughter. Agnes' hands flew up defensively. "I didn't mean it like that, you bunch of dirty perverts!"

When that laughter died down, Sydney poured her neighbor more coffee. "Between you and Cara, I guess I've got some competition, huh?"

She took a sip of her coffee. "You betcha."

Cara's head snapped around. "So you admit he spent the night? I thought maybe his cruiser broke down."

There was no point denying it. Sooner or later they'd know everything, and the truth wasn't pretty, but she might be able to sugar coat it a little and lessen the questions. "No, he stopped over."

"Why?" Hailey asked, hopping up to sit on the counter, all ears now.

He never had explained it to her. "I'm not exactly sure. But when he got there, he saw something in the house."

Luke had sauntered closer and that caught his attention. "What did he see?" he asked suddenly interested.

"A shadow."

"A shadow?" Luke asked, skeptical.

"Yes, he said he thought a man was in the house."

"Did you ever see this man?"

"No," she said, sensing where he was going with this. "But he knocked over a table as he was climbing out the window. And the door was broken into."

"You saw this? With your own eyes?"

"I saw the open window and the toppled table if that's what you're asking."

"No. I'm asking if you saw a man, a shadow, or any proof, other than things that Wade *told* you? He could have done all that stuff to make it look like this *intruder* existed."

There was a strained silence between the two. Both of their body languages screamed tension and everyone around them had gone silent, not daring to get in the middle of their heated exchange. Arms crossed, Sydney growled, "No. I didn't." Luke gave her an 'I told you so' look that flared her temper. "I trust Wade."

Three little words, the complete truth, but said in anger, were like a visible blow to Luke. He gave her a slow nod of understanding before patting the back of the chair he was standing beside two times. "Just be careful. Everyone in this town forgets his sins too easily. They make like he's perfect, but he's not. And they all know it. Be careful. He's not the man you think he is."

When he turned to walk away, Sydney stormed into the kitchen. She liked Luke. He was a nice guy unless the topic of Wade came up, then he turned into a raving lunatic. She had been planning to ask Melissa what the story was between them, but never got the chance.

It was time to do a little research of her own on Wade, and see what she could find.

CHAPTER 12

LATE THAT AFTERNOON, WHEN her shift ended, Sydney walked outside feeling relieved. Wade hadn't come into the diner to interrogate her, and other than her uncomfortable run-in with Luke, things had been pretty laid back once they fixed the flaming toaster. With a smile on her face, she pulled around to the front of the diner, but what she saw stopped her dead in her tracks.

Wade's truck was off to the side of the parking lot and he was standing in front of it talking to a woman. She was very pretty, with perfectly styled dark brown hair. Sydney had never seen her before, but there was something about the way she stood there touching him that she didn't like. Which was ridiculous, because Sydney had no claim on Wade. From the way they were standing, she couldn't get a good view at his face, only hers, and from the looks of it, she was having the time of her life, petting him like a giant cat. When the woman went up on her tiptoes to kiss him, Sydney's hands tightened on the wheel. Her foot slammed down on the gas and she pulled out of the parking lot faster than she should have, sending an arc of stones into the air behind her. Only then did Wade turn his head and she could see him frowning at her as she sped away.

I dare you to give me a ticket for speeding, she thought as her car raced down the road. She decided it was time to get some answers about Wade.

There was no denying she was jealous and it annoyed her that she would react in such a childish way to what she saw. It was her own fault for letting herself fall for the guy without knowing more about him. Melissa had thought he was perfect, but she always saw the best in everyone, something Sydney knew first-hand could come back and bite you in the ass. Luke definitely didn't like Wade and maybe she should have paid more attention to his concerns instead of staring into Wade's eyes like some lovesick schoolgirl.

She had trusted Wade. That was the hardest pill to swallow. For the first time since that awful night almost six years ago, she had allowed herself to trust someone to look out for her and to keep her and Faith safe. But maybe Wade wasn't worthy of it. And if that was in fact the case, then there was no way they could stay in Elton. She knew that now. It was time to make some difficult decisions.

So she went to the one person who couldn't help but bluntly tell her the truth.

"Sydney." Agnes greeted her with a welcoming smile like she did every day. "Faith started some art project a few minutes ago. It's something for her birthday party, but she's not quite done. Why don't you come in and have some chicken. I've got plenty left."

"Thanks," she said as she scooted inside. From the outside, Mrs. Whittman's looked like any other home in Elton; modest, neat and well-maintained. It was only when you were inside that you saw the world Agnes lived in. To most people the multiple locks and security monitors inside might be off-putting, but to Sydney they were a comfort. If that wasn't enough, the 150 pound German Sheppard named Diablo was enough to stop the toughest heart. When Faith was here, Sydney knew she was safe.

"How was the rest of your shift? Did Luke stay all afternoon with that sour look on his face?" An enormous pile of potatoes and a chicken breast were placed on the plate before her. Sydney smiled appreciatively.

"Thank you." Her hunger had her digging into the potatoes within seconds. "He stayed a while after you left, but didn't really say anything. He just read the paper."

"Mommy!" Faith said with a smile as she ran into the kitchen, an empty roll of tape in her hand. "I'm making a new creation. Can I finish it before we leave?" When Sydney agreed, Faith turned to Agnes, her expression becoming serious. "I have a code red." She waved the plastic packaging in the air. "No more tape."

With a laugh, Mrs. Whittman went to a drawer by the phone and pulled out a new spare. Faith's eyes lit up at the sight. "To be clear, Faith, my dear, lack of tape is not a code red. It's not classified as a matter of life or death or national security. A code yellow, or maybe it could be a code orange if you were wrapping a gift to give someone, but not a matter of life or death. Understand?" The little girl's head bobbed up and down in understanding, but her eyes never left the circular roll in her hand.

"You go finish up your project while your mother eats." Without another word, Faith sprinted out of the kitchen and went back to work in the other room. "Whiskey or wine?" Agnes held up both, her standard offering at the end of the day. She swore the whiskey was the key to longevity, but Sydney wasn't up for immortality. She did however need some form of liquid courage for the conversation she wanted to have, so she didn't refuse.

"Wine, please." Sydney thanked her as she placed a very generously filled glass of red wine beside her plate. Agnes had her traditional two fingers of whiskey, neat.

"Long day?" Agnes asked as she slid into the chair across the table. "Or is the late night finally catching up with you?" For a mature woman, she certainly enjoyed teasing Sydney.

Sydney wadded up her napkin and launched it over the table at her. "You're as bad as the rest of them." Agnes took a long sip of her whiskey. Sydney could see that she was mulling something in her head.

"Do you believe Wade when he said there was someone in your house last night?"

The perfect opening had been given, so she took it as she played with the chicken on her plate. "Should I?"

Mrs. Whittman shrugged her shoulders. "That's for you to decide."

"I had decided, until I saw him in the parking lot of the diner kissing some woman. Now I'm not so sure." It was Sydney's turn to take a long sip of her wine while Agnes sat wordless across the table. The corners of her lips pulled down into a deep frown.

"Kissing someone you say?" Sydney speared a piece of chicken and nodded her head. "Did she have dark hair and kinda look like the devil incarnate?"

"She was definitely thinking about sin when she was stroking his chest, if you ask me."

"Damn that girl," Agnes spat the words out with a sudden burst of anger. "She won't leave him alone."

"He didn't seem to mind her attention," Sydney grumbled, taking another drink. She was starting to warm from the inside out as the alcohol took effect. She leaned forward in her chair. "Tell me about Wade."

Agnes played her cards very close to her chest. She thought of Wade like a son, and was going to protect him if necessary, it seemed. "What do you want to know?"

"Why does Luke hate him?"

"Why didn't you ask Luke or Wade?"

"Because I didn't think either of them would tell me." Sydney had considered cornering Luke, but he was always so emotional when it came to Wade, she knew no good would come from it.

"Why not?"

"Will you stop answering my questions with questions?"

"Sorry. Those two have a long history and I think it's their story to tell. Why is it so important to know?" Again, Agnes cautiously avoided answering.

"Luke's a friend, I guess, but sometimes it's hard because Wade…"

"Might be something more?"

Sydney didn't answer right away, instead pausing to organize her thoughts before she spoke. "You know there's a lot I can't tell you, right? I've kept my secrets since we came to town. And I trust you to watch Faith when I'm not around. I can tell you that trust doesn't come easily for me." Her eyes drifted to the other room where her daughter played happily, making decorations for her birthday party. One Sydney hoped she'd be able to have in Elton, if it was safe. "I trust Wade. At least I did until today. Things are…catching up with me and, right now, I need to make a choice between leaving Elton or staying. But I can't stay if I can't trust Wade to keep his word. Right now, after seeing him in the parking lot, I have to say, I'm more inclined to run so if there's something you can tell me to change my mind, please do. I'm begging you. Our lives might depend on it."

"Both of those boys are as trustworthy as they come. Their problems are between them. Pride and jealousy are powerful emotions that are hard to let go. For everyone involved, that is." When Sydney didn't say anything but looked at her imploringly, Agnes tossed back the rest of her whiskey. "Screw it. Whole town knows anyway. It's public knowledge. I was hoping you'd talk to Wade about it, then maybe share whatever it is you've been hiding. Now don't look at me that way, child. I wasn't born yesterday. Your confession doesn't surprise me at all. I know evasive techniques, and you've been practicing them so long I bet you don't even think about it anymore." Sydney's head dropped. "But since I can see you're as stubborn as an old mule I once had," Mrs. Whittman said with a cheeky smile, "I'll tell you what I can."

"Thank you," Sydney said softly, still plagued by guilt for always being the one asking for things from people but never willing to give anything in return. It was a difficult way to live and she was getting tired of it.

"Luke and Wade grew up together and were never close friends. But their dislike of one another grew deep when their hormones kicked in and they began chasing skirts."

Faith ran in for some juice then disappeared back into the living room. "They're opposites, as you've noticed. Luke was the outgoing one and Wade was more of the quiet, mysterious type."

The picture was becoming clearer for Sydney and she knew exactly how the girls would react to them. Luke would be charming and pursue girls constantly and Wade would give off the air of danger that would attract girls like flies. Then the conflicts would arise and the posturing, probably mostly on Luke's part. His insecurity, his distrust of Wade made a lot of sense, but he was so vehement about it. There had to be more.

"After high school, Wade went into the military. The female population around here wore black for a month when he was deployed. His parents were so proud of him for going into the service. Bragged about him to anyone who would listen – which was just about the entire town. Drove Luke crazy."

"That's still not the end of their story, is it?" There had to be more to it and whatever it was, Agnes was reluctant to tell her. That had all her internal alarms ringing.

"No. When Wade came home, he met this girl, Tara. I'm pretty sure she's the one you saw pawing him in the parking lot today. The girl was either an unidentified mental patient or Lucifer's niece. One of the two."

"Don't hold back, tell me what you really think."

"She was rotten, but a skilled liar. Her family had moved to town a few months before Wade got back and she'd been *dating* a number of the men in town but the moment she saw Wade, she was like a heat-seeking missile and wouldn't let go."

Green's so becoming on you, Sydney, she told herself as her gut churned. "Let me guess, Luke had his eye on her before Wade came home?"

Agnes' nodding head confirmed it. "He had more than his eye on her—they were pretty serious. At least Luke thought they were. Then

Wade came back and you have to understand, Wade had been in the thick of it in Iraq. From what I heard from my husband, he saw some horrible stuff and he wasn't himself those first few months." She took Sydney's empty plate to the sink and went to refill her glass. "George talked to him a lot. Being a veteran, he understood some of what Wade was going through. The two of them became close."

"That's why Wade is so important to you." She smiled in confirmation and before coming back to the table Agnes looked in on Faith and checked her monitors.

"Yes. While he was getting his feet back under him, Tara swooped in and dug her claws in deep. He was hurt and lonely and she took advantage of that. Worm that she was." The nasty tone Agnes' voice took on when she mentioned Tara spoke volumes.

Tara was scum.

"How she got him to marry her was anybody's guess."

The air in the room seemed to vanish as Sydney sputtered for breath. "M-Married? Wade's married?" Not only was Tara scum, she was Wade's scummy wife.

Great.

"You don't like the idea of Wade married, do you?" The smug grin on Agnes' face made Sydney's heart pound. "Good. Then you're really gonna hate the next part." She grabbed another glass and poured Sydney some whiskey of her own, which she quickly sipped. "Tara became pregnant."

Sydney gripped the table when the room began to spin, either from the whiskey burning a hole in her stomach or the thought of the baby.

Wade had a child.

"He was so excited. He told George that he saw the baby as his future, his hope. It brought him out of the funk he was in after his tour." Something on one of the monitors caught her eye, distracting her mid-sentence. "Speak of the devil." She tapped the monitor. "This her?"

Sydney craned her neck and was shocked to see the woman she now knew was Tara standing on the sidewalk, staring at her house.

"Yes. What is she doing?" They watched her pace back and forth between their two houses before getting into her car and driving away.

"Who knows? Her parents moved a few towns over. I'm sure they've passed on the gossip from the festival and she came to mess with Wade again. She's a disturbed girl." Agnes sat back down and sighed. "Now where were we?"

A feeling of dread slid down Sydney's spine. She wasn't sure if she wanted to hear any more of the story. "Wade was having a child with Satan's niece."

"Ah, yes. Well, the day before she was due to have the baby, she told him it wasn't his."

"Are you kidding me?"

"No."

"And it was true?"

"Yep. Paternity test proved it a few months later."

Sydney sprang to her feet, unable to stay still a second longer. "That's horrible! Who does that?"

"Apparently you missed the part of the story where I called her a mental patient…"

Her feet stopped and she became rooted to the floor. "Oh my God, poor Wade."

"*Devastated* was putting it mildly." Every word out of Agnes' mouth was breaking her heart. "Max was born the next day. Tara refused to allow Wade to be in the delivery room for the birth, so he only saw him through the window of the nursery. Overnight, Wade's world changed. He would have done the right thing by that boy and raised him, but Tara told him she'd never let him be a part of Max's life. Wade was crushed when he had to walk out of that hospital alone."

"Oh, God." Sydney knew exactly what that felt like to think for months you were going to leave the hospital with a tiny angel and then that dream is snatched away. She had more in common with Wade than anyone else in the world.

Agnes shook her head. "From there, Wade went directly to the court-house and filed for a divorce. It got very ugly. She insisted on living in their house with the baby, so Wade moved to his parents but whenever he saw her, it ripped his heart out. Then the rumors started."

Her blood chilled. "What rumors?"

"Tara," Agnes spat her name in anger, "that conniving witch started telling people that Wade hit her and that was the reason they were getting a divorce. The killer was, people believed her. She had played so many folks in this town, she had them eating out of her hand. Especially when she waved that beautiful baby in their faces."

"Wade would never hit a woman! Who would be dumb enough to believe her? Most of the people in this town grew up with him!" Then it hit her. "Luke believed Tara."

"Yep. But you have to remember, he was still bitter about her choosing Wade over him. His pride was hurt something awful so he wanted it to be true. He wanted Wade to be the louse he always hoped he was. Made his anger easier to fuel." She paused, shaking her head. "There never was any proof, not a scratch on her miserable head. So she started breaking things in her house, bumping into things to bruise herself up a little and telling people Wade came over in a rage and did it. I don't have any proof that's what she did, but no way Wade would walk into his home and trash the place no matter how mad he was. He made his choice. He simply walked away from her. It was all circumstantial evidence at best, but those who had an axe to grind with Wade bought into it. Still do, to this day."

"What about the baby?" The question slipped from her lips before she could stop it. "Who was the father?"

Agnes shook her head sadly. "Don't know. That's something Wade would never talk about. I don't think it was Luke's. He would have chased after Tara to the ends of the earth if there was even a chance of it being his. The whole thing was a horribly sad mess created by one nasty woman looking to grab everything she could from the folks around her."

It took Sydney a few minutes to collect her thoughts. This thing between Luke and Wade went deep and it wasn't a quick fix. But one thing was crystal clear in her mind—Wade would never hit a woman. And it was difficult not to think less of Luke for thinking he would.

"So why was he kissing her today if she's so horrible?"

That brought a smile to Agnes' face. "You said you could see her but not him, right?" Sydney's nodded her head. "Well, then I'm guessing if you could have seen him, he'd have looked like he was on the verge of throwing up." She looked out the window thoughtfully before she spoke again. "If she's back, she wants something from him. She either wants money or to cause trouble. That's the only time she comes around him now."

"Why did you decide to tell me this?"

"Because Wade's too damn proud to share it himself. And I wanted you to understand that he has been alone for so long, by his choice, that the fact that he is showing interest in you, Sydney, is huge. I think you're good for him. You are genuine and selfless. And he's as trustworthy as they come. If he offers you his protection, he'll die before he'd let anything happen to you or your daughter. If you want my opinion, and even if you don't, here it is: You and Wade would be good for one another. So stay. Stay with Wade and fight whatever demons might come after you."

Agnes had given her a lot to think about as she loaded Faith and her toilet paper roll castle into Sydney's arms a short while later. Finding out Wade had been married was a shock. Part of her was furious he hadn't mentioned it, but the rational part of her understood. She had plenty of things in her past she wanted to keep dead and buried—why should he be any different?

He wasn't a liar, which made her feel somewhat better. She hadn't been wrong about him. But two people with as much in their pasts standing between them as Wade and Sydney had, there was very little chance of a happy ending. She had to be honest with herself about that much at least.

The smartest thing to do was to push all thoughts of Wade out of her mind. That's what she hoped this conversation with Mrs. Whittman would do—allow her to find a reason, any reason to keep away from him. But then she heard about his wife, the child that he lost, the future he was robbed of, and she couldn't get him out of her head. If anyone could ever understand why she did what she did, he might.

Might.

Or he could find her as vile as the woman who had stolen everything from him and throw her in jail. And was Sydney really any better than her? She took a child from her family. It wasn't up to Sydney to judge them unfit, maybe there were grandparents who could have given Faith everything and protected her from her father while allowing her to be with her relatives. Instead of looking into that, Sydney took the little girl who was so horribly offered and ran, using her tiny body and unconditional love to soothe the ache in her chest. She was worse than Tara.

Tara.

The image of her staring at the house stuck in her mind. What kind of trouble was she going to cause? Sydney had enough on her plate. She didn't need to add a jealous ex-wife into the mix, especially one as volatile as Tara sounded.

As soon as she stepped into her living room, Wade consumed her thoughts. She remembered him sleeping on her couch, walking through her house with no shirt on and making himself at home with her daughter, and she liked it. Way too much. What she wouldn't give to see what could happen between them. But to try could cost her everything.

The phone rang, breaking her sullen train of thought. She hurried into the kitchen and when she picked it up for the third time today, there was no one there. Just breathing on the other end. So Sydney made the only choice she could.

It was time to run.

CHAPTER 13

AFTER TWO SLEEPLESS NIGHTS and two longer days of avoiding Wade and his phone calls, Sydney had made up her mind. They needed to leave. It had nothing to do with Wade and Tara, she kept telling herself. That was ancient history. But every day at work she saw the faces of people who could be hurt if *he* came to town to exact his revenge on her and she couldn't stand to see a single one of them harmed because of her. For their safety and Faith's she decided it was time to leave Elton.

She'd been quietly packing things up, telling Faith she was cleaning the house for her upcoming birthday party. A party she wouldn't ever attend because they'd be long gone. But Sydney pushed the thought of her daughter's impending heartbreak out of her mind and focused on sorting things into the suitcases and getting rid of anything that could leave behind any information about them.

She had stared at a map online late at night, trying to decide where to hide this time. Big city or small? East Coast or West Coast? If it wasn't so late in the fall she might have considered a trip up to Alaska, but then she didn't think it wise to test fake passports at the borders. She'd settled on Arizona, hoping the warmth and scenery would make it up to Faith that she wouldn't get to celebrate her sixth birthday with her friends in Elton.

Everything was packed and ready to go. Sydney had to wait another day to get her last paycheck from Pete and Cara, then they'd be off. The night before they were set to leave, Faith had woken up with a high fever. The poor thing was miserable with a sore throat and cried all night. She couldn't possibly steal her from her sick bed and start off on an eighteen hour trek across country without a doctor around if she needed it.

So instead, Sydney stayed home, locked the doors, and nursed her daughter back to health. It was a good thing she had stayed because it ended up being strep throat. Had she left that night, God knows how sick Faith could have gotten over the course of their trip. Countless popsicles, bowls of Jell-O, and glasses of ginger ale later, she began to perk up.

When she walked out the door to work this morning, Sydney was already exhausted, but Faith was ecstatic because it was her first day back to school and she had missed her friends desperately.

Friends Sydney was planning on ripping her away from tonight, now that she was better.

It was going to do more than tear out Faith's heart to leave; Sydney wasn't going to make it out unscathed, either. But they had to go. There were more phone calls with no one on the other line. Once she heard a man's deep chuckle before the line went dead. Now, when a phone rang, Sydney jumped a mile and approached it like it was a living thing out to do her harm.

Countless times she had felt like she was being watched when she was home alone with a sick Faith. Especially in the middle of the night, when she'd come downstairs to get a glass of water or a cool rag to take down her daughter's fever, she'd shiver, feeling an unknown pair of eyes on her. So many times she reached for the phone, wanting to call Wade, or Cara and Pete, but then stopped herself, knowing there was no point in leaning on him or anyone else in town. It'd only make leaving that much harder.

She hadn't seen Wade since the night she spoke to Agnes about his past. It wasn't something she ever planned to ask Wade about. It was his past, his business. If only he'd give her the same respect, they wouldn't have an issue. But he was busy with work and she was busy with a sick child, so circumstances had helped her stay away from him.

Not that it kept her from thinking about him constantly.

The FBI appeared in town, interviewing people and asking more questions. Their presence was part of the reason she'd been able to avoid Wade the last two days. He'd been busy, too. And fortunately she'd been spared their attentions while Faith was sick. Word around the diner was they believed there was a link between the diner murder and the woman they found outside town a few weeks earlier, but they weren't sharing much with the local police. The investigation was taking up all of Wade's time and energy, which was fine with Sydney. She didn't want him to suspect she was getting ready to leave, and with his keen observation skills, he'd probably figure it out in a second.

"You okay?" Cara touched Sydney's shoulder and she nearly screamed, having worked herself up thinking about Wade and the strange phone calls. "What's wrong? You've been so jumpy today. When the phone rang before, you turned white as a sheet."

"I don't know, maybe I've caught a touch of what Faith had."

Cara pressed the back of her hand to Sydney's forehead. Her brow furrowed with concern. "No fever. Maybe you should go home and rest. Strep is very contagious. You have to be exhausted. Taking care of her alone isn't easy. I wish you would have let me come over and help."

As much as Sydney would have loved her company, she couldn't let anyone come over and see the bags she had packed. She was saved from the conversation by Luke.

"Well this day just got brighter. My favorite girl is back at work!"

"Hi, Luke." Sydney was happy for a reason to get away from Cara before she was forced to make up another lie. "What can I get you?"

"Coffee and a southwestern omelet." He flashed a wide grin. "I missed you. Hailey's nice but she doesn't put extra salsa and sour cream on my omelet like you do. I heard Faith was sick. Is she feeling better?"

"She went back to school today. I think missing class made her feel worse than the strep throat." Sydney laughed. "I know I definitely wasn't like that as a kid. If there was an excuse to get out of school, I used it."

"Same here," Luke said, slapping his hand on the counter in amusement. "She must have gotten that from her father."

At the mention of Faith's father, Sydney froze. Images of him with the bloody bat flooded her mind. It wasn't Luke's fault, he had no idea what those words had set in motion, but her reaction was too strong, it was impossible to hide and he picked up on it right away.

"Syd? Honey, talk to me, what's wrong?" When she stood there unmoving, he reached across the counter and took her hand, even though she tried to pull away. "Are you okay?"

"Why don't you take your hand off her and let the lady catch her breath," a voice said from behind Luke. There was no mistaking the warning in Wade's voice. Sydney could see Luke thinking of a response. She must have looked fragile enough that he thought better of engaging Wade in an argument at the moment, and he released her wrist. Sydney took a few steps away from the counter and tried to collect herself.

"I'm getting really tired of you telling me what to do, Sheriff."

"Guys, please don't fight," Sydney said softly, pressing a hand to her queasy stomach.

Wade ignored Luke's comment and made a bee line for Sydney, coming right behind the counter uninvited. She tried to wave him off, but he ignored her flailing hand.

"Make yourself at home," Luke mumbled into his mug, but Sydney heard and gave him a stern look. She didn't want to be the cause of another fight between them. Tomorrow she'd be long gone and they would still be in town together.

She allowed Wade to take her into the corner of the kitchen. Pete and Cara immediately exited and busied themselves in the dining room, giving them some privacy.

"Next time Luke touches you, do me a favor and deck him." He stepped toward her and brushed his fingers lightly over her wrist.

Even with as much as she had been avoiding him, Sydney had to admit, it felt good to be around Wade again. He had a way of pushing away the bad things and making her feel safe. More like herself. "I hear the sheriff frowns upon assault here in Elton."

"I'd make an exception." Somehow Wade made even a simple wink look sexy. His long lashes and full lips made Sydney's mouth water, forgetting the conversation with Luke that shook her so badly.

What was it about this man that made her feel so alive?

"Luke was trying to make me feel better." She was surprised to feel a stirring of anger toward Wade, but she did. The image of Tara kissing him flashed into her mind. So much so, she wanted to check for lipstick on his cheek.

"You want to talk about the other day?"

"I have no idea what you're talking about," she said dismissively as she stared over his shoulder refusing to meet his eye.

"Sure you do. If you didn't, you wouldn't be so angry with me right now."

With a shrug she said, "I have my secrets, and you have yours. Why don't we leave it at that?"

"You don't care you saw someone kissing me?"

"Not particularly." What a lie. Probably one of the biggest she'd ever told, but there it was. For a second she thought Wade would call her on it, but he stayed quiet and tried to control his temper.

"I was coming to the diner to see you. To talk to you." When Sydney rolled her eyes, he dropped his voice to a whisper. "I didn't want to kiss her. I don't want anything to do with her."

Something about his confession broke through her jealousy and comforted her. He did care about her, and most importantly, about what she thought about him.

"Why not?" Sydney bit her lip, knowing she was baiting him but unable to stop herself. It wasn't fair to either of them, since she was leaving in a few hours, but he didn't know that yet. This could be the last time she laid eyes on Wade and she was tempted to make this encounter something to remember. And fortunately, Wade seemed inclined to oblige.

Without another word between them, he pressed her against the cold tile wall as he kissed her, the heat from his body deliciously enveloping her. His tongue stroked hers aggressively as he took control, and Sydney was happy to yield to him. She wanted someone else to be in charge for a change. She was tired of being the one to take care of everything. In this moment, she gave herself to him completely in the only way she could: with her kiss.

If she could have, she would have stayed locked together with him, forever.

"You're under my skin, Sydney," he murmured against her lips. "I think about you all the time. It's crazy what you do to me." She could feel the rock hard evidence of that grinding against her hip as his hand crept under her shirt. Thoughts of rolling around in her bed with this man electrified her. "You're the only woman I want." She clung to him and returned his attention with an aggressive side that she didn't know she possessed.

Together, they made the rest of the world melt away and all Sydney could think about was Wade and how wonderful he made her feel. Their kiss had a tempo that would grow to a frenzied pace, then ebb into gentle pecks that were just as arousing before starting to build again. Their hands explored one another, the thought of someone walking in on them exciting Sydney even more. Soon her head was spinning and she broke away, gasping for air.

"What are we doing?" she asked, her chest heaving as she looked into his eyes. He was struggling for control, the fire still burning behind his eyes.

"I have no idea. I never lose control like this, ever." He ran his hands up and down her arms when she shivered. Her emotions were all over the place, so she lowered her head to his chest, hiding her face.

"Ditto."

He held her for a while and didn't say a word. The silence gave her time to think and remember that this was it. This was her goodbye. Her bags were packed, she was leaving Elton. After tonight she'd never see him again. She reached up on her tiptoes and gave him a gentle peck on the lips. "You're an amazing man, Wade Jenkins. One I could easily see myself falling for." The confession was the least she could do. She couldn't even think about walking away without leaving some part of herself with him.

"I have something to ask you."

Here it comes, Sydney thought. Her bubble of happiness was going to be shattered all because of a question. One that she wouldn't be able to answer no matter how much she wanted to.

"How's Faith?"

Had he pushed and interrogated her, she would have gone on the offensive, but the way he spoke with kindness and somehow knew where her heart was, never ceased to amaze her.

"She's fine. Back at school." Sydney's words trailed off. "Oh my God, look at the time!" With lightning speed she grabbed her purse and keys and ran for the back door. She was almost ten minutes late to pick Faith up. Add in the drive time and she was going to get there twenty minutes later than she should have. She was fumbling with her phone to call the school as she shoved her way past Wade. "I have to get her."

"Sydney," Wade's sharp command had no effect on her as she threw open the door and ran to her car. She knew she looked like a lunatic but she'd never been late. Images of Faith sitting alone on the sidewalk flooded her head, the repercussions of her being left alone enough to make her vomit.

With trembling hands, she tried to jam her key into the lock with little success. She paused long enough to take a deep breath and gently slide the key into the door, springing it to life. Once she was behind the wheel she braved a look in Wade's direction. He was storming toward her car, with a frown on his face. There wasn't time for an argument, so she started the car only to hear a faint clicking noise that repeated every time she turned the key.

"No, no, no," she whispered hitting the steering wheel as she tried the ignition again and again but it remained silent. Irrational panic overtook her at the thought of not being able to get to Faith.

"Get out of the car." Wade loomed outside her window with an irritated scowl. "Your alternator is dead." When she refused to budge and futilely turned the key again, Wade wrenched open the door and stuck his face right next to hers. "You might not want to trust me with your secrets, but I can damn well drive you to school to pick up your daughter. Now let's go before you snap your key in half. Faith is waiting."

She focused all her fury on Wade. It was all because of him that she had been distracted. Again. He made her lose track of time with his kisses and attention. She shoved him in the chest to get him out of her way then slammed her door shut. Sydney didn't acknowledge him at all as she stormed toward his cruiser and climbed inside. When he didn't hurry, she laid on his horn which caused the windows of the diner to fill with curious faces.

Without a word, Wade climbed into the seat beside her and, unlike her car, his roared to life. Rocks kicked up behind his vehicle as he sped out of the parking lot and onto the road. At least five minutes passed before either of them spoke.

"I'm sorry." The words slipped out as Sydney watched the mailboxes fly past her window one by one. She hated that he saw her so desperate.

"She's fine." Wade glanced over at her, but his cold expression didn't change.

"That's not the point," Sydney snapped.

"And since you won't tell me what the point is, I'll just shut up and drive." Even as furious as he was, he still tossed his phone over to her.

"Thanks," Sydney said softly and quickly dialed the school. She was relieved to hear Faith was in the office, waiting for her. The principal had just called the diner and Pete told them she was on her way so Faith was helping make some copies for the following day at school.

A day Faith wouldn't ever get to see because they'd be long gone, if only her stupid car would start.

Could this day get any worse?

She pushed that thought from her mind as the school came into view. Wade had made it there in record time. If Sydney wasn't so mad, she would have kissed him. But kissing him was what had put them in this situation. He had barely stopped the car when she hopped out the door and took off running for the office.

"Ms. Ross." Faith's teacher met her in the hallway outside the office where other parents were retrieving their children. "Faith's inside with Miss Anna."

The secretary gave her a warm smile as she walked through the door. Faith was neatly arranging a stack of pink papers on the worktable.

"Mommy! Look what I made."

"She's a great helper." Miss Anna smiled and gave Faith a warm hug. Tears burned in her eyes and Sydney had to look away. Elton was a very special place, full of special people that she couldn't bear to leave. But she had to.

"Hi, Wade!" Faith surprised Sydney by grabbing his hand and pulling him into a hug. "Did you come with Mommy to pick me up?"

The scowl that had been on his face minutes ago was replaced by a radiant smile. One that was so genuine it made Sydney's heart thunder against her chest. "You bet I did."

"Good, because I missed you."

He gently tugged on one of her pigtails. "I missed you too, princess." When she threw open her arms, he scooped her up and slung her backpack over his shoulder. "Let's get you home."

The sight of them together was too sweet for words. The big, brooding Wade was tamed by the curly-haired little girl. To say she had him wrapped around her finger wasn't an exaggeration. Sydney followed behind them, entranced. While Faith chatted on and on about school, Wade smiled and nodded asking questions as if it was the most interesting thing he'd heard all day. His kindness overwhelmed Sydney. Even though he was furious with her and she was beyond irritated with him, he still went out of his way to be kind to Faith.

"Thanks," Sydney said as she reached past him to buckle her daughter into the backseat. When she stepped back, Wade was still standing there, watching her with a strange look on his face.

"You don't have to keep thanking me. I want to help. Why is that so hard for you to believe, Sydney?"

"I have trouble trusting people."

Wade gave a sarcastic laugh. "I never would have guessed." He opened her door but caught her arm when she tried to slip inside. "We need to talk."

"I know." Sydney didn't dare look at him, afraid of what he might see in her eyes.

"Good, because this time you're not hiding from me. Now let's get you two home."

AT THE HOUSE, FAITH disappeared inside, anxious to get back to her latest building project. Armed with another roll of tape and some construction paper she grabbed an apple and headed upstairs, leaving Sydney alone with Wade. He didn't waste any time starting the interrogation.

"I need to know a few things."

Sydney steeled herself for the questions, excuses at the ready when it came time to answer. "Like what?"

"You moved here almost six months ago. And before that you were working for a dry cleaner in Indianapolis and a supermarket outside of Nashville."

There was no harm in answering those, so she shrugged. "Yeah, so?"

"And where did you work before that?"

Her stomach rolled and turned sour. He knew. The pricey identification she'd paid for hadn't been good enough to fool Wade. Without giving anything away, she narrowed her gaze. "Why do you want to know?"

He made himself at home at the kitchen table while she nervously paced back and forth. "Because you don't seem to have a past beyond eighteen months ago, Sydney. Did you know that?"

"That's ridiculous."

"Your employment history, rental history, bank statements all end." When she made no effort to explain, he continued. "I'm guessing that's when you bought the new social security number? The license is very well done. It must have cost you a pretty penny."

"I have no idea what you're talking about."

"Dammit, Sydney. Why won't you talk to me?" Now he was the one on his feet and pacing but he looked more like a tiger ready to pounce. Sydney leaned against the counter, watching him. "You can trust me. I could help you. I know you're running from someone. If you'd just tell me who it is, I could help." When she didn't budge, he went in for the kill. "That little girl up there deserves to be safe. If there's danger…"

"If there's any danger, I'll take care of it just like I've been doing since she was a newborn!" Sydney hissed, not wanting to raise her voice and have Faith hear any of this.

"Let me help you," he said as he extended his hands out at his sides, offering himself to her. Completely. All she had to do was reach out and accept.

But she couldn't.

"I. Don't. Need. Help." Her shoulder bumped against his chest as she pushed her way past him, desperate to put space between them so she could pull off this charade and let him get on with his life. "Faith is my daughter, not yours." There was such pain in his eyes as she spewed the hateful words at him, probably reminding him of Tara in that moment.

He folded his arms across his chest but said nothing. His body language screaming with fury, but Sydney didn't let up. She couldn't.

"If she needs anything, I'll take care of it. We don't need your help, and I sure don't remember asking you to play white knight and save us. This whole situation is none of your business." She jerked her chin toward the door. "I think you need to leave."

Wade's anger hit her like a tidal wave. It poured off him and filled the tiny kitchen. She could see the muscles in his jaw clenching as he struggled to keep his mouth shut. It took everything in her not to cry.

Just wait a minute, Sydney, she told herself. Give him another minute to let it all sink in and he will leave. It's better for both of you if you break it off like this. He deserves better and you need to take care of Faith. You can't do that by staying here.

Without a word he grabbed his keys and stormed out the door, ripping Sydney's heart further from her chest with each step he took. What she wouldn't have given to have tried to make a life here, with him.

Then the tears started to fall.

"Where's Wade going?" Faith popped her head around the corner, with some papers in her hand.

Sydney quickly ran her fingers under her eyes. "He, um, had to go to work."

"He probably had a bad guy to catch." The little girl held out the papers to Sydney. "Here, these were in my backpack. Miss Anna said the envelope's for you. Someone left it in the office." The weekly newsletter and latest fundraiser information she laid on the table, trying to get her mind off of Wade and how angry he must be at her. And in a few more minutes she was going to have Faith furious at her too when she told her they were leaving.

But it was all for the best, she told herself as she slipped her finger under the flap of the envelope. Inside there was a single piece of paper. Her heart stopped and terror filled her body. She read it twice and felt the bile rise up the back of her throat.

I'm coming for her.

The words filled her with terror. He'd been at her school. He was here in Elton and coming for them. There was no time for Sydney to think. Without a working car, she was trapped. Still clutching the note in her hand, she acted on pure instinct and ran out the door as fast as her feet would carry her. She heard a shrill screeching noise and realized it was coming for her but she didn't stop. There was only one thing she could do to protect herself and Faith.

She threw herself into the road.

Right in front of Wade's moving car.

He slammed on the brakes, the edge of his bumper brushing against her leg, but she was too terrified to worry about nearly being hit by a car. Faith was in danger and she swore she'd never let that happen.

He jumped out of the car and ran over to her, demanding to know what she was doing. When he saw the tears pouring down her face he opened his arms to her, and this time she ran to him and held onto him for dear life. She started crying harder when she felt him gently stroking her hair, whispering that he was there and everything would be all right.

It was time to tell the truth and let the chips fall where they may.

CHAPTER 14

THERE WAS SOMETHING THAT Sydney found extremely soothing about running her hands through soapy water as she washed the dinner dishes. And tonight, she needed all the calm she could get. After her hysterical episode in the middle of the street, Wade had carried her back inside and told Faith she was crying because she saw a spider and got scared. He pretended to smash something in the corner to complete the charade so Faith wouldn't be upset. Then he proceeded to make himself at home, cooked them dinner, helped Faith with her homework, and was currently reading her a book before bed.

All of that without asking her a single question.

He was amazing.

Sydney tried to enjoy it while she could. She knew when he came downstairs he was going to expect her to start talking and tell him everything, and she was prepared. She only hoped that the kindness he was showing them would continue once he knew the truth about what a horrible person she was. The plan to leave Elton was temporarily on hold. If this conversation with Wade didn't go well, Sydney had already gathered up their emergency pack with cash, ID's, and essential paperwork. Her knife was inside, as well as a gun that she hated carrying but, to protect Faith, she found she'd do anything. Even steal a car if that's the only way they could get out of town. She was putting away the last of the dishes when she heard his heavy footsteps coming down the stairs.

"She's all tucked in," he said taking two mugs out of the cabinet and pouring coffee into them. He looked relaxed while Sydney felt like she was going to throw up.

"She adores you." The words came out as a squeak as she wiped the last of the dishwater from her hands, guilt swamping her. "Listen, I'm so sorry for what I said before about her not being yours, that was awful of me and I didn't mean to hurt you…like she did."

He didn't acknowledge that she knew about his past, he simply nodded and sat down at the table across from her. "Why did you run into the street to stop me?"

Was she really going to do this?

Her heart pounded as she looked into his eyes, eyes that were calm and strong and promised to listen to every word she shared. Unfortunately they gave her no indication as to what his reaction would be, and that was the part that terrified her. So before she shared anything, she needed some guarantees from him. Promises that, once he made, she knew he'd keep. Because that's the kind of man he was.

"The things I'm going to tell you aren't pretty. They're actually quite ugly. The hardest part in all of this is that they will change the way you look at me. But I can deal with that, if I know Faith is safe. She's my number one priority. Having said that, I need you to make me a promise."

"What?"

"No matter what I tell you, you have to make sure Faith is protected. If, after you hear everything, you think she shouldn't be with me, I'm asking you to personally guarantee her safety. She's not going into the system with Child Protective Services or anything like that. She's not going to anyone you don't hand pick. Heavens, she adores you. Keep her, for all I care, just don't let her get hurt after all of this." Desperation and fear choked her. She fisted her hands to keep him from seeing how badly they were shaking as she waited for his word.

"You have my word, I'll keep her safe."

Sydney relaxed and let out the breath that she had been holding. He would keep his word, and she knew he'd never send Faith back to that man. No matter what happened to her, Faith was going to be all right. Knowing that gave her the courage to begin.

"My senior year of high school, I got pregnant. My boyfriend was a complete jackass and demanded I get an abortion. I refused, so he told everyone in school it wasn't his and that I was a cheating whore. Because I was nothing more than another pregnant teenager in their eyes, they believed him." Wade's jaw ticked, the only tell that he was unhappy with what she was saying.

"My mother wasn't a very stable person. She struggled with mental illness and was very religious. A dangerous combination for the mother of an unmarried, pregnant teen. She found out about the baby and threw me out of the house with the clothes on my back and a hundred dollars. I lived in a shelter for a few weeks. I wasn't going to let anything hurt my baby so I got a job afterschool as a waitress," she smiled at the irony, "and made whatever money I could. One of the ladies at the shelter noticed how hard I was working and offered to let me have a room in an apartment building her brother owned. It wasn't great. As a matter of fact it was pretty disgusting, but it was mine."

As she went on, Wade sat there silently allowing her to tell her story without interruption. She was sure there would come a point where he would ask questions, but for now, he was content to listen. That helped give her the strength to continue.

"About a month before I was due, I didn't feel well and had started to have some contractions. I went to the clinic where I had been getting my prenatal care and they did an ultrasound. They told me," she covered her face and braced herself to say the words that she'd never had the courage to utter before, "they told me that my baby was dead."

A low curse slipped past Wade's lips and his anger somehow comforted her. "I'm so sorry."

There was no way she could pause even long enough to accept his sympathy. She had to press on. "I was devastated, to say the least. They induced my labor and I delivered this perfect, beautiful, tiny baby girl. She had ten fingers and toes, a dusting of blonde hair, but no heartbeat. I was allowed to hold her, and I told her how much I loved her and all the things that I had dreamed for us. It felt like my heart was being shredded with each second that passed because I knew it wouldn't last. I named her Hope and I remember kissing her tiny head and promising to love her forever."

Wade reached across the table and wiped the tears from her cheeks.

"Handing her back to the nurses was the hardest thing I've ever done. When they left, I remember lying in the bed, staring at the ceiling and wondering what I was going to do. My boyfriend wouldn't care. He'd be happy and tell me it was for the best. My mother would tell me it was a punishment from God for my sins and that I deserved it. I had already pushed aside dreams of college when I found out I was pregnant, but now, I didn't even have Hope to dedicate my life to. I had nothing. I watched the sun rise out my window and I knew it was time to leave. Not just the hospital, but my life in California as well."

His voice was raspy when he spoke. "What did you do?"

She pulled her hair back into a ponytail then dropped her hands into her lap. "I filled a bag, gassed up my car, and drove. I had no idea where I was going. All I knew was, with every mile farther away I drove, the better I felt. But I was consumed by images of the baby and retracing my actions over the last few days. Did I do something to hurt her? What could I have done differently?"

At that point he interrupted his voice gentle and words unexpected. "You know it wasn't your fault, right? The doctors, the nurses, someone had to have told you that."

She offered him a weak smile. "I know. I knew it then, but when something like that happens, you can't help but ask yourself why. I found hours had passed before I would come out of my own thoughts and I'd have to look at the GPS on my phone to see where I was. I barely made it through the mountains before it got dark. I wanted to get off the highway for a while so I started off on some country roads. I was somewhere south of Billings, Montana, when it happened."

He could sense her anxiety spike and he froze, sitting very still and giving nothing away with his expression. "What happened?"

"It was dark, and I was exhausted. I thought about Hope's tiny face and couldn't stop crying so I pulled over next to this cornfield. God, it was like I was surrounded by mountains of corn. I don't know if I was on a highway, the interstate, or Farmer Brown's road anymore but I remember the stalks were so tall. I just sat in the car and cried until I couldn't cry anymore." She wiped her eyes and took a few deep breaths and prepared to lay her sins in front of this man that she cared so much about.

Trust him, her inner voice whispered. She held onto that thought and continued.

"I was getting ready to leave when I looked out the windshield and there was this woman. She was disoriented and staggering toward the car, covered in blood. She was in a dirty nightgown with little yellow flowers on it. Don't ask me why I remember that, but they looked to be the same shade as the corn." Sydney lost herself in the memory for a second before snapping back to the here and now. "She looked like she had been attacked by an animal or something so I jumped out of the car and tried to help."

Wade leaned forward on his elbows, intently listening to her every word. She could see him recreating every nuance of the scene in his mind. She was sure he had a million questions, but he waited and let her tell the story.

"Right when I got to her, she collapsed and shoved something at me. At first I thought it was a wad of blankets until I looked closer and I saw there was a newborn baby in them." Sydney glanced over at the stairs thinking of how much bigger that tiny girl was now, but still in the same danger. Nothing had really changed for either one of them.

"There was so much blood. She could barely talk. I wanted to call an ambulance but she just kept begging me to take the baby and get her away from him."

"Who?" Wade asked, knowing a name would be a solid fact he could use to verify in this insane story.

"I didn't know, exactly. The woman said, *He's trying to kill her* and *I couldn't let him have her.* "

"Did you ask her what her name was?"

"M-Marcy. Her name was Marcy, but there wasn't time for me to ask her much more. I could hear rustling in the corn and someone coming closer. She panicked, begged me to go and take the baby. I offered to take her to the police but that freaked her out even more. I was about to drag her to my car when I heard him yelling terrible things. He was saying he would kill her when he found her and make her pay."

"Jesus, Sydney."

"I had blood all over me from trying to help her, but it didn't do any good. I couldn't stop the bleeding enough to help her. When I looked over at the baby, I realized there was one thing I could do to help her. The only thing I could. The stalks right next to us started shaking and I could hear him breathing. Watching us. I grabbed the baby and ran for the car as fast as I could."

Wade was like a statue beside her. His expression was calm but she could feel his anger vibrating beneath his skin. The silence was slowly killing her but if he interrupted, she didn't know if she could continue.

"The keys were still in the ignition, so I started to drive away. He jumped through the corn but I didn't stop. He watched me drive away, and the last I saw of him, he was standing over Marcy and had raised what looked like a baseball bat over his head. I couldn't watch anymore so, like a coward, I sped away." Years had passed but the emotions were still raw as if it all had happened yesterday. She covered her face and tried to stop shaking. Wade settled into the chair beside her and rubbed his hand along her back.

"I drove. I didn't stop until the car was almost out of gas. The baby was content and just sat in my arms making all those great noises newborns make. I remember looking at her in the moonlight and wondering if this was God's way of giving me back what he had taken. Logically, I know it doesn't work that way, but to me, at that time, it was sign that we were meant to be. I took it on faith."

"That's where her name comes from."

"Yes." Sydney turned to look into his eyes, something that had terrified her before she started this whole confession but now she needed the truth. If he believed nothing else, he would have to believe this. "I love her as if she were my own. I love her more than that because I love her enough for me and for her mother who couldn't see her grow up. I owe Marcy that. She entrusted me with her daughter and I have every intention of keeping the promise I made her that night. Faith has never wanted for anything. I've worked every day to make sure she is happy, healthy, and well fed. I love her, Wade. I swear that to you."

He took her hands in his and held them for a second before he spoke. If he said she was under arrest she would crumble. "Anyone with eyes knows you love her, Sydney. I appreciate you trusting me enough to tell me all of that. It couldn't have been easy." Sydney bit down on her trembling lip as he continued. "I knew you've been hiding something but I never guessed it was all of that."

Her heart fell at the disappointed tone in his voice. She pulled her hands away from him and clasped them tightly in her lap. "You think I'm an awful person. It's okay, I know I'm a horrible woman. You won't be telling me something I don't tell myself every night."

"Actually," he said lifting her chin so he could look her in the eye, "I think you're an angel. If you hadn't taken Faith she could have died that night like her mother at the hands of a monster. Her mother asked you to take her and protect her which I can say you've done. That little girl is happier and healthier than most kids today. You're a good mother, Sydney."

His kind words reopened the floodgates and she cried. She cried for her baby, for Marcy and for all that was taken from Faith by her father.

She cried knowing that she would never get to have the life she wanted with Wade and Faith in Elton. It all was going to be taken away from her because of her decisions that day, but she would gladly sacrifice it again for Faith.

"Being a good mother is not necessarily the same as being a good person."

He surprised her when he scooped her up and pulled her into his lap. Sydney had prepared herself to be shouted at or arrested, but the thought that he would still want to have anything to do with her after he knew the truth threw her off balance. She was completely dumbfounded when he brushed the hair out of her face and kissed her. It wasn't a gentle kiss either, it was passionate. If his goal was to use his lips to make her forget everything, including her name, mission accomplished.

"So you don't hate me," she gasped when she came up for air. Her whole body warmed at the sound of his deep chuckle.

"No, I don't hate you." He kissed her again, slowly this time, allowing her to savor it and run her hands over his chest. In the arms of this man, she could believe the impossible was possible.

"I have some questions, though," he said as he ended the kiss. "Are you up for it?" Not trusting her voice, she nodded her head. "Good. Do you know who's after you? I need a name."

"I think it's Faith's father. I did some research a few years back. I went online and began trying to retrace what route I might have taken from California. I know it's ridiculous, but I really wasn't paying any attention at all. I have a general idea where in Montana I was when I pulled off the highway. I started looking online at land records to find farms in the area near that exit, and who owned them. It took me months, but I think I finally found the right one. There was a farm owned by a man named Ronald Washington. He was a farmer and a member of the local sheriff's department so that explained why Marcy wouldn't have wanted to go to the police." Wade's head nodded in the affirmative.

"Was there a birth certificate on record for Marcy or a death certificate? Are you sure Washington was her last name?"

Sydney's head swayed from side to side. "I never could find one. But there's a lot of land out there in Montana. Plenty of places to get rid of a body. It breaks my heart to think that he might have buried her out there somewhere."

"Unfortunately, you could be right. Especially if they weren't married. She could have been a woman he had an affair with, too. No way to know. But someone should have reported her missing, I would imagine. I'll look into that when I get back to the station."

Sydney gave him the date this happened and the towns she could remember from when she exited the highway. It was almost six years to the day that Faith came into her life. Wade seemed confident that something would come from his search to give them a lead and he was interested in looking into the police angle. In a small town, it would explain the fear Sydney described in the woman when she brought up the police or 911.

"The only marriage Ronald had was to a woman named Amanda Washington a year later," Sydney said as she searched her mind for the tiniest of details she had found about Ronald.

"Is he still married?"

"I don't know, I haven't checked in a while."

"Did you get a good look at Ronald that night, or have you seen him since? Could you give me a description?"

"No. That night is crazy in my head. I've had so many nightmares about it, and him in particular, that I wouldn't know what was real and what was my imagination anymore. And even though I've felt him watching us or thought that he was coming after us, I never had any real proof until now. There were times I was worried it was all going on in my head, to tell you the truth."

"Because of your mother." She nodded in affirmation as she fidgeted with the button on her shirt, not wanting to think about having anything in common with her mother.

"The first year we moved around a lot. It was easier because Faith was so small and we didn't have too much to take with us. Then we started staying longer, but odd things would always happen after a few months. Mysterious phone calls, dead animals, something destroyed in our yard. Again, things that could have been explained away by kids, vandals, or honest mistakes, but in my heart I knew it was him."

"So why did you change your last name a year and a half ago? What happened to make you take that step?"

"I started getting calls, daily. The first one came when I was running around trying to make dinner. Faith was crying and someone asked for Sydney Jackson. Because I was distracted, I said 'Yes, that's me', not even thinking. He immediately hung up and I knew I'd made a grave mistake. From then on, whenever we got a call, the person on the other end would sit there and just breathe."

"I assume you had the cops trace the number that was calling you?"

She shook her head. "What was I going to tell them? The father of the baby I stole is harassing us?"

"You could have said he was a boyfriend or something."

"And what if they actually tracked him down? I'm sure he would have been more than happy to tell the cops how I stole his daughter. Then I'd be the one in jail and he'd have Faith. There was no record of Marcy's death. I couldn't prove anything on my end, but with a simple blood test he could prove Faith was his child, not mine."

Wade held her and remained silent for a long time. She knew he was digesting every word and it surprised her he wasn't more critical. He hadn't condemned her or questioned her judgment yet, but she could feel it coming.

"You know about my past."

It wasn't a question he asked, just a simple statement of fact. The tone of his voice told her he wasn't going to discuss it, he was making a point.

She whispered, "Agnes told me."

Wade nodded. "We all make mistakes and do things we aren't proud of. But I think it's what you do after the mistake that speaks the loudest about what kind of person you are. Did you make a mistake that's going to have major legal ramifications for you? Yes. But have you given that child a life beyond what she would have had if you had left her behind? Absolutely. No one can question your love and devotion to her."

"Are you disappointed in me?" It felt silly asking him that, but his opinion mattered. She had to know how he saw her, even if it wasn't good. The not knowing was going to kill her.

"I'm disappointed I wasn't there years ago to help you. You did the best you could under the circumstances, Sydney. I can't tell you what I would've done because I haven't walked in your shoes. But what I know of you now, is amazing." He kissed her on the forehead and slid her off his lap so he could stand up.

"I need to go to the station to look into a few things. I want to know exactly who we're up against and see what I can find out about custody of Faith." Sydney tensed at the mention of Faith and reflexively looked at her emergency pack. Wade picked up on it and took her by the shoulders.

He knew exactly what she was thinking.

"Don't you dare run off on me, Sydney. I swear I don't want to take Faith away from you. I want to make sure you can keep her. Let me help you stop him. You don't have to do this by yourself anymore."

His words seemed like an answered prayer. She wasn't alone anymore. After six long years, she had someone else in this world she could count on. It was invigorating and terrifying to think about. It was everything she had longed to hear, but she still doubted his truthfulness. "Really?" she asked as she reached up to brush her hand along his jaw, to make sure he was real. "I don't know how I can ever thank you."

"Don't leave."

"I don't want anything to happen to you, Wade. I'd never forgive myself if you were hurt because of me."

He caught her chin between his fingers. "I'll be fine. And I swear, I won't let him hurt you or Faith."

She closed her eyes and in a show of extreme trust, picked up her emergency kit with everything they needed to run, and she put it in his hands. A look of relief washed over his face. He nodded and slung it over his shoulder.

"I'm going to make sure the house is secure and then I want you to go to bed and get a good night's sleep. I'll be down at the station and I'll have someone drive by every hour. If you hear anything or think something's not right, you call me and I'll be here in five minutes."

She watched him check every window, door, and closet before he left. As the lights of his car disappeared into the darkness, Sydney crawled into bed with a sense of peace that she hadn't experienced in a long time. Telling him was the hardest thing she'd ever done, but now that it was over, she realized she wasn't alone anymore. She had Wade by her side.

Ronald Washington wasn't gonna know what hit him.

CHAPTER 15

"YOU'RE STILL HERE?" SAM asked Wade just before dawn as he arrived to start his shift. Wade hadn't slept since he left Sydney's and his mood reflected that. The middle finger Wade extended to Sam in welcome answered the question. "Sorry, boss. Who knew you weren't a morning person." Sam went to his desk and began slathering cream cheese onto his bagel.

The great thing about living in a small town was you knew everybody in the area. The bad thing about living in a small town was that everyone knew everyone else's business. Be it relationships, employment, or schedules, nothing was a mystery in Elton which was why Sam was very aware of the fact that Wade had been up all night, a night that wasn't his shift.

"How's Sydney?"

An innocent question but one that still raised Wade's hackles more than it should have.

"She's fine. What do you care?"

His deputy threw up his hands in surrender. "Last night I heard on the scanner you asked for hourly patrols. I thought maybe there was more trouble at her place."

"I'm sorry," Wade said with a groan as he rubbed his hand across his whiskered face. He got up from his chair and poured another cup of coffee. He ignored the tiny grounds that floated as he forced the thick black sludge down his throat. There was still more work to do. "I've been staring at the computer all night trying to figure something out."

"Anything I can do to help?" Sam offered. He was a good kid, hard-working and honest. More than anything, he knew how to keep his mouth shut and was a whiz with computers.

Wade leaned back in the chair at his desk. "I'm trying to find information on someone but I don't have much to go on. I think the name is Ronald Washington and he's from Montana. Six years ago he was living on a farm way outside of Billings. I know he was married to a woman named Amanda, but then about three years ago, they both vanished."

"A lot of folks in that area like to go off the grid from time to time. Anti-government and such. I have a cousin up there who says the mountains are covered with people doing just that. They live off the land, do odd jobs, and get paid cash under the table. Maybe that's what this guy did." Sam skimmed the papers Wade passed him. "He sold his farm for a fair amount, but the money never made it into his bank account. If he and his wife did go underground, they would've had a bit of cash to do it."

"But after that sale, I can't find a hit on his social security number for anything. No credit cards, no driver's license, no banks, taxes, or insurance."

"Is he in the system?" Sam's fingers flew over the keys of his computer. "Nothing here in the national database but let me see something." He leaned closer to the screen, his brows furrowed. Wade craned his neck to get a look at what the kid was doing. "Here. There are a bunch of guys with the name Ronald, Ron, or Ronnie Washington in the penitentiary system in Montana. Is it possible one of these guys is your man? You know cons give bad socials all the time or use fake identities to try and avoid priors following them. Might want to go through their mugshots and see if you can find him that way. Want me to print this list?"

"Can you cross-reference anyone with that name who might have been a recent release, too?"

"For that, I'd have to make a formal request but it should come back in the next day or two. I'll get it to you as soon as it arrives."

They both stood up and Wade clapped Sam on the shoulder. "Thanks."

Sam nodded in acknowledgement and headed out to start his shift. Knowing the deputy as well as he did, before long Sam would end up finding his way over to Pete's for an early morning cup of coffee and the newspaper. Wade also happened to know the kid was interested in the newest hire at the diner, none other than the coffee scorching Hailey.

Wade returned to his desk to try and finish up a few things, but he was distracted by thoughts of Sydney. He had been thinking a lot about her confession and everything she had told him. In his heart, he knew Faith was better off with Sydney than she ever would have been with her abusive father, but the cop in him, the part of him that believed in the law and rules, was conflicted by her choices.

No matter what happened, he was glad she trusted him enough to share her past, but he found himself struggling with the details. If she was lying about any of it, he was done with her. It wouldn't be easy—he was more attached to her than he realized—but he'd fallen for a liar once, and he swore he'd never do it again. He'd been taken advantage of, had his heart ripped out, and all for nothing. No matter how gorgeous and sweet a woman she was, if Sydney lied, it was over.

Fortunately, everything he'd found so far corroborated her story. She didn't know all the details he had on her before she made her confession, or that he had already connected Sydney Ross to the pregnant high school girl reported by her unstable mother as a runaway, but her story matched exactly with what he knew. He made a few calls overnight and found that she had used a different name when she was at the clinic, probably trying to avoid her mother's, and potentially her boyfriend's, snooping.

On some level, he was more than a bit disturbed at how well she lied. But when he stepped back and looked at it, she did it when she was protecting someone. Her baby, or Faith, especially. She didn't lie for her own gain. That eased his mind somewhat, but the uncertainty lingered.

In all his searching, he couldn't find anything on Marcy. There was no Marcy Washington that he could link with Ronald at any time before or for that short window of time after the incident when he was still on the farm. It was as if she didn't exist. He could search missing children and runaway reports from the western third of the country, but that could take weeks. There were a few Jane Does that had been found in Montana in the months after Sydney found Faith, but before he could begin the process of matching one of those bodies to the woman who was killed by Ronald, he would need a DNA sample from Faith and he was willing to bet his life Sydney would never go for that.

The day had flown past when he was startled by a text message. What flashed across the screen made him feel like a hypocrite.

We need to talk. I'm tired of waiting.

Tara. She'd been harassing him for about two weeks. She blew into his life every now and then, usually when she needed money, or if she was in trouble with the police somewhere. Mostly she did it just to parade Max in front of him and tear out his heart for the fun of it. He was an idiot for ever getting involved with her. It was ridiculously early for a text from her but she probably had been out all night drinking, or whatever she was into these days, and was just getting home.

Sydney knew the town gossip version of his past and from what she said, she'd caught an eyeful of the two of them in the parking lot, but he highly doubted she knew how often his ex-wife was still slinking around his life, asking for things and threatening to cause trouble.

You have your secrets and I have mine. Sydney's words came back to him and he couldn't help but shake his head. He was just as guilty as she was of withholding the details of his past, and yet he had the nerve to be irritated with her for concealing things from him?

Nice double standard.

He was going to have to tell her the ugly details soon. Tara was becoming more obnoxious. And jealous. She was threatening to tell

Sydney her version of events and how he had wronged her. The woman could weave a tale of lies that even a saint would believe. Everything would be carefully designed to ruin what Wade and Sydney might have built together. Tara was a very convincing liar, and before she appeared on Sydney's doorstep, Wade felt obligated to warn her.

He had no idea how long he had been staring at his computer but the sun was up when he heard his name. "Wade, you have a call on line one," Mrs. Watts, the receptionist, said over her shoulder. "It's a David Post?"

This was a call he'd sat by the phone all night waiting for. Thank God Dave, one of the men he had served with, was a lawyer on the east coast and still liked to get up early. He'd emailed him shortly after leaving Sydney's last night to share with him a hypothetical situation and was interested to get his thoughts on it.

"Dave," Wade said with a smile as he cradled the receiver against his shoulder.

"Rip, how are you, man?"

Wade winced at hearing his handle from their time together in Iraq. "I'm good, how about you?"

His friend laughed. He had a solid practice back in Boston, and in all the years he'd known Dave, he was someone Wade never argued with, because against Dave, you'd lose every time. "There are plenty of bad guys to keep me busy, that's for sure. So I got your email."

"Yeah? And?" The anticipation was killing him. He needed to know how badly Sydney was screwed.

"And I'd say you have a hypothetical shit storm on your hands, my friend. Do you have some time to talk? Hypothetically, of course."

Over the next forty-five minutes, Dave painted a somewhat grave picture of the situation. If Ronald Washington was Faith's father, according to Montana law, he could take her away from Sydney. There was no legal adoption of Faith, in fact Sydney would probably be facing jail time for transporting a minor across state lines, kidnapping, and a slew of other offenses they could charge her with. Even if Marcy herself came back from the dead and said she wanted Sydney to keep Faith, Ronald would still have a claim to her as the biological father.

He was beginning to agree that her only chance of keeping Faith was to run.

For someone who had sworn to uphold the law, he was certainly bending his fair share of them on Sydney's behalf lately, and he wasn't quite sure how he felt about it. Up to this point, he'd tried not to think about how far he was willing to go to protect them, but sometime soon he was going to have to look himself in the mirror and account for all of his choices. The one thing that wouldn't change was his need to keep Sydney and Faith safe. She'd made a mistake in taking Faith back then, but the little girl might not have survived that night if Sydney hadn't intervened, or worse, grown up with an abusive father who would have done God-knows-what to her. Honor or not, he needed to see this thing through with Sydney or he'd never forgive himself.

Strangely enough, when he hung up the phone, he knew the second Sydney walked into the station. It could have been the exaggerated greeting he heard come from Mrs. Watts, or the faint smell of her perfume, or maybe the fact that she was so far under his skin, she was in some ways already a part of him. He met her eye and waited for the awkward smile and wave she'd offer.

God, he really needed to get a life.

He relaxed in his chair and enjoyed the show as she approached his desk. The way she moved was a gift from heaven. She wasn't even trying to be sexy. If she had, it would have been a turnoff, but the fact that she had a natural seductive quality really caught his eye. She was young, beautiful, and nervous as hell from the way she as wringing her hands together.

"Hi," she said, playing with her ponytail as it hung over her shoulder.

"Hey." He motioned to the seat across the desk and she perched herself on the edge. She looked like she was ready to bolt, so he tried a little small talk to try and put her at ease.

"Faith at school?"

"Yeah, I just dropped her off. I-I was actually on my way to work."

"So what are you doing here?"

"I don't really know." She shook her head and seemed to be mustering her courage. "I just wanted to see if…if we're okay?" she asked in a rush.

"I wasn't planning on arresting you today at the diner, if that's what you're asking."

She tilted her head to the side as she considered something. "You've been here all night."

"Yep." He rubbed his hand against the whiskers on his cheek as if to prove it.

The fiery look in her eyes was comical. She tried to put out this tough façade to the world, but he knew, probably better than anyone, just how vulnerable she was. But he let her take her shot at him. "Up all night checking out my story?" She splayed her hands out on his desk, leaning forward.

He took a swallow of coffee just to let her stew and tried not to stare at her chest. "I'd be an idiot not to."

"And?"

"Everything you told me checks out. I already knew quite a bit about your past before our conversation." When he saw her eyes flare wider, he explained. "I ran your prints the day I pulled you over. I got your real name and knew about what happened to you up until the time you left California."

"You illegally acquired my fingerprints?"

He ignored her question and continued on to the information she really wanted to know about. "Ronald Washington disappeared from public record a few years ago. I have a couple of leads out to try and piece together where he's been so we know what we're dealing with." He didn't miss the way her body visibly relaxed when he said 'we.' "I can't find anything on Marcy. She's a ghost with nothing to legally tie her to Ronald. I'm gonna keep looking, though. Don't worry."

She looked defeated as she leaned back into her chair, the yellow Pete's T-shirt she wore every shift bringing out the gold in her brown eyes. "This is such a mess. And with you being the sheriff, it's even more complicated. I'm sorry I dragged you into it."

"You didn't drag me into anything." He came around the desk and sat on the edge so he could face her. "We all have things in our past we'd just as soon forget." It was as good an opening as he was going to get, so he took it. "There's something I want to talk to you about. It's important. Do you think you could be a few minutes late for work?"

She slipped her cell out of her purse and smiled. "Cara? I'm going to be a little late." She paused and picked at a piece of thread on her jeans, refusing to meet his eye. "I'm with Wade," she nearly whispered into the phone. Her eyes rolled at whatever Cara said. "I'm at the station, so that would be a little difficult to pull off, Cara." With a few quick words, she returned the phone to her purse.

"Follow me." As he led her down the hall to one of the interrogation rooms, he dreaded the impending conversation. If he'd learned one thing over the years, it was that women weren't fond of stories about baggage from your pasts. Especially when the baggage was female.

Her eyebrows shot up when he closed the door and checked to make sure the privacy blinds were drawn. "Should I call an attorney?"

Wade shot her a wry grin. "There aren't many private places in this building. It was this or the supply closet. Maybe we'll go check that out after we talk."

"Have mercy." The words slipped out, causing Sydney to clamp her hand over her mouth and turn bright red. She fanned her flaming cheeks and muttered to herself under her breath. "Y-You said you wanted the talk to me?"

"You told me about a mistake you made, and I feel like it's only fair if you hear about Tara from me." The tension in the room shot up with the mention of her name. "Tara was…" He nearly laughed when Sydney bit her lip to keep herself from blurting something out. "A nightmare. But not at first. I was lonely, and she said and did all the right things. I was the sucker who wanted to believe everything she spewed, and I ended up paying for it."

After four years, it shouldn't have been so difficult to talk about. He was young, and stupid, fresh out of combat and she took advantage of him. And he let her. That's probably what bothered him more than anything. He let Tara make a fool of him. Even with everyone around him telling him to be careful, he'd fallen for her lies. All of them.

"When she told me that the baby she was carrying wasn't mine, it was the worst pain of my life. Nothing I went through in Iraq came close to that night. And all because I wouldn't buy her a diamond necklace as a *birth present*, she called it. I wanted to use the money I'd saved to get us a bigger house once the baby was born, but she thought she deserved a gift for going through the trouble of giving birth. She was big on flashy gifts, especially for herself. I wasn't. When I refused, she told me it was just as well because I wasn't even the father, and maybe she'd go ask *him* for that necklace since he had far more money than I did."

Sydney winced at the cruelty of Tara's words. Wade had relived the moment so many times in his head, he forgot how truly despicable it had been. "When Max was born, I had to go see him, at least once. Maybe I was a glutton for punishment, or just stupid. I'd spent the last nine months of my life loving him. Whatever it was, I needed to say goodbye to him and that part of my life."

When he finished, tears swam in Sydney's eyes but she didn't let them fall. She took every horrible memory of that time and gave him the strength to keep talking. That was what impressed him the most about her. Sydney had amazing strength of character, even if she didn't realize that about herself.

"I wish that was the end of my story with Tara, but it isn't." Sydney's eyes locked on his, a million questions floating in them, but she waited and let him fill in the details. "She likes to pop into my life like a thunderstorm from time to time. She dumps a ton of crap on me, floods the fields with her evil, then disappears as quickly as she arrives." He crossed his arms and leaned back against the wall and prepared himself for her reaction. "Tara's been texting me. She knows about you, and isn't happy about it."

For the first time in fifteen minutes, Sydney spoke. Her voice was calm but strong. "What does that mean?"

"She wants to meet you, and I've refused. It's what she does about once a year. She gets all dramatic, offers to let me spend time with Max, tries to get me into bed. When that doesn't work, she asks for more money. Most of the time she goes away when she realizes I'm not going to give her what she wants, but this time it's different. Because of you."

"Me?" Wade nodded his head. "How do I fit into your ancient history?"

Wade debated how much to say, then threw caution to the wind. If he was going to clear the air between them, then it had to include his feelings. "She knows I have feelings for you."

"Y-You said that to her?"

"No. Not in so many words, but her parents are still in the area and, apparently you and I are hot gossip these days. Ever since I spent the night at your place."

"Why are you telling me all of this?"

"Because you were brave enough to tell me about your past, I thought you should know about mine. I mentioned Tara because I think she might approach you sometime soon, and I wanted you to hear the details from me, not her. She's manipulative and vindictive and will make up lies in a heartbeat, so if she does corner you, make sure there are other people around who can corroborate your side of what happened and what was said. I wanted you to be prepared."

"Is she dangerous?"

"No."

"She's been outside my house."

"What? When?"

Sydney paused and waited for him to calm down. "A few days ago, Agnes and I saw her standing on the sidewalk in front of the house. She didn't go into the yard or do anything. It was weird."

He paused, debating whether to share the last bit of information or not. It was always better to be prepared, so he told her. "In the beginning, I thought she might be the one harassing you." That caught Sydney's attention. She went completely still.

"What do you mean?"

"She made some comments. Threats against you. I wouldn't put the random phone calls past her either. The thing you need to know is Tara's all bark and little bite. She had nothing to do with the man in your house and all the other things that have been going on. I'm sure of it. My suspicions were also before I knew your whole story." He unfolded his arms and moved closer, since Sydney looked visibly shaken.

"I guess there's just something about me that makes people hate me," Sydney mumbled sadly looking down into her lap.

Wade leaned over, putting his face right near hers. "There's nothing wrong with you. Tara's a psycho, but her beef is with me. If she comes within a hundred feet of you again, I'll slap a restraining order on her."

"Why haven't you done that to keep her away?"

"I don't know." Wade walked to the other side of the room to keep his emotions from showing. His reason wasn't something he wanted to share. It made him feel weak.

"Max," Sydney said softly. "Sometimes, when she comes around, you get to see Max, don't you?"

He considered denying it, because it wasn't something he was all that proud of, to throw his Achilles' heel out there for the world to see. But it wasn't the world, it was Sydney, and she had trusted him with her secrets, it was his turn to go all in. Not sure his voice would work Wade gave a curt nod in confirmation.

"You love him. Even though he's not yours, you still love him."

"He's a great kid, despite who his mother is. He likes trains."

She stood up and, with her eyes locked on his, she came at him, unafraid and strong. The top of her head barely reached his chin. With her big brown eyes turned up to meet his, she didn't say a word when she wrapped her arms around his waist and buried her head against his chest.

Platitudes would have sounded hollow. Things were a mess in both their lives right now. She was being pursued by a ghost from her past and he was being plagued by a stupid mistake he had made in his. The whole thing was a disaster in the making, and yet, holding her against him like this, in the dingy little interrogation room, for the first time he felt like everything would be all right. Someday, losing Max and the life he thought he was going to have might stop hurting. And Sydney was the one who was helping him see that.

But first he had to make sure nothing happened to her.

Tara had to be dealt with and sent packing. The two local murders were still unsolved, but Wade had a sickening feeling they were somehow related to the things that were happening around Sydney. If Ronald was already in Elton, as he suspected, then there would be more trouble to come.

"You should get to work," he said in a rougher voice than he would have liked. Immediately her arms dropped. But there wasn't time for apologies. There were still countless leads he had to follow if he was going to find Ronald in time. Plenty of people he had to question to see if they've seen anyone new in town. He was lost in his own thoughts until he heard Sydney clear her throat.

"Yeah," she said in a soft voice. "I should go." There was hurt in her eyes as she headed for the door.

He could have told her everything would be all right, but it would have just been words. Until he figured out what the hell was going on in Elton, he couldn't promise her anything, and she knew it.

She glanced back, wanting to say something, but with a shake of her head she thought better of it and disappeared out the door.

Now it was time to find the bastard.

CHAPTER 16

T UNA ON RYE, UP!" Pete called from the window ringing the bell like a mad man.

Hailey elbowed her in the side. "You gonna get that before his head explodes?"

"What? Oh jeez. Sorry, Pete." Sydney rushed to the window and loaded the plate onto a tray. The last few days since she had told Wade the truth about her past finally started to catch up with her. She must have looked as scattered as she felt.

Pete's anger was quickly replaced by concern. "You okay, kiddo?"

"I'm great." Sydney flashed him a fake smile, hoping he'd buy it. Of course, he knew her well enough not to be fooled.

"Cara, get out here and figure out what's wrong with our girl. She looks like someone ran over her puppy." Sydney rolled her eyes and went to deliver her order to Luke who was in one of the booths waiting.

"Tuna on rye," she said as she laid the plate onto the table. They hadn't really talked much since the other day when he tried to warn her away from Wade. She still didn't know how she felt about him, knowing his view of Wade was tainted by the feelings he had for Tara. It was all still jumbled in her head.

"Thanks. How are you doing? You've been pretty quiet around here the last few days." So he'd noticed her mood, too. Great. She already had Cara waiting behind the counter to interrogate her, and now Luke wanted to play psychologist on her too. "You and Wade have a fight?"

Had he simply asked what was bothering her, he might have gotten away unscathed, but bringing up Wade made her snap. "I've got a lot of things on my mind, that's all. Faith was sick and a woman was murdered and dumped behind the diner. Not much for me to be jumping up and down about lately." The words came out harshly and she felt a twinge of guilt when he recoiled, but she was tired of putting on a happy face. Some days sucked, and today was one of them. "Sorry, that was obnoxious of me. I'm just dealing with a lot of stuff."

"Yeah, okay." There was an awkward pause, then he said, "You know Wade isn't the only man in town who's interested in you."

There it was, the real reason he hated the idea of her with Wade. He had feelings for her. Not that he'd ever done anything to let her know or hinted that he wanted to be anything more than friends. But it wouldn't have mattered. Her heart was already spoken for. Even if she had to leave it behind someday.

"Unfortunately, Wade is the only man I'm interested in. I'm sorry, Luke." He didn't try to hide his hurt. He simply turned his attention to his sandwich and dug in. But before she walked away, she had to try and reach out to him one more time.

"Friends?" She held out her hand and waited.

With a nod, he took what was offered. "Sure."

It should have made her feel better to have cleared the air with Luke, but it didn't. She had hurt him, just like she'd hurt Wade when she was eventually arrested for all her transgressions. In her wake, she would leave a lot of pain for some really good people to deal with.

Cara had been watching the whole situation with Luke, and as soon as Sydney reached the counter, she wasted no time in intervening. "Hailey, go take care of Sydney's tables. I need to talk to her for a while. And for the love of God, don't touch any of the appliances unless I tell you to." Hailey's grousing died down as she crossed the dining room to refill drinks.

They sat side by side on two of the stools. Cara rested an elbow on the counter giving Sydney her full attention. "Talk to me."

Sydney buried her face in her hands unsure where to start. Her head and her heart were a mess, but she had to keep so much from Cara it was killing her. How could she ever explain what was going on inside of her when she didn't understand it herself?

"How about if I start and tell you what I think? Then you can jump in if I say something wrong, okay?" Sydney nodded her still covered head, not brave enough to look Cara in the face.

"I know Agnes told you about Wade and Tara." That got Sydney's attention, her head popping out of her hands instantly. "Relax, she's been worried about you too and told me, that's all. She suggested I lock you and Wade in the freezer until you two work all this out. I opted to talk about it." Her warm smile nearly sent Sydney into tears, but over the last few days she realized the tears do nothing but make her face wet. If she was going to start weeping over all the woes in her life, she'd never stop. There'd always be something. From now on, she was saving her tears.

"Now, here's where I'm guessing, but Wade looks like he ate some bad cannoli. Snapping at folks and all that. Did you two talk?"

Sydney's head bobbed up and down. "Yeah."

"Did you share…everything…with him? Does he know whatever it is you need to keep quiet?"

"Yep." Sydney tapped her nails in a nervous rhythm on the counter. "The whole ugly truth."

"Oh, sweets. How did it go?"

"It was okay, I think." She gave a sarcastic laugh. "I'm not in jail, so that's a good sign." Cara made the sign of the cross and mumbled something to the sky. "It's been a couple days since I told him, but the next morning, we talked at the station and it was awkward. He had stayed up all night checking out my story. Then he told me everything about Tara, I think mainly to warn me she might give me a hard time."

"That little witch." Cara pointed her finger at the kitchen. "If she shows up, you call us and I'll send Pete over to get rid of her."

"I can handle Tara, she doesn't scare me. I've dealt with far worse than a jealous ex-wife."

"So is that why you're feeling so down? Tara?"

Sydney snorted. "No, I haven't given her a second thought, to tell you the truth."

"Then what?"

Was she really considering telling her? To have the thoughts in her head and in her heart was one thing, but to voice them out loud made them that much more real—Sydney didn't know if she was ready for that. Once they were out, there was no taking them back. And what were the odds things would work out the way she wanted?

"Tell me, bambina." The motherly tone in Cara's voice crumbled her defenses. She needed someone to confide in, and with Melissa gone, Cara was her closest and dearest friend.

"I-I think," Sydney took a deep breath and let the words fly. "I have feelings for Wade. Big, giant, scary feelings." Her head immediately fell into her hands to hide from Cara's reaction, but it wasn't exactly what she was expecting.

"Well, duh."

Sydney looked up, her brows furrowed. "Excuse me?"

"Oh, honey, anyone who looks at the two of you would know there was something brewing. A crush, lust, or love, whatever it was it was getting bigger and bigger each time he strolled through that door and ordered some pie as an excuse to see you. I'm happy for you."

"Thanks?" Sydney said, not intending it to be a question but her voice squeaked, not sure Cara understood the situation. "There's just one problem."

"What's that?"

"I'm not sure he feels the same way."

A huge barking laugh came out of Cara. There was nothing about what she said that should have been remotely entertaining, but Cara seemed to think she was the funniest person alive at the moment from the way she was carrying on. "Oh, sweets, I don't want to embarrass you, but that man undresses you with his eyes every chance he gets. He wants to get you into bed, bad. Even an old bat like me can see it. Heck even Pete said so. How can you miss it?"

"I don't think you understand."

Cara waved her hand through the air dismissing the question. "Have you kissed him?"

"Um, yes."

"And how was it? A peck on the cheek like you'd give your cousin, or a hot steamy kiss that made you think of silk sheets and sweaty bodies?"

"Cara!"

"I remember how it was when I was falling in love with Pete."

"That's not what's going on here."

Cara gave her a knowing look. "Isn't it?"

Oh, crap. Sydney shook her head from side to side as if that would somehow keep Cara's words from ringing true. She did have feelings for him, and what made them big and scary was that they were love. She was hopelessly in love with Wade, and she didn't know if he even wanted to talk to her anymore.

Great.

"He might have been interested before I told him about my past, but now, I don't think he wants anything to do with me. I haven't seen him at all since that morning at the station when I hunted him down. Not a phone call, not a piece of pie, nothing."

"He's got a lot on his plate with the murder. That weighs on him, heavily."

"I know, and I'm not trying to be whiney or anything. I just can't help but wonder if he thinks I'm too much trouble."

Cara considered that for a moment then a wicked smile curled her lips. "So let's find out!"

"You're scaring me."

"Hailey," Cara called over her shoulder with a grin, "you still drive around with that enormous makeup case in your car?"

"Of course," she said with a shrug. Like everyone had a portable salon with them, everywhere they went.

"Bring it in, girl. We've got work to do."

"Oh, no you don't." Sydney threw up her hands and stepped away from the counter and Cara. She was almost at the kitchen door when Hailey came flying through it, pinning her in place.

"Who we making over?"

"Sydney."

Hailey scrambled out the door with a smile on her face.

"No, no, no." Sydney moved away from Cara, searching for a way out of her grasp. "We did this once. I'm not doing it again."

"You want to know how he feels about you, right? Then let's give him something to look at and see if he bites."

At that moment, Hailey returned with a massive box in her hand and a pearl of wisdom of her own. "Kinda like you do with a nice big trout. Put a pretty lure out there to get his attention. That's what my dad always taught me," she said as she unstacked the oversized makeup case.

"You don't even know if he's coming into the diner tonight." It was her last ditch effort to get them to stop, but when Cara's hands landed on her shoulders and she was shoved onto a stool, she knew she was toast.

"Then there's no harm in playing." Cara gave some directions to Hailey whose painted lips curled up into a grin, then she disappeared to take care of the few remaining tables.

"You don't have to do this," Sydney whispered to Hailey, hoping to get the girl on her side.

"Sure I do," she said with two hair pins clenched between her teeth. "I've got ten bucks on you and Wade hooking up before next Friday."

"You what?!"

The pins flew out of Hailey's mouth as Sydney spun around and startled her with a glare. "Calm down. It's just a bet I made with his deputy, Sam. We've been talking lately," she said with a shy smile.

"He thinks Wade will be able to hold out longer because he's so disciplined, or something stupid like that." Hailey rolled her eyes and picked up the tiny hairpins that had spilled onto the floor. "Sam's cute, don't you think?"

From there, Hailey began chattering on and on about how wonderful Sam was and all the reasons she wanted to date him. As long as Sydney nodded and smiled at all the right places, Hailey was happy.

It felt like an hour had passed but it was probably only fifteen minutes at most. Many diners gave her the thumbs up or wished her luck, so yeah, it was nearly public knowledge that she was being primped and pressed for Wade's benefit. And still, she didn't know if it was even worth it. He still might not even show up, and then all the work Hailey did would be a waste.

"One last thing to do. Oops," Hailey said as she fanned Sydney's eye. "Too much adhesive."

"I'll get it." Sydney stood up and rushed to the back.

On her way to the bathroom, Sydney tried to wipe the blob of glue from the false eyelashes. She needed a mirror to see the damage. When she flipped on the light and looked in the mirror, she was stunned.

Her hair was down, not up in a knot or pony tail. It looked longer than she remembered, definitely less frizzy, with big curls at the ends that framed her face. Her makeup was spectacular. Hailey knew what she was doing. It wasn't too much, and it wasn't too little. The eyelashes made her eyes pop against the dark shadow she used on the lids. Her face glowed. It looked like she had spent the afternoon in the sun with the hint of pink Hailey brushed onto her cheeks. The nearly-nude color of her lips was a nice contrast to the color around her eyes.

"Holy smokes," Sydney whispered, tilting her face at different angles to better appreciate all of Hailey's work.

A loud whistle scared her half to death. Cara burst through the door and crammed herself into the tiny bathroom to get a better look. "Wow!" She clapped her hands together in excitement. "You look amazing, bambina. He's gonna drool when he sees you."

Sydney shooed Cara out the door and followed behind her. She grabbed a clean apron and wrapped it around her waist, ready to get back to work now that the dress up session was over. "*If* he shows up, Cara. You have no idea if he's even going to come in."

A knowing grin on her face Cara asked, "Are you working?"

"Obviously," Sydney said as she finished tying her apron.

"Then he'll be in," she said in a sing-song voice. "That's the only reason I'm not complaining that you have your hair down while you're serving food. The hell with the health department. It'd be a shame for all that work to go to waste." Cara dodged the door to the dining room and made a bee line for Pete before Sydney could get her hands around her boss's neck.

"Coward," Sydney called into the kitchen after Cara. Feeling happier than she had all day, Sydney hit the door with her shoulder so she could get back to work. It was only a few seconds before her breath left in a rush when she noticed Wade's truck pulling into the parking lot.

"Oh, hell."

"Game on!" Hailey declared with a fist pump and a broad smile.

"Shut up, Hailey," Sydney hissed, grabbing a towel and wiping the nearest surface she could find to look busy. Cara and Pete popped out of the kitchen window to witness his entrance. "You guys," Sydney whined desperate to not make a spectacle of herself just *one time* when Wade walked into the diner. Her waving arms did nothing to make the pair go away. In fact, they leaned out farther to see where he parked.

Nerves were a normal part of her day where Wade was concerned, as well as the verbal diarrhea, but now, she was especially self-conscious with the ridiculous makeup on. She could only hope and pray he didn't notice. But who was she kidding, the guy noticed everything. It was part of his job description.

She was screwed.

When she saw his tall profile walk past the front window, flanked by someone who was also in uniform, she did the only mature thing she could think of, she dove behind the counter and prayed he'd go sit in Hailey's section.

"Wade, Sam. What a surprise!" Hailey gushed in an overly perky voice.

"Um, you invited us over for a cup of coffee," Sam said with a nervous hitch to his voice.

Sydney resisted the urge to drag Hailey to the ground and beat her. Instead, she pinched the back of her knee, knowing full well she'd been set up. Hailey probably called Sam while she was in the back and asked him to come in and bring Wade with him, sneaky little traitor that she was.

"It's not funny," she mouthed to the couple who seemed to think the situation was downright hysterical based on their reactions.

"That's right, I forgot." Hailey reached under the counter for a clean mug. Sydney had two in her hands waiting for her. There was no escaping this, because Hailey was seating them at the front counter, smack in the middle of Sydney's section.

"I'll make a fresh pot for you both," Hailey said with a smirk as she took a step toward the new coffeemaker, which she was forbidden from touching. On reflex, Sydney sprang to her feet and jumped between her and the machine.

"I'll do it."

"Hi, Sydney," Sam said stunned to see her pop out from underneath the counter. "Didn't know you were down there."

"Yeah, I was getting this knife that was stuck under the thingy for Pete." She turned to the window and threw the dirty utensil at him. "Here you go Pete, now go cook something." It was the most pathetic excuse she could come up with since her brain had stopped functioning. Her face was so hot it felt like it might melt off. She dumped fresh coffee grounds in and braved a peek at Wade from beneath the veil of her hair. She found him staring at her with a shocked expression.

"Syd?"

"Hi, guys." She made her way to that part of the counter, bumping Hailey out of the way with her hip. The entire time Wade's eyes were fixed on her, the heated look in them unmistakable.

Well, I'll be damned.

"Can I get you something?" She looked first at Sam, enjoying the way Wade kept watching at her. Normally he wasn't as blatant with his attentions, but considering how much she'd missed him over the last few days, she relished it.

"Yeah, I'll take a bacon cheeseburger."

"Fries okay with that?"

"Yeah, thanks." Sam waved Hailey over and the two began a hushed conversation that Sydney couldn't pick up any part of, so she turned her attention to Wade.

"What can I get you, Sheriff?" she asked Wade in a seductive voice she barely recognized. Wade was as surprised as she was because he fumbled with his menu, nearly dropping it on the ground. It brought a smile to her face to see the normally composed Wade Jenkins flustered.

"I told you so." She heard Cara laugh behind her before dragging Pete back into the kitchen.

"I-I'll have the, um…"

"The turkey club, extra mayo, hold the tomato, right?" She leaned toward him, pointing to it on the menu just as an excuse to get closer to him. "It's right here." She could smell the rich cologne he wore and it sent a tingle of awareness through her body.

If she had her way, she would have crawled into his lap and buried her face in his neck right now. But that would have to wait.

"I know what I want," he said slowly, his composure regained. Wade's eyes never left hers except to dip down to her lips. Everything feminine in her responded, and immediately, thoughts of the two of them wrapped in an erotic kiss filled her mind.

Hailey snickered from behind Sydney. "Now, now, let's keep it PG, you two. There *are* kids in this diner. Don't make me throw a bucket of water on you."

"Go away, Hailey," Wade said with a deep rumble of sound from his chest.

With a laugh, she grabbed Sam by the hand and led him to a booth. "You bet, Wade."

Sydney could have kissed her.

"What did you do to your hair?" Wade asked as he captured a curl and rubbed it between his fingers slowly.

"It was slow around here today. Hailey got bored," she said with a shrug. "Do you like it?" With a flick of her head a pile of platinum waves came pouring over her shoulder nearly hitting him in the face. Flirting was something that was foreign to her, but from the look on his face she was doing just fine.

Maybe they were going to be okay after all.

"I think you know I like it." The muscles in his neck tensed as he struggled to control himself. Knowing the effect she had on him made Sydney feel powerful.

She leaned forward and whispered in his ear, "Good." She allowed her lips to lightly brush against the shell of his ear.

"Careful, Sydney," he said darkly, "or I'm coming over this counter, and taking you out that back door straight to my place."

"Oh my," Sydney whispered, stunned by his brazen declaration.

"Oh my, indeed." He took a sip of the coffee she handed him to cool the flames that had erupted between them. "You look beautiful."

The sincerity in his voice made her heart flutter. "Thanks. We were just goofing around."

"I've missed you." They were the words Sydney had been holding out hope to hear and she couldn't stop the wide smile that spread across her face.

"I missed you, too," she said shyly. She went over to the window and put his order in, ignoring the big grin on Pete's face and the way Cara was fanning herself beside him.

"You two are terrible," Sydney whispered with a laugh.

Cara stuck her head out the window and waved to Wade. "That's why you love us, Syd."

Funny thing was, she was right. From the crazy couple in the kitchen to the loony waitress trying to strong arm a deputy into dating her to the dear friend on a European adventure to the primal male who threatened to drag her to bed if she wasn't careful, she loved all of them, and more than anything, she wanted to stay in Elton and make a life for herself and Faith.

Wade's phone rang, and she could tell by the tone of his voice it was work. She took care of her other tables while he took the call, not wanting to intrude. When she came back to the counter and handed him his food, he was tucking his phone back into his pocket.

"Any chance I can get that sandwich to go?"

She did her best not to show her disappointment as she took his barely touched plate off the counter. "Sure, let me go box it up." She was digging in the closet for a Styrofoam box when she felt someone standing behind her. Her senses on high alert, she took a deep breath and spun around ready to strike. Fortunately she stopped herself when she saw it was Wade.

"You scared me to death."

"Sorry," he said coming closer, trapping her against the storage rack. It was amazing how he always seemed to fill the space around her. "What are you doing after work?"

"I-I was going to head home and see Faith. She's been with Agnes all day."

"Any chance she could stay a little longer? I want to take you out, for a drink, maybe? Things have been crazy lately, and I need one night of normal."

"Wade Jenkins, are you asking me out on a date?"

He flashed his teeth at her. "I think I am."

"It's the hair, isn't it? Hailey will never let me live it down."

"It's all you, Sydney. The hair and the makeup are just the icing on the cake."

She bit her lip, suddenly feeling nervous and shy. "I get off at seven. Will you be done by then?"

"I'll pick you up here at seven. If Agnes can't watch Faith, call me. We can hang out at your place instead." He brushed his fingers across her cheek. "I just want to be with you tonight."

"I'd like that."

He gave her no warning, but in the blink of an eye he was on her, his tongue sweeping past her lips and brushing against hers. He was taking complete control, and all Sydney could do was hold onto his shoulders for dear life and enjoy the moment. It was what she'd wanted, what she'd been thinking about the last few days. There was nothing like being kissed by Wade. Fire raced through her veins with each slide of his tongue. The feel of his rock hard body pressed against hers was heaven. His hand knotted in her hair, pulling back, giving him better access to her pliant body. When she thought she might pass out from lack of oxygen, she finally broke the kiss, both their chests heaving from the passion that blossomed between them.

"Later, Sydney."

"Oh my," Sydney said again with a smile.

"Definitely," he said with a quick peck on the lips. He grabbed the Styrofoam box with a wink and disappeared out the door, leaving her stunned in a supply closet. Sydney took a second to try and fix her tousled hair and twisted shirt before she walked back into the kitchen where, of course, Cara and Pete were waiting.

"Your lipstick looks a little smudged there, Sydney," Cara pointed out as Sydney walked past.

"Wade certainly was in a good mood when he left," Pete yelled after her, but Sydney just kept walking back to the dining room.

With a big goofy smile on her face.

CHAPTER 17

YOU CAN'T BE SERIOUS." Hailey stood behind Sydney glaring at her reflection in the mirror. Wade was going to be at Pete's in fifteen minutes to pick her up and she was checking her hair to make sure there wasn't a French fry, crusted over mustard, or some other weird condiment in it for their date.

"What's wrong now?"

"You're not wearing that!" Hailey said, tugging at the bright yellow Pete's T-shirt. "He's taking you out. You want him to look at you and think 'Damn, she's hot,' not 'I wonder what the phone number for Pete's Place is?'"

Sydney put her hands up in frustration. "I don't have time to run home, Hailey. This will just have to do. He liked it enough when he was in here earlier." That was an understatement. The way he'd kissed her and the obvious arousal she felt pressed against her in that supply closet, he thought she was hot, ugly T-shirt and all.

"I don't get old people," Hailey said, dropping a black shirt into Sydney's hands.

"You're crazy! I'm only five years older than you."

"Then why are you dressing like my mom when you have a date with the hottest guy in town? Next to Sam, of course." Her lips turned up in a wry grin because she knew she had her.

There was no reasoning with Hailey, and she was right, a Pete's T-shirt wasn't sexy. "Get out of here so I can put this on. Will it even fit me?"

"I said you're old, not fat. Yes, it will fit. And you won't smell like a burger in it. Trust me, he'll love that top." She waggled her eyebrows at Sydney's reflection. "It shows plenty of cleavage."

As much as she hated to admit it, the shirt did look great. It was a black wrap that clung to her like a second skin. The plunging neckline did give a tantalizing view of her breasts just like Hailey said it would. It was amazing how much a simple thing like changing her shirt could boost her confidence and settle her nerves. Gone was the anxious flutter in her stomach, and in its place was the slow burn of desire and excitement for what was to come. As she gave herself a final once over, her phone rang.

"Mommy!" Faith's excited voice always made her smile.

"Hi, baby. How are you?"

"I'm good. Mrs. Whittman and I are going to have a sleepover!"

"A sleepover? No honey, you're just staying a little longer than usual. I'm going out for a little bit after work, but I'll be home later."

She could hear Faith's curls brushing against the receiver as she shook her head. "Nope, Mrs. Whittman said sleepover. She said Wade is taking you on something called a hot date. It sounds like fun! Here, you talk to her."

A deeper, more mature voice came over the phone. "Sydney."

"Agnes, I won't be out late."

"That's not what I heard from Cara."

"When did you talk to Cara?"

"Doesn't matter. She filled me in on what went down this afternoon. Said the temperature shot up about a hundred degrees when a certain sheriff walked into the diner. Lots of fireworks, from what I understand." In the background Sydney could hear Faith complaining that she missed the fireworks.

If only she knew.

Sydney walked through the kitchen and gave Cara the stink-eye for her gossiping ways. She just smiled and blew Sydney a kiss, then went back to loading a rack of glasses.

"Listen, Agnes, I appreciate you offering to keep Faith, but I *will* be home tonight."

"Mhmm," the woman sighed into the phone not trying to hide her disbelief. "Tell me this, how long has it been since you went on a date? And don't lie, I asked Faith."

"Agnes!"

"Answer the question, Sydney."

There was no point in lying. She'd had no life since the day she told her loser boyfriend she was pregnant. That had been over six years. "A ridiculously long time. Years. Honestly, a lifetime ago."

"And the last guy you dated, was he as good looking as Wade?"

She couldn't contain the snort that escaped when she imagined the scrawny Bobby beside the chiseled muscle of Wade's body. "No."

"Yeah, then like I said, Faith and I are having a sleepover. Just in case."

"You're crazy."

"Not the first time I've heard that, and I know it won't be the last. Listen, I'll keep her safe, no worries about that. The alarms are on, the cameras are working, and my .45 is loaded. Diablo will be with us all night. We're tucked in snug as a bug in a rug here."

There was a rustling on her end of the phone, then Faith came back on. "Have fun with Sheriff Wade. I like him. He's really nice."

"He is nice, isn't he?" Sydney leaned back against the counter, smiling. It warmed her heart that Wade had made an impression on Faith too.

"And he tells really good bedtime stories." Wade was a good man, the real deal. She only hoped he could help her out of the trouble she was in so they could stay in Elton and make a life for themselves.

With him.

"I have to go, baby, he'll be here any minute."

"Have fun, Mommy!"

The phone passed to Mrs. Whittman, and before the line went dead, she spouted one parting bit of Agnes wisdom. "And remember, Syd, no glove, no love."

Sydney just blushed and stared at her phone when the line went dead, lost somewhere between wanting to laugh and die of embarrassment.

"Have a nice chat with Agnes?" Cara asked with a cackle as she poked her head out from behind the window.

"You two are a dangerous combination." Sydney finally laughed as she folded her apron and tucked it under the counter.

Cara gave her a playful pat on the cheek. "And don't you forget it." The door of the diner opened, turning both their heads. "Well, well, well," Cara said with a cluck of her tongue. "Someone else cleans up nicely, now, doesn't he?"

Wade walked through the door with the same air of confidence he always did. Nothing intimidated him, and that was something Sydney found extremely attractive. If that wasn't enough, he looked like a dream. In place of his uniform he wore a pair of well-worn jeans that were tight in all the right places. The tight black T-shirt hugged his chest and showed every delicious ripple of muscle underneath. A black leather jacket and a pair of black boots completed the look. She looked cute, but he looked downright edible. And dangerous.

"You ready?" Sydney didn't trust her voice to come out as more than a squeak with him looking so good, so she opted for a quick nod of her head. " 'Night Cara."

"Bye, Wade!" She gave Sydney a shove, sending her stumbling out from behind the counter. "Take good care of Sydney. You two kids have fun."

"Don't do anything I wouldn't do," Hailey called from across the restaurant. Pete's head popped out from the window.

"Just behave, and treat her right."

Wade took all the teasing in stride, and offered her his hand. She loved the calloused feel of his fingers as they twisted with hers. The heat and the strength surrounded her hand and traveled up her arm. "Let's go."

Grabbing her purse, Sydney followed him out the door and cast one last look over her shoulder to Cara and Hailey who were both grinning from ear to ear. Sydney motioned to Wade's back with her free hand. "Oh my God," she mouth to them, sending them into a laughing fit as the door closed behind her.

"What a beautiful night," Sydney whispered as Wade led her to his truck. It was cool, but not frigid yet. Her long sleeve shirt was okay for now, but later, she'd be wishing she grabbed a coat.

He stopped her at the side of his truck. "If you'd rather, we can go back to your place and hang out with Faith. I know you haven't seen her much today." It was the way he said it that melted her heart. She had no doubt he would drive her home and spend the evening with a rambunctious five-year-old, all for her. He'd listen to her ramble on and on about her birthday party that was coming up in a few days, and smile through every ruffled detail she shared. He wouldn't mind, wouldn't do it grudgingly, he'd do it, for her. And knowing that made her want this night out with him all the more.

She placed her hand on his cheek and smiled. "I squeezed myself into this top of Hailey's and let her play beauty salon with my head. You're taking me out for a drink. Agnes is probably teaching Faith Morse code or something useful like that. She's fine." She pressed a gentle kiss to his lips because she couldn't stop herself. "But thank you for offering."

MURRAY'S WAS ON THE edge of town, so the drive out there gave them plenty of time to talk. It was comfortable and they were never at a loss for things to discuss. From Faith, to the diner, to the crazy things that had happened in his day, nothing was off limits. He was open and honest, voicing his frustrations with work and the federal agents who had overrun the town. The conversation was easy, like they had known each other for years.

In addition to the talking, there was plenty of touching. Wade held her hand as he drove, his thumb feathering back and forth, leaving a trail of fire in its path. The tingle that started in her fingers traveled the length of her arm and soon her entire body was hyper-aware of Wade and the way he was touching her. As innocent as the contact was, there was a definite air of seduction about it. He knew exactly what he was doing to her body. She couldn't stop her mind from wandering to him touching her other places, and she thanked God it was dark in the cab of the truck or he would have caught her blushing like a schoolgirl.

At Murray's, he turned off the truck and leaned across the cab. "You any good at darts?"

"We'll find out," she said with a cheeky grin as she jumped out of the truck and met him on the sidewalk. Hand in hand, they walked into the bar for the entire town to see.

"Sydney!" a number of people shouted her name, definitely surprised to see her there. Apparently, after Pete's closed up for the night, many of her regulars headed over to Murray's for a drink and some pool. "What are you doing with the likes of Wade?" one of them yelled in good natured fun.

"I bet she lost a bet," Mr. Forte yelled from the bar as he held up his beer with a smile. Sydney pulled Wade with her to the bar and gave the aging man a kiss on the cheek.

"More like I won." She winked at Wade then leaned in and said conspiratorially to Mr. Forte, "You have any hints about how to win at darts?"

The man let out a big belly laugh. "Yeah, don't play Wade!"

SYDNEY HELD HER OWN during their game. Mainly because she insisted Wade play left handed. Unfortunately for her, enough people had used that strategy with him in the hopes of getting a win that he was getting pretty good at it, and she still lost.

"Best eleven out of thirteen?" she asked, half joking but her competitive streak had come out, and she wanted to win at least once before they left.

"Sure." He leaned down and kissed her gently. "You set it up and I'll go get you another beer."

"I think you're trying to keep me from winning."

He caged her in his massive arms and dipped his head to her ear where he whispered, "Maybe I'm getting you drunk so you can win…later."

She sighed as his hot breath fanned over her neck, then took advantage of his proximity to rub against him and send him a little message of her own. "I'm up for anything you might want to play, later." His eyes flared and when it looked like he was going to pick her up and carry her out of the place, he stepped away and gave her a slow, sexy smile.

"I'll go get those beers now. I'm suddenly very thirsty."

Sparks were flying between them and Sydney didn't know how much longer she could keep her hands to herself. She was pulling the last dart from the board when someone crashed into her shoulder and she felt something wet splash down the front of her shirt.

"Oh gosh, I'm sorry," a cute brunette in a black hat said as she set her drink down on a nearby table. She shook the excess liquid that had spilled on her hand onto the floor. "Let me get you a towel."

"It's fine," Sydney said, tugging the material from her body. "I'll go wash up in the sink." She looked around the room. "Do you know where the bathroom is?"

A slow smile spread on the woman's face. "First time here?" Sydney gave a quick nod trying to place the woman who was suddenly looking familiar. "It's down that hall, around the corner, third door on the left."

"Thanks."

"I'll tell tall, dark, and gorgeous where you went, no worries." There was something about the woman's smile that made Sydney uncomfortable.

Sydney hurried down the long hall, concerned about getting the sticky mess off the front of her shirt. Since it was Hailey's, she didn't want to return it to her a mess.

At the end of the hallway, the music became softer. She was so far from the main bar area that things quieted down. She made the turn and started counting doors. Her hand was about to come down on the knob when the lights flickered, the hall going temporarily dark. Sydney stifled a scream and flattened herself against the wall, reaching blindly for the knob. When she felt the cool metal bulb against her hand, she yanked it open and light flooded the hall. Her heart was pounding by the time she closed the door behind herself.

Quickly she rubbed a paper towel over the front of her shirt, dabbing as much of the sticky drink out of the fabric as she could. She tried not to think about having to navigate down that dark hall to get back to the main bar, but at this point, she was so spooked she would have run across fire to get back to Wade. She wiped a few more towels over the damp spot to dry it as much as possible before she left the dingy bathroom.

Taking a deep breath, she wrenched open the door and was relieved to see the lights had turned back on. She hurried down the corridor, turned right and immediately she could hear the music and the laughter from the bar. Her anxiety started to fade. A few more steps and she'd be back with him. As soon as she came through the archway, her eyes went to the dartboard in search of Wade. When he wasn't there, she scanned the bar until she found him by the front door with a woman. The woman who had dumped her drink on Sydney. From the look on Wade's face, he wasn't happy to see her and the pieces fell into place.

Tara.

The previous times Sydney had seen her, she had either been busy sucking on Wade's face, or on a small video monitor or across the parking lot, so Sydney hadn't been able to pick up her features clearly. However, the dark hair and the build were the same. The look on Wade's face right now was one of restrained rage. There was only one person who made him that uncomfortable, and Sydney was not about to let her ruin their night. She locked eyes with Wade and headed straight into their conversation.

"You listen to me," Sydney heard Tara hiss when she got within earshot. Wade gave nothing away to Tara even though he had seen Sydney coming the whole time. He continued to glare at her with nothing but contempt. Sydney put on her best fake smile and bumped Tara as she passed her to get to Wade. She wrapped her arm around his waist and could have kissed him when she felt the weight of his arm settle around her shoulder and pull her close.

"Thanks for keeping him company, honey. Bless your heart, but you're helpful. I'm sure there's got to be somebody in this place who might be happy to see you. Right, Tara?"

Tara looked at her incredulously, unable to believe Sydney dared to dismiss her. "You little witch." She took a swipe at her, but Sydney just stepped back and out of reach, using Tara's momentum against her, Sydney pinned her arm behind her back. All those months of self-defense finally paid off.

"Now here's what's gonna happen. You're going to walk away and leave us to enjoy our evening. It's been a pretty crappy week for both of us. And if this shirt is ruined, you'll be getting a bill for the dry cleaning. Goodnight, Tara." With a tiny shove she sent the woman stumbling toward the crowd at the bar. Only then did Wade say something.

"Ready to get out of here?"

Without a second glance at Tara she laced her fingers with his and they bid goodnight to their friends at Murray's, many of whom had stood up to keep Tara from following them. Her protests muffled behind the closed door as they stepped outside.

"Sorry about that," Wade said without looking at her. Sydney stopped in her tracks and turned him to face her. He was shaken, either with anger or distress, but it didn't matter. She wasn't going to let that woman ruin another second of Wade's life. So she did the only thing she could think of to snap him out of his funk.

She kissed him.

It wasn't a friendly kiss or one of encouragement; it was a full frontal assault on his senses, one that hopefully would erase the bad memories and fill his mind with thoughts of her. The dark shadows of the parking lot made her feel brave and protected from prying eyes. At first he seemed stunned, unsure of her intentions. When her hand trailed down the front of his jeans and brushed against his growing erection, there could be no question and he let go, picking her up off her feet and returning the kiss with all the fervor she had shown, and then some.

"Sydney," he growled, his hands fisted into the back of her shirt.

"Your place. Now." He laughed when she wrapped her legs around his waist and whispered, "Hurry," into his ear.

Without a missing a beat, he carried her to the truck, buckled her into her seat, then jumped in the truck and they peeled out of the parking lot, gravel kicking up from their speedy exit. Wade kept a death grip on the steering wheel as he weaved through town, headed for his house. Sydney's heart was pounding with excitement. No matter what, she knew she would remember this night for the rest of her life. A man like Wade Jenkins didn't come around every day, and if for some reason she did have to run, or if she did eventually get taken into custody, the memory of this night was going to get her through the rough times.

It had to.

He pulled into the driveway, the car jerking to a stop as his foot slammed down on the brake. The fact that he wasn't hiding his need excited her even more. She lunged across the cab and kissed him again, her hands wandering over his chest and under his shirt. His skin trembled as her nails lightly raked over his abdomen.

"I need to get you out of this truck or I'm going to take you right here and now." He threw open his door and dragged her out after him. The urgency in his movements amplified everything Sydney was feeling. By the time they hit the front porch, she was absolutely desperate for him.

The lights never made it on once they made it through the doorway. She heard the lock click behind her and then she was pinned against the wall, the weight of Wade's body nearly stealing the breath from her lungs in the darkness. His hands were everywhere, touching, petting, squeezing her, fanning the fire that was already raging inside her even more.

"You're so beautiful, Sydney." His voice was tight as he tried to keep himself in control. "I've dreamed of touching you like this so many nights."

A groan escaped her lips as his mouth began devouring her neck. Small nips turned into warm swirls of his tongue and he explored every inch of her neck and shoulders. He followed the neckline of her shirt and began kissing the swells of her breasts. Sydney's hands knotted in his hair, urging him on. His hand slipped under the waistband of her jeans and she froze. It had been a lifetime since a man touched her like this, and never a man like Wade.

What if she wasn't experienced enough for Wade? Doubts began to flood her mind.

"If you want me to stop, all you have to do is say the word, Sydney. Whatever you want." She could hear the strain in his voice and his panting breath, but he hadn't moved an inch, waiting for her answer.

"Just like riding a bike," she mumbled to herself then widened her stance and plunged his hand deeper into her panties. He groaned when his fingers found her wetness between her legs.

"Oh, baby." He slumped against her, as if his knees had gone weak. "You're so hot and soft. I bet you taste sweet too. Will you let me taste you, Sydney?"

"Less talking, more kissing." Sydney pushed the jacket off his shoulders then pulled his T-shirt up and over his head. When her hands landed on his chest she felt the lightest dusting of hair and muscle. She wanted to run her tongue over every ridge and valley on him. "Where's your bedroom?"

He led her through the dark, up a staircase at the back of the house. The second floor was one huge room with a sitting area and desk to one side, and a king sized bed on the other. Moonlight poured in through the huge picture window across from the bed. From it, you could probably look out over the farms and see the tiny row of lights that beckoned downtown. This time of year the view had to be spectacular with all the fall colors painting the scenery, but she didn't pause to look when the bed and the man standing beside it were calling to her.

Wade sat on the edge of the mattress and watched her approach. Sydney liked the feel of his eyes on her, the seductive side in her springing to life. She slowly kicked off her shoes as she walked, letting them land in a pile off to the side. Her hands went to the bottom of her shirt and paused. Even though it was dark, she could feel him watching her every move in the moonlight and it empowered her to keep going. With a swift pull, her shirt came off and her jeans soon followed. Wade fisted his hands into the comforter to keep from grabbing her and ending the show. Knowing he was that close to losing control made Sydney smile.

"You're being so well behaved." She straddled his legs and perched herself on his lap. His hands immediately landed on her hips then began to explore her curves, brushing over her thighs and cupping her bottom gently. The tremor that went through him told her how much he was holding back.

And she wanted more than anything to see him let go.

"Touch me." The words came out somewhere between a purr and a plea and she didn't have to ask twice. His hands cupped her breasts, squeezing before he feathered kisses across them. He sucked her nipple through the thin material of her bra, and she could feel her arousal swell. Nothing in her life had ever felt so good.

He turned and pressed her into the mattress, his weight collapsing on her. His hot, hard flesh rubbed against hers and they both groaned in pleasure. His power was palpable with his every movement and she wanted to feel all he had to offer. Her hand dipped between them, but Wade grabbed it before she could reach her destination, pinning her wrist over her head.

"My turn to play." The way he said it sent a shiver down her spine. There was nothing playful about his tone, only a promise of heat and fire and pleasure like she had never imagined before.

His free hand slowly made its way up her thigh, his knuckles brushing lightly over her panties. Sydney writhed from side to side, desperate for more of his touch. "So impatient," he whispered against her breast. He flicked his finger under the clasp of her bra, her breasts spilling from the material, giving his mouth better access.

"Oh, God," Sydney said as his tongue flicked over her nipples, the moisture from his mouth making them peak and harden.

He sat her up and slipped the scrap of lace from her arms, tossing it onto the floor with the rest of her clothes. When he tugged her panties down her thighs, she was left completely naked in his arms.

"God, Sydney. You are such a miracle." His fingers slipped through the dampened curls between her legs, finding exactly where she was begging to be touched. A cry escaped her as a single finger pushed inside, filling her.

"You're so tight," he gasped, his erection grinding deliciously against her stomach. Her hips moved in rhythm with his fingers, the intense pleasure nearly overwhelming her.

Sydney reached for his jeans, unbuttoning them. Her heart pounded harder when he rolled off her and slid them down over his hips revealing every naked inch of him.

"Oh my," Sydney sighed.

"You say that a lot," he said with a smile as he returned to the bed.

"You're just an 'Oh my' kinda man, Wade Jenkins. You have to know that."

He poised himself above her, his hips settling between her thighs. When he looked into her eyes, they were the only two people on the planet. No demons from their pasts, no complications or baggage; just a man and a woman and the potential for pleasure beyond words. The time for teasing was over, they were starved for one another, and with each touch of his hands, Sydney found herself begging him for more.

Finally, with one forceful stroke, he slipped inside of her and they both cried out at the sensation. Nothing had ever felt so right. They were together in the most intimate way imaginable and, in that moment, Sydney thought anything was possible.

They made love well into the night, falling asleep only to be woken up by playful strokes of the other's hands. With the same intensity, they came together time after time, never tiring of one another, and never getting their fill. They shared their dreams and fears. They shared their hearts with one another in the darkness as the hours ticked by, time seeming to move faster when they were together. Finally Sydney collapsed with exhaustion, a well satisfied smile on her face.

Dawn was barely breaking when she felt Wade stir. She was already so attuned to his presence, that she knew the moment he left her side. A few minutes later he returned with breakfast in bed: two cups of coffee and two bowls of cereal.

"Sorry if I disturbed you, but I thought you'd like to be home before Faith woke up." He settled the tray over her legs, and sat down beside her.

Those were the little things about Wade that made her care for him even more. Most men would have snored away until noon, but he was up, and had even made her breakfast, all so she could get home to her daughter. He was one special man.

"What are you thinking in that beautiful head of yours?"

"That you're amazing." She devoured the cereal, not realizing how hungry she was. *That's what a night of wild sex will do to you,* she thought to herself with a smile. They finished their breakfast then Sydney padded around his bedroom wearing nothing more than his T-shirt that hung to her knees as she collected her clothes which were strewn about the room. Hailey's blouse that she had worn last night was all stuck together from Tara's nasty drink.

"I'm borrowing this," she said as she slipped her jeans on underneath. She knotted the bottom of his shirt to give it a better fit. Her face paled suddenly when she glanced at the clock. She shoved her feet into her shoes as she hurried to the door, pulling him by the arm. "Come on, we have to go. We have to get my car before Pete and Cara get to the diner or they'll know I spent the night with you. I swear I'll never hear the end of it!" When Wade looked unaffected by the whole thing, she pinned him with a glare. "Um, you won't think it's funny when she's picking out wedding invitations for us, now let's move."

They headed out for the diner just as the sun was breaking over the horizon. The beautiful colors filled the sky, giving it a radiant glow. A wonderful night, with a wonderful man and now she was rewarded with a sunrise for the ages.

Life was good.

Sydney's spirits were high as they pulled into the diner. She was flooded with relief to see the lights were still off inside. They had managed to beat Cara and Pete there.

"Thank you for last night, Wade. It was something I'll never forget." She rested her hand on his thigh and leaned over to kiss his cheek. He stopped the truck and gave her a kiss she felt all the way to her toes.

"It wasn't a one night stand, Sydney. You're important to me." She must have let her twinge of panic show on her face, because he pulled her close and smiled. "I know you're scared, and I know there are things from your past we have to deal with, but I want you to promise me you won't run without telling me." He brushed her hair out of her face. "I don't think I could take it if you left without saying goodbye."

"I'm not going anywhere." She kissed him again but when his hands started wandering, she moved out of his reach. "Don't start that again or I'll never get home in time."

They were still laughing and making plans to see each other again when Wade pulled around the back of the diner. Something looked off about her recently repaired car from a distance, but she couldn't put her finger on it. The closer they got, the more obvious it was. The moment Sydney saw it, she shrieked in distress.

Someone had slashed Sydney's tires and smashed every window in her car.

CHAPTER 18

"Mommy! Look what Pete made." Faith came barreling into the kitchen with a beautiful cake covered in tiny chocolate teddy bears. Two of her friends from school were at her side. "This is the best birthday ever," she squealed on her way out of the room.

Sydney put the cake on the counter and took a deep breath. She looked out into the living room where Cara and Pete stood talking to Agnes. Sam and Hailey were cuddled up on the couch, their heads together, and a warm smile on Hailey's face. Luke placed himself on one side of the room, as far away from Wade as possible. A couple of the deputies and countless children from school filled the rest of the room, and leaning against the wall with his eyes glued on Faith was Wade, their fierce protector. How had he grown to mean so much to her in so little time?

Sydney's paranoia was at an all-time high since her tires were slashed. She was obsessive about not letting Faith out of her sight, and even had considered cancelling the birthday party. Her driving patterns had all changed and her safety routines had increased as she did what she could to reassure herself that she and Faith were safe. But it wasn't helping.

Wade had a few clues on who had vandalized her car. When they went to look at the damage, he was insistent that it had been Tara.

'Whore' and 'Bitch' had been scribbled on the hood of her car in lipstick. Swearing, he had stormed toward the vehicle, but paused when he found what appeared to be boot prints in the soft dirt beside her car. If that wasn't enough, Tara had disappeared and left town that night, without a word, so Wade couldn't question her about any of it.

Every deputy in the area had been called to the diner. They looked for fingerprints, but found none. Then they took photographs of everything they could find. Footprints, sprays of glass, the location of random cigarette butts and the total annihilation of her car were all documented. By the time Pete and Cara arrived at the diner that morning, the parking lot was full of flashing lights and police cars. Pete turned white, probably assuming the worst and flashing back to the night they found Angie's body. Sydney had rushed over and explained that it was her car that was damaged, but everyone was fine. Once he heard that, anger replaced his worry, and Pete was livid that someone was damaging cars on his property.

That had been two days ago. Since then, Wade had rarely let Sydney out of his sight. During the day, he worked and stopped into the diner as often as he could, always there to make sure she made it in and out of work safely. At night, he'd come to the house, and hang out with them like he'd been doing it for years. Faith was falling for him just as hard as Sydney was. She'd beg him to carry her upstairs and tuck her in. Once she was fast asleep, he'd turn his attention to Sydney. Already she was getting far too attached to falling asleep in his arms.

It was the only thing keeping her in town.

The urge to run was overwhelming. She constantly thought about packing a bag, picking up Faith from school and then just driving as far and fast from town as possible. However she had no functioning car, so that was out of the question. Any thoughts she had of hopping a bus were negated by the promise she made Wade that she wouldn't leave without telling him, and she'd given him all their emergency papers. But staying was slowly killing her.

With another look around at all the people who had gathered to celebrate Faith's birthday, she smiled. These people, this eclectic collection of friends—she wanted this. A place to call her own, a life for her and Faith.

A family.

Wade walked into the kitchen and helped himself to a beer from the refrigerator. "You ready to cut the cake? Those kids are about ready to burst over there."

"Here." Sydney handed him Pete's masterpiece. "Go put this on the table and tell them not to touch it until I get there. Use your mean sheriff face if you have to." He made a playful grab for her but she laughed and dodged him, sneaking around and hiding behind the door of the refrigerator.

"Chicken," he said with a smile as he picked up the cake and tried to grab her around the door.

"Don't drop the cake or Pete will have your head. Or worse, Faith will cry."

"Like I'd let that happen." He kissed her and then started out of the kitchen just as the phone rang. The sound made her tense.

There had been countless hang ups lately, and with half the town in her living room, there wasn't anyone else left to call her. Wade must have sensed her distress because he set the cake on the table amongst the screaming girls and made eye contact with her just as she picked up the receiver.

"H-Hello?"

There was a long pause and Sydney was just about to hang up the phone when a male voice finally spoke. "How could you do that to her?" Her heart stopped beating.

"I-I," she stammered unable to breathe let alone speak.

"I hope you're having fun with your stolen baby on her birthday. Which do you celebrate more, her birth or the fact that you took her?"

The pale look on Sydney's face had Wade mowing a path through the crowd to get to her. His deputies picked up on his movements and followed him into the kitchen.

"Who is this?" Her voice came out as a desperate breath. Thick, deep laughter roared through the receiver.

"Don't you worry, I'll take care of you soon enough just like I did Marcy, little girl."

Sydney fell back against the wall and Wade snatched the phone from her ear, but not before she heard the voice yell, "By the way, that red dress makes you look like the whore you are." Wade wrapped his arm around her and cursed.

He can see me. She closed her eyes and buried her face in Wade's chest, praying she didn't pass out.

"Listen, you son of a bitch, you come near her and I'll kill you. I won't hesitate and I won't miss." Wade's voice had a cold, lethal tone to it that terrified Sydney. She knew he was serious. If Ronald came anywhere near her or Faith, Wade would kill him.

How could she ask him to do that? He had a life, a job, a family.

"Damn it," Wade growled and let the phone drop to the ground as the line went dead. Sydney crumpled into a ball on the floor. Wade sank down beside her and pulled her into his arms. "Listen to me, you are fine. Stay calm."

Sam peppered Wade with questions. "What's going on? What do you need?"

"She just got a threatening phone call."

"The guy who's stalking her?"

Wade nodded his head. "Probably." A shiver went down Sydney's spine as she thought about Ronald being that close to Faith. "He could see her, so he's got to be outside somewhere. I need you to cover the doors. Look for anyone lingering around outside that you don't know. A strange car, a dog you've never seen before, whatever. I want to know about it. No one goes in or out of the house without us knowing." Their heads turned when Pete hoisted Faith up to the table to look at her birthday cake. "No one else knows what we're doing, got it? We aren't ruining that little girl's birthday."

They exchanged a few more words then Sam's voice disappeared. Sydney braved a look up at Wade who was stroking her back, trying to reassure her with his gentle touch. When she met his eyes, she saw the fierce determination in them. "Nothing will happen to you while I'm here. Do you trust me?"

With a courage she found deep within herself, she nodded her head. There were few things she had been able to count on in her life, but Wade was one of them. He didn't know how to fail. He was going to keep them safe, or die trying. She just prayed it didn't come to that because she couldn't live with herself if anything happened to him.

"Good girl." He kissed her gently and gave her a little shake. "Faith is ready to cut her cake and then open her presents. Sam and the boys are at the doors and watching out the windows. I'm going to slip outside and see if I can find him." Sydney clutched his arm, terrified at the thought of Wade going after Ronald or him lying in wait to ambush Wade.

"I'll be fine. The boys will watch my back." He cradled her cheeks in his hands. "You can do this, Sydney."

She dug deep inside and steeled herself, burying her terror and focusing on her daughter. "For Faith." With a deep breath, Sydney pulled herself together and stood up. "Who's ready for cake?" Sydney asked with feigned excitement. Only Agnes looked at her funny, picking up on the tension in her voice. The rest of the room, especially the children, exploded with cheers. They hushed as the candles were lit to sing to Faith.

As the birthday girl attacked her cake, Sydney glanced out the window, looking for some sign of Wade. He'd been gone less than ten minutes, but until he was safe and sound in her living room, she couldn't help but worry. Sam gave her a slight shake of his head to warn her away from the window as he casually took up his position beside the front door. At some point in the last few minutes he'd locked the deadbolts and thrown the chain, probably on Wade's command. The guests were so engrossed in the party that they hadn't noticed anything was out of the ordinary.

"Can we do presents now, Mommy?" Faith asked as she bounced up and down with chocolate cake smeared from one end of her face to the next. She'd come so far, this little girl who she'd had thrust into her arms and life six years ago today. Every moment with her had been a blessing.

She offered a silent prayer to God asking for many more. Sydney gave her face a wipe with her napkin then agreed.

"You sit down on the floor." *Away from the doors and windows,* Sydney thought to herself. "I'll bring the presents to you."

With Cara at her side, they took the gifts from the table and piled them all around Faith on the floor. Her friends crowded around, jockeying for the best position to see what was being opened. As she picked up each package, she'd lift it into the air and ask, "Who is this from?" ignoring the card that was attach to the gift.

Dolls, games, and everything pink you could find in a store was spread out on the floor by the time she was done. She was wearing the tiara Cara and Pete had bought her along with a whole wardrobe of dress up clothes. Agnes Whittman had gotten her a metal detector and tiny spy camera she refused to put down. Melissa had even managed to send a gorgeous mini Eiffel Tower from France. Sydney missed Melissa so much right now, but was glad to know she was safe and sound, thousands of miles away.

In front of Faith, there sat one last present. It was too big for her to lift up so she planted her hands on her hips and shouted. "Who got me this *giant* one?"

"I did." Wade's voice came from behind Sydney, startling her.

She wanted to throw her arms around his neck and check every inch of him to make sure he was whole, but instead, she reached a hand behind her and felt Wade's strong, warm hand grasp hers. Then she finally relaxed. He was back, and he was okay.

There wasn't time for questions because Faith tore into the beautiful yellow wrapping without a second thought. As soon as she realized what it was, her excited squeals filled the room. "Mommy, it's an easel, and paints, and paper, and crayons and brushes and a whole set of markers…and more tape!" Her voice got more excited with each thing she listed. She ran over to Wade and jumped up into his arms. "That is the best present ever." She placed a big, wet, kiss on his cheek and Sydney swore she saw him blush as Faith gushed on and on about how wonderful it was.

"Glad you like it," he said as he put her back down on the ground. "Now, go thank your guests for the presents and for coming to your party." When she was out of earshot, he pulled Sydney into his arms and kissed the top of her head. "You holding up okay?" Sydney nodded her head against his chest, her throat thick with relief that he was back.

Cara and Pete were cleaning up the shredded wrapping paper while Luke tried, unsuccessfully, to hide his displeasure with seeing Sydney being held so intimately by Wade.

"Thanks for coming, Luke."

"I wouldn't have missed it. Faith is a sweet kid." He looked back and forth between the two of them with a curious expression on his face. "What happened earlier? I saw Wade disappear outside and Sam and the boys rushing around? Anything I can do?"

Sydney felt Wade go very still beside her, a warning to not say too much. It was difficult enough thinking about Wade in danger because of her, but the last thing she needed was Luke running around half-cocked and getting himself hurt. Wade surprised her when he asked Luke a question. "See anyone new in town lately?"

"Other than your ex-wife?" Luke retorted, closely watching Sydney's reaction. "Where'd she go by the way? Rumor has it you had a bit of a run-in with her at the bar." Sydney kept her face calm but dug her fingers in Wade's hand to release some of her displeasure.

"I have no idea," Wade said, his face calm but his body tense. "I'm just glad she's gone."

"What did you do to her this time?"

Wade's jaw clenched, as he reigned in his temper for Sydney's sake. If they hadn't been standing there, surrounded by children, she was pretty sure Wade would have punched him, and it seemed like Luke was looking for a fight. "I didn't do anything. Just like I didn't do anything to her all those years ago." He wrapped his arm around Sydney, holding onto her for support. "Interesting that she disappears the same night Sydney's car was trashed, don't you think? But you believe what you want. Tara's a liar and a user. She used you back then, and then threw you to the side to see what she could get from me. When I wasn't profitable enough for her, she left, but not before she dragged my name through the mud. Be happy you avoided her full wrath. I'm still paying for my mistake."

For the first time, Luke seemed to really be considering what Wade said. He had to know what happened between him and Tara, or didn't happen, had nothing to do with Wade. For all they knew, Tara was on the run for the damage she did to Sydney's car. Maybe he was finally starting to realize that.

"Now that we got that out of the way," Wade said as he rubbed the back of his neck, uncomfortable with the turn the conversation had taken, he asked again, "I do need some help. Have you seen anyone new in the last couple of days? A person, truck, or car you haven't seen before?"

Maybe it was the tone of his voice or the way he had laid all his cards on the table with Luke, but whatever the reason, Luke's expression became very serious as he thought about the question. "There was a black sedan near the diner one day. Out of state plates, but there was no one but Elton folks inside eating."

"Do you remember what state?"

Luke shook his head. "I want to say California, but I could be mistaken. I assumed it was one of the feds with a rental. Why?"

Faith's friends from school interrupted their hushed conversation, thanking Sydney for the wonderful party. Faith handed out the goody bags while parents gave a wave as the party started to wind to a close. When the house cleared of invited guests, those who were left were her dearest friends. Cara and Pete, along with Agnes, came to join the conversation, somehow picking up on the urgency between Luke and Wade.

Agnes looked back and forth between the two men. "Why are you asking about strangers, Wade? We got trouble?"

Sydney looked up at Wade, searching for what to do or say. He gave her an encouraging nod and the flood gates opened up.

"Someone from my past may be in town. At least I think he's in town. There's a lot I want to tell you, but I can't because it could put all of you in danger. All I can say is he's out there, and he's after me…and Faith. He really wants her." She choked up and took a deep breath, leaning on Wade for strength. "So if something happens to me, you all have to promise me you will protect her. Don't let him get her, and if he does, you have to find her and get her back. No matter what it takes. Please."

"Oh, my God, Syd." Pete opened his arms and Sydney flew into them needing a fatherly hug more than she could explain at that moment. "It's gonna be fine, sweets. No one will hurt you or your baby girl."

"He dangerous, Wade?" Agnes asked, in her typical no-nonsense way of speaking. "If so, I'm taking Syd out to the shooting range tomorrow morning and getting her comfortable with a gun." When he didn't say anything she raised an eyebrow at him. "Don't give me that look, Wade Jenkins. She needs to be prepared."

"Who is this guy? And what can I do to help?" Luke asked, the first civil words Sydney heard him say to Wade. "Anything."

"I appreciate the offer," Sydney said, not wanting Wade to be the one to shoot Luke's question down, "but I can't tell you more than his name is Ronald. It's a long story and there are some legal issues, if I shared any more…" Her voice trailed off as she tried to gauge their reaction. Not a single one of them blinked an eye.

"Wade? What can we do?" Luke asked again, unaffected by a thing Sydney had said.

"Keep your eyes open. Let me know if you see anything or anyone unusual. I'm especially interested in out of state vehicles. He's nearby and he's hiding, but he was also arrogant enough to call her in the middle of the party. He was close enough to see what Sydney was wearing. He's getting too close for comfort, so I'd appreciate extra eyes out there." He looked directly at Agnes. "Call me if you see something in the area. Do not go after anyone on your own. If it is him, he's going to be armed and dangerous. I don't want a wild shootout in town. Understand, Agnes?"

Agnes smiled at Sydney. "Shoot one purse snatcher in the buttocks and this one will never let me live it down."

They all shared a laugh at Agnes' expense, and it was just enough to lighten the mood. They stayed a few more minutes then filed out, each having a word with Wade before leaving. When she saw him share a handshake with Luke, she couldn't help but smile despite her fear.

She gathered up a couple plates with cake on them and tossed them into the trash. Faith busied herself with her gifts and dolls up in her room. Sydney could hear her chattering to herself as she played. The sound of the deadbolts locking on the front door was like music to her ears. They were all gone. She turned around and Wade stood in the doorway to the kitchen, his arms spread wide. Sydney fell into his arms and held on for dear life.

"Did I ruin the party?" she mumbled against his shirt.

"You did a great job. Faith had a wonderful time and no one knew you were upset."

She looked up into his green eyes for strength. "Did you find anything outside?" When he nodded, the bottom fell out of her stomach. "What?"

"Footprints under your dining room window and the kitchen windows. Bastard hid in the bushes, that's how he saw you. And it looks like he's been there a few times. The prints matched the ones from around your car." When she started shaking, Wade held her tighter. "Sam's spending the night camped outside in an unmarked car, watching the place. And I have Billy looking into a few things back at the station. You're gonna be fine. I'll put someone at school with Faith, too."

Not wanting to sound completely desperate, Sydney tried for a breezy tone, but her question, "Do you have to leave?" came out more hysterical than she intended.

He looked her in the eye and flashed a wicked smile. "You aren't getting rid of me that easily. I thought we'd have a sleepover." Then, as if nothing happened, as if a psychotic lunatic hadn't been crouched under her window an hour earlier, he started cleaning her house.

CHAPTER 19

THE DOOR OF THE diner chimed and out of nervous habit, Sydney glanced over to see who walked in. When she saw the reverend and his wife, she swallowed her fear and gave them a polite smile, then got back to work.

Calm down, Sydney, you're being paranoid.

How many times had she said that to herself today? From the moment she got to work, she'd had the distinct feeling she was being watched. She checked out all the windows as she waited on her tables and saw nothing unusual. She'd called Agnes five times to make sure that Faith was okay and there wasn't anything suspicious going on by them. It was pathetic that she'd been reduced to an emotional basket case, but she always knew in the past when danger was close, and the way she felt, she was readying for a knife in the back.

Luke walked in and made a bee line for the counter. "Hey," he said as he sat down on the stool in front of her. "How you doing?"

"I'm great," Sydney said a little too fast as she poured his coffee, accidentally spilling the steaming liquid over the top.

"You're a mess," Luke said with an understanding smile as he grabbed the towel from her hand and wiped up the spill. He looked around the diner. "Where's your guard dog?"

"I thought you and Wade declared a cease fire of sorts," she said giving him a stern look.

"Who said anything about Wade? I was talking about Agnes."

"You're terrible!" Sydney laughed, as she got him a new, and not overflowing, cup of coffee.

"Since you brought him up, does Wade have any leads on that car? I went down to the station and gave him a description of everything I could remember." Luke looked over the menu, trying to make light of his visit, but Sydney wasn't fooled. She was touched that he would not only do that, but put his differences aside and work with Wade to help her. It was nice to see them being civil to one another.

"Thanks for doing that," she said as she tugged down on the menu he was half-hiding behind. "And I'm glad you and Wade are playing nice." The door opened again and she immediately checked to see who it was. Relief washed over her when she saw Hailey show up, on time for once, for her shift. She gave a wave then ran into the back to put her stuff away.

"You expecting trouble today?" Luke asked, following her gaze to the front door. "Or are you expecting lover boy any minute?"

"No. He's working and I'm just being silly."

"Did you see someone?" He immediately took a closer look around the diner and out the window. All he saw were the usual folks from town. Nothing out of the ordinary, but still, she couldn't relax.

"No. That's the thing. There's nothing going on, I'm just acting like a lunatic."

Luke immediately looked guilty. "Did he tell you about Tara?"

That got her attention. "No. What about her?"

With a slow exhale, Luke set down the menu. "I talked to her this morning. More like she called me around four A.M., drunk." Sydney didn't say a word but her eyebrows shot up toward her hairline. "Yeah. Basically she admitted to smashing your windows and slashing your tires. After that run in she had with you at Murray's, she saw your car parked at the diner and decided to take a few whacks at it."

"Classy."

Luke laughed. "Now that's the one thing I don't think that woman's ever been called."

"Well, at least we know the truth about my car." It should have relieved some of her anxiety to know it was Tara and not Ronald who smashed her car, but it didn't. Maybe she was the one responsible for the phone calls too. And if that was the case, what about the footprints by her car and outside her window? Was it Ronald following her around, or was it all Tara? She voiced her thoughts to Luke and he shook his head.

"Wade doesn't think it was all Tara. She might have done the damage, but he still thinks Ronald was there, surveying the situation and lying in wait for you to come back to the car."

"Great," Sydney growled, her fears renewed.

"I'll pay for the damages to your car," Luke offered.

"You'll do no such thing."

His face fell. "Are you going to press charges against her?"

"No. I want nothing to do with her. I already have one psycho after me, I really don't need another." Luke didn't so much as crack a smile at her little joke, because it was true. And not funny. "If I did, it would only give her another reason to come back into Wade's life, and yours. I think it's best to let her stay away."

Luke nodded. "I'll pay her parents a visit and let them know how generous you're being in not pursuing this legally. Hopefully they can encourage her to finally leave us all alone."

"I honestly have no idea what you and Wade saw in her."

He paused as if to think of a way to explain it to her. Finally he shrugged. "If she was happy, she'd make you happy. She knew how to have a good time. But if the smallest thing didn't go her way, she'd make everyone within a five mile radius miserable. She was spoiled rotten by her parents and she expected men to do the same."

It was impossible for Sydney to imagine either one of those men putting up with Tara's brand of crazy for as long as they had. Luke seemed to be taking her off the pedestal and was seeing her for more of who she was, not who he wanted her to be. "She sounds charming."

"She was exciting, annoying, aggravating and fun all rolled into one tiny person. The problem was, I only paid attention to the fun, and overlooked the rest of it. For a while."

"And now?" It was none of her business, but she needed to know where Luke stood on Tara, if there was any hope of he and Wade moving past this anger they shared for one another.

"Now I know she's not who I made her out to be in my head. And since I'm making life altering realizations I have one more to lay on you." He leaned across the counter and whispered, "Wade isn't really all that bad. But if you ever repeat that, I'll deny it until the day I die."

"You're a nice guy, Luke Rollins. You deserve to find a girl who will treat you right."

"Since you turned me down, by any chance do you have a sister?" he asked hopefully, causing Sydney to smack him in the shoulder and laugh.

"You're incorrigible."

With a big toothy smile, he put his hand over his heart. "Guilty as charged." It was in that moment that she knew Luke and Wade would be all right. They would get past this thing with Tara and find a way to be, if not friends, then polite acquaintances. The animosity was gone and Luke looked like he felt twenty pounds lighter for it. It was the first thing that had made her feel hopeful about the future days.

She treated Luke to lunch and sent him on his way, well-fed and with a smile on his face. She really did hope he'd find someone special. He deserved to be happy.

When Luke left, things slowed at the diner and she had more time to herself to think, and the fact that she still hadn't seen Wade all day wasn't helping. He was her anchor, the one getting her through the endless days while they waited for Ronald to make his next move. Today, however, Sydney had been left to wallow in her fears and already with hang ups for the day she was convinced it was Ronald taunting her at work. Or maybe it was still Tara.

"Hey, Sydney?" Billy, one of Wade's deputies and her current babysitter waved her down.

"What's up? You want more coffee?"

"No, I just got a call about a tractor trailer accident a few miles away. They need some backup so I have to run."

Sydney waved her hand to send him on his way. "Go then. I'll be fine."

He tossed a few bills onto the table to settle his check. "You sure? Wade knows I'm leaving so I expect he'll be over here soon."

"I'm a big girl, Billy. I can take care of myself." She hoped he didn't hear the way her voice wavered. He headed out, and Sydney went back to busying herself with cleaning.

Cara accidentally dropped a plate and Sydney nearly jumped on the counter.

"Syd, why don't you head home? You're a mess today. I'll cover for you." Sydney was already stripping off her apron before Cara had finished talking. "I'll call Wade and let him know you're leaving."

Wade had warned her this morning he'd be tied up most of the day. The federal agents were back and had hinted they had found evidence, something new about Samantha's murder, but there were still no clear leads on Angie's murder. That ate at Wade, night and day. While their fancy lab in St. Louis ran countless tests, all they could do in Elton was wait.

Sydney looked around the diner, which was empty except for a lone customer who was getting ready to pay. All in all, it was a slow night. If she left a little early, Cara and Pete wouldn't be swamped with work. As a matter of fact, they might close up early for a change. Feeling less guilty, Sydney hastily made her exit.

"Thanks, Cara." She placed a peck to the woman's cheek. "I don't know what's wrong with me tonight." She quickly said her goodbyes to Pete then gathered up her purse. "I'll see you guys in the morning."

"Wait for Pete. He'll walk you out."

"Bye, Cara," Sydney called over her shoulder without stopping. She needed to feel comfortable in her own skin again. If she couldn't walk to her car—an ugly rental the insurance company had dropped off—by herself she was going to be useless to Faith if trouble did come knocking. She needed to suck it up and take care of herself for a while.

It was dark outside when Sydney stepped out the back door, the late fall sun setting much earlier now that it had even a few days before. The air was crisp and she could smell the slightest hint of snow in the breeze. All the sounds of night serenaded her on the way to the car, the rustle of the dried up field grasses blew in the wind as she crossed the parking lot.

A parking lot where a dead woman was dumped. The thought slipped into her mind before she could stop it, sending a shiver down her spine.

Sydney paused as if the night air would bring encouragement and tell her everything would be fine, but the silence she was met with only saddened her more.

There was a strange crackling noise that came from the field beside the diner. Around her, everything went silent. Sydney's heart slammed in her chest as she fished wildly around in her purse trying to find her car keys. Wade had told her a million times to have them out and ready when she walked to her car, especially at night. Yet here she was, alone, and searching for them in the dark.

Her feet shuffled to the side of the car, using the steel frame of the vehicle to hold her shaking body upright. Another rustle came from the same direction and Sydney was two seconds from screaming when her fingertip brushed against a metal loop at the bottom of her purse. She yanked out the keys and jabbed them into the lock, freeing the door and allowing herself to climb safely inside just as Pete ducked out the back door of the diner, calling her name.

Too scared to wait, Sydney threw on her headlights and started her car, roaring out of the parking space and nearly running over the orange and white cat that leisurely strolled out of the field in front of her. She shook her head and laughed at herself.

"Move, you stupid cat. You nearly gave me a heart attack!" With a quick beep of the horn goodbye to Pete, she scared the cat back into the field and she was able to pull out of the parking lot and head home.

It had been days since she drove home alone at night. Wade typically followed her from the diner, his headlights being that extra sense of security that would calm her nerves and make her feel safe.

Sydney turned onto the long stretch country road that ran the length of the Cooper's farm. There were no streetlights so she kept her attention on the road, not knowing what other kind of wildlife was planning on jumping in front of her car tonight. She had gone about a hundred yards when a pair of headlights flashed in the rearview mirror behind her. For a second she panicked and worried she hadn't backtracked as much as she typically did, but she wanted to get home tonight for some reason. Her knuckles turned white as she gripped the steering wheel for a few moments until it dawned on her who it was.

Wade.

When Cara called him, he must have jumped in the car to follow her home. A smile spread across her face at his thoughtfulness.

The car came up behind her quickly, holding at about three car lengths behind as she crept down the dark, hilly road. A minute later, flashing lights signaled from behind her. She looked at the speedometer and knew she wasn't speeding. Then a slow smile spread across her face at the thought of Wade stopping her. He probably wanted to check on her and see how she held up today. Sydney found a small patch of gravel and pulled off to the side of the road. She glanced back in her mirror to quickly check her makeup and adjusted her sadly disheveled ponytail. The next thing she knew, she was startled by a loud tapping on her window.

She was laughing as she lowered the window. "Thanks for the heart attack, Wade." But immediately she could tell it wasn't him. From the build of the officer standing outside the window, to the flashlight shining directly into her eyes, she knew whoever this was had a much smaller frame than Wade. The uniform was nearly hanging off them. When the light dipped, she caught sight of a dark braid hanging over the shoulder of the officer.

I didn't know there were any female officers in Elton, she thought to herself as her anxiety rushed back, full force.

"License and registration," the female officer said sharply, the bright light making Sydney's eyes water.

"Um." She reached for her purse which was sitting on the front seat, stunned and even more confused as to why she'd been pulled over if it wasn't Wade. And the stern way the woman was speaking to her was unexpected. There was no professional tone to her voice only a harsh edge that rattled Sydney's nerves. "Here." As she handed the officer her identification, she tried to get a look at her badge, but the handle of the flashlight was in the way. "Was I speeding?"

The officer ignored her question, only snapping, "Turn off the car." When Sydney didn't immediately comply, the woman raised her voice and barked, "Now!"

"S-Sorry." Sydney's internal alarms were sounding, but before she did anything, she needed to get an idea of who this woman was. Maybe she was new and didn't know about Sydney's situation, so she dropped Wade's name in the hope that the woman would take the hint, and back off a little. All she wanted to do was get home to Faith. "I-I didn't know there were any female officers on the Elton police force. Wade, Sheriff Jenkins, hadn't mentioned it."

"I'm sure there's lots of things *Wade* doesn't tell you." With that, the female officer strode back to her car, with Sydney's identification in hand.

"Think," she growled. Wade had never really checked her license but this woman seemed like she was very serious about it, and if she looked hard enough, she might discover it was a fake and that would be a disaster. She didn't dare drive off or create a huge issue for Wade at the station. Instead, she tried to get a hold of him and see if he could talk down his overzealous officer.

With her phone hidden in her lap she texted, "Did you hire a female officer? She pulled me over and…" before she could type any more, she saw the light of the officer's flashlight approaching the car again. She cursed and hit send, hoping it would get to him soon enough.

"Come on, Wade," she whispered as she rolled her window back down. "Is there a problem, officer? I wasn't speeding. Are the plates expired? It's a rental. I'm sorry for all the questions. I'm just confused as to why you pulled me over."

"Get out of the car."

"What?"

She knows.

Sydney was horrified at the thought of being put into the back of a police cruiser and driven to the station in handcuffs where her secrets were going to be spilled in front of so many people she knew and cared about it.

"Get out of the car, now."

"Can't you call Sheriff Jenkins? He knows me. Can you talk to him? He's your boss, right?" She stopped talking the second she saw a gun muzzle pointed at her face.

"I'm not asking again. Get out of the car, or I'm going to shoot you." The matter of fact way she said it made Sydney's blood run cold.

On the outside, Sydney somehow managed to stay calm, but inside, she was screaming. Something wasn't right, she could feel it. She was on a deserted strip of road with one of two evils. The woman pointing a gun at her was either an officer who knew, after checking her identification, that she was a fraud with no past beyond eighteen months ago and wanted to lock her up, or this officer wasn't who she seemed and intended to do her serious harm. Either way, she had to be very careful if she ever wanted to see Faith again. She glanced to the passenger seat where her phone sat, just out of reach.

"Ok," Sydney said softly, raising her hands for the officer to see and slowly reaching to release her seatbelt. "I'll get out of the car. Could you put the gun away, please?" There was no way to get away from her from inside the car, but outside, she could run and get lost in the fields, if she was lucky.

All she wanted to do was get to Wade.

"Move it," the woman all but screamed at her, the hysteria in her voice telling Sydney she was in serious trouble.

Sydney stretched all her movements out, hoping and praying that another set of headlights would come up over one of the hills and send this woman running for cover, but as she shut the door behind her, there were no other cars in sight.

Without a thought, Sydney swung her arm out toward the woman's face, landing a crushing blow to her nose. The flashlight dropped to the ground as the woman screamed in fury. Sydney ran as fast as she could to the officer's car, desperate to put as much distance between herself and this woman as possible. If she made it home quickly enough, she could grab Faith and they would disappear before anyone found the woman.

The click of a gun being readied to fire froze Sydney in her tracks.

"Touch the car and you're dead."

"Why are you doing this to me?" Sydney pleaded as the woman approached.

With the flashlight gone, Sydney's eyes had finally adjusted to the darkness and she could begin to make out the woman's features. When she realized who was standing in front of her, she did the only thing she could do.

She screamed and everything went black.

THE NEXT THING SYDNEY knew, she found herself in a moving car, her head throbbing from the fall she must have taken. She was in so much pain, she squeezed her eyes shut and waited for the nausea to pass. Then she heard the woman beside her mumbling.

"Dammit, Charles, what have you done now?"

She kept her eyes closed, trying to piece together what had happened. Sydney's head made a dull thud as it banged repeatedly against the window of Wade's cruiser. She could smell his cologne in the leather. There was no sound to be heard except the soft mutterings of her captor. The blow to her head still had her feeling disoriented. She had no idea how close or far from Elton they were. Part of her was afraid to open her eyes and find out.

Her shoulders burned as her arms began to cramp. Little bits of rock and grass covered her clothes, new aches and pains reminding her of her

VICTORIA MICHAELS

earlier ordeal on the side of the road. At some point, her hands had been tied behind her back, her wrists pinched so tight she couldn't even feel her fingers. There was warm, sticky blood trickling down the side of her face from where a ghost from her past had hit her with the butt of her gun. Not a ghost really, but a woman she long assumed dead.

Marcy.

Seeing her face had been a shock. All these years Sydney had been so certain she was dead. There was no way she could have survived that incident with Ronald. She'd lost so much blood and when he raised the bat over her head, Sydney couldn't imagine anyone surviving that. But she had.

Marcy was back, but why?

She had looked very much the same, just older. Wade had asked her to describe Ronald once and she couldn't, but Marcy's face was seared into her brain. Probably because Faith resembled her mother so much, the image never truly left her. But the anger and the violence, that was something she never expected from this woman, the woman who sacrificed herself so her daughter could live. Or so Sydney had thought.

It must have taken superhuman strength for Marcy to haul Sydney's limp body into the car. She was definitely taller than Sydney but their builds were similar. Something she hadn't noticed all those years ago. The car bounced wildly as they drove down the country road. Sydney braved a look out the window to get an idea of where they were, but her vision was so blurred it made her nauseous. *Probably a concussion,* she told herself. In an effort to save her energy, she slammed her eyes shut. And prayed.

"I know you're awake." Marcy cranked the wheel hard to the left, the tires screeching under the force.

Sydney's battered body pressed tighter against the door until they finished making the turn. For a second, she debated finding a way to open the door and fling herself out of the car, but she had a feeling she knew where they were headed and there was no way Sydney was letting this woman go there alone. She'd just have to bide her time and wait for another moment to run.

230

They drove a while longer, and then the car jerked to a stop. Sydney's suspicions were confirmed when she saw the fuzzy outline of her home in front of them.

"What do you want?" Sydney's voice was rough as if she hadn't used it in months. "Where's Wade?"

The woman spun on her so fast, Sydney didn't have time to dodge Marcy's hand as it slapped across her face. "Sorry to do that but you need to sit back and relax. We have a little situation going on at the moment. Just be quiet and let me think, please." She flashed a knife and tapped the edge on the steering wheel. The silver of the blade reflected in the moonlight. "What do I want? If I'm being honest, I really don't want anything from you. I, for one, am glad you have Faith. But the others, well, they're not. They're really angry and—" Marcy winced, grabbing her head. "They're fighting me on this. They have been ever since that night." She looked toward the house, her eyes wild. "I was right to give her to you, but they're going to take her from you. And not you, or your hunky boyfriend, are going to be able to stop them."

"No! You can't have her." Sydney screamed and tried to ram the woman with her shoulder, but she was swatted away like she weighed next to nothing. Marcy's hand slammed down hard on Sydney's neck, pinning her face against the dashboard and cutting off her airway. When she spoke again, Marcy's voice was noticeably rough, deeper.

"Now listen here, you bitch. Touch me again and I'm gonna start snapping bones. We understand one another?"

All she could do was nod her head and stare at the woman strangling her. In the course of a few seconds she had changed, not just her temper but her face and voice too. There was a roughness to Marcy that hadn't been there before and it terrified her. And Sydney couldn't help but wonder who were the 'others' Marcy kept mentioning? Was she working with someone? Had Ronald and Marcy been together, stalking her all along?

Marcy released her and Sydney gasped for air. "I-I love Faith."

"So does her mother!" she growled, the knife, now in her right hand, sliced wildly through the air as she stabbed at the leather beside Sydney in anger. There was a momentary flurry of motion and curses until Sydney once again felt the tiny prick of the knife positioned against her side. "You do remember her, don't you? The woman who carried her for nine months, loved her, sang to her, and dreamed of a life with her." She leaned across the seat, her face inches from Sydney's while the steel of the blade dug deeper into her side drawing blood. "Do you know what you did to her when you took her baby? You broke her!"

The way Marcy kept referring to herself in the third person was alarming. Sydney's internal warning alarms were going off. The mood swings and the rage were scary, but strangely familiar. She thought back to her mother's ranting and the months she spent in the women's shelter. She'd grown up around mental illness all her life. This woman obviously wasn't stable, but just how 'broken' was Marcy?

CHAPTER 20

Evenings around the Elton sheriff's office were typically uneventful. At least they had been until two murders rocked the small town to its very roots. Add to that the nightmare that was going on with Sydney. Now Wade's days were full of conference calls, questions, and visits from all branches of law enforcement, it seemed. What he wouldn't give for a quiet evening right about now.

Wade glanced at the clock to find the hands had barely moved at all since last he checked. Earlier in the day, he had reached out to an old bird at a local police station in Montana that was so small it made Elton look like a metropolis. He was hoping this would be the lead he needed to confirm who this man from Sydney's past was so they weren't tracking a ghost. But the person he needed to speak with hadn't been in, so Wade left an urgent message. And he was slowly going insane from the wait.

He had been searching the Internet for days to pin down the exact town where Sydney had been when she left the highway that night. He was hoping to confirm that one of the men who worked there years ago, a volunteer deputy, was named Ronald Washington, or 'Donny' to his friends. Wade dug further and found that, even though Donny had been with the sheriff's office, he was a sleaze with a string of arrests for assault, a number of domestic charges, and restraining orders that were all later dropped by his wife, Amanda.

The calling card of a habitual abuser, Wade thought to himself.

A little more than three years later, he had disappeared. Maybe he went on the run, maybe his wife finally took a shot at him, or maybe he found a secluded cabin and became a mountain man. Whatever the reason, the guy was a ghost now, which really bothered Wade.

The piece of information that didn't add up was the fact that his wife was named Amanda, not Marcy. Sydney suggested that maybe Marcy had been a girlfriend he kept on the side, which was a definite possibility. However, if that was true, it was going to make it difficult to connect her to Faith without more information. If he confirmed Ronald's identity it would at least be a starting point. Wade was desperate for something to sink his teeth into on this case. He was hoping this local sheriff's office would give him answers rather than raise more questions.

Until then, he considered several 'what if' scenarios with the facts he had.

What if this guy got a partial plate on Sydney that night? She said he watched her drive away. If he wanted to find her, he had a lead. It'd be a long search, but if he was in with the law enforcement, he had connections. It would explain how he would have been able to track her over the years and how he could find her when she moved. As far as Marcy went, if Sydney was right, Ronald could have easily disposed of her body that night in the mountains of Montana and then went back to his life with Amanda. Stranger things have happened. The problem was, Wade liked to deal in facts, not speculations. And right now, he was praying for just one fact he could work with to help Sydney.

His eyes wandered to the clock again. "Seriously? How busy can they be in nowhere, Montana?" Wade stood up and raked his fingers through his hair in frustration. He wasn't used to standing around waiting. The inaction was killing him.

"Easy, boss. There's probably an escaped cow or two they have to get off of the highway." Sam laughed, trying in vain to lighten Wade's mood.

He'd been pacing all afternoon and the guys knew something had him stressed. They assumed it had to do with what was going on with Sydney. Everyone at the station believed it was a simple case of harassment, but they didn't know the half of it. "You know Billy went to check on that injury accident in Hightown?"

"Yeah," Wade scrubbed his hand down his cheek, "I'll swing by the diner and get Sydney when her shift ends."

So much had happened in the last few weeks that Wade found himself sifting through the images in his head. The woman they found dead at the edge of town, then Angie's lifeless body was dumped behind the diner, Sydney's face when he told her that there had been someone in her house, Wade making love to Sydney, waking up with her draped across his chest, the smile Faith gave him when she opened his present, the shattered windows on Sydney's car. The good all intertwined with the bad into a never ending nightmare.

Frustrated, Wade grabbed the file on Angie's murder off his desk and thumbed through it again. Right on top was the picture of her, face down and covered in stab wounds beside the dumpster. A dumpster he found a picture of Faith wedged behind. Wade stared at the scene for the thousandth time, looking for something small he might have missed. He couldn't help but feel like it was right in front of him.

Sam looked over his shoulder and shook his head. "You have to stop staring at that picture. You could probably draw it from memory by now."

"I'm missing something. There's something here." Wade set it aside and flipped through the countless lab results done on the blood and tissue samples found near her body. Nothing out of the ordinary, of course.

"Wade, you're doing everything you can to find her killer. Whoever this was, they were good, and the sonofabitch took their time. They did their homework and planned this out."

Wade froze, and grabbed the photograph again, holding it from a distance and compared it to the woman they found in Greenville. He'd been thinking the same thing since he arrived on the scene that night, but he hadn't dared to say the words out loud. The build, the hair color, and age were a match in both pictures.

Dead ringers for Sydney. Coincidence or design?

He was in Elton. Ronald killed both of these women on his way to town and he'd been there for days.

Wade let his mind acknowledge the truth he had been avoiding. He grabbed the file the FBI had left about the other murders they were trying to connect these ones to. As he flipped the pages, all the women were blonde and early twenties. On his second pass he noticed the cities they were from all aligned with where Sydney had lived recently. Indianapolis, Nashville, and he'd bet if he were to ask Sydney, she would confirm she had, at one time, been in Decatur, too.

"Shit," he said as he threw the file onto the desk. "He's been following her all along. But he seems to miss her by a few months every time."

"What are you talking about?" Sam reached down and picked up a paper that had rolled under the fax machine. He absently looked at it, before his eyes went wide with surprise and he handed it to Wade.

"I don't care about another fax from the Feds."

"You'll care about this." He thrust the paper at Wade more forcefully. "I think we found the guy you're looking for."

Wade skimmed the fax from a California court of records and found a J. Ronald Washington's date of birth…and death. "It's not him," Wade mumbled but he kept reading, looking for anything that could help. Was he the brother of their man? There was a case number scrawled at the bottom, so he had Sam pull it up on the computer. He barked at Mrs. Watts to call the diner and tell Sydney to stay put until he got there.

"Oh, Cara called about fifteen minutes ago, Wade. You were on the phone with the guys from Greenville. Sydney headed home early. She wasn't feeling well."

"This isn't happening," Wade muttered as he scrambled around the office, searching for his phone on his desk. He needed to hear her voice, then he could calm down and figure out what all this meant. But for now he had to know she was safe.

Because something told him she wasn't.

"His wife, Amanda, killed him." Sam's head popped up over his monitor with a grim look on his face. "It was a total bloodbath. He was stabbed over a hundred times. Amanda was on the run for a long time. Her lawyers claimed insanity and she's been locked up for the last two months in Atascadero which is a mental hospital outside of Fresno. That explains why you couldn't find them in Montana."

He had started to dial Sydney's number when he found her text message. "We don't have any female officers," he said to himself then realization slowly started to hit him. The events of the last weeks fell into alignment, and the one common thread to all of them was Sydney.

He grabbed Sam by the collar. "Go find Sydney and call Billy back, now. One of you take the route from the diner that goes past the pond, another one of you go past the farm and I'll go to her house. I want to know the moment you see her headlights, understand?" He didn't wait for a response, he grabbed his jacket and started calling Sydney's cell phone repeatedly, praying she'd pick up. When it clicked over to voicemail, he thought his head was going to explode. He was almost out the door when Mrs. Watts screamed his name.

"I don't have time for this." He went outside and drew up short when he realized his cruiser was missing. "Where the hell is my car?"

"Wade, it's a doctor from a hospital in California. She said she had to speak with the sheriff, that it's an emergency."

"I have to find Sydney!" he bellowed, his fear and frustration bubbling over until he felt a trembling hand on his arm.

"I think this is *about* Sydney," she whispered, turning his blood to ice. With a vile curse, he stormed back inside and grabbed the phone off her desk.

"What?" he snarled into the mouthpiece, unable to keep from pacing as he listened. He had too much adrenaline in his body, too many places he needed to be.

"Sheriff? Is this the sheriff?"

"You need to start talking, now. I'm in the middle of an investigation and you're holding me up. Talk fast."

The rage in his voice made her cut to the chase. "My name is Dr. Margaret Lee and I'm a physician at Atascadero. There's a woman, a patient of mine, headed in your direction, I believe." She rattled off her name and DEA number as proof of her identity. Mrs. Watts took the piece of paper Wade handed her and ran to his computer to check it out. When she confirmed the woman's identity, Wade started peppering Dr. Lee with questions.

"The mental hospital? You work in California?" The car Luke saw in town had California plates. What were the odds?

"Yes. I believe someone is in grave danger which, you know, exonerates me from doctor patient privilege. I have a patient, a very disturbed woman by the name of…"

Wade didn't wait for her to finish, his worst fear coming to life. "Amanda Washington."

"You know her?" She sounded somewhat relieved, but Wade's irritation was growing by the second.

"I know *of* her. Why is she coming here? From what I understand, she killed her husband and is locked up."

"She *was* locked up. Then, about four weeks ago, she escaped. Somehow she snuck out during a shift change in the infirmary, but that's irrelevant. She's been my patient for the last six months while she was awaiting trial, and in that time I got to know her very well. When she's on her meds and lucid, she's reasonable but when she's off them, I have serious concerns." The woman was rattling off the information as fast as she could, but it was still taking too long to get to the point.

"A crazy woman is coming to Elton. Tell me why?"

"Do you know a woman named Cindy or Sydney? The last name I have for her looks like Jackson, but I think she's going by something else now. I'm sure there's more than one Sydney in town, but she has a little girl who goes to—East Elementary? I tried calling the school, but they refused to give me any information."

"What does Amanda want with this woman?"

The woman was quiet for a moment and when Wade was about to demand an answer to the question, she finally spoke. "Have you ever heard of DID or Dissassociative Identity Disorder?" Every word out of this woman's mouth was ratcheting Wade's anxiety higher. He kept looking at his phone, hoping and praying for a message from Sam or Billy saying they found Sydney.

His throat closed up, but he managed to grind out, "It's like multiple personalities, right?"

"Right. Amanda is the main personality. She's cripplingly depressed. If left to her own devices, she'd sit in a dark room and not speak unless spoken to. She has other personalities that aren't as…docile."

"You need to talk faster. Much faster." Wade's knuckles went white on the receiver of the phone. Mrs. Watt's eyes were huge as she eavesdropped on his side of the conversation, clearly not liking the part she could hear.

"She has a personality named Marcy who is her caretaker. She's the one who was the peacemaker for Amanda. She always tries to smooth over things and make Amanda's life easier. Her other personality, he's more explosive. Charles is her guardian. When Amanda cannot defend herself or feels physically threatened, he surfaces and he can be incredibly violent, so use caution. He broke her husband's arms and fractured his skull multiple times before he died."

A thought came to Wade. "Is he a smoker?" When the doctor confirmed his suspicion, Wade let out a string of curses. The cigarette butts on the shattered glass from Sydney's car made sense now. Tara may have done the damage, but this Charles personality had also been there.

"I think she's already here."

"I was afraid of that. I got a letter a few days ago, saying she was going to, I'll quote her, *'Take back that which was rightfully hers and stolen from her by a whore in the night.'* The writing sounds like Charles to me, his violent nature showing in it. Next, I received a picture of a woman and a young girl walking down a sidewalk. Off in the corner I could make out the name of the school. You have no idea how many East Elementary schools there are in the United States. Then today, in the mail, I received the article from your local paper about the woman who was killed at a diner."

"She's killing women that look like Sydney," Wade mumbled to himself.

"That's what the note indicated. I believe that Charles is the one exacting his vengeance here. Amanda desperately wants her baby back, but she isn't capable of searching for her, or even caring for her if they were reunited. But Charles comes out and will go off like a rabid dog after her heart's desire."

"I think she might have Sydney." It chilled him to the bone to admit that, but neither Sam nor Billy had called to say they'd found her. Mrs. Watts was on the phone, jotting something furiously on a notepad. She didn't look happy as she handed him the paper.

Found her empty car by Connor's field.

"I have to go," Wade ground out through gritted teeth, his anger barely contained.

"Wait!" the woman yelled in desperation.

"She has her!" he shouted, taking his aggression out on this faceless stranger. "I don't think you understand me."

"The girl is who Amanda's after. She claims she wants her daughter back. I have no idea if the child is real or not."

"She's real. I've met her." Wade gripped the phone tighter as his stomach turned.

"Then, Sydney is just a means to an end for her."

"Send me everything you have, including a picture." He thrust the phone at Mrs. Watts and grabbed the other set of keys she offered, bumping into Luke on his way out the door.

"Hey, something's up with Sydney," Luke said jogging to keep up with Wade as he stormed through the parking lot. "She left work early and said she felt like someone was watching her all day. Where the hell is your cruiser?"

Wade stopped in his tracks with a curse. A thousand questions came to him, but in the end, they didn't matter. "Sydney's been kidnapped."

Luke was visibly shaken. "I-I just saw her at the diner."

Wade wrenched open the door of his truck, his fury barely contained. "Found her car, empty, over by the Conner's place. I have to get there and see what else I can find." Desperation made strange bedfellows. Wade swallowed his pride for Sydney's sake. "I need a favor."

"Name it." His instant agreement stopped Wade short. No smart ass comment, no arguing. Maybe they really were moving past their bullshit.

"Go to Sydney's house, see if anyone's there. I have no idea where this person took her, but I think Faith is in danger too. If you see anything, call me. Do not try to intervene. The woman who has her is armed and dangerous."

Luke's eyebrows arched in disbelief. "Woman? I thought she said it was a guy after her."

"I don't have time to explain. Can you do that for me?" Unable to stand still another second, he climbed into the truck and slammed the door. He heard Luke's voice loud and clear through the glass.

"On my way."

Luke pulled out of the parking lot behind him. Wade watched him peel off in the opposite direction. As he sped toward the farm, his fingers tapped a furious rhythm on the wheel. He was relieved to have another person helping in the search, as long as Luke didn't do something stupid like get himself shot.

As he flew down the road, Wade punched numbers into his cell. "Come on, pick up the damn phone." He knew exactly where Sydney's car would be, the desolate stretch where there wasn't a sign of life for miles.

Damn Sydney and her backtracking.

If she had just gone straight home, he thought as he slammed his hand against the wheel.

"What do you want, Wade?" Agnes asked, unamused by the curse he let fly when she finally answered. "Sydney isn't here, you know."

"She's missing."

Her voice was cool as ice. "What are you talking about?"

"I don't have time to explain. I'm on my way to where they found her car." He paused, unsure how the rest of this conversation was going to play out. He only had one shot with Agnes.

"Middlemist Red," Wade said and held his breath not sure what her reaction would be. The silence that followed stopped his heart.

"What did you say?" the strangled question came through the receiver so softly Wade almost didn't recognize Agnes' voice.

"Middlemist Red. Your cheeks were the color of Middlemist Red the night you met George."

"H-He told you?" The quiver in her voice only made this more difficult.

"He wanted me to watch over you when he was gone and he told me if there was danger and I ever needed you to listen and do what I said without hesitation, this was the way to ensure your cooperation. No matter the request."

There was an uncharacteristic sob quickly covered by the rough clearing of her throat. The tough-as-nails version of Agnes Whittman returned to the phone. No one messed with Agnes. "Tell me what to do."

"Take Faith to the safe room. Don't bother denying it, George told me about that, too. The underground one with all the guns. And prepare for anything. Lock yourselves in there and be silent as mice. No matter what you hear, even if it's Sydney. Do not come out until I get there." He could hear her calm and shallow breathing on the other end of the line. "Can you do that, Agnes? Someone has Sydney right now and they want Faith. They will kill her to get to Faith. No matter what, don't come out unless I'm the one with Sydney."

"Done." He could hear her rustling around in the drawers of her kitchen, probably grabbing some last minute supplies.

"You don't have long. It might only be a matter of minutes before they get there."

"Then you better stop talking and let me do what I need to do," she snapped, calling Faith's name away from the phone. "And Wade," she said, the tone of her voice one he knew never to doubt. "I'll protect this girl with my life, but don't you dare try and open that bunker door without first saying that phrase or I'll blow your head off right through the door. Even if you *are* with Sydney."

"Good," Wade said breathing easier knowing Faith would be safe. It was the only thing he could do for Sydney right now. "If I try, I want you to shoot me and anyone else that's around because if I don't say it that means someone with me is coming for Faith, and I can't stop them."

"Done."

CHAPTER 21

WITH A FLICK OF her wrist, a noticeably calmer Marcy signaled Sydney to get out of the car. The gash in her side was seeping blood through her shirt by the time Sydney climbed out of the car. If she ran now, she wouldn't get more than twenty feet before Marcy was on her. She had to be patient, calm, and do whatever Marcy asked. An opportunity would present itself and when it did, Sydney would fight for not only her life, but Faith's as well.

"Don't make a sound," Marcy hissed in her ear as she smiled. Hiding the gun in her waistband Marcy made it look, to anyone who might be peeking out their window, as if they were old friends on a stroll. She even managed to hide Sydney's tied hands with a jacket she pulled from the backseat of the cruiser.

It was cold, and Sydney could see each of her panting breaths fogging up in front of her face as they walked around the car. With the knife in her hand, Marcy led Sydney across the lightly frosted grass of her front yard and over to Mrs. Whittman's door. Diablo barked wildly as they approached. The dog was giving a clear signal to alert her owner that there was a stranger on their property but Marcy didn't hesitate. Sydney prayed Agnes would see the knife or the blood on the surveillance monitors inside and call the police.

Marcy was calm as they made their way up Agnes' driveway—eerily so. The barking dog had no effect on her, her facial expression placid as if she truly were out on an evening stroll, but the woman was on high alert, ready for anything. Her face may have looked relaxed, but her body was as taut as a bowstring.

"Do that cute little knock to tell her it's you." It was terrifying to think how long Marcy might have been following them and how close she got to Faith.

She could have killed me at any time. A shudder went down her spine at the thought. Marcy knew where they lived, when they came home, the routes she drove, where Faith was after school, and those were just the things Sydney was aware of. Any night she could have climbed in the window while Sydney was sleeping, slit her throat, and stolen Faith away, never to be found again. No one ever would have known. So why hadn't she done that rather than risk a sloppy altercation with Sydney?

Wade.

He'd been at the house the last three nights, keeping watch over both of them. He was the reason she was still alive. All the while he was holding her, whispering sweet words in her ear, as he made love to her over and over again, he was protecting her, and neither of them had any idea that there was an unstable woman yards away, watching. What she wouldn't do to feel Wade's arms around her once more.

How had Marcy gotten Wade's car? A terrible question plagued Sydney. Was he still alive? Had Marcy killed him, finally clearing the way for her to come after Faith? If he was dead, Sydney would never recover.

Marcy cut the tie that had been securing Sydney's wrists so she could reach her bloodied hand to the door and tap out the cadence Agnes had taught her. The reddened smear she left on the door was a disgusting reminder of how much blood was flowing down the front of her shirt, but she couldn't look at it. She needed her wits about her, not hysterics. She pushed the pain away and waited for the chance to strike. On the third hit of her fist, the door slowly swung open. Sydney hid her surprise as best she could at the unsecure state of Agnes' home. She never left a door or window unlocked.

Never.

Unless something had happened to her, too. Her trembling hand flew to cover her mouth at the possibility. What did Marcy do? Her worst fears raced through her head. *She killed Agnes and Wade first, then came after me.* That macabre thought turned into panic for Faith's well-being.

"Looks like the old bat was expecting us." Marcy kicked in the door with her boot, mud flying off her sole and crumbling onto the pristine floor. Diablo, the hulking German Sheppard launched herself at Marcy and attacked. One quick slice across the dog's throat ended its life. Blood poured out of its lifeless body and spread out across the floor, forming a horrible red stain. Sydney swallowed a sob while Marcy sneered at the dog. "Sit, Lassie." She kicked the dog aside, slamming the door shut behind them. The super secure home that once was a comfort to Sydney now became her prison. A prison she was trapped inside of with a mad woman.

The coppery smell of the blood made Sydney nauseous, but Marcy was unaffected as she tracked bloody footprints all over the kitchen floor. Sydney leaned against the wall to keep from passing out. That wouldn't help with anything. She needed to focus and be strong right now. Time was running out and Faith needed her.

The house looked the same, no signs of trauma inside, just Agnes' well-lit kitchen. No bodies, no one bound and gagged. Not a single sign of either Faith or Agnes. As Marcy dragged her through the growing puddle of blood, she couldn't help but sigh with relief.

Somehow Agnes had known to leave or hide.

Focusing on the positive, Sydney knew Wade couldn't be dead. If he sensed trouble, there was no doubt he would move heaven and Earth to help her. Sydney was willing to bet her life on it. But she would have to give him time to work. As calmly as possible she stalled and tried to get her mentally unhinged assailant talking.

"M-Marcy, listen." She made the mistake of reaching out and touching the woman's arm. She grabbed Sydney's wrist, twisted her arm, and tripped her to the ground, landing on top of her. Any air that had been in her lungs was driven out, and Sydney found herself wincing in pain as her cheek slammed into the wood floor, blood splashing into her face.

A furious voice hissed in her ear. "Marcy isn't right now, blondie. You're stuck with me, and I promise you, I'm not nearly as nice as that gal." That deep, rough, voice was back making Marcy sound like a stranger again. Sydney closed her eyes as the woman kept talking in her new cadence. It was the same one she had used earlier in the car when she was angry. "Now you're gonna sit in one of these chairs, nice and easy. Put your hands on the top of the table, then you're gonna tell me where they are."

The more Marcy talked, the more Sydney thought she recognized the voice. It was the person who called during Faith's party. The man she assumed was Ronald…or maybe it wasn't. She mulled it all over in her head.

Two ways of talking, two temperaments, two names, two…personalities. Sydney was no psychiatrist, but the woman before her was homicidal and acting like two completely different people. There was a much more masculine tone to her voice now. She'd watched enough TV, and had lived for years with a mentally ill mother, to get an idea of what was going on. Marcy had more than one personality. The question was, how many were there?

On a hunch, she asked, "W-What's your name?" Sydney gasped as the woman rolled off her back and yanked her up by her hair. Tears filled her eyes at the searing pain, but she quickly wiped them away, refusing to show weakness. She planned on fighting with everything she had when the time came. Tears wouldn't help with that, but information would.

"I'm Charles, and I'm *not* the nice one." She retracted the blade on the knife then slipped it back into her pants pocket. It was amazing the way her whole body posture changed when she was Charles. Her legs were farther apart, her shoulders more rounded forward. She gave the collar of the shirt a tug and yanked the top two buttons open, offering a deep sigh of relief as she rolled up the sleeves and pulled out the gun from the holster on her belt.

"Shut up," Charles growled, grabbing her forehead and giving her head a shake as if trying to clear her thoughts. "I know what I'm doing."

While her captor was distracted by her inner demons, Sydney looked around the room for a sign of where Faith and Agnes might be hiding, but found nothing. No clue, no hint, no trail of breadcrumbs for her to follow. She tried to block out the incoherent mutterings and listen for any sort of sound in the house that might give their location away. Sydney wasn't leaving until her daughter and Agnes were with her. However, if Faith was already safely away, then Sydney could run at her first opportunity. She needed something to go on.

The problem was she had no idea what to do.

"Can I have a dish towel?" Sydney asked timidly, hoping to stop some of the bleeding in her side and distract the woman by getting her talking. If she knew what Marcy—or Charles—had planned, she'd be able to better strategize her next move. There had to be something nearby she could use to defend herself if it came to that. She just had to find it.

Charles grabbed a dishrag off the counter and threw it in her face. "Anything else, ma'am? I'm your humble fucking servant."

"No, thank you," she said softly as she pressed it to her side, wincing. At this point, the less she said, the better. Marcy's personality, Charles, was looking for a reason to hit her, and she'd be damned if she'd give it to her.

"Poor baby got a boo-boo?" With a disgusted snarl, she ripped open her shirt and bared her horribly scarred torso. "You wanna see some messed up shit? Look at this train wreck. This is what livin' with Ronald for years does to you." The scars crisscrossed her abdomen before disappearing around her side. She'd obviously had no medical attention for the wounds, the jagged scars thick and raised, even all these years later. "And that's just the stuff you can see on the outside." She tapped her temple. "You don't want to know the nuthouse rolling around in here. Right, guys?"

The words, "I'm sorry," fell from Sydney's mouth before she could stop herself. And she truly was. No one should have to live that way, but she wanted out of this house and away from this woman. Sydney tried to get a look at the clock but Charles stepped in front of it blocking her view. She pleaded in her head, *Wade, where are you?*

There was a wild look in Charles' eyes that nearly stopped her heart. "I don't want your pity, you whore. I want Amanda's daughter back!" The gun slammed down onto the table beside her and she held her breath, certain the thing was going to misfire and kill her at any second. "Where are they?"

The name Amanda echoed in her head and chilled her to the bone. The haze of her concussion finally started to lift. Amanda was the woman who had married Ronald months after that night in the cornfield. But what if she had been there when Marcy gave her the baby, buried beneath her other personalities. A baby that came from her body, but maybe not…her mind.

All the puzzle pieces began to fall into place and the image they created was more horrific than she could have imagined.

Marcy, Charles…and Amanda Washington were the same person. Three distinct personalities trapped in one body. So many things suddenly made sense. The realization hit her, and she wanted to vomit. For all these years she had kidnapped another woman's baby. A woman she knew existed. One she could have returned Faith to at any time. If she had, would Amanda have been this disturbed, or would she have been able to pull herself together for the sake of her child?

"I asked you a question. Where are they?"

Sydney buried her guilt. Right now, she needed to stay alive. "I have no idea."

"Liar!" Charles grabbed Sydney's elbow and bent her arm at an awkward angle, sending an intense pain shooting through her shoulder. If she applied any more pressure Sydney was certain her shoulder would dislocate. She gasped for breath and swallowed her pain.

"You've been watching Agnes," Sydney gasped, the darkness threatening to close in on her. If she fainted, she was dead. She had no doubt Charles would see her as useless and kill her in a heartbeat. She fought to find her voice, sweat beading on her forehead from the intense pain.

"This place is a vault, you have to know that. She has even more hidey holes in this house than you can imagine and she isn't big on sharing that information."

"You'd never leave Amanda's daughter and not know where she was."

"When I left her here, I knew she was safe. That's all I ever wanted for her. To be safe. From Ronald." Sydney took a big chance bringing him up, the mere mention of the name potentially enraging Charles, but it was the one bit of common ground they had. Their fear of Ronald brought them together and Sydney was frantic to make a connection with her. One that would allow her to see Sydney as a mother, not a monster. The death grip Charles had on her elbow loosened and Sydney took the opportunity to pull her arm away.

"You have no idea what you're talking about." The woman shook her head from side to side, not wanting to hear Sydney's words.

"He was awful, evil. That night on the road, you asked me to take her. You begged me to save her for you and keep her away from him." Tears streamed down her cheeks, desperate to get through to the unstable woman. "I thought he killed you. All these years…" She made eye contact with the woman, hoping some of what she was saying was resonating with her and that, even with her thin grasp of reality, she would remember what happened that night with some clarity.

"I-I tried to take you with me, remember? I wanted to take you and Faith to the hospital."

Marcy's body shook and she stumbled, bumping into the chair and clutching her head. Sydney thought about running, but then Marcy's eyes popped open. Eyes that were wide and frightened as they took in the kitchen in wonder. "Jenny. Her name is Jenny." A new, calm and docile voice came out of Marcy's mouth. One that gave Sydney a little hope.

"Marcy?"

"N-No, I'm Amanda. And my daughter's name is Jenny." The woman's eyes fixated on the blood and the dog. "I-I did that, didn't I?" Sydney nodded, afraid to move much or say anything out loud, unsure how the woman before her would respond. The woman, Amanda, looked at the gun in her hand and flung it onto the kitchen counter like it was radioactive. "Why won't he just stop hurting people?" she mumbled to herself.

At least for the moment, Sydney felt safer.

"What's the date?" Amanda asked, her hand fluttering to her throat as if she had forgotten how to speak.

"It's the fifth. November fifth."

"Four weeks," she gasped, tears welling up and spilling from her eyes, "I was gone four weeks this time." Her forehead wrinkled as she looked at Sydney. "You." She stumbled forward again, unable to operate her own body. "You're the one who has her."

"I didn't take her, Marcy begged me…" Amanda raised a hand, halting Sydney mid-sentence.

"I don't know how long I have left. Do you have a picture of her?"

Sydney frantically patted her pockets hoping she could stay on Amanda's good side long enough to escape. "My phone. It's back in my car but Agnes might have a picture somewhere." Carefully Sydney reached for one of the drawers hoping to find a picture, or get closer to the gun. At this point she didn't care, she just wanted to find her daughter and get the hell out of there.

The first drawer she opened had dishtowels in it, no hidden gun or false bottom, much to Sydney's dismay. Amanda stood between her and both the gun and the kitchen door, so running was out of the question. Charles could come back at any minute and she needed to think fast and keep Amanda as calm as she could. Hopefully she could use Amanda's guilt against her. She inched her way toward the drawer that she knew held the silverware.

Amanda moaned and stumbled, clutching her head as she slid to the ground at Sydney's feet. *Just like she had all those years ago.* A shiver slid down Sydney's spine at the memory, and she jumped away from the woman like she had done back then, reliving the terror.

Leaning back against the cabinets, Amanda offered Sydney a teary smile. "What does she look like? Describe my baby girl to me. Let me see her in my mind, just one more time." The sorrow and desperation in her voice were heart wrenching. Sydney looked away and saw the gun on the counter a few feet past Amanda. If she took advantage of Amanda's sadness, it was her chance to escape. She slowly moved closer, offering tiny details about Faith with each step.

"She has gorgeous brown curls. The color of your hair, actually. It's past her shoulders and a real bear to comb in the morning." She was about four feet away from the gun that was teetering on the edge of the kitchen sink like a beacon. "Her eyes are big and round, the color of sapphires, a very deep shade of blue, and she has the sweetest dimple on her left cheek."

The deranged woman grabbed her hand, pulling her to the ground beside her, putting Sydney further from the gun she so desperately wanted in her hand. She didn't appear to want to hurt Sydney like she had before. Now she was clinging to Sydney for dear life, her hands trembling uncontrollably. "Is she happy?"

As she sat on the floor, the scene surrounding her was surreal. The woman beside her was back from the dead. All around them the floor was crimson from Diablo's blood. And Sydney's. Bloody footprints tracked over the floor in a macabre trail. She winced as her fingers brushed against her injured side. Sydney's blood loss was starting to affect her more, her vision coming and going if she moved too fast. Instead of shoving Amanda out of the way and running for the door, she looked at the broken woman before her and did the unthinkable. She answered the question because it took more energy to avoid it. In a twisted way, she felt she owed Amanda that much for all the joy Faith had brought to her life.

"She's very happy. Ronald never touched her, he never hurt her. You saw to that, Amanda. You protected her." She tried to smile encouragingly but when Amanda tipped her head back and started mumbling to herself she knew another personality was about to emerge and depending on who it was, her time was limited. "Let me go and I can continue to make her happy. I promise that I'll spend the rest of my life putting a smile on her beautiful face."

"That's very sweet of you, dear," she said in a motherly tone. "I knew you'd be good for the little one the night I gave her to you."

"Marcy?" Hope spiked through Sydney with this personality's return. "You're back." She was at least reasonable and knew Sydney didn't steal Faith, so maybe she was her best chance of getting out of here before someone else was hurt. Unfortunately for Sydney, Marcy didn't release the death grip on her wrist or let her go.

"I wish the others would have agreed with me. We could have spared ourselves so much trouble these last few years. Charles is terribly blood-thirsty, I'm afraid." She shook her head, reflecting on whatever horrors the personalities living within Amanda Washington had committed. "I tried to keep him from finding you, but eventually, it was going to happen. I'm glad the girl has you. Amanda never could have cared for her, and Ronald would have done terrible things." Marcy shuddered and bile rose up the back of Sydney's throat at the mere thought of Ronald being anywhere near Faith.

"I never meant to keep her from you, but I truly believed you died that night," Sydney said, inching her body down the base cabinets and toward the sink. When the room started to spin, Sydney closed her eyes and took a deep breath.

It was time to make her escape. She was running out of time. The police hadn't shown up with guns drawn, and there was no sign of Wade which was terrifying her. What if he had approached Marcy, not knowing who she was and Charles came out and attacked him? Wade would have been caught off guard and wouldn't have stood much of a chance. He could be alone and hurt somewhere, or worse. The shaking started again as the fear consumed her.

Where are you, Wade? She screamed in her head and her heart, on the verge of a panic attack.

There still hadn't been any sign of Agnes or Faith. On one hand, it was a relief to know that they were either far away or hidden so well that Sydney was confident Marcy would never be able to find them. Unless she burned the house to the ground. Sydney pushed that thought aside;

Marcy and company would never jeopardize Faith's life. That was the only thing keeping her from hysterics.

If she ran now, there was a chance she could get away and find Wade before it was too late. Together, they could come back, take care of Marcy, and get Faith safely out of the house if she moved fast enough. If she took too long, there was always the possibility Marcy could find Faith and disappear with the little girl forever. While she decided what she was going to do, she again mumbled, "I thought he killed you."

Marcy let out a rough chuckle. "Sure you did." She sneered in disbelief, her personality again shifting. From the change in posture and hatred in her eyes, Sydney knew Charles was back. It set off every panic alarm Sydney had in her body. Her eyes were crazed, but calculating. "I'm holdin' up pretty damn well for a dead person. Don't you agree?" Charles raised a bloodied fist and Sydney braced herself for a blow that never came. "No worms crawling, feasting on me. Ronald ain't so lucky."

Sydney took a deep breath and fought to clear the lightheaded feeling that was coming over her. She couldn't wait or try to reason her way out of this anymore. She was losing too much blood. With a burst of speed, she stood up, spun and reached for the gun. She watched in horror as it fell into the sink because of her clumsy movements. The gun clanged into the metal basin, Sydney chasing it clumsily as it slid and twisted away from her hand. When she finally had a finger on the gun, Sydney was rammed in the back, the weight of the woman behind her forcing her to bend over the counter. Her head dangled into the sink basin while her injured side screamed in pain. Charles used Amanda's height and a surge of insanity-driven adrenaline to hold Sydney down forcing her long blonde hair to swirl down the drain as she was pinned in place. The gun was ripped out of her hand and slid well out of her reach. She found herself once again, defenseless.

"If I turn on the disposal, I can watch the hair be ripped from your head," Charles growled in her ear. Sydney could feel the pinch of the knife at her neck. "Did you like the present I left you at the diner?"

Sydney forgot about the pain and the danger and shoved back as hard as she could, outraged. Weak from blood-loss, her thrashing did little to dislodge the woman who continued to laugh and tighten her grip while Sydney's blood pooled on the counter. She didn't know how much longer she could fight.

Sydney tried to no avail to get her feet under her, to kick Charles, but she was bent so far over the counter, her toes were barely touching the ground. She had no leverage to do anything and was at the mercy of Amanda's alternate personality, which terrified her. Charles was more than a brute, he was deadly.

"Put your hands behind your back. Make a move for the gun again and I'll slit your throat." The zip tie stung as it was slipped around her wrists, cutting off circulation to her hands once again. Sydney was shoved into a chair while Charles tucked away the knife and methodically checked all of Mrs. Whittman's security cameras.

"I'm taking Amanda's daughter back." With a mocking smile she added, "And then killing you." Charles wasted no time and dragged Sydney to her feet, the gun now in hand. "Now, let's go find Jenny."

CHAPTER 22

CHARLES LED SYDNEY THROUGH the house, barking out Faith's name, doing nothing to disguise the hatred that contorted Amanda Washington's beautiful face each time she said the name. They systematically searched the rooms with Charles banging on the walls and slamming a foot onto the floor, listening for any differences in the density of the surfaces as she hunted for a hidden door.

Charles had obviously done some research on Agnes.

After some searching, Charles managed to find one of the hidey holes in the guest bedroom that Faith often slept in when she was there. Sydney held her breath, praying that Agnes and Faith were far, far away from the house. If they were on the other side of the door, she was afraid that, in a fit of rage, Charles would kill them all. Sydney screamed when Charles shot open the lock, terrified that Faith might have been on the other side. When Charles threw open the door and there was no one inside, Sydney sagged with relief. Charles gave no reaction but a single curse under her breath.

"I'm getting tired of this. If you can't help me find them then I have no use for you, blondie." She motioned with the gun. "Kneel down, let's get this over with."

"N-No, no wait. I do know of one safe room, but there's a key we need to find because it's a steel door. I-I'm just not sure where the key is." Sydney had no idea where the lie came from, but it was enough to make Charles pause and buy her some more time.

"Then what good are you?"

Where Amanda was overly emotional, Charles was controlled rage. Marcy hinted that Charles had been the one to stand up to Ronald and the thought that this personality had been able to inflict damage and ultimately kill someone as violent as Ronald was beyond frightening. Faith was probably the only person safe from Charles. She'd kill Sydney and Agnes without a second thought.

The only way to defend herself was to find a weapon, and fast. She had to make a guess where Agnes was most likely to have an extra gun lying around.

"It has to be in the kitchen. She spends most of her time at that table eating and playing solitaire," Sydney said in a rush, praying Charles would bite. There had to be a weapon in the kitchen, if only she could find it before it was too late.

She seemed to consider it, and thanks to George Whittman's excellent home construction skills, Charles didn't know where else to look, so she agreed. Annoyed, but willing.

"Tick, tock. You have two minutes." Charles shoved her into the kitchen and smiled as if it was going to be great entertainment. She tucked the gun into the back waistband of her jeans and leaned against the counter to watch Sydney's frantic search. She pulled out her knife, clicking it open and motioning Sydney to turn around. With a flick of her wrist she cut the tie, and Sydney had use of her hands again. It felt like a thousand pins and needles were stabbing her as blood flow returned to her fingers but she didn't pause. She rummaged through the drawers, praying she'd find a key. Or a gun.

At this point, either would work.

It was difficult to search, not knowing what she'd find inside each drawer. She knew Agnes would never leave a gun out where Faith might find it, so it wouldn't be in plain sight, but she'd have one handy, some-where. The butter knife wasn't much of an option. With the way Charles was handling the huge blade in her hand, Sydney would never get the chance to use it. She quickly searched the drawers she hadn't opened, hoping to find some random key she could distract Charles with until she could find a weapon. She found a box of bullets in the back of one drawer. Sydney knew little about guns, but she slipped two out of the package, holding them inconspicuously between her fingers as she con-tinued to search for a gun that would hopefully be able to fire them.

"Find the goddamn key!" Charles barked as she continued to click the knife open and shut, open and shut. The noise grated on Sydney's frayed nerves. All of the drawers had been searched, so Sydney scoured the counter. The one thing that stood out and was large enough to hide anything was the electric fryer.

"Thirty seconds." Charles stared at his watch, unwilling to give her any extra time. When Charles turned to check out the security monitors, Sydney dove at the fryer, her hands shaking as she threw open the lid. Her hand hit a bulky metal object and she nearly cried with relief. But she had no idea if it was loaded or if she needed to put in the bullets she found. She should have paid more attention to Agnes at the firing range.

Charles noticed her fishing around and appeared amused watching Sydney flounder. Her eyes locked on the bullets that had somehow fallen out of Sydney's hands and were rolling on the counter.

"So," she pulled the gun from her waistband and pointed it at Sydney's head, "I'm guessing you found a gun." She tsked Sydney's lame efforts at subterfuge. The sad thing was, if Sydney wasn't so terrified, she'd probably have done the same to herself.

"Think you can shoot me before I shoot you?" Charles laughed at the spilled ammunition. "I know my gun is loaded, and you…don't."

Loud banging came from the front door, interrupting Charles' tirade. "Agnes, it's Luke. Open up. Hurry, Agnes! Sydney's in trouble." He con-tinued pounding on the door and yelling Agnes' name to the point that Sydney thought his knuckles must be bleeding. Then he went silent.

And all the while, Charles smirked at the monitor.

"Another man desperate to save you, Sydney. Hope it works out better for him than it did for the cop." Sydney tried to remain calm. She knew that was the best option, but at the mention of Wade, all her anxiety came out in a rush of anger.

"Where is Wade? What did you do to him?"

"This." Without a moment's hesitation Charles unlocked the front door and fired a single shot at Luke. Sydney watched in horror as he collapsed onto the ground in front of the house. It had all happened so fast, Sydney hadn't had any time to react. She hadn't even been able to scream in warning to Luke. On the monitor, she could see the blood staining the sidewalk around him.

"How could you?"

Charles shrugged and locked the door back up. "Quite easily. All those years brawling with Ronald taught me well. That guy out there means nothing to me. The only people I care about are Amanda and Jenny. Everyone else can kiss my ass." Charles was so far gone that she hadn't even flinched as she shot a man in cold blood. God only knew what she had done to Wade.

"You're out of time, blondie." She pointed the gun at Sydney's face. Inside the fryer, Sydney's blood covered fingers blindly grasped the other gun, releasing the safety. It was time for her to act. She said a silent prayer and readied herself. If she was going to die, by God, she was going to die a fighter.

"You never should have taken Jenny." Without pause, Charles pulled the trigger.

Sydney closed her eyes and waited for the impact of the bullet, the last six years with Faith flashing before her eyes. She wouldn't change a second of it, but she knew she'd die with one regret. She'd never told Wade how she felt about him. That somehow in the last few crazy weeks, she'd fallen desperately in love with him. She couldn't keep a peaceful smile from spreading across her lips as she waited for the explosion of the bullet leaving the chamber.

She loved Wade.

But instead of a horrific death, she was met with silence. Her eyes flew open and she found Charles angrily pulling the trigger of the gun, but the only sound was an insipid clicking.

The gun never fired.

"Damn you, Marcy." Charles hurled the useless gun to the floor and reached for the knife. "You stupid, bitch. It's no problem, I'll just gut you instead." She lunged, the knife slashing across Sydney's arm as she tried to defend herself.

Charles was rearing back for another attack when Sydney fired her gun, and by some miracle, hit Charles. Sydney wasn't exactly sure where the bullet made contact since she had closed her eyes, something Agnes would kill her for later, but it had worked. Charles dropped to the ground like a stone. Blood seeped from her side as she lay on the ground looking more like a sleeping child than a blood-thirsty murderer.

Sydney numbly stood in the kitchen, staring at the woman who had given birth to her daughter. A woman she might have just killed. How would she ever explain it all to Faith? She'd just taken a life.

Sydney ran over to the sink and threw up.

She set the gun on the counter and splashed water on her face, trying to keep herself from going into shock. As she wiped her mouth she had a decision to make. Stay or go? She had to find Faith, she couldn't leave if there was even the slightest chance she was still inside the house. She grabbed the phone to call the police but there was no dial tone. Furious, she threw it at the wall and paced through the kitchen, her eyes avoiding the monitors. The last thing she wanted was to be reminded that Luke was dead a few feet outside the door because of her.

And still no sign of the police. Or Wade.

Where was he?

She hadn't allowed herself to think about him much, but the fact that he hadn't driven his truck through the wall trying to get to her made her heart sink. Charles must have killed him. That, or he was so severely injured that he couldn't get to her. There was no other explanation as to where he could be or how Marcy had gotten his cruiser. Nothing else would have kept him away. With a rage and fury she had never known, she screamed.

"Faith!" Sydney ran through the house, shouting her name and calling out to Agnes, begging them to come out. "We have to get out of here, hurry!" But the house remained silent. She ran into Agnes' bedroom thinking that would be the most likely place for another safe room. Crazed, she began pounding on the walls and jumping up and down on the floor trying to get their attention wherever they were hiding. Hysterical and now desperate to find her daughter, she grabbed a bookend and started tearing into the wall, hoping to reveal a secret panel or something that would lead her to Faith. Tears streamed down her face as she clawed at the drywall.

"We have to go. Come out! I swear it's safe now, but we need to go. Faith, where are you?" Her desperate pleas were met with silence. She threw the bookend across the room, her anger finally flaring at being left to deal with all of this alone.

He swore he'd protect her and keep them safe. How many times had he told her he wouldn't let anything happen to them? But when she needed him most, he was nowhere to be found.

"Where are you, Wade?" she screamed to the heavens as if somehow he was going to magically appear. "I *need* you!" The possibility of Wade's death sent Sydney staggering.

As she frantically scanned the room one more time for a clue as to where Faith might be, something on Agnes' dresser caught her attention. Right in the center of the walnut antique was a framed picture of Sydney, Faith, Melissa and Agnes, one they had taken at the Fall Festival. The four of them looked so happy together as they stood next to the town's largest pumpkin, which she remembered had tipped the scales at just over four hundred pounds this year.

So much had changed since then.

She was tracing the elaborate swirl along the edge of the frame when an odd thought popped into her head. If only she'd known this picture was here, she could have showed it to Amanda and let her see her daughter once before she killed her. She could see so much of Amanda in Faith. All the emotions she had buried bubbled to the surface.

"Oh, Faith, what did I do?" Sydney asked as she reached up and clutched the frame to her chest.

"You left the gun in the kitchen, idiot," Charles laughed from behind her. "And now you're going to die." She stood inside the bedroom, blood dripping down her shoulder where Sydney's bullet had made impact. The arm hung limp at her side but the other had a firm grasp on the gun as the barrel pointed at Sydney's head.

Sydney considered making a run for the door when there was a flash and the gun fired.

She screamed then fell back, hitting her head on the dresser. In the darkness that followed, she heard Wade shouting her name, telling her to run. She staggered to her feet and saw him wrestling with Charles for the gun.

"Get out of here, run to the front door!" Wade barked out the order as the gun skidded out of their reach and Charles connected with a nasty right hook to Wade's face.

She'd never been so happy and terrified to see someone in her whole life.

"She also has a knife, be careful!" Sydney screamed, unwilling to walk away and leave Wade on his own with a crazy woman who had shown near superhuman strength earlier. The silver of the knife flashed and soon Wade had smears of red all over his chest and arms as his skin was ripped open by Charles with each movement of the knife.

His eyes met hers and she saw how desperate he was to get her to safety. He would take care of Charles and whoever else might pop out of Amanda's sick head. He had to, because Sydney couldn't imagine her life without him in it any more.

Wade knocked the knife out of Charles' hand, blood spattering as it crashed into the wall beside them. Somehow, Charles spun and lunged for the gun that was then immediately pointed up at Sydney. She was running from the room when Wade shouted her name then a gunshot rang out behind her. A sharp pain hit her side and then she had the sensation of falling. For a second, she thought she had been shot, but then she realized it wasn't a bullet that hit her. Wade had tackled her to the ground, knocking the breath out of her as he catapulted her into the hallway.

As fast as he had hit her, he was gone. The weight of his body vanished, leaving Sydney disoriented and shivering on the ground. She could hear things breaking in the bedroom and tried to go help, but her vision was blurred by the blood running down her face and into her eyes. There was more commotion, then a single gunshot rang out.

A chilling silence followed.

The thought of anything happening to him was too much to process. "Wade!" Sydney closed her eyes and screamed his name until her throat burned. Sydney felt herself pulled down the hallway. She tried to fight at first but when she felt the warm press of Wade's body she relaxed, and didn't stop moving until they hit the kitchen.

"Are you okay? You're bleeding." He was out of breath as his hands frantically ripped open her shirt exposing the deep puncture wound from where she had been stabbed in the car earlier and the other cuts from Charles' knife. He grabbed a towel from the counter and began wiping away the blood so he could get a better look at her injuries. He held the towel in place and applied pressure to the one on her abdomen to try and slow the bleeding.

"We have to go. We have to get out of here!" Sydney dug her fingers into Wade's shoulder and knew she was hysterical as she tried to writhe out of his grasp, but she couldn't help herself. She'd been trapped in this house with a crazy woman and all she wanted was to get herself, and Wade, to safety. "We have to find Faith before we leave. Do you know where she is?"

Never in her life had she been so torn. She wanted to be leave and run away from this house, but she *needed* her daughter. No matter how scared she was, Faith was probably more frightened and she'd die before she'd let Marcy or Charles get her hands on Faith.

"Where's the gun?" Sydney asked. Wade tightened his grip on her, holding her in place. She had to make him understand, they had to be able to protect themselves. Charles wanted them all dead. "Did you leave it in the bedroom? We have to go back for it."

"You're not going in there." His voice was stern and calm, the complete opposite of Sydney's agitated state. Wade's eyes roamed over her face, his jaw clenching as he released her with one hand to wipe the blood off her forehead.

Desperate to get away from the awful scene around them, she pushed him away. "Stop. We have to get Faith out of here, Marcy will come back."

He looked her right in the eye and gave a single shake of his head. "She's dead. I killed her." Sydney's eyes roamed over his pale face. The exertion from the fight and blood loss was starting to take its toll on him physically.

"S-She had the gun and w-was going to shoot me," Sydney stammered, unable to stop shaking. Everything had happened so fast there hadn't been time to process everything, but now it hit her how close she had come to dying.

Wade shook his head. "I pushed you into the hall and then went back." Sydney let out a strangled gasp at his admission. "I got the gun away from her and killed her. A shot to the head. She's dead, Sydney. And she can't hurt you, or Faith, anymore."

It was too good to be true. All these years, whenever she thought she was safe, the danger would return. Could it really all be over? She almost didn't dare hope. "Are you sure, Wade?"

"I wouldn't lie to you about this. She's dead. She'll never hurt you or Faith again." The truth was in his eyes. Any doubts she'd had vanished when she saw the look on his face. Her happiness was short-lived. "Luke!" Wade yelled, still tending her wounds.

"H-He's dead, Wade. Charles shot him." The words stung as they came from her mouth, the guilt she felt a bitter reminder of her part in his death.

"He's too stubborn to be dead," Wade grumbled as he stormed to the front door and threw open the locks. Luke limped in, his thigh bleeding through his jeans. "Send in Sam and Billy. Then tell the ambulance it's safe to come now."

Luke nodded. The pain appeared to be more than he wanted to admit. He gave Sydney a brave smile and tried to lighten the mood when he noticed her concern. "Chicks dig scars, I hear."

"You're okay?" The words came out as a strangled whisper. "I thought you were dead."

"He's fine. He was wearing a vest. If she'd have shot him in the chest, he wouldn't have had a mark on him," Wade said thumping Luke in the chest for good measure.

"Next time you need help, you go cause the diversion and I'll save the beautiful woman."

Wade offered Luke his hand with a genuine smile on his face and the two shook hands. "Agreed."

Luke stepped out of the house and Wade returned to her side, inspecting her other injuries. All the while he worked on her, blood ran down his arms from the gashes Charles had inflicted. His wounds dripped blood onto the floor at his feet, but he didn't seem to notice the pain he had to be feeling. His entire focus was on Sydney.

"You're bleeding, and your eye is swelling shut. You need a doctor, Wade."

He kissed her forehead. "I'm fine."

"No, you're not! Those cuts…there are so many of them and blood's everywhere. You could have a concussion—" Her hysterical rant was cut off by his massive arms wrapping tightly around her.

"I'm fine."

"She said she shot you like she shot Luke." Sydney shuddered against his chest.

"She lied."

"How'd you get into the house?"

"Secret passage way."

Sydney sat back in surprise. "Seriously?"

"Yes," Wade said with a grin. He wiped the blood from her face with such tenderness, it melted her heart. But it wasn't over yet. And they still had to find Faith.

"Faith." Her daughter's name flew out in a rush. Her heart rate speeding up as the panic returned. "W-We have to find her. I-I can't find my baby. I looked everywhere, Wade." Sydney broke down into hysterics, the emotions she had kept hidden overwhelming her. The pain, the fear, and the desperation were too much to contain. Her past had caught up with her and there was enough death and destruction in Agnes' house to prove it. Every awful thing she ever imagined happening paled in comparison to the truth as she looked around at the blood stained kitchen.

However, in Wade's arms, she knew it was finally safe to let it all go. So she cried, and screamed, and wailed until she nearly hyperventilated, and he held her through it all.

With a gentle strength, he held onto her as tightly as he could, rocking her back and forth like a child, telling her she was safe. He knew where Faith was hidden and he promised her that her daughter was fine. But even his reassurance couldn't ease the tears.

"I was so scared for you," Wade admitted when Sydney's sobs had finally run their course. "George had built a bolt hole, but the door wouldn't give." He shuddered. "I was afraid I'd make noise prying it open so I had Luke start banging on the door to distract Amanda and cover up any sounds you might hear. I didn't know if I'd get to you in time. I damn near ripped the door off its anchors, but the moment it opened, I ran all the way here." Sydney glanced down at his hands and saw his bloody fingers were horribly swollen and bruised. Proof of how hard he tried to reach her.

"I love you." The words had been at the forefront of her mind since the moment he rushed into Agnes' bedroom to save her. Now they slipped effortlessly from her lips, without regret or hesitation. In that moment, the wide smile that crossed Wade's face assured her that everything would be all right. They would be all right.

"I love you, too."

"Oh, Wade," she gasped, caught off guard for a moment by his admission. Then Sydney kissed him, her head still spinning with the knowledge that he loved her too. It wasn't the trauma of the evening or the fear she had felt, it was the knowledge that he was someone she could count on, in any situation for the rest of her life. He'd seen her at her worst and stood by her side. And loved her. How did she get so lucky?

"When I thought something happened to you…" Her voice trailed off, unable to find the words to express the fear and anguish she felt. A hollow feeling filled her at the mere thought, but then Wade cradled her face in his hands and kissed the pain away.

"Nothing on this Earth could ever keep me from you. I'll always come back to you, Sydney." The sincerity and strength behind his words left no doubt in her mind: he was the one. There would never be anyone else. They were going to make a wonderful life together, with Faith.

But first they had to end this ugliness and face whatever legal issues stood in their way. As if reading her mind and sensing her worry, Wade offered her a smile.

"It's over."

Was it really? Amanda Washington was dead along with Charles and Marcy. Wade had killed them and now the police were going to be involved. It was only a matter of time before the truth of it all came out. It was only a matter of time before there was a chance Sydney could lose Faith. For good.

"I need Faith." With a wince, Sydney pushed herself to her feet, the edge in her voice not going unnoticed by Wade.

"I know this is taking a while, but I don't want Faith to be scared when she sees you. She's a smart kid and is going to know something's up. You are cut and bruised from head to toe, Syd. I don't want to scare her so let's get you cleaned up a little more before we see her. I swear on my life, she's safe."

Wade asked Sam to go look around the house for a clean shirt for Sydney. Luke happened to have a spare sweatshirt in his car and brought that in for Wade so he could get rid of his shredded T-shirt.

Numb, Sydney sat in a chair and drank a large glass of water while Wade tended to the rest of her cuts as best he could. The paramedics quickly wrapped the worst of her injuries but agreed to let Wade transport her to the hospital as soon as she saw Faith. She had a number of visible cuts and scrapes that they wouldn't be able to hide from Faith, but at least the bleeding had let up and she wasn't as dizzy anymore.

"When we see Faith, we'll tell her there was an accident and we're fine but you need to spend the night in the hospital, okay?" Wade watched her reaction closely, making sure she felt like composed enough to see Faith without terrifying her. "Are you ready?"

"Absolutely," she murmured, lacing her fingers in his outstretched hand.

She tried not to wince as she moved. Now that the adrenaline was gone, her injuries seemed to hurt a lot more than they had earlier. He led her out of the kitchen and toward the guest bedroom where Charles had found the safe room. Sydney shook her head vehemently. "She's not in there. Earlier C-Charles found the room but they weren't there."

"Actually, they were. She just didn't look closely enough." Wade led her inside the safe room and pulled back the door all the way, exposing the small five by five room. He ran his finger along a nearly invisible seam in the concrete. Finding what he was looking for, he smiled and pressed a tiny black button.

"Middlemist Red, Agnes. Middlemist Red." There was such relief in his voice as he pulled Sydney against his chest and kissed the top of her head. He wasn't the least bit surprised when the concrete moved to the side and he found Agnes standing at the top of a narrow staircase, with a shotgun aimed directly at his chest.

"Better safe than sorry," she said with a shrug as she lowered her weapon. "Jesus, you two look like hell. But I'm damn glad to see you."

They followed her into a huge underground bunker that probably took up half the yard beside her house. It was enormous, stocked with enough food to last a few years from Sydney's guess. It had all the amenities of home as well as a full arsenal of weapons locked up somewhere, she heard Agnes explaining to Wade. Just then she saw Faith curled up in a beanbag chair watching a movie on the tiny television in the corner. The headphones on her head kept her from even noticing they had walked into the bunker.

"Is the woman dead?" Agnes asked, startling Sydney. She motioned to the tiny monitor that showed not only the guest room but the safe room as well. "I saw her drag you in there, but I knew she'd never find the door to the bunker." She beamed with pride. "My George was one hell of a construction man."

"He was at that," Wade said ruefully as he held out his bloodied hands. "I had a heck of a time breaking into the bolt hole he put in the garage."

"The old coot told you about the tunnel, too? Sonofabitch, that man couldn't keep a secret for anything." With a teary laugh Agnes pulled them both into a hug. "I was so scared for the two of you. And if you tell anyone I said that, I'll smack you both."

"I cannot ever thank you enough for what you did for Faith today, Agnes. She's my whole world. I hope you know that, and remember that even after you f-find out what I did to bring all this upon us."

Agnes touched her face gently, careful to avoid her many cuts and bruises. "I don't care what you did. There's nothing that's going to change how I feel about you. We're family. Now and forever."

They embraced and shared a more tears until Faith finally noticed they were in the room. She yanked off the headphones and ran over, stopping a few feet short.

"Mommy! Wade! What happened to you?" Her blue eyes were wide with worry as she looked at their injuries.

With careful movements, Wade crouched down in front of her and smiled. "Hi, doll. We were in a bit of an accident. I want to take your mom to the hospital to see if she needs any stitches. Would that be okay?"

Faith's beautiful eyes looked back and forth between them, trying to process the cuts on her mother's face and Wade's hands. Sydney knew if she looked half as bad as Wade, Faith was probably terrified, but to her credit, she didn't act like it.

"Are you okay, Mommy?" She took a few steps closer, nervously chewing on her lower lip.

"Yes, baby. I'm good, but I could really use a hug." When she opened her arms the little girl smiled and gingerly wrapped her arms around Sydney's waist. "I love you, Faith, don't ever forget that."

"I love you too, Mommy. Forever and always."

EPILOGUE

SYDNEY PACED OUTSIDE THE courtroom, the click of her heels echoing throughout the marble cave that surrounded them. Her arms remained tightly wrapped around her chest as if she were physically trying to hold herself together. Wade calmly sat on a bench with his elbows resting on his knees, watching her teeter on the edge of a nervous breakdown.

"Syd, come here for a minute and then you can get back to wearing a hole in the floor." He held his hand out to her and smiled.

She was a ball of nerves waiting for the lawyers and the judge to decide their fate. The men and women on the other side of the door had the power to either make her the happiest woman alive or to literally tear her heart from her chest and never let her see Faith again. Either way, when they came out, her life was going to be forever changed.

The not knowing was killing her.

"I don't know what I'll do if—" she started, but Wade cut her off, silencing her with a tender kiss.

"We aren't going to talk like that. You've done everything they asked. We both have."

Time had seemed to slow down over the last few months as they had struggled to sort the whole situation out. Sydney had been arrested the moment she was discharged from the hospital. Wade had been her rock and stayed by her side through it all, until he, too, had been named in Amanda's death. Some young DA looking to make a name for himself tried to paint the picture that Wade had killed Amanda so Sydney could keep Faith. It was thrown out of court, but it forced Wade to stay in Missouri and tie up loose ends while Sydney had been sent back to Montana to face her charges.

David Post, Wade's friend from Boston who took her case without hesitation, was every bit the brilliant lawyer she had hoped and prayed he was. He managed to get Agnes appointed as Faith's foster parent, provided she moved to Montana while all of this was being settled. He even managed to get Sydney supervised visitation once a week with her little girl. It was difficult to see her so infrequently, but considering that she thought she might never see her again after that night, Sydney was grateful for every second she could get.

Wade came to Montana as soon as he could and he brought with him Pete and Cara who closed the diner for a few days once a month so they could stay with Sydney. Never in her life had she known such unconditional love and support as she did in the days after returning to Montana. Even though she was terrified and heartbroken about being away from Faith, she knew that, no matter what, she had people in her life who loved her.

And that would get her through whatever may happen.

"Did you talk to Faith this morning?" Wade asked, trying to occupy her mind with something more pleasant for a while as they waited.

"I did," Sydney laughed and ticked off all the messages Faith had told her to give to Wade. "She says hello, she misses you, and of course, she wants to know when you're going to come over again. She has a new recipe she wants you to try."

Wade laughed and shook his head. "It can't be any worse than the marshmallow and sunflower seed creation she made me eat last time." He poked Sydney in the side. "She takes after her mother."

He meant the words to be teasing, but all they did was bring tears to her eyes. She so desperately wanted to be Faith's mother. Legally and irrevocably. She glanced at the door.

"Did you talk to Melissa, too?"

"Yes. Thunderstorms in New York have grounded her flight. She'll be in tomorrow. Poor thing sounded exhausted." Melissa had flown home the minute she heard about Sydney's arrest. She put everything on hold and came back to support her friend. It was only at Sydney's insistence that she returned to Europe to finish her trip. There was no point in both of them feeling trapped. She begged Melissa to go travel through Europe for her. It would give her something to dream of. "I thought she'd never come home. She's changed her return flight four times now."

Wade's hand massaged her shoulder. "Don't worry about that now. Melissa's on her way home."

As her foot tapped out an impatient rhythm, Sydney glared down the hall toward the courtroom. "What's taking so long, Wade? This has to be a bad sign."

"Stop." He kissed her temple. "You're going to drive yourself crazy."

They sat, holding hands in a comfortable silence for a few minutes, then the door to the courtroom creaked open and Sydney shot to her feet, her heart slamming against her ribs. David stuck his head out and, with a less than encouraging smile he waved for them to come inside.

It felt as if all the air had been sucked out of the building as Sydney tried to take a breath. Her anxiety spiked, and Wade pulled her into his arms. "It's going to be all right. Whatever they decide, we're going to get through it. Together." He tipped her face up and placed a gentle kiss on her lips. The determination in his eyes gave her the courage she needed to put one foot in front of the other and walk through that door, with Wade's hand in hers.

Through the enormous doors, the judge sat behind his elevated desk, a stern look on his face. The district attorney and the woman from family court made brief eye contact with Sydney then went back to their conversation. Neither one of them gave any indication with their expressions or body language what the decision had been. On Sydney's side of the room her probation officer, David, and a few other people had their heads tucked together so Sydney didn't recognize them until they looked up. Then appreciation and shock slammed into Sydney.

"Cara? Pete?" She launched herself into Pete's outstretched arms, confused by their presence, but thrilled beyond words to see both of their faces. Cara had tears in her eyes as she wrapped her arms around Sydney, too. If things didn't go her way, she was going to need all the support she could get. "What are you two doing here?"

"Sydney and Wade, this is Jason, our son-in-law and this is his brother Michael who happens to be a family law attorney. When Jason told him about your custody situation, they flew out here from Chicago to consult with David because Michael found a precedent he thought might help."

Wade's hand immediately extended to both men. "I appreciate you taking the time to come all this way for us."

"I don't know if we did any good or not. This judge has one of the best poker faces I've ever seen in a courtroom. I've argued before some pretty stern characters, but he takes the cake," Michael said with a glance up at the judge who was still shuffling some papers on his desk.

"How are you holding up, honey?" Cara asked, with a motherly smile. "Wade's taking good care of you, I hope."

Without hesitation Sydney laced her finders with his. "I'd be lost without him."

Cara reached up and patted Wade on the cheek. "Good boy."

"I-I still can't believe you're here."

"Well, believe it, sweets. Luke and Hailey send their love. The two of them are running the diner while we're gone." Pete laughed. "Hopefully they don't burn the place down."

"You're both crazy," Sydney said with tears in her eyes.

"We both love you," Cara said with a sniffle. "And there's no way we weren't going to be here for you."

The judge cleared his throat and all talking in the courtroom ended. Sydney took her place beside her attorney, with Wade on her other side.

"This case is most unusual." The deep baritone of the judge's voice echoed off the marble walls. "I've listened to the arguments. I've spoken extensively to Mrs. Washington's former psychiatrist, as well as listened to the recommendations of the representatives from children's services and your probation officer." He pinned Jason and Michael with a hard look. "I've even been woken up at a most inappropriate hour this morning to hear yet another person willing to spout antiquated precedents that support your request for custody, Miss Jackson."

"Oh, please. It was seven o'clock," Jason hissed under his breath earning a smack from Cara.

"Shh, you behave."

"As I was saying, this whole case is unusual. If you just would have turned the girl into the authorities that night, you could have begun the legal adoption process and we wouldn't be here." Sydney felt her cheeks flush red, the burden of her guilt and the potential consequences making it hard to breathe. She opened up her mouth, ready to offer yet another apology to the judge. Even if he wouldn't give her custody, she would plead for visitation. There was no way she could cut Faith out of her life. It would kill her.

Sensing the direction of her thoughts, Wade gave his head a slighted shake and put his arm around her shoulder, holding her in place. Sydney leaned into him and allowed his strength to support her at the most terrifying moment of her life. Staring down the barrel of Charles' gun was nothing compared to this.

"You have been the model parolee. I see that you've met with the court appointed psychiatrist on a regular schedule, and that you've completed the community service requirement, and then some." He pulled off his glasses and folded his hands on the massive desk, looking directly at Sydney. "But that doesn't change the fact that you kidnapped a young girl."

"Are you gonna let him talk about Sydney that way," Agnes barked out, sending Sydney's attorney to his feet.

"Your honor," David started, but the judge sent him back to his seat with a glare and threatened to throw Agnes out of the courtroom if she spoke out again.

"I'd like to see him try and get me out of here," she mumbled under her breath, making Cara chuckle.

"Dr. Lee has been an advocate for you getting custody, as have your psychiatrist, the social worker, pretty much every person in this room." He waved his arm at the crowd and Sydney was moved to find everyone nodding in agreement. Tears flooded her eyes and spilled down her cheeks. She knew what he was going to say next, and her heart was breaking.

"I wish I could, but with the charges against you, I can't set that precedent in the eyes of the law. Imagine what other attorneys could argue down the road."

Wade held her tighter when she started to sway in her seat on the verge of fainting. There was no way she could even comprehend a life without Faith. Without her laughter and smile, or her hugs.

The judge did not miss her distress and called out to the bailiff. "June, get her a glass of water. She's white as a ghost down there." He waited until the water arrived and she took a sip. The whole room was holding their breath, wondering what decision he had made about Faith.

"What am I going to do?" Sydney whispered to Wade.

"Be brave. And trust me." He pressed his lips to her temple and Sydney could feel him pouring all his strength and love into her at that moment. She did trust him, and she trusted the people surrounding her in the courtroom. Cara's hand rubbed gently on her back giving her what comfort she could. Pete mumbled to Jason, who was doing his best to keep his father-in-law from jumping the barrier and "letting the judge have it," over his disagreement with what the judge was saying. If she wasn't so heartbroken, Sydney would have laughed at it all.

But the one person she needed more than any of them wasn't there.

"This morning I had another person petition for custody of Faith." The words froze Sydney in her chair. Throughout this whole ordeal of returning to Montana, the one thing Sydney had working in her favor was that Ronald and Amanda had no living relatives who were interested in adopting Faith. All their immediate family had passed away and the relatives social services *could* find were very distant cousins who wanted nothing to do with a child of Ronald's. But now, hearing that, Sydney felt the bile rising up the back of her throat.

Blood relatives would trump an outsider's petition in a court of law.

"He had been quietly going through the process of being cleared by family services. I know you were hoping for custody, Miss Ross, but this person has no criminal record, they have not been implicated in the kidnapping of Faith and he is an upstanding member of the community as countless people have testified."

Sydney's heart sank with each positive quality the judge was rattling off about this applicant. It was over. She'd lost Faith.

"Therefore, it is my decision to grant full custody of the minor, Faith Jenny Washington, to Mr. Wade Arthur Jenkins on this, the twenty first of October." He rapped the gavel down on his desk when the room erupted in chatter.

With eyes as big as saucers, Sydney turned to Wade who was grinning as proudly as she'd ever seen. Cara was weeping behind her and Agnes patted him on the shoulder in congratulation. "You sly fox, Wade. Well done."

"Y-You applied for custody?" Wade nodded his head slowly, letting her take it all in. "Why?"

"It was your idea, remember? Months ago, you made me promise not to let her end up in someone else's care. Your exact words were 'keep her for yourself,' so I did." He would have custody of Faith. It was a done deal. But what about her? Had she just lost both of them?

"Your honor!" Sydney sprang to her feet and once again silencing the courtroom with her outburst. The judge looked over the top of his glasses at her with raised eyebrows.

"Yes, Miss Jackson?"

"Wade and I are...involved. Dating. Serious about one another." She took a deep breath and tried to stop making a fool of herself in front of the man who would decide her fate. "I love him."

The corner of the judge's mouth turned up in a grin. "I can see that."

"But if he has custody of Faith, does that mean I have to give up both of them? Because I don't know what I'd do..."

"I don't think you understand my ruling, Miss Jackson. Mr. Jenkins has full custody of the child now. As her custodial parent it's up to him to decide who the child is able to be around. If he deems you a suitable person in the child's life," he shrugged his wide shoulders and sat back in his padded chair, "then who am I to say who can and cannot be a part of this sweet girl's life?"

Sydney's heart sprang back to life. "S-So I can see her?" The woman from Children's Services led a smiling Faith into the courtroom.

"I think he wants you to do more than see her." The judge motioned back towards Wade who had slipped out of his chair and was beside her, down on one knee with a gorgeous sparkling ring in his outstretched hand.

"Oh, my." Sydney's eyes filled with tears as her hand fluttered over her heart.

"Sydney Ross-Jackson, will you do me the honor of marrying me and spending the rest of your life with me and our beautiful daughter?"

"Say yes, Mommy!" Faith squealed in excitement as she ran over and wrapped her arms around Sydney's waist, jumping up and down. "Do it, do it!"

"I love you so much," Sydney said looking into Wade's eyes which were filled with love and adoration. "Yes, I'll marry you."

Wade put the ring on her finger and scooped her up into his arms, pouring all his love and joy into a single kiss. The courtroom erupted into cheers. Everyone from their friends, to the courthouse staff, and even the judge clapped and offered their congratulations as they filed out of the room, giving Wade and Sydney some privacy.

"Are you sure you want to do this?" She already knew the answer, it was written all over his face. He was thrilled with the idea of being a father and a husband.

"You and Faith are the two most precious things in my life. I love you both."

Sydney threw her arms around his neck and held onto the man she loved. She never would have guessed what fate had in store when she climbed into her car all those years ago, but she made it through the heartache, and along the way, finally found where she belonged. She laced her fingers with Wade's and led him toward the door.

"Let's go home."

ACKNOWLEDGMENTS

I am beyond thankful for the amazing people in my life who have helped me along the way. Thanks to Patty who takes a peek to tell me if I'm on the right track. To Niki and Heather who both put up with my inability to correctly place a comma to save my life. I thank you both for your editing skills, your ability to help me avoid my nemesis, the semicolon, and above all else, for your honesty.

None of this would be possible without my dear friend Barb who has been with me since the very beginning of it all. She is the voice of reason yet cracks the whip when necessary. She constantly inspires and helps me with the things I stink at like cover design, web layout, and formatting. This wouldn't be nearly as much fun without you, Barb, so I thank you from the bottom of my heart.

Last, but never least, to my wonderful family who makes me laugh and continues to inspire me in ways they never even imagined. I love you and our crazy cats more than I can say.

ALSO BY VICTORIA MICHAELS

Boycotts & Barflies
Trust in Advertising

ABOUT VICTORIA

Victoria Michaels is a wife, and mother of many who lives her life in what seems like a constant state of motion. Kids' sports, meetings, homework and general family fun take up twenty-seven hours of her day. In her thirty seconds of free time, Victoria likes to read, write and travel the country with her husband. She most enjoys writing about love and laughter, two things that are central to her everyday life.

If you would like to know more about what's coming next from Victoria, please check back at www.victoriamichaels.net for updates, news and sneak peeks of future releases, or follow her on twitter @vic_michaels.

www.ingramcontent.com/pod-product-compliance
Lightning Source LLC
Chambersburg PA
CBHW060358180626
46817CB00007B/2469